THE WORL

A WOMAN
AND OTH

ANTON CHEKHOV was bo

son of a poor grocer. At the age of nineteen he followed his family to Moscow, where he studied medicine and helped to support the household by writing comic sketches for popular magazines. By 1888 he was publishing in the prestigious literary monthlies of Moscow and St. Petersburg: a sign that he had already attained maturity as a writer of serious fiction. During the next 15 years he wrote the short stories—50 or more of them—which form his chief claim to world pre-eminence in the genre and are his main achievement as a writer. His plays are almost equally important, especially during his last years. He was closely associated with the Moscow Art Theatre and married its leading lady, Olga Knipper. In 1898 he was forced to move to Yalta, where he wrote his two greatest plays, *Three Sisters* and *The Cherry Orchard*. The première of the latter took place on his forty-fourth birthday. Chekhov died six months later, on 2 July 1904.

RONALD HINGLEY, Emeritus Fellow of St Antony's College, Oxford, edited and translated The Oxford Chekhov (9 volumes), and is the author of *A Life of Anton Chekhov* (also published by Oxford University Press).

THE WORLD'S CLASSICS

ANTON CHEKHOV

A Woman's Kingdom and Other Stories

Translated with an introduction and notes by

RONALD HINGLEY

Oxford New York

OXFORD UNIVERSITY PRESS

1989

Oxford University Press, Walton Street, Oxford OX2 6DP
Oxford New York Toronto
Delhi Bombay Calcutta Madras Karachi
Petaling Jaya Singapore Hong Kong Tokyo
Nairobi Dar es Salaam Cape Town
Melbourne Auckland
and associated companies in
Berlin Ibadan

Oxford is a trade mark of Oxford University Press

This selection first issued as a World's Classics paperback 1989

British Library Cataloguing in Publication Data
Chekhov, A. P. (Anton Pavlovich) 1860–1904.
A woman's kingdom and other stories, (World's classics).
1. Short stories in Russian 1800–1917, English text.
I. Title II. Hingley, Robert.
891.73'3 [F]
ISBN 0–19–282209–8

Library of Congress Cataloging in Publication Data
Chekhov, Anton Pavlovich, 1860–1904.
[Short stories. English. Selections]
A woman's kingdom and other stories/Anton Chekhov; translated with an introduction and notes by Ronald Hingley
p. cm. — (The World's classics)
Translated from the Russian. Bibliography: p.
Contents: The seizure—My wife—The two Volodyas—The black monk—A woman's kingdom—At a country house—Murder—My life—In the hollow.
1. Chekhov, Anton Pavlovich, 1860–1904—Translations, English.
I. Hingley, Ronald. II. Title. III. Series.
PG3456.A15H56 1989 891.73'3—dc19 88–25529
ISBN 0–19–282209–8 (pbk)

The text of the seven stories in this volume is taken from volumes 4, 6, 7, 8, 9 of the Oxford Chekhov, translated and edited by Ronald Hingley.

Printed in Great Britain by
Hazell Watson & Viney Ltd.
Aylesbury, Bucks

CONTENTS

INTRODUCTION

The nine stories in this volume all present features consistent with the traditional picture of Chekhov. For example, all run true to form by being composed, or at least partly composed, in the minor key of literary cliché. They exploit trivial details. They project an unnerving brand of anti-climax through tantalizing hints, haunting half-statements, and deafening silences. They display masterly economy, anguished yearnings, poignant lyricism, pastel colours, and the rest of all that.

Yet there is more to Chekhov than these formulae convey. He is as disinclined as any other major author to repeat himself mechanically, or to deal in fictional stereotypes. He is always poised to astonish by transcending any conceivable definition of his norm.

Two of these stories in particular will surprise those who associate their author too obsessively with the trivial round and the common task, however adroitly transmuted by the Poetry of Everyday Life. They are *Murder* and *In the Hollow*, each of which achieves a sensational level of brutality and violence. *Murder* not only flies homicide at its masthead, but handles the theme with gruesome relish, one memorable detail being the murderer's fear of his feet skidding in blood-boltered boiled potatoes. Still more harrowing is the passage of *In the Hollow* which describes the scalding of Lipa's baby. Can this be the most powerfully portrayed of all the many spectacular murders in Russian literature? Arguably so, even though Chekhov gets through it with characteristic brevity. He does not need the scores of pages required by Dostoyevsky to set up the axing of his pawnbroker in *Crime and Punishment* and the shooting of Shatov in *Devils*.

Still more laconic is the grim evocation (earlier in *In the Hollow*) of Lipa's wedding night—a scene all the more painful for being left to the reader's imagination through one of the most thunderous of all literary silences. Nor does Chekhov's technique desert him when he goes on to portray the young mother's grief for her murdered baby.

Birth, copulation, death—here they all are, these basic human themes, Chekhov or no Chekhov. And they are so powerfully purveyed as to challenge any lingering conception of our author as a bard of banality content to measure out his characters' lives with coffee spoons. Even so—and even in so tragic a tale as *In the Hollow*—the adroit deployment of the trivial remains crucial. All these major horrors are drawn together, summed up, and put into perspective at the funeral feast where an unctuous cleric so fatuously seeks to console the stricken and bereaved mother in what could qualify as the most Chekhovian sentence that Chekhov ever wrote.

'"Grieve not for the babe, for of such," said the priest, picking up a fork with a pickled mushroom on it, "is the Kingdom of Heaven."'

Another important theme is social commentary. Chekhov was not of course writing as a sociologist, and his work is grossly distorted by those who exaggerate this element. But it would be equally mistaken to ignore it entirely. All these items have it to some extent—and especially, once more, *In the Hollow*. As a study of Russian village life this appealed to contemporary Russian Marxists, conforming as it did with their view of the peasantry as a backward and reactionary force. A comparably coarse and primitive impression is conveyed by the peasant scenes of *My Life*, as also by the whole of the influential story *Peasants*.[1]

Chekhov knew little and cared less about Marxists or any other ists. His apparent pandering to their notions was as accidental in the peasant context as it also was in the occasional pictures of industrial life to be found in certain stories. *A Woman's Kingdom* is one of these, being thematically linked with two more: *Three Years* and *A Case History* (neither included in the present volume). In these works Chekhov studies the Russian merchant or business class from a standpoint of his own. His workers and humbler employees are background figures, never developing into major characters. They are all shown as victims of the 'system', so that these works can be read, by those who wish to do so, as indictments of burgeoning Russian capitalism. But none of them offers a black-and-white confrontation of grasping employer and victim-worker; far from it, for the employers are portrayed, despite their wealth and potential freedom of action, as equally helpless victims of a situation from which they seem to derive

[1] *Peasants* appears in an earlier World's Classics selection from Chekhov, *The Russian Master and Other Stories*.

nothing but frustration. In *A Woman's Kingdom* this role is played by the factory-owner Anne Glagolev, trapped in a predicament from which she is as ill equipped to escape as are the humblest of her sweated labourers. Exactly the same is true of Alexis Laptev in *Three Years* and the Lyalikov heiress in *A Case History*.

Anne Glagolev also happens to be one of the many women in Chekhov who would like to get married and are expected to do so, but who are unable to find a suitable partner. The exceptional feature here is that the only serious candidate for her hand is so much her social inferior—the vigorous Pimenov, one of her own employees and only a rung or two above the humblest. This potential romance fizzles out, as almost everything in Chekhov fizzles out, when she realizes that she feels closer to the most corrupt and effete of the lounge lizards in her immediate circle than she can be to the intelligent artisan who attracts her as a man.

The conflict between social classes, again in the context of potential wedding bells, is portrayed in the short and unjustly neglected *At a Country House*, where the pathetic snob Rashevich so idiotically discourages his guest—a possible husband for one of his two bored and eligible daughters—by insulting the man's honourable working-class background in a long and richly comic tirade. This is, incidentally, one of many passages in which Chekhov the master of understatement opts for overstatement on the grand scale. The technique here much improves on what it also closely resembles: that deployed in the comic stories which he had churned out as an apprentice author in the early 1880s.

In *My Life*, one of his longest and most important stories, Chekhov gives a special twist to social relationships in that his hero takes the deliberate decision to leave one class and join another. Misail Poloznev rejects the kind of professional career appropriate to the architect's son which he is and joins the ranks of the proletariat, ending up as a house-painter after various false starts. But though Misail is treated with sympathy by his creator there seems little doubt that Chekhov believed him mistaken and that the story was conceived as a polemic against such a decision to cultivate the simple life.

That this story is at the same time an attack on the views of Leo Tolstoy, the great missionary of the simple life, might not be immediately obvious to the modern reader because Tolstoy's name does not occur in the text. But it is clear from Chekhov's tone that he believes his hero to have taken the wrong road in life. And that Chekhov thought of him as having done this under Tolstoy's influence is put beyond doubt when we collate the many references to Tolstoy and his theories in Chekhov's correspondence. While discrediting his hero's way of life Chekhov simultaneously implies approval of those among Misail's associates who are anti-Tolstoyan in openly enjoying such amenities as soft carpets, cultured surroundings, and professional or business careers. These devotees of bourgeois élitism are the talkative Dr Blagovo, the railway tycoon Dolzhikov, and Misail's estranged wife Masha, who grievously sins against Tolstoyan morality by pursuing a career as an opera singer and—more heinously still—by possessing the attribute of physical beauty.

It is typical of Chekhov to imply that he feels more affection for his philosophically discredited hero than he feels for those characters in the story whose views are more or less his own. As this illustrates, he did not like to seem to preach, and he effectively softened any didactic impact which *My Life* might have had through this device of showing antipathy towards those who made the right choice while displaying sympathy for the man who fell into error. Anti-Tolstoyan the story most certainly is. But no reader of it can feel buttonholed by a rabid anti-Tolstoyan crusader.

The Tolstoy theme recurs in an earlier and very different story, *The Seizure*.[2] It describes a sensitive young man, Vasilyev, touring the brothels of Moscow with fellow-students not disqualified by inhibitions such as his from availing themselves of what is on offer. When Vasilyev moralizes about prostitution, lamenting the effect on a typical whore of sexual intercourse with, say, five hundred strangers, his art-student friend objects. 'You look at me with hatred and revulsion, but I say you'd do better to build a score of brothels than to go round looking like that.' There is, the art student goes on, more real vice in Vasilyev's facial expression than in all Moscow's 'red-light' Sobolev Alley. But these rough words do not console Vasilyev. He suffers a nervous collapse brought on by his brothel experiences—which do not, incidentally, include sampling Sobolev Alley's wares.

Such squeamishness was too much for Tolstoy. The virile

[2] This story is also known under the title *A Nervous Breakdown*, and appears as such in The Oxford Chekhov, vol. iv.

greybeard disliked Chekhov's story, and quipped that the flaccid Vasilyev should at least have 'had a go' at one of the girls. Still, despite this robust objection, there was no fundamental difference between Chekhov and Tolstoy on prostitution, for both regarded it as a particularly obnoxious evil. Here, then, is a pro-Tolstoyan story to set against the later anti-Tolstoyan *My Life*.

We know that Chekhov himself occasionally visited Moscow brothels: but in the spirit of a medical or sociological researcher, not as a gratifier of the flesh. It was as a qualified doctor keenly interested in the pathology of human behaviour, and certainly not as a lust-crazed fornicator, that he approached this sensitive subject. For this reason stories such as *The Seizure* have been called 'clinical studies'. Another clinical study, and one still more harrowing, is *The Black Monk*, which so movingly depicts the cruel treatment of an innocent young wife by her insane husband. But it might be misleading to dwell too heavily on the author's sympathy for the pathetic Tanya and on his antipathy for the crazed Kovrin; he seems in fact to bear Tanya a grudge for the crime of trying to domesticate her man. Chekhov himself long resisted attempts by his family and friends to persuade him to marry, instead writing stories (this being one of them) which stress the undesirability of the married state.

Linked with Chekhov's fear of domesticity is his tendency to condemn most forms of self-indulgence, whether in love-making, eating, drinking, gambling, or being rude to servants. This theme is a prominent feature of *The Two Volodyas*. Visits to restaurants, brandy-swigging, loud laughter, too much talking, casual fornication: these are some of the misdemeanours severally or individually attributed to the heroine as well as to her husband Volodya, to her lover the other Volodya, and to her chain-smoking friend Rita. How eloquent a contrast they offer to the clean, austere world of the well-scrubbed, modest, silent nun Olga. The colouring of Olga and her milieu is insistently monochrome, with all the emphasis on pallor and blackness—a feature typical of Chekhov's invocation of purity in a naughty and dirty world. Not that Chekhov himself was as ascetic as some of these stories might seem to imply. He led a lively social life, but with an un-Russian tendency to avoid excess in this and all other matters.

In *My Wife* an ill-starred marriage is again one of the main themes. Another still is gluttony as depicted in the Rabelaisian scene where the wealthy landowning hero is found tucking into a ten-course dinner with a fellow squire, having access to unlimited food in an area where peasants are perishing of starvation all around them. These guzzling philanthropists argue amiably about the horrors of the famine and express their sympathy for the victims while lustily disposing of sucking pig, horse radish, sour cream, cabbage stew, pork, buckwheat gruel, home-made liqueurs, pigeon, tripe, duck, partridge, cauliflower, fruit dumplings, curds, jelly, pancakes, and jam.

As this story reminds us, Chekhov's work by no means lacks echoes—however sparse, disguised, and muted—of his personal experiences. In the winter of 1891–2 the famine described in *My Wife* was devastating parts of south-eastern European Russia even as he wrote about it. He himself visited the stricken area in a vain attempt to organize effective relief measures, and found himself dining with similar gluttonous bigwigs who expressed their profound sympathy for the starving through mouthfuls of pudding. Nowadays, of course, anyone with a television set can actually watch people starve while eating his dinner, a possibility denied to Chekhov's unenlightened age.

Further biographical echoes are found in *Murder*. The social milieu is similar to that in which Chekhov spent his childhood as the son of a struggling grocer. It touches on the world of village traders, railway officials, innkeepers, horse dealers, and so on. Here the element of religious mania and addiction to church ritual owes something to the model of Chekhov's father, who was much given to religious observance and to inflicting it on his children. At the end of the story Chekhov draws on his experiences as a traveller in the year 1890, when he crossed Siberia to visit the convict settlement on Sakhalin Island. We find the murderer Jacob Terekhov among the inmates of Voyevoda Gaol, the grimmest prison in the entire settlement and one which Chekhov himself has described as such in his book *Sakhalin Island*.

Murder is one of those many Chekhov stories which seem not to have attracted their rightful share of attention. If so this is a pity, since it is one of his most powerful works. It shows, as do these nine stories as a whole, how much wider his range can be than is sometimes implied by those who seem to dismiss him as a gifted miniaturist.

SELECT BIBLIOGRAPHY

W. H. Bruford, *Chekhov and his Russia: A Sociological Study* (London, 1948).

The Oxford Chekhov. Tr. and ed. Ronald Hingley. Nine vols (London, 1964–80).

Letters of Anton Chekhov. Tr. Michael Henry Heim in collaboration with Simon Karlinsky. Selection, Commentary and Introduction by Simon Karlinsky (New York, 1973).

Letters of Anton Chekhov. Selected and edited by Avrahm Yarmolinsky (New York, 1973).

T. Eekman, ed., *Anton Chekhov, 1860–1960* (Leiden, 1960).

Ronald Hingley, *Chekhov: a Biographical and Critical Study* (London, 1950).

—— *A New Life of Anton Chekhov* (London, 1976).

Robert Louis Jackson, ed., *Chekhov: a Collection of Critical Essays* (Englewood Cliffs, N.J., 1967).

Karl D. Kramer, *The Chameleon and the Dream: the Image of Reality in Čexov's Stories* (The Hague, 1970).

Virginia Llewellyn Smith, *Anton Chekhov and the Lady with the Dog*. Foreword by Ronald Hingley (London, 1973).

A CHRONOLOGY OF ANTON CHEKHOV

All dates are given old style.

1860 — 16 or 17 January. Born in Taganrog, a port on the Sea of Azov in south Russia.

1876 — His father goes bankrupt. The family moves to Moscow, leaving Anton to finish his schooling.

1879 — Joins family and enrols in the Medical Faculty of Moscow University.

1880 — Begins to contribute to *Strekoza* ('Dragonfly'), a St. Petersburg comic weekly.

1882 — Starts to write short stories and a gossip column for *Oskolki* ('Splinters') and to depend on writing for an income.

1884 — Graduates in medicine. Shows early symptoms of tuberculosis.

1885–6 — Contributes to *Peterburgskaya gazeta* ('St. Petersburg Gazette') and *Novoye vremya* ('New Time').

1886 — March. Letter from D. V. Grigorovich encourages him to take writing seriously.

First collection of stories: *Motley Stories.*

1887 — Literary reputation grows fast. Second collection of stories: *In the Twilight.*

19 November. First Moscow performance of *Ivanov*: mixed reception.

1888 — First publication (*The Steppe*) in a serious literary journal, *Severny vestnik* ('The Northern Herald').

1889 — 31 January. First St. Petersburg performance of *Ivanov*: widely and favourably reviewed.

June. Death of brother Nicholas from tuberculosis.

1890 — April–December. Crosses Siberia to visit the penal settlement on Sakhalin Island. Returns via Hong Kong, Singapore and Ceylon.

1891 First trip to western Europe: Italy and France.

1892 March. Moves with family to small country estate at Melikhovo, fifty miles south of Moscow.

1895 First meeting with Tolstoy.

1896 17 October. First—disastrous—performance of *The Seagull* in St. Petersburg.

1897 Suffers severe haemorrhage.

1897–8 Winters in France. Champions Zola's defence of Dreyfus.

1898 Beginning of collaboration with the newly founded Moscow Art Theatre. Meets Olga Knipper. Spends the winter in Yalta, where he meets Gorky.

17 December. First Moscow Art Theatre performance of *The Seagull*: successful.

1899 Completes the building of a house in Yalta, where he settles with mother and sister.

26 October. First performance of *Uncle Vanya* (written ?1896).

1899–1901 First complete edition of his works (10 volumes).

1901 31 January. *Three Sisters* first performed.

25 May. Marries Olga Knipper.

1904 17 January. First performance of *The Cherry Orchard*.

2 July. Dies in Badenweiler, Germany.

THE SEIZURE

I

ONE evening a medical student, called Mayer, and Rybnikov—a pupil at the Moscow Institute of Painting, Sculpture and Architecture—went to see their friend Vasilyev, a law student, and suggested a joint expedition to S. Street. It was some time before Vasilyev would agree to go, but in the end he put his coat on and left with them.

He knew of 'fallen women' only by hearsay and from books, and never in his life had he been in their 'houses'. He knew that there are immoral women, forced to sell their honour for money under pressure of dire circumstances—environment, bad upbringing, poverty and so on. They know nothing of pure love, they have no children, no civil rights. Their mothers and sisters mourn them as dead, science treats them as an evil, and men address them slightingly. Yet, despite all this, they have not lost the semblance and image of God. They all acknowledge their sin, hoping to be saved, and means of salvation are lavishly available to them. Society does not forgive people their past, true—and yet St. Mary Magdalene is no lower than the other saints in the sight of God. When Vasilyev chanced to recognize a prostitute on the street by her dress or manner, or to see a picture of one in a comic paper, he always remembered a story that he had once read: a pure, self-sacrificing young man loves a fallen woman and offers to make her his wife, but she considers herself unworthy of such happiness and takes poison.

Vasilyev lived in one of the side streets off the Tver Boulevard. It was about eleven o'clock when he left home with his friends, it had just begun to snow for the first time that winter, and all nature was under the spell of the fresh snow. The air smelt of snow, snow crunched softly under the feet and everything—the ground, the roofs, the trees, the boulevard benches—was soft, white and fresh, so that the houses looked quite different from the day before. The street lamps shone more brightly, the air was clearer, the carriages' rumble was muffled. In the fresh, light, frosty air, a sensation akin to the feel of white, fluffy, newly fallen snow seemed to obtrude itself on one's consciousness.

The medical student began singing in a pleasing tenor:

'Against my will to these sad shores
An unknown force has drawn me.'

The art student chimed in:

'Behold the windmill, now in ruins——'

'Behold the windmill, now in ruins,'

repeated the medical student, raising his eyebrows and shaking his head sadly.

After pausing, rubbing his forehead and trying to remember the words, he sang out so loudly and professionally that passers-by looked round at him:

''Twas here that I did once encounter
A love as carefree as my own free self.'

The three men called at a restaurant, and each drank two glasses of vodka at the bar without taking off his overcoat. Before they gulped their second vodka Vasilyev noticed a piece of cork in his. He raised the glass to his eyes and peered into it for some time, squinting short-sightedly.

The medical student did not understand his expression. 'Hey, what are you staring at? No metaphysics, please. Vodka's for drinking, sturgeon's for eating, women are for consorting with, and snow is for walking on. Do behave like a proper human being for one evening.'

'I, er, I'm all for it,' laughed Vasilyev.

The vodka warmed his chest. He looked dotingly at his friends, admiring and envying them. How well poised these healthy, strong, cheerful fellows were, how well rounded and smooth their minds and spirits! They sing, they adore the stage, they sketch, they talk a great deal, they drink without having headaches next day, they are romantic and dissolute, tender and bold. They can work, protest indignantly, laugh for no reason, talk nonsense. They are ardent, decent, self-sacrificing, and no worse human beings than Vasilyev himself—so careful of his every step and word, so squeamish, so guarded, so ready to make mountains out of molehills. And so he felt the impulse to spend one evening like his friends, to let himself go, to fling caution to the winds. Was there vodka to be drunk? Then drink it he would, even if it meant a splitting headache next morning. Were there girls to be visited? Then he would visit them. He would laugh, play the fool, respond cheerily to contact with passers-by.

He came out of the restaurant laughing. He liked his friends, the one with his parade of artistic unconventionality and crumpled broad-brimmed hat, the other in his sealskin cap—a man of means, but with an air of academic Bohemianism about him. He liked the snow, the pale street lamps, the sharp black imprints made on the fresh snow by the feet of passers-by. He liked the air, and especially the limpid, tender, innocent, almost virginal atmosphere that nature displays only twice a year—when everything is covered with fresh snow, and on bright days or moonlit nights when the ice breaks up on the river in the spring.

He sang in an undertone:

'Against my will to these sad shores
An unknown force has drawn me.'

For some reason he and his friends had this tune on the brain as they went along, all three of them rendering it unthinkingly, not in time with each other.

In ten minutes, Vasilyev imagined, he and his friends would knock on a door and creep along dark passages and dark rooms to the women. Taking advantage of the darkness he would strike a match, and suddenly illumine and behold a martyred face and guilty smile. The unknown woman, fair or dark, would surely have her hair down and wear a white nightgown. She would be scared of the light and terribly embarrassed.

'Heavens, what are you doing?' she would say. 'Put that light out.'

It was all very frightening, yet piquant and novel.

II

The friends turned off Trubny Square into Grachovka Road and quickly entered the side street which Vasilyev knew only by hearsay. He saw two rows of houses with brightly lit windows and wide open doors, and heard the merry strains of pianos and fiddles fluttering out of all the doors and mingling in a weird medley, as if an unseen orchestra was tuning up in the darkness above the roofs.

He was surprised. 'What a lot of houses!'

'That's nothing,' said the medical student. 'There are ten times as many in London. There are about a hundred thousand of these women there.'

The cabbies sat on their boxes as calmly and unconcernedly as in any other street. Pedestrians walked the pavements as in other streets. No one hurried, no one hid his face in his coat collar, no one shook his head reproachfully. This unconcern, that medley of pianos and fiddles, the bright windows, wide open doors—it all struck a garish, impudent, dashing, devil-may-care note. There was obviously just the same sort of bustle and high spirits, with people's faces and walk expressing just the same offhandedness, at slave markets in the old days.

'Let's begin at the beginning,' said the art student.

The friends entered a narrow passage lit by a lamp with a reflector. When they opened the door a man in a black frock-coat, with an unshaven, flunkeylike face and sleepy eyes, slowly arose from a yellow sofa. The place smelt like a laundry with a dash of vinegar. A door led from the hall into a brightly lit room. In this doorway the medical student and the artist stopped and craned their necks, both peering into the room at once.

'Buona sera, signori and gents.' The art student gave a theatrical bow. 'Rigoletto, Huguenotti, Traviata!'

'Havana, Cucaracha, Pistoletto!' added the medical student, pressing his hat to his breast and bowing low.

Vasilyev stood behind them, also desirous of giving a theatrical bow and saying something nonsensical, but he only smiled, feeling an embarrassment akin to shame, and impatiently awaiting further developments.

In the doorway appeared a small fair girl of seventeen or eighteen, crop-haired and wearing a short blue frock with a white metallic pendant on her breast. 'Don't stand in the doorway,' she said. 'Do take your coats off and come into the lounge.'

Still talking 'Italian', the medical student and the art student went into the lounge, followed by the irresolute Vasilyev.

'Take off your coats, gentlemen,' said a servant sternly. 'This won't do.'

Besides the blonde there was another girl in the lounge—very tall and stout, foreign-looking, with bare arms. She sat near the piano playing patience on her lap and paying no attention whatever to the guests.

'Where are the other young ladies?' asked the medical student.

'Having tea,' said the blonde. 'Stepan,' she shouted, 'go and tell the girls that some students have arrived.'

Soon afterwards a third girl came in wearing a bright red dress with blue stripes. Her face was heavily and unskilfully made up, her forehead was hidden by her hair, and there was a look of fear in her unblinking gaze. After entering she at once began singing some song in a powerful, crude contralto. After her a fourth girl appeared, and then a fifth.

Vasilyev found nothing novel or interesting in any of this, feeling as if he had seen it all several times before—the lounge, the piano, the mirror with its cheap gilt frame, the pendant, the dress with the blue stripes, the blank, indifferent faces. Of the darkness, the stillness, the secrecy, the guilty smile and all that he had expected and feared to meet here he saw no trace.

Everything was ordinary, prosaic, boring. Only one thing slightly piqued his curiosity—the dreadful and seemingly intentional bad taste evident in the cornices, in the inane pictures, the dresses and that pendant. There was something significant and noteworthy about this lack of taste.

'How cheap and silly it all is!' Vasilyev thought. 'This trumpery that I see before me—what is there in it all to tempt a normal man and make him commit the fearful sin of buying a human being for a rouble? I understand sinning for the sake of glamour, beauty, grace, passion, good taste, but this is different. What's worth sinning for here? But I must stop thinking.'

The fair woman addressed him. 'Hey, you with the beard, treat me to some porter.'

Vasilyev was suddenly embarrassed. 'With pleasure.' He bowed politely. 'But you must excuse me, madame—I er, shan't drink with you, I'm not a drinking man.'

Five minutes later the friends were on their way to another house.

'Now, why did you order porter?' the medical student raged. 'Think you're a millionaire? That's a complete waste of six roubles.'

'Why not give her the pleasure if she wanted it?' Vasilyev riposted.

'The pleasure wasn't hers, it was the Madame's. They tell the girls to ask the customers for a drink, because they're the ones who make the profit.'

'Behold the windmill, now in ruins,' sang the art student.

Arriving at another house, the friends stopped in the hall, not entering the lounge. As in the first house a figure wearing a frock-coat, with a sleepy flunkey's face, got up from the sofa in the hall. Looking at the fellow, his face and shabby frock-coat, Vasilyev thought: 'What an ordinary simple Russian must have suffered before landing up on the staff of this dump!' Where had he been before, what had he done? What future had he? Was he married? Where was his mother, and did she know he was employed here? From now on Vasilyev could not help paying particular attention to the servant in each house. In one of them—he thought it was the fourth—there was a frail, emaciated little flunkey with a watch-chain on his waistcoat. He was reading *The Leaflet*, and paid no attention to the visitors. Glancing at his face, Vasilyev somehow fancied that a man with a face like that was capable of robbery, murder and perjury. And his face was really interesting—the big forehead, the grey eyes, the squashed little nose, the small, pursed lips, and an expression simultaneously blank and insolent, like a young whippet's as it chases a hare. Vasilyev felt he would like to touch the man's hair to see if it was soft or coarse. It must be coarse like a dog's.

III

After two glasses of porter the art student suddenly became drunk and unnaturally animated.

'Let's go to another,' he commanded, flourishing his arms. 'I'll take you to the best of the lot.'

After bringing his friends to 'the best of the lot', he evinced an urgent desire to dance a quadrille. The medical student muttered something about their having to pay the band a rouble, but agreed to join him. They started dancing.

It was just as nasty in the best house as in the worst. Mirrors, pictures, coiffures, dresses—all looked just the same as before. Scrutinizing the appointments and costumes, Vasilyev realized that this was by no means lack of taste, but something worthy to be called the taste—the style, even—of S. Street. A quality to be found nowhere else on earth, it had the integrity of its own ugliness, and—far from being accidental—it was the outcome of a lengthy evolution. After visiting eight brothels he was no longer surprised at the colour of the dresses, the long trains, the gaudy ribbons, the sailor suits or the thick, mauvish rouge on the cheeks. He realized that it was all as it should be—had even one of the women been dressed like a human being, had but a single decent engraving hung on any of the walls, then the general tone of the entire street would have suffered.

'How clumsily they market themselves,' he thought. 'Can't they see that vice is seductive only when it's attractive and hidden—when it's packaged as virtue? Modest black dresses, pale faces, sad smiles and darkness would be far more potent than this tawdry glitter. The imbeciles! If they can't see it for themselves, couldn't their clients have taught them or something?'

A young lady in a Polish dress trimmed with white fur came and sat by him. 'Attractive dark man, why aren't you dancing?' she asked. 'Why do you look so bored?'

'Because I *am* bored.'

'Then give me some claret and you won't be bored any more.'

Vasilyev made no answer.

'What time do you go to bed?' he asked after a pause.

'About half past five.'

'And when do you get up?'

'Sometimes two o'clock, sometimes three.'

'And what do you do when you get up?'

'We have coffee, and we have our dinner at about half past six.'

'And what do you eat?'

'Nothing special. Soup or cabbage stew. Beefsteak, dessert. Madame looks after the girls very well. But why ask all these questions?'

'Er, for something to say'.

There was a great deal that Vasilyev wanted to discuss with the girl. Where had she been born? Were her parents still alive, and did they know that she was here? How had she come to enter this house? Was she happy and contented? Or sad and oppressed by gloomy thoughts? And had she any hope of escaping from her present predicament? He felt a strong urge to discover these things, but where to begin and how to frame a question so as not to seem indiscreet—that was quite beyond him.

'How old are you?' he asked after a long pause for thought.

'Eighty,' joked the girl, laughing as she watched the art student, who was waving his arms and legs about.

Then something made her suddenly burst out laughing, and she brought out a long, obscene sentence in full hearing of everyone. Vasilyev was aghast, and, not knowing how to look, gave a strained smile. He was the only one to smile, and all the others—his friends, the band and the women—did not even glance at his companion, and seemed not to have heard her.

'Get me some claret,' she repeated.

Repelled by her white fur trimming and her voice, Vasilyev left her. He felt stifled and hot, and his heart began pounding with slow, powerful hammer-like thuds.

'Let's go.' He pulled the art student's sleeve.

'Just a moment—let me finish.'

While the art student and the medical student were completing their quadrille Vasilyev scrutinized the band so as to avoid looking at the women. At the piano was a venerable, bespectacled old man resembling Marshal Bazaine. The violinist was a young man dressed in the latest fashion and sporting a fair beard. Far from looking haggard, his face seemed intelligent, clever, youthful, fresh. He was fastidiously and tastefully dressed, and played with feeling. Problem: how did he and that respectable-looking, venerable old man get here, and why weren't they ashamed to be in this place? What did they think of when they looked at the women?

Had the pianist and the fiddler been ragged, starving, saturnine, drunken with haggard or stupid faces, their presence might have been understandable. As it was, Vasilyev understood nothing. He remembered the story about the fallen woman that he had once read, but that image of humanity with the guilty smile had nothing in common with the present scene, he found. He was not watching fallen women now, he felt, but another, utterly peculiar, alien, incomprehensible world. Had he seen this world previously, on the stage, had he read of it in a book, he would never have believed in it.

The woman with the white fur trimmings gave another loud guffaw and uttered an obnoxious phrase in a loud voice. Overcome by revulsion, he blushed and went out.

'Wait, we're coming too,' the art student shouted after him.

IV

'My partner and I had a conversation as we were dancing,' said the medical student when all three had come out into the street. 'We spoke of her first love affair. Her knight in shining armour was some Smolensk bookkeeper with a wife and five children. She was seventeen —living with her father and mother, who sold soap and candles.'

'How did he win her heart?' asked Vasilyev.

'Bought her fifty roubles' worth of underclothes, damn it.'

Yet the medical student had contrived to worm out his young woman's love story, which is more than I could, thought Vasilyev.

'Well, I'm going home,' he said.

'Why?'

'Because I don't know how to behave here. Besides, I'm bored and disgusted. Where's the fun in it? If only they were human beings—but they're savages and animals. I'm going, do what you like.'

'Ah Gregory, my dear old Greg!' wheedled the art student, putting his arm round Vasilyev. 'Let's visit just one more, and then to hell with them. Come on, Gregorius!'

They persuaded Vasilyev and led him up a staircase. The carpet, the gilt banisters, the porter who opened the door, the vestibule panelling —all had the S. Street touch, but in perfected and imposing form.

'I really must go home,' said Vasilyev as he took his coat off.

'Now, now, my dear chap.' The art student kissed him on the neck. 'Don't be naughty, Greg, old son—be a pal. We came together, so we'll leave together. What a chump you are, really.'

'I can wait in the street—this place disgusts me, honestly.'

'Now, now, Gregory! If it's disgusting you can observe it. Just observe it—see?'

'One must take the objective view,' said the medical student sententiously.

Vasilyev went into the lounge and sat down. There were several other visitors there besides him and his friends: two infantry officers, a baldish, white-haired gentleman in gold-rimmed spectacles, two beardless youths from the College of Surveyors and a very drunk man who looked like an actor. The girls were all busy with these guests, and paid no attention to Vasilyev. Only one of them, dressed as Aida, gave him a sidelong glance and smiled.

'A dark stranger has arrived,' she yawned.

Vasilyev's heart pounded and his face burned. He was ashamed to face the other visitors—a loathsome, agonizing sensation. It was agony to realize that he, a decent, warm-hearted man, which was how he had always thought of himself, hated the women and felt only revulsion for them. The women, the band, the staff—he was sorry for none of them.

'That's because I don't try to understand them,' he thought. 'They all resemble animals more than people, yet they are human, of course, they do have souls. One must understand them before judging them.'

'Don't leave, Gregory, wait for us,' shouted the art student, and disappeared.

Soon the medical student too had disappeared.

'Yes, I must try to understand them, one mustn't be like this,' continued Vasilyev's train of thought.

He began staring intensely at each woman's face, looking for a guilty smile. But either he failed to read their expressions, or else not one of them did feel guilty, for on each face he detected only a crass look of banal, humdrum boredom and complacency. Stupid eyes, stupid smiles, harsh, stupid voices, immodest movements—that was all. In the past they had evidently all had their affair with the bookkeeper and the fifty roubles' worth of underclothes, and the only bright spots in their present existence were the coffee, the three-course meals, the wine, the quadrilles and sleeping till two in the afternoon.

Not finding a single guilty smile, Vasilyev tried to see if there was anyone who looked intelligent, and his attention was caught by one pale, rather sleepy, exhausted face—that of a dark woman, no longer young, in a dress covered with spangles. She sat in an armchair, looking at the floor, plunged in thought. Vasilyev paced up and down the room and sat by her side as if by accident.

'I must start with some commonplace, and then gradually become serious,' he thought.

'What a nice dress you have.' He touched the gilt fringe on her shawl.

'Oh, do I?' said the brunette listlessly.

'Where do you come from?'

'Eh? From a long way off—Chernigov.'

'That's a nice area. It's nice there.'

'Absence makes the heart grow fonder.'

'A pity I'm no good at nature descriptions,' thought Vasilyev. One might be able to move her with descriptions of the Chernigov scenery. No doubt she was fond of it if she was born there.

'Don't you get bored here,' he asked.

'Of course I do.'

'Why don't you leave then, if you're bored?'

'Where should I go? Want me to beg for my living?'

'Begging would be easier than living here.'

'How do you know? Have you tried it?'

'Yes I have—when I couldn't pay my tuition fees. And it would be obvious even if I hadn't. At least a beggar's a free man, but you're a slave.'

The dark girl stretched and sleepily watched a waiter who was bringing glasses and soda-water on a tray.

'Get me some porter.' She yawned again.

'Porter, eh?' thought Vasilyev. 'But what if your brother or mother walked in here now? What would you say? And what would they say? They'd give you porter, I'll be bound!'

Suddenly the sound of weeping was heard, and from the adjoining room—to which the waiter had taken the soda-water—swiftly emerged a red-faced, angry-eyed fair-haired man, followed by the tall, plump Madame.

'Who said you could slap girls' faces?' she screeched. 'We have classier guests than you, and they don't make trouble, you rotten fraud!'

Such a din arose that Vasilyev was frightened and turned pale. In the next room someone was sobbing the heartfelt sobs of the grievously ill-used. Now he realized that the people in this place were genuine human beings who were ill-treated, who suffered, who wept, and who called for help like people anywhere else. His deep loathing and abhorrence gave way to a sensation of acute pity and of anger against the transgressor. He rushed into the room from which the sobs proceeded, and discerned a martyred, tear-stained face between rows of bottles on a marble table top. Holding out his hands towards the face, he took a step towards the table—only to recoil at once, aghast. The weeping girl was drunk.

His heart sank as he made his way through the noisy crowd gathered round the man, and he felt childishly scared, fancying that the denizens of this weird, mysterious world wanted to chase him, beat him and shower him with obscenities. He snatched his coat from the hook and rushed headlong downstairs.

V

Huddling against the fence, he stood near the house and waited for his companions to emerge. The strains of pianos and fiddles—cheerful, reckless, insolent, mournful—blended into a sort of chaotic medley that again sounded as if an unseen orchestra was tuning up in the darkness above the roof. If you looked up into this darkness the black background was spangled with moving white dots—falling snow. As the snowflakes came into the light they floated round lazily in the air like feathers, and descended still more languidly to the ground. A host of them whirled round Vasilyev, clinging to his beard, his eyelashes, his eyebrows. Cabmen, horses, pedestrians—all were white.

'How can snow fall in this street?' Vasilyev wondered. 'Damn these blasted brothels!'

His legs were buckling with fatigue from running all the way downstairs, he was panting as if he was climbing a hill, and he could hear his heart pounding. He was consumed by a desire to escape from the street quickly and go home, but even stronger was his desire to wait for his companions and vent his ill humour on them.

There was much about the houses that he did not understand, and the doomed women's mentality was still a closed book to him, but it was evident that things were far worse than he could have imagined. If that guilty woman—the one who had poisoned herself in the story—was to be called 'fallen', then it was hard to find a suitable name for all those now dancing to the musical pandemonium and mouthing their long, obscene sentences. They were not so much doomed as damned.

'There is vice here,' he thought. 'But there is neither the sense of guilt nor the hope of salvation. They are bought and sold, they flounder in strong drink and other abominations, they're as silly as sheep, they're casual and insensitive. God, God, God!'

He also saw that everything covered by the terms *human dignity*, *individuality* and *God's semblance and image* was defiled, becoming—in drunkards' parlance—'utterly smashed', and that the street and the stupid women were not the only factors responsible.

A group of students passed him—white with snow, cheerfully chattering and laughing. One, tall and slim, stopped and looked at Vasilyev's face.

'It's one of our lot,' said the drunken voice. 'Been overdoing it, old boy? Ah well, my dear fellow, never mind, you have a good time. Push the boat out! Don't be downhearted, old son!'

He took Vasilyev by the shoulders, placed his cold, wet moustache against his cheek, then slipped and staggered. 'Hold on! Don't fall!' he shouted, throwing up both arms, and rushed to catch up his companions with a laugh.

Through the hubbub the art student's voice was heard. 'How dare you hit a woman? I won't have it, blast you! Rotten swine!'

The medical student appeared in the doorway, glanced about him, and spotted Vasilyev. 'So there you are,' he said in a worried voice. 'I say, one should never go out with Yegor, honestly. I just can't make him out. He's made a scene! Hey, Yegor, are you there?' he shouted into the doorway.

'I won't let you hit a woman!' It was the art student's piercing voice, carried from aloft.

Then something awkward and lumbering rolled downstairs. It was the art student flying head over heels, evidently being thrown out.

He picked himself up from the ground, shook his hat and brandished his fist upwards with a look of outraged spite. 'Bastards! Swindlers! Bloodsuckers!' he yelled. 'I won't have any beating! To beat a weak, drunken woman! Oh, you——'

'Yegor! Come, Yegor!' the medical student implored him. 'I swear I'll never go out with you again—my word, I won't.'

The art student gradually calmed down and the friends set off for home.

The medical student started singing.

> 'Against my will to these sad shores
> An unknown force has drawn me.'

A little later the artist chimed in:

> 'Behold the windmill, now in ruins.

What snow, heaven help us! But why did you leave, Gregory? You're a lily-livered coward, and that's a fact.'

Vasilyev walked behind his friends and examined their backs.

'We can't have it both ways,' he reflected. 'Either we only imagine that prostitution is an evil and we exaggerate it. Or else, if prostitution really is as great an evil as is commonly supposed, then my dear old pals are slave-owners, rapists and murderers just as much as the inhabitants of Syria and Cairo caricatured in *The Meadow*. There they are singing, roaring with laughter, and reasoning so sagely. But haven't they just been exploiting hunger, ignorance and stupidity? They—well, I was a witness to it. Where's their humanity, their medicine, their painting? The learning, the art, the lofty sentiments of these assassins remind me of the piece of bacon in the story. Two robbers cut a beggar's throat in a wood, begin sharing his clothes between them, and find a piece of bacon in a bag. "Very nice—let's eat it," says the one. "Are you mad?" asks the other, aghast. "Have you forgotten today's a Wednesday—a fast-day?" So they didn't eat it. First they cut a man's throat, and then they come out of the wood thinking what good Christians they are! These two are the same—buying women and then strutting about thinking what great artists and scholars they are.'

'Listen, you!' he said abruptly and furiously. 'Why do you come here? Can't you see the horror of it? Well, can't you? Medicine teaches you that every one of these women dies before her time from tuberculosis or some other cause. And the arts tell us that she's morally dead long before that. Every one of them dies from entertaining an average of five hundred men in her life. So each one's murdered by five hundred men. And you're two out of the five hundred! Now, if you each visit this or similar places two hundred and fifty times, in the course of your lives, it follows that you'll be jointly responsible for murdering one woman. Can't you see it? And isn't it appalling? To conspire with one, two, three, five others to kill one foolish, hungry woman! My God, if that isn't horrible what is?'

The art student frowned. 'I knew it would end like this. We should never have brought this blithering idiot along. You think your head's full of grand ideas and notions, don't you? Hell knows what they are, but ideas they are not. You look at me with loathing and disgust, but in my view you'd be better occupied building another twenty brothels than going round with that look on your face. There's more immorality in your eyes than there is in the whole street. Come on, Volodya, and to hell with him. He's no more than a blithering idiot.'

'We human beings do kill each other,' said the medical student. 'It is immoral, of course, but talking about it won't help. Good-bye.'

On Trubny Square the friends said good night and parted. Left to himself, Vasilyev quickly strode off down the boulevard. He was scared of the dark, scared of the snow falling on the ground in large flakes and apparently wanting to envelop the entire globe. He was scared, too, of the lamplight dimly glinting through the clouds of snow. An unaccountable, craven fear took possession of him. Though occasional passers-by came his way, he fearfully kept his distance, feeling as if women and only women were coming at him and staring at him from all sides.

'It's starting,' he thought. 'I'm having a breakdown.'

VI

At home he lay on his bed, shivering all over. 'They're alive, alive—ye Gods, alive!' he said.

He gave his imagination free rein, fancying himself now as the brother of a fallen woman, now as her father, now as the woman herself with her painted cheeks—and it all appalled him.

For some reason he felt he must solve the problem immediately at all costs, and that it was his personal problem, no one else's. He strained every sinew, fought back his despair, sat on his bed, clutched his head in his hands, and began wondering how to save all the women he had seen that day. As an educated man he was familiar with the procedure for solving all manner of problems, and, agitated though he was, he followed that routine rigorously. He called to mind the history of the problem and its literature, pacing his room between three and four o'clock in the morning as he tried to remember all the modern techniques of rescuing women. He had many good friends and acquaintances with lodgings in St. Petersburg—at Falzstein's, Galyashkin's, Nechayev's and Yechkin's. Among them were a good few honourable and self-sacrificing men, some of whom had tried to rescue women.

'These few attempts can all be divided into three groups,' thought Vasilyev. 'One lot have ransomed a woman from her brothel, rented her a room and bought her a sewing-machine, and she has become a seamstress. The rescuer has, willingly or reluctantly, made her his mistress, and has then disappeared after graduating and consigning her to some other decent fellow as though she were an object. But fallen the fallen woman has remained. Others, having redeemed one, and having likewise taken a separate room for her—and also bought her the regulation sewing-machine—have further brought to bear homilies, writing lessons and books. As long as this has remained an interesting novelty to the woman, she has stayed and done her sewing. But then she has become bored and begun to entertain men without the knowledge of the homily-deliverers. Or else she has run off back to the place where she can sleep till three in the afternoon, drink coffee and have plenty to eat. A third group, the most ardent and selfless of all, have taken a bold and resolute step. They have married the girl. And when this brazen, crushed, spoilt or stupid animal has become a wife, the mistress of a home and then a mother, her life and outlook have been so transformed that it has been hard to recognize the one-time fallen woman in the wife and mother. Yes, marriage is the best means, and perhaps the only one.'

'But it's impossible,' said Vasilyev aloud, sinking on to his bed. 'I'm the last person to get married. For that one needs to be a saint, incapable of feeling hatred and revulsion. But let's suppose that the medical student, the art student and I all overcame our scruples and each married one—suppose they all got married. What would the result be? The result would be that while they're getting married here in Moscow your Smolensk bookkeeper will be debauching another batch, and this other lot will come rushing here to fill the vacancies along with girls from Saratov, Nizhny Novgorod and Warsaw. And what about London's hundred thousand whores—not to mention those of Hamburg?'

The oil had burnt down in his lamp, and it had begun to smoke, but Vasilyev did not notice. He began pacing to and fro again, still brooding. He was now posing the problem differently: what must be done to remove the demand for fallen women? This presupposed that men—their purchasers and murderers—must appreciate the immorality of their slave-owning role and recoil from it in horror. The men it was who needed saving.

'Obviously the scientific and artistic approaches lead nowhere,' thought Vasilyev. 'Missionary work is the only answer.'

He imagined himself standing on the street corner on the next evening, and asking every passer-by where he was going and why. Why? 'Have you no fear of God?'

He would address the apathetic cabmen. 'Why are you waiting here? Where are your feelings of indignation and outrage? You believe in God, don't you? You know that it's a sin, that people will go to hell for it, so why don't you speak up? They're strangers to you, true, but they too have fathers and brothers just like you, don't they?'

A friend of Vasilyev's had once described him as a gifted man. There are literary, theatrical and artistic talents, but his special flair was for human beings. He was keenly and splendidly sensitive to pain in all its forms. As a good actor reflects others' movements and voices, so could Vasilyev echo another's hurt in his soul. Seeing tears, he wept. In the presence of the sick he himself became ill and groaned. Witnessing an act of violence, he would feel as if he personally were the victim, take fright childishly and run off in panic for help. Others' pain irritated him, stimulated him, aroused him to ecstasy, and so on. Whether the friend was right I do not know, but Vasilyev's reaction to having, as it seemed, solved his problem was akin to inspiration. He wept, he laughed, he spoke aloud the words that he would say on the next day, feeling the keenest affection for those who would hearken to him and stand by him on the street corner to preach. He sat down to write letters, swore vows to himself.

His reaction also resembled inspiration in proving short-lived, for he soon tired. The whores of London, Hamburg and Warsaw bore down on him with their collective weight as mountains press on the earth, and he quailed, disconcerted by their sheer bulk. He remembered that he had no talent for speaking, that he was craven and cowardly, that apathetic persons would hardly wish to hear and understand him—a law student in his third year, a quaking nonentity—that true evangelism involved deeds as well as pious words.

When it was light, and carriages were beginning to rumble in the street, Vasilyev lay quite still on his sofa, staring into space. No longer was he brooding on women, men or evangelism, his entire attention being focused on the spiritual anguish that tormented him. It was a dull, abstract, undefined hurt akin to misery, despair and terror in the ultimate degree. He could indicate its location—in his chest, beneath his heart—but there was nothing to which he could compare it. He had suffered acute toothache, pleurisy and neuralgia in his time, but all that was nothing to this spiritual agony. With pain like this life seemed utterly repugnant. His academic thesis, an admirable composition already completed, the people he was fond of, the rescue of fallen women, together with all that had evoked his sympathy or indifference on the previous day—it exasperated him now, as he recalled it, no less than the carriages' clatter, the scurrying of the servants in his lodging house, the daylight. Had anyone now performed some great deed of mercy in his presence, or an outrageous act of violence, he would have been equally repelled by both. Among all the notions idly drifting through his head there were only two that did not irk him: one, that it was within his power to kill himself any moment, and the other that his sufferings would last no more than three days. This he knew from experience.

After lying down for a while he stood up, wringing his hands, and paced the room in a square, along the walls—not from corner to corner as usual. He glanced at himself in the mirror. His face was pale and cadaverous, his temples were hollow, his eyes bigger, darker and less mobile, as if they belonged to someone else, and they expressed intolerable mental anguish.

At midday the art student knocked on the door. 'Are you in, Gregory?'

Receiving no answer, he stood for a minute, pondered and answered himself in southern dialect. 'He bain't here. Danged if he haven't gone off to that there mooniversity, drat 'im!'

He went away. Lying down on his bed, his head under the pillow, Vasilyev began crying in his agony, and the more profusely the tears flowed the more terrible his spiritual anguish became. When it grew dark he remembered the excruciating night that faced him, and was overwhelmed by sheer despair. He dressed quickly, ran from his room, leaving the door wide open, and drifted without aim or reason into the street. Without thinking where he was going, he set off rapidly down Sadovy Street.

Snow was falling as heavily as yesterday, but it was thawing. Thrusting his hands into his sleeves, shuddering, scared of the clatter, the tram-bells and the pedestrians, he walked down Sadovy Street to Sukharev Tower and the Red Gate, and then turned into Basmanny Street. He went into a tavern and gulped a large vodka, but felt no better for it. Reaching Razgulyay, he turned right and strode down side streets where he had never been in his life. He reached the old bridge where the Yauza murmurs and from which you can see the long rows of lights in the windows of the Red Barracks. Wanting to relieve his mental anguish with some new sensation or different pain, but not knowing how to achieve this, he unbuttoned his overcoat and frock-coat, weeping and trembling, and bared his chest to the sleet and the wind. But that did not alleviate his sufferings either. Then he bent over the railings on the bridge, gazed down at the black, turbulent Yauza, and was prompted to throw himself in head first, not because he recoiled from life, or wanted to commit suicide, but to replace one pain with another, if only by smashing himself up. But the black water, the darkness, the deserted snowy banks—they were all so frightening. He shuddered and went on. He went past the Red Barracks, and then came back again, went down into a copse and came back out of it on to the bridge again.

'No, I'll go home. Home,' he thought. 'It will be easier there.'

He set off and, on arriving home, tore off his wet overcoat and cap, and began pacing along the walls, continuing to do so without stopping until morning came.

VII

When the art student and the medical student came to see him next morning he was lurching about the room groaning with pain, his shirt torn and his hands bitten.

'For God's sake!' he sobbed on seeing his friends. 'Take me where you like, do what you want, but in pity's name hurry up and save me. I shall kill myself.'

The art student was taken aback and turned pale, while the medical student—though also near to tears—felt that the medical profession should be cool and composed in all emergencies, and he remarked coldly that Vasilyev was having a nervous breakdown. 'But it's all right—we'll go to the doctor's at once.'

'Anything you like, but for God's sake hurry!'

'Don't get so excited. Try and control yourself.'

The art student and the medical student put Vasilyev's coat on with trembling hands, and took him into the street.

'Michael Sergeyevich has wanted to meet you for ages,' said the medical student on the way. 'He's a charming fellow, very good at his job. He only graduated in 1882, but he has an enormous practice already. He's very matey with students.'

'Hurry, hurry!' said Vasilyev.

Michael Sergeyevich, a stout, fair-haired doctor, received the friends with frigid courtesy and dignity, smiling on only one side of his face. 'Mayer and your art student friend have told me of your illness. I'm glad to be of service. Now, sit down, pray.'

He sat Vasilyev in a big armchair near the table and moved a box of cigarettes towards him. 'Now then,' he began, smoothing the knees of his trousers. 'Let's get to work. How old are you?'

The doctor asked the questions and the medical student answered them. He asked about Vasilyev's father. Had he had any particular illnesses? Did he drink to excess, was he remarkable for cruelty or any other aberrations? He asked the same questions about his grandfather, mother, sisters and brothers. On learning that his mother had a fine voice, and had sometimes performed on the stage, he evinced sudden signs of animation.

'Excuse me,' he said, 'but was the stage a positive obsession with your mother, do you recall?'

Twenty minutes passed. The doctor kept stroking his knees while saying the same thing over and over again, and Vasilyev found this boring.

'So far as I understand your questions, Doctor,' he said, 'you wish to know if my illness is hereditary or not. It is not.'

The doctor proceeded to ask whether Vasilyev had had any secret vices as a boy. Had there been any head injuries, fads, vagaries, obsessive proclivities? Half the questions commonly asked by painstaking doctors may safely be left unanswered without risk to health, but Michael Sergeyevich, the medical student and the art student all wore expressions suggesting that, should Vasilyev fail to answer a single one, then all was lost. On receiving the replies the doctor jotted them down on paper for some reason, and on learning that Vasilyev had taken a degree in natural science and was now studying law, he cogitated deeply.

'He wrote a first-rate dissertation last year,' said the medical student.

'I'm sorry, but don't interrupt me—you're stopping me concentrating.' The doctor smiled on one side of his face. 'Yes, of course, that too plays a role in the evolution of the case. Intense intellectual work, exhaustion—. Ah, yes indeed.' He addressed Vasilyev. 'And do you drink vodka?'

'Very seldom.'

Another twenty minutes passed. Speaking in an undertone, the medical student began stating his view on the immediate cause of the attack, explaining that he and the art student had accompanied Vasilyev to S. Street two days earlier.

The offhand, neutral, nonchalant tone in which his friends and the doctor alluded to the women, and to that wretched street, struck Vasilyev as most peculiar.

'Tell me one thing, Doctor,' he said, making an effort not to speak rudely. 'Is prostitution an evil or isn't it?'

'No one denies that, my dear fellow, no one at all,' said the doctor, his expression suggesting that he had long ago found answers to all such questions.

'Are you a psychiatrist?' Vasilyev asked rudely.

'Yes sir, I am.'

'Perhaps all of you are right, you may be.' Vasilyev stood up and paced the room. 'But I find it most remarkable. For me to have studied in two faculties rates as a heroic exploit. My authorship of a thesis which will be neglected and forgotten in three years' time—that's a reason for lauding me to the skies. But my inability to allude to fallen women as casually as I might to these chairs—that is a reason for taking me to a doctor, for calling me insane, and for being sorry for me!'

Vasilyev somehow felt immense pity for himself, for his companions, for all the people he had seen two days earlier, and for the doctor. He burst into tears and collapsed in the armchair.

His friends looked enquiringly at the doctor. With an air of fully comprehending the tears and despair, and of feeling himself a specialist in that line, he went up to Vasilyev, silently gave him some drops to drink, and then, when he had calmed down, got him undressed, and began investigating the sensitivity of his skin, his knee reflexes and so on.

Vasilyev began to feel easier. When he left the doctor's he felt ashamed of himself, he was no longer exasperated by the carriages' clatter, and the weight beneath his heart was growing lighter and lighter as if it was melting away. He was carrying two prescriptions—the one for bromide, the other for morphia.

He had taken all that stuff before!

He stood in the street and thought for a while, then said good-bye to his friends and sauntered languidly off towards the university.

MY WIFE

I

I RECEIVED a letter, as follows.

'Dear Mr. Asorin,

'Not far from you, in the village of Pyostrovo, there are some deplorable goings on which I think it my duty to report. The villagers all sold their cottages and possessions and went off to settle in Tomsk Province, but turned back and came home again. There is nothing for them here any more, of course, it all belongs to others. They have moved in at three or four families to a hut, so that each hut houses at least fifteen persons of both sexes, not counting small children. It comes to this: there is nothing to eat, they are starving, there's a mass epidemic of spotted or famine fever. Literally everyone is ill.

' "You go into a hut and what do you see?" the district nurse tells me. "All of them are ill, all are delirious. Some are roaring with laughter, others are going right round the bend. The huts stink, there is no one to give them a drink or fetch water and they have nothing to eat but potatoes spoilt by frost."

'The nurse and Sable, our local doctor . . . what can they do when there isn't any food, and when food is needed more than medicine? The Council won't help because these people have been taken off the books and are registered with Tomsk now, besides which there is no money anyway.

'Informing you of this and knowing you as a humane man, I beg you not to refuse immediate help,

'A WELL-WISHER'

This was obviously written by the district nurse herself or else by the doctor with that zoological name. Many years' daily experience has convinced the local doctors and nurses that they can do nothing whatever. Yet they still draw their salaries from people who live on frozen potatoes and they still think they have the right to assess my claims to be regarded as humane.

Worried by this anonymous letter, by certain peasants coming into my servants' kitchen every morning and begging for food on bended knee, and by someone breaking into my barn one night and stealing twenty sacks of rye—worried also by a feeling of general depression fostered by conversations, newspapers and foul weather—I was working listlessly and ineffectually. I was writing a history of the railways, which meant reading masses of Russian and foreign books, pamphlets and magazine articles. I must click my counting-frame, leaf through logarithm tables, think, write—then read, click, think all over again. But barely had I picked up a book or started thinking before my ideas would become muddled. I would frown, get up from my desk with a sigh and pace the large rooms of my deserted country house. When I was bored with walking about I would pause by my study window. Looking across my broad courtyard, pond and bare young birch plantation, across the large fields covered with a recent fall of snow now thawing, I could see on a hill which marked the horizon a huddle of brown huts whence a muddy black track ran down the white field in an irregular stripe. This was Pyostrovo, subject of my anonymous correspondent's letter. Were it not for the crows swooping and cawing above pond and fields as harbingers of rain or snow, were it not for a knocking in the carpenter's shed, this little world that was causing so much trouble would have seemed like the Dead Sea, so quiet, still, lifeless and dreary was everything around.

I was too worried to work and concentrate. What the matter was I didn't know: disillusionment, I liked to think. I had actually given up my job in the Ministry of Transport, and had moved out here to the country to live quietly and work on sociological literature. Such had been my long-cherished dream. But now I must say farewell to my quiet life and my reading, I must drop everything and busy myself exclusively with peasants. There was nothing for it since the famine victims of our county had absolutely no one else to help them, I was pretty sure of that. I was surrounded by uneducated, immature, callous people. The greater part of them were dishonest. Or else they were honest but unbalanced and frivolous, like my wife for instance. One could neither depend on such people nor could one leave the villagers to their fate, so I had to bow to the inevitable and tackle their rehabilitation myself.

I began by deciding to give five thousand silver roubles to famine relief. Yet this did not relieve my worries, it merely aggravated them. Standing by my window, pacing my quarters, I was tormented by a new problem: to what use should I put this money? To have food bought, to go from hut to hut doling it out: that was more than one person could cope with single-handed, not to mention the risk of giving twice as much in one's haste to those who already had enough, or more than enough, as to the starving. I had no faith in officialdom. These local magistrates and tax inspectors were all young people, and I was suspicious of them—as I am of all our modern youth, so materialist, so lacking in ideals. Nor did the Rural District Council, the parish councils, and the county offices as a whole inspire in me the faintest wish to ask for their assistance. That these institutions were sponging on local and central government funds I knew, and they went round with their tongues hanging out all day in search of further juicy pickings.

I thought of asking the local squires over with the idea of setting up some committee or centre in my house as a focus for all subscriptions, and as a source of aid and dispositions throughout the county. With facilities for frequent consultation and a broad, loose system of control, such an organization would reflect my views precisely. But I pictured the buffet meals, dinners and suppers, not to mention the fuss, the futility, the verbiage and the bad taste which this motley gaggle of provincials would perforce bring into my home. So I quickly dropped the idea.

As for my own household, that was the last place where I could look for help or support. Of the large, bustling family once headed by my father, only the governess remained: Mademoiselle Marie or, as she was now called, Old Mary—a personage utterly insignificant. This neat little old lady of seventy looked like a china doll in her light grey dress and white-ribboned bonnet. She was always reading a book in the drawing-room.

'What else do you expect, Paul?' she always asked when I passed, for she knew why I was so preoccupied. 'I've always told you what would happen, you have only to look at our own servants.'

My second family—my wife Natalie, that is—lived on the ground floor, which she occupied entirely. She ate, slept and received callers down there without in the least caring how I ate and slept, or whom I received. Our relationship was straightforward and relaxed, but cold, empty and dull, as between two people who have drifted so far apart that they can even live under one roof without any semblance of intimacy. Of that passionate, disturbed love, now sweet now bitter as gall, which Natalie had once aroused in me, nothing remained. Gone too were the former outbursts, the loud altercations, the reproaches, the complaints, as also the eruptions of hatred which had usually ended with her going abroad or to her relatives, and with my sending money: in small but frequent instalments so as to wound her pride the more often. (My wife is a proud woman with a sense of her own importance. She and her relatives live at my expense, and she can't manage without my money, much as she would like to, which gave me satisfaction and was my sole consolation in my distress.) When we ran across each other in the downstairs corridor or yard nowadays, I would bow and she would give a friendly smile. We would talk of the weather, we would say that it was about time to fit the double window-frames for winter and that someone had driven over the dam with carriage bells ringing.

'I am a faithful wife,' her expression seemed to tell me. 'I don't disgrace the good name which means so much to you, while you are sensible and don't bother me. So we are quits.'

I tried to tell myself that my love had died long ago, that I was too engrossed in my work to give serious thought to my relationship with my wife. But these were mere thoughts, alas. When she was talking down below in a loud voice I would hang on her words, even though I could not distinguish a single one of them. When she played the piano down there I stood up and listened. When her carriage or horse were brought to the door I went to my window and waited for her to come out of the house, after which I would watch her getting into her carriage or mounting her horse and leaving the premises. I felt a prey to discordant emotions and was afraid of being given away by the look on my face. I would watch her leave and then await her return, hoping to glimpse again through my window her face, her shoulders, her coat, her hat. I was bored, sad, and subject to a vague feeling of infinite regret. I felt an urge to walk through her rooms while she was out and I hoped for a speedy solution to the problem which the two of us had been precluded by clash of temperament from solving: a solution which should come about naturally and in the normal course of events. I hoped, in other words, that this beautiful, twenty-seven-year-old woman would hurry up and grow old, and that my head would hurry up and turn grey or bald.

One lunch-time my manager informed me that the Pyostrovo villagers had taken to stripping thatch from their roofs to feed their cattle. Old Mary looked at me in fear and perplexity.

'But what can I do about it?' I asked her. 'One can't do everything single-handed, and I have never felt so lonely in my life as I do now. I would give a lot to find just one individual in the whole county that I could rely on.'

'Then ask Ivan Bragin over,' Mary said.

'Now, what a good idea!' I thought delightedly.

'*C'est raison,*' I carolled, going into my study to write Ivan Bragin a note. '*C'est raison, c'est raison.*'

II

Of the whole crowd of friends who had taken food and drink in my house twenty-five or thirty-five years ago, who had visited us wearing fancy dress, who had fallen in love, married and bored everyone about their wonderful hounds and horses, Ivan Bragin was sole survivor. At one time he had been very active, voluble, rowdy, amorous: renowned both for his radical leanings and for a peculiar facial expression which charmed men as well as women. But now he had aged and run to fat, and he was maundering on bereft of charm and radical leanings alike. He arrived the day after my letter reached him, in the evening when the samovar had just been put on in the dining-room and little Mary was slicing a lemon.

'Glad to see you, friend,' I greeted him merrily. 'Why, you're stouter than ever.'

'Not stout—swollen up,' he answered. 'It all comes from bee stings.'

With the familiarity of one mocking his own girth he put both arms around my waist, laying his large, soft head on my chest (the hair was combed down on to his forehead, Ukrainian-style) and uttered a thin, senile peal of laughter.

'Now, you look younger every day,' he brought out through his laughter. 'I don't know what you dye your head and beard with, but you might give me some.'

Wheezing and gasping, he embraced me and kissed my cheek.

'You might give me some,' he repeated. 'Why, you're not yet forty, are you, old man?'

'Indeed I am,' I laughed. 'I'm forty-six.'

Bragin smelt of tallow and cooking, which suited him. His large, bloated, clumsy body was confined inside a long, high-waisted frock-coat like a coachman's caftan, with hooks and eyes in place of buttons, and it would have been odd if he had smelt of eau-de-Cologne, say. In his double chin—bluish, bristly as a burr, long unshaven—in his goggling eyes, in his wheeze, as in his entire lop-sided, slovenly figure, in his voice, his laughter and his words it was hard to recognize the well-built, attractive chatterbox who had once made the local husbands jealous.

'I badly need your help, friend,' I said as we had tea in the dining-room. 'I want to organize famine relief, but I don't know how to tackle it, so perhaps you will be kind enough to advise me.'

'Yes, yes, yes,' sighed Bragin. 'Quite so, quite so.'

'I wouldn't have bothered you, my dear fellow, but there is really absolutely no one else I can turn to. You know what people are like round here.'

'Quite so, quite so. Yes.'

It occurred to me that we were embarking on a serious practical discussion in which anyone, whatever their situation or personal relations, could take part. So why not invite Natalie?

'*Tres faciunt collegium*,' I said happily. 'How about inviting Natalie? What do you think?'

I turned to the maid. 'Fenya, ask Mrs. Asorin to come up: at once if possible. Tell her it's most important.'

A little later Natalie came in. I stood up to greet her.

'Excuse us troubling you, Natalie,' said I. 'We are discussing something very important and we have had the happy idea of taking your kind advice, which I'm sure we can count on. Sit down, please.'

Bragin kissed Natalie's hand, and she kissed his head. Then, when we were all sitting round the table, he looked at her with tears of joy, leant towards her and again kissed her hand. She wore black, her hair was carefully arranged and she smelt of fresh scent. She had obviously dressed to go out, or was expecting someone. Coming into the dining-room, she held her hand out to me in a direct and friendly way, and gave me as warm a smile as she had given Bragin, which pleased me. But she twiddled her fingers and kept jerking back in her chair as she spoke. She talked rapidly, and her jerky speech and movements irritated me, reminding me of her home town of Odessa, where local society, both male and female, had once wearied me with its bad taste.

'I want to do something for the starving,' I began.

'Money's the great thing, of course,' I went on after a short pause. 'But to confine oneself to subscribing money, and leave it at that, would mean buying one's way out of trouble. Assistance must be in financial form, but it must be properly organized on a serious basis, that's the main thing. So let's think it over, friends, and take action.'

Natalie looked at me quizzically and shrugged her shoulders as if asking what on earth this had to do with her.

'Yes, indeed, famine . . .' muttered Bragin. 'Actually. . . . Yes, indeed.'

'The situation's serious,' I said, 'and relief is urgently needed. Indeed, urgency must presumably take priority among those principles which we are about to elaborate. "First size things up," as they say in the army, "and then up, boys, and at 'em!" '

'Yes, quite,' Bragin brought out drowsily and listlessly, as if dozing off. 'Except that there's nothing anyone can do about it. The crops failed and that's that. No amount of sizing things up and shock tactics will get you anywhere. It's the elements. You can't go against God and fate.'

'Yes, but what use is a man's brain if not to fight the elements?'

'Eh? Yes. Quite so, quite so. Yes, indeed.'

Bragin sneezed into his handkerchief, brightened up, and looked at me and my wife as if he had just woken from sleep.

'My crops failed too.' He laughed a shrill laugh and gave a crafty wink, as if this was really quite a joke. 'I'm out of money, I'm out of food and my place is full of workers, like Count Sheremetev's. I'd like to kick them out, but I haven't the heart, somehow.'

Natalie laughed and began questioning Bragin about his domestic affairs. Her presence gave me more pleasure than I had known for some time and I feared to look at her lest my glance somehow betray my secret feelings. Such was our relationship that these feelings might seem surprising and comic. She laughed and talked to Bragin, not in the least embarrassed by the fact that she was my guest and that I wasn't laughing. I waited for a pause.

'Well, you two, what of it?' I asked. 'First we'll open a subscription as quickly as we can, I should think. We shall write to our friends in St. Petersburg and Odessa, Natalie, and ask them for donations. Then, when we have a certain sum in hand, we'll start buying food and fodder. Now, will you, Bragin, kindly take on the distribution of relief? Having every confidence in your innate tact and efficiency, we for our part shall merely venture to hope that you will acquaint yourself with all the details on the spot before issuing any relief. Will you also ensure —and this is vital—that food is given only in cases of genuine hardship, and on no account to drunkards, loafers and the kind of peasant who exploits his neighbour?'

'Yes, yes, yes,' muttered Bragin. 'Quite so, quite so——'

Oh, we shall get nowhere with this drooling old fogy, I thought, irritated.

'I'm sick and tired of these famine victims, bother them,' Bragin went on, sucking lemon peel. 'They're so frightfully touchy. The starving have it in for those who aren't starving, while those with food have a grudge against those without it. Yes, indeed. Famine makes a man crazy, stupid, savage. It's no joke, famine isn't. A starving man swears, he steals—and worse, maybe. You must try to understand these things.'

Bragin choked on his tea, coughed and shook all over with squeaky, suffocating laughter.

'And thereby hangs a t-t-tale,' he brought out, waving both arms to ward off the laughter and cough which prevented him speaking. 'Let me tell you about it. There was a famine in two local districts a couple of years after the serfs were freed, and dear old Theodore, who has since passed on, came and asked me over to his place. "Come on, come on," he kept pestering me, as if he had a knife at my throat. Well, why not? "Let's go," said I. So we upped and went. Evening was drawing in and it was snowing a bit. As we came up to his farm night had already fallen. Suddenly there's a loud bang from the woods, and then another. Bang, bang! Oh, to blazes! I jump out of the sledge to look, and someone's rushing me in the darkness, floundering knee-deep in snow. I get one arm round his shoulders, so, and knock the gun out of his hands. Then up pops another and I clout him on the back of the head, so he grunts and plops nose down in snow—I was pretty tough in those days, quite a punch I packed. I fix two of them and then I see Theodore astride a third. We hold on to these three stalwarts, see, we tie their hands behind them to stop them injuring themselves or us and we take them into the kitchen, the fools. We are furious with them, yet we're ashamed to look them in the eye. They are peasants we know, decent folk at that, and we're sorry for them. They are scared out of their wits. One cries and asks forgiveness, another glares like a wild beast and swears, the third gets down on his knees and prays.

' "Don't hold it against them," I tell Theodore. "Let the swine go."

'He gives them food and a sack of flour apiece, and lets them go, tells them to go to blazes. That's how it was. May he rest in peace, poor fellow. He understood, he didn't bear them any grudge. But others did, and what a lot of lives they wrecked! Yes, indeed. The Klochkovo inn case alone, that put eleven men behind bars. Yes, indeed. And it's the same now, see? Anisyin, the local detective, spent last Thursday night at my place, and he was on about some landowner. Yes, indeed. One night they break down his barn wall and steal twenty sacks of rye. The squire finds out about this outrage next morning and fires off a telegram to the Governor on the spot, then another to the Public Prosecutor, a third to the local magistrate, a fourth to the detective.

People are scared of these busybodies, of course, so the authorities panicked and there was no end of a to-do. Two villages were searched.'

'Now, look here, Bragin,' I said. 'It was I that was robbed of the twenty sacks of rye, and it was I telegraphed the Governor. I wired St. Petersburg too—not because I'm a busybody, as you put it, or because I bore a grudge. I always take my stand on principle. Whether you steal with a full belly or an empty one, it's all the same in the eyes of the law.'

'Yes, yes,' muttered Bragin, put out. 'Of course, quite so.'

Natalie blushed.

'There are some people,' she said, and paused. She was doing her best to seem cool, but couldn't help looking into my eyes with the hatred that I knew so well.

'There are some people,' said she, 'for whom starvation and human misery serve solely as an object to vent their rotten ill nature on.'

Embarrassed, I shrugged my shoulders.

'I want to put it in general terms,' she went on. 'There are some people utterly callous and devoid of feeling, yet they can't leave others alone in their misery, but meddle because they're afraid of those others being able to get on without them. Nothing is sacred to them, they're so conceited.'

'And there are also some people,' said I quietly, 'who have characters like angels, yet express their sublime ideas in such a form that the angel becomes difficult to distinguish from an Odessa fish-wife.'

Not the happiest of remarks, I confess.

My wife looked at me as if it cost her immense effort to hold her tongue. Her sudden outburst followed by her ill-judged eloquence about my wish to help the starving . . . they were uncalled for, to put it mildly. When inviting her upstairs I had expected quite a different attitude to myself and my intentions. Just what my expectations had been I cannot say, but the prospect had stimulated me pleasantly. Now, however, I saw that to go on talking about the famine victims would be tiresome and perhaps foolish.

'Oh yes, you know Burov, the businessman?' Bragin murmured irrelevantly. 'He must be worth four hundred thousand roubles or more. "Let the starving have a couple of hundred thousand, Ivan," I told him. "You'll die anyway, you can't take it with you." He was offended. But die he must, mustn't he? It's no joke, death isn't.'

Once more silence ensued.

'So all I can do is make the best of things on my own,' I sighed. 'One can't cope with everything single-handed. Oh, all right then. I'll try to struggle through on my own, and with any luck my war on famine will go better than my war on callousness.'

'I am expected downstairs,' said Natalie.

She got up from the table and addressed Bragin. 'You will come down for a minute, won't you? I won't say good-bye now.'

She left.

Bragin was on his seventh glass of tea, gasping, smacking his lips, and sucking by turns at his moustache and a lemon rind. He muttered something drowsily and dully, but I was not listening, I was waiting for him to go. He stood up to say good-bye at last, looking as if drinking tea had been the sole purpose of his visit.

'So you haven't given me any advice,' I said as I saw him out.

'Eh? I'm just a doddering old fool,' he answered. 'What use is my advice, anyway? You shouldn't take things so much to heart. Why you worry so I really don't know. Stop bothering, old man.

'It's quite all right, believe me,' he whispered affectionately and earnestly as if soothing a child. 'It's all right.'

'What do you mean, all right? The peasants are stripping their roofs, and there is said to be typhus about.'

'Well, what of it? If there's a good harvest next year they'll have new roofs. And if we die of typhus others will survive. We're all going to die sooner or later anyway, so stop worrying, there's a good fellow.'

'I can't help it,' said I irritably.

We were standing in the dimly lit hall, and Bragin suddenly took me by the elbow. Evidently about to say something very important, he looked at me for half a minute in silence.

'My dear Asorin,' he said quietly, his fat, torpid face and dark eyes suddenly flashing that peculiar expression for which he had once been famous, and which really was enchanting.

'I'm telling you as a friend, Asorin, do try and change your ways. You're such a bore. A bore, old boy.'

He stared into my face. The charming expression dimmed, the eyes lost their lustre.

'Yes, yes, indeed,' he muttered, wheezing lethargically. 'Forgive an old man. All a lot of poppycock, this! Yes, indeed.'

Lumbering downstairs, spreading his arms to balance himself and showing me his great hulking back and red neck, he produced the disagreeable impression of some sort of crab.

'You ought to leave here, my dear sir,' he muttered. 'Go to St. Petersburg, go abroad. Why fritter away the best years of your life around here? You're young, you're healthy, you're rich. Yes, indeed. Oh, if I were only younger I'd be out of here like a bat out of hell.'

III

My wife's outburst reminded me of our life together. At one time each eruption had left us irresistibly attracted to each other, and we would come together, loosing off all the high explosive accumulated within us in the meantime. Now, after Bragin's departure, I felt strongly drawn to my wife. I wanted to go down and tell her that her tea-time behaviour had insulted me, that she was cruel and petty, and that her plebeian brain had never been up to comprehending *my* sayings and doings. I spent some time walking about my rooms, thinking what to say to her and guessing her answers.

That evening, after Bragin had left, I experienced a particularly irritating form of the worry which had been troubling me of late. I could neither sit nor stand, but walked and walked, choosing only the lighted rooms and staying closest to the one where Old Mary was sitting. I had a sensation very like what I had once felt in a storm on the North Sea, when everyone thought that our steamer would capsize because she carried no load or ballast. This evening I realized that my worry was not disillusionment, as I had thought, but something else. Just what I couldn't tell, and that annoyed me even more.

'I'll go and see her,' I decided. 'I can find an excuse. I'll say I needed Bragin, that'll do.'

I went downstairs and strolled over the carpets in vestibule and hall. Bragin was sitting on the drawing-room sofa, drinking tea again and muttering, while my wife stood opposite him holding the back of an arm-chair. Her face wore the calm, sweet, docile expression with which people listen to saintly idiots and simpletons, attributing some special hidden meaning to trivial words and mumblings. It struck me that there was something morbid, something of the convent, in her expression and posture, as also in her rooms with their antique furniture, sleeping cage-birds and smell of geraniums. Low-pitched, half-lit, very warm, these rooms were like the quarters of an abbess or a pious old lady whose husband was a high official.

I entered the drawing-room. My wife showed neither surprise nor confusion, but looked at me severely and calmly as if she had known I would be coming.

'Excuse me,' I said gently. 'I'm so glad you're still here, Bragin, for I forgot to ask when we were upstairs: do you know the first names of our Rural District Council chairman?'

'Andrew Stanislavovich. Yes, indeed.'

'Thanks,' said I, taking out a book and noting it down.

A silence followed during which my wife and Bragin were probably waiting for me to leave. My wife didn't believe I had any need of the Council chairman, I saw that in her eyes.

'Well, I'll be going, dear lady,' muttered Bragin after I had walked across the drawing-room once or twice and sat down near the fire-place.

'No,' Natalie said quickly, touching his hand. 'Stay another quarter of an hour, I beg you.'

She obviously did not want to be left alone with me without witnesses.

All right then, thought I, I'll wait a quarter of an hour too.

'Why, it's snowing,' I said, getting up and looking out of the window. 'What marvellous snow.

'What a pity I don't hunt, Bragin,' I went on, pacing the drawing-room. 'Hare-coursing and wolf-hunting in snow like this . . . it must be terrific fun, I should think.'

Standing still and looking out of the corner of her eyes without turning her head, my wife was observing my movements. Her expression suggested that I had a sharp knife or revolver concealed about my person.

'You must take me hunting some time, Bragin,' I went on gently. 'I shall be grateful indeed.'

At that moment a visitor came into the room. It was an individual unknown to me: a man of about forty, tall, thickset, bald, with large fair beard and small eyes. From his manners and rumpled, baggy clothes I took him for a parish clerk or teacher, but my wife introduced him as a Doctor Sable.

'Very pleased to meet you, I'm sure,' said the doctor in a loud, high-pitched voice, firmly shaking my hand and giving a naïve smile. 'Very pleased.'

He sat down at table and took a glass of tea.

'Do you have a drop of rum or brandy by any chance?' he asked in a loud voice.

'Be a good girl, Olga, and look in the cupboard,' he told the maid. 'I'm perished.'

I sat down by the fire again, watching, listening and inserting an occasional word in the general conversation. My wife smiled cordially at her guests, keeping a wary eye on me as if I were some wild beast. My presence irked her, which aroused my jealousy, my annoyance and a stubborn urge to wound her. This wife, these snug rooms, this ingle nook . . . these things are mine, thought I, they've been mine for ages. So how can some doddering Bragin or Sable have more right to them than I?

Now that I no longer see my wife through the window, but near me in her usual domestic surroundings—that very domesticity which is denied to me now that I am getting on in life—I long for her despite her loathing for me, as I used to miss my mother and my nanny when I was a little boy. Now that I am on the verge of old age my love for her seems a purer, higher thing than of old. That is why I want to go up to her and bring my heel hard down on her toe to hurt her, and smile as I do so.

I turned to the doctor. 'How many hospitals have we in the county, Dr. Raccoon?'

'His name is Sable,' my wife corrected me.

'Two, sir,' answered Sable.

'And how many deaths do you get per hospital per annum?'

'I must have a word with you, Paul,' my wife told me.

She excused herself to the visitors and went into the next room. I got up and followed her.

'Back upstairs with you this instant,' she said.

'You are extremely bad-mannered,' I told her.

'Back upstairs with you this instant!' she repeated sharply, looking into my face with hatred.

So close was she standing that if I had stooped a little my beard would have touched her face.

'But what's the matter?' I asked. 'What have I done wrong all of a sudden?'

Her chin quivered, she hastily wiped her eyes and she glanced at herself in the mirror.

'This has all happened so often before,' she whispered. 'Of course you won't go. Have it your own way then, I'll go and you stay.'

We returned to the drawing-room, she with resolute countenance, I shrugging my shoulders and trying to smile sardonically. More visitors had arrived: an elderly lady and a bespectacled young man. Neither greeting the new arrivals nor saying good-bye to the old, I went off to my own rooms.

After the tea-time scene in my room, and now this business downstairs, I realized that our domestic drama, which we had already begun to forget over the last two years, was starting all over again for some ridiculous, pointless reason. Neither my wife nor I could stop ourselves now, and within a day or two of this outburst of hatred—as I knew from previous experience—something disgusting was bound to happen, something which would upset the whole balance of our lives. So we hadn't become any wiser, cooler or calmer in the last two years, I thought, starting to walk up and down my rooms. So there would be more tears, shouts, curses, suitcases and journeys abroad, followed by my obsessive, morbid fear that she would disgrace me somewhere abroad with some Italian or Russian fop, that I should once more refuse her a passport. There would be more letters, more utter loneliness, more yearning for her, followed five years later by old age and grey hair. I paced about imagining the impossible: how she, grown handsomer and more buxom, would embrace some unknown man. Now certain that this was bound to happen, I wondered frantically why I hadn't given her a divorce during one of our old, old quarrels. Why hadn't she run away then and made a clean break? That would have freed me from my present longing for her, freed me from hatred and anxiety, and I should have lived out my life quietly working, without brooding about anything.

A carriage with two lamps drove into the yard, followed by a wide sledge pulled by a three-horse team. My wife must be giving a party.

Until midnight all was quiet below and I heard nothing, but at midnight there was a shifting of chairs and a clatter of crockery. They must be having supper. Then they moved the chairs again and a noise reached me through the floor. They seemed to be cheering. Old Mary was already asleep and I had the whole upper storey to myself. The portraits of my forebears, those cruel mediocrities, gazed down at me from the dining-room walls and the reflection of my lamp winked disagreeably in the study. Jealous and envious of the goings-on downstairs, I pricked up my ears.

'I am the master of this house,' thought I, 'and I can send these gentry packing this instant if I want.'

But I knew this was nonsense, I knew I couldn't send anyone packing, I knew that the phrase 'master of this house' was meaningless. It is possible to be quite obsessed with one's status as householder, husband, wealthy citizen and man of position, yet not to know what all these things mean.

After supper someone downstairs started singing in a tenor voice.

'Nothing special has happened, has it?' I urged myself. 'So why am I so upset? I won't go down and see her tomorrow, that's all, and our quarrel will be over.'

At a quarter past one I started going to bed.

'Have the downstairs visitors left?' I asked Alexis as he was undressing me.

'Yes, sir, they have, sir.'

'What was all the cheering about?'

'Mr. Makhonov has given a thousand sacks of flour and a thousand roubles for famine relief. And an old lady whose name I don't know, sir . . . she has promised to run a soup kitchen for a hundred and fifty people on her estate, sir. The Lord be praised, sir. And Mrs. Asorin decided that all the ladies and gentlemen should meet every Friday.'

'What, downstairs in this house?'

'Yes, sir. And they read a piece of paper before supper to say that since August Mrs. Asorin has collected eight thousand roubles in cash, not to mention food. The Lord be praised, sir. What I think, sir, is that if the mistress takes the trouble—to save her soul, like—she'll collect a lot of money, sir. It's a rich neighbourhood, this is.'

Dismissing Alexis, I put out the light and pulled the bedclothes over my head.

'Really, why do I worry so?' I wondered. 'What *is* this force that draws me to the starving peasants like a moth to the candle? I don't know them, now, do I? I don't understand them, I've never seen them, I don't like them. So why worry?'

I suddenly crossed myself under the quilt.

'But what a woman!' I told myself as I thought of my wife. 'Holds regular committee meetings in the house without telling me! Why the secrecy, why the conspiracy? What have I done to them?'

Bragin was right, I ought to leave.

I awoke next day with the firm intention of leaving as soon as possible. Yesterday's incidents had wearied me—the tea-time conversation, my wife, Sable, the supper, my fears—and I welcomed the prospect of release from surroundings which brought back such memories. While I was having coffee my manager reported at length on sundry matters. He kept the juiciest tit-bit till last.

'They have found those thieves who stole our rye,' he smilingly reported. 'The detective arrested three peasants at Pyostrovo yesterday.'

'Get out of here!' I shouted in a terrible rage.

On a sudden impulse I seized a basket of sponge-cakes and hurled it to the floor.

IV

After lunch I rubbed my hands together and thought of going to my wife and telling her I was leaving. But why? Who cared? Nobody, I told myself. But then, why *not* tell her, especially as it would only give her pleasure? Moreover, it would not be altogether tactful to leave without a word after yesterday's quarrel. She might think I was frightened of her, and the idea of having driven me out of my own home would, perhaps, irk her. Besides, it would be just as well to tell her that I was subscribing five thousand roubles, to give her some hints on organization, and to warn her that in so complex and responsible a matter her inexperience might produce most lamentable results. I felt an urge to see her, in short, and even as I was concocting various excuses for calling on her I had already quite made up my mind to do so.

It was still light when I went in and the lamps were still unlit. She was sitting in her work-room, which forms a corridor between drawing-room and bedroom, and was writing something rapidly, bent low over the table. Seeing me, she started and moved away from the table, adopting a pose seemingly designed to shield her papers from me.

'Excuse me, I shall only be a minute,' I said, embarrassed for some reason. 'It has come to my ears that you are organizing famine relief, Natalie.'

'Yes, I am. But that's my business,' she replied.

'Certainly it is,' I said gently. 'And glad I am it is because it accords precisely with my own intentions. Have I your permission to join in?'

'I'm sorry, but I can't permit that,' she answered, and looked away.

'But why not, Natalie?' I asked quietly. 'Why not? I too have enough to eat, and I too wish to help the starving.'

'I don't know what this has to do with you,' she said with a contemptuous laugh, shrugging one shoulder. 'No one asked you to butt in.'

'Well, nobody asked you to either, but that hasn't stopped you setting up a regular committee in *my* house.'

'I *was* asked, but *you* won't ever be, you can take my word for that. Go and offer your services somewhere where you're not known.'

'For heaven's sake don't take that tone with me.'

I tried to be easy on her, making a most earnest effort to keep my temper. For the first few minutes I found her presence delightful. I felt an aura of gentle domesticity, youthful femininity and extreme elegance: just what was so lacking on my own floor of the house, as in my life altogether. She wore a pink flannel house-coat which made her look strikingly young, lending gentleness to her swift, sometimes jerky movements. Her magnificent dark hair, the mere sight of which once stirred my passions, had fallen loose through her sitting for so long with her head bowed, and looked untidy. But that only made it richer and more voluptuous in my eyes. That's a cheap and vulgar way of putting it, though. Before me stood an average woman, neither beautiful nor elegant perhaps, but still my wife, with whom I had once lived, with whom I should still have been living to this day had it not been for her unhappy character. She was the only person on the face of the globe that I loved. Now I was about to leave, and I knew that I shouldn't even see her through my window any more. And severely unbending as she was, haughty and derisive as was the smile with which she answered me . . . even so I found her enchanting, I was proud of her and I confessed that the thought of leaving her was a horrifying impossibility.

'For two years we have kept out of each other's way, Paul,' she said after a short pause, 'and we've lived at peace. So why this sudden urge to resurrect the past?

'Yesterday you came to insult and humiliate me,' she went on, raising her voice, her face flushed, her eyes flashing hatred. 'But you must control yourself, Paul, you mustn't behave like this. I shall put in for a passport tomorrow and leave. I'll leave, I tell you. I'll go into a convent, a widow's home, an almshouse——'

'Why not a lunatic asylum?' I couldn't help shouting.

'All right then, a lunatic asylum. Better still!' she shouted, flashing her eyes. 'In Pyostrovo today I envied the starving, sick village women because they weren't living with a man like you. They are honest women, they're free, but I . . . thanks to you I am a parasite, I'm pining away in idleness. I eat your food, I spend your money, but I pay with my freedom and a kind of faithfulness which is no use to anybody. As you won't give me a passport I am forced to protect your good name, non-existent though it is.'

I had to keep silent. Clenching my teeth, I quickly went into the drawing-room, but came back straight away.

'No more,' said I, 'I do most earnestly entreat you, of these assemblages, plots and conspiratorial hideouts in my house! I only admit people I know to this house. As for these friends of yours, if the swine choose to indulge in philanthropy let them do it somewhere else. I'm not having people in this house who cheer for joy in the middle of the night because they can exploit a neurotic like you.'

Wringing her hands, uttering a protracted groan like a toothache-sufferer, blenching, my wife rapidly strode across the room. I gave a gesture of despair and went into the drawing-room. I was choking with rage, while also shaking with fear of losing my temper, and of doing or saying something that I should regret for the rest of my life. I clenched my fists hard, thinking to control myself thereby.

I drank some water, calmed down a little and went back to my wife. She was standing in her previous pose as if shielding her table and papers from me. Down her cold, pale face tears were slowly trickling. I paused for a moment.

'How little you understand me,' I said bitterly, but without anger. 'You are so unfair to me. I swear I came to you with the purest of motives, only wishing to do good.'

She crossed her hands on her breast and her face adopted an agonized, suppliant expression like that of a frightened, crying child begging not to be punished. 'I'm quite sure you'll refuse, Paul, but I'm asking you all the same. For once in your life force yourself to do the decent thing. Leave this place, I beg you. That's the only thing you *can* do for the starving peasants. Go away, and I'll forgive you every single thing.'

'There's no need to insult me, Natalie,' I sighed, suddenly overcome by a strange impulse of humility. 'I had already decided to leave, but I shall not go before doing something for the starving. It's my duty.'

'Oh, really!' she said gently, frowning impatiently. 'You can build a first-class railway or bridge, but you can't do anything for the starving, I'd have you know.'

'Indeed? Yesterday you reproached me for not caring, for lacking compassion. How well you know me!' I laughed. 'You believe in God. Well then, as God is my witness, I worry day and night——'

'I see you do, but that has nothing to do with famine or compassion. You worry because the starving peasants can manage without you, because the Council, and the welfare workers in general, don't need your guidance.'

I paused briefly to choke back my irritation.

'I came here to talk business,' I said. 'Do sit down. Sit down, please.'

She remained standing.

'Sit down, please,' I repeated, pointing to a chair.

She sat. I sat down too and thought for a moment.

'Please take this seriously,' I said. 'Now, look here. You have been moved by love of your fellow men, and you've undertaken to organize famine relief. I have nothing against that, of course, I fully sympathize, I am prepared to co-operate in any way, whatever terms you and I may be on. But much as I respect your intelligence and your good heart . . . yes, and your good heart,' I repeated, 'I cannot agree that so difficult, complex and responsible a matter as relief organization should be in your hands exclusively. You are a woman, you're inexperienced, you know nothing of life, you're too trustful and expansive. You have surrounded yourself with helpers whom you don't know at all. I shall not exaggerate if I say that, under the aforesaid conditions, your activity is bound to entail two deplorable consequences. Firstly, the county will be left entirely without relief. Secondly, you will have to pay for your mistakes, as for those of your helpers, with your reputation as well as your pocket. The losses and deficiencies I shall make good, granted. But who will restore your good name? When inefficiency and neglect breed the rumour that you, and consequently I, have pocketed two hundred thousand roubles over this affair, will your helpers come to your aid then?'

She remained silent.

'Not through vanity, as you claim,' I went on, 'but wishing neither to deprive the famine victims of their relief nor you of your reputation, I believe it my moral duty to interfere in your affairs.'

'Be brief,' said my wife.

'You will be so kind,' I went on, 'as to show me how much has been subscribed to date and how much has been spent. Thereafter you will inform me daily of each new contribution in cash or in kind, and of each new outlay. You will also give me a list of your helpers, Natalie. They may be perfectly respectable people, I don't doubt it. Still, inquiries must be made.'

She said nothing. I stood up and paced the room.

'To work then,' I said, sitting down at her table.

'Are you serious?' she asked, looking at me bewildered and terrified.

'Do be reasonable, Natalie,' I begged her, seeing the protest in her face. 'You may have every confidence in my experience and probity.'

'I still can't see what you want.'

'Show me how much you have collected and spent so far.'

'I have no secrets, anyone can look. There you are.'

On the table were half a dozen school exercise-books, some sheets of writing paper covered with scribbling, a map of the county and lots of bits of paper of various sizes. It was growing dark, and I lit a candle.

'I can't see anything yet, sorry,' I said, leafing through the exercise-books. 'Where is your register of incoming donations?'

'You can get that from the subscription lists.'

'Indeed so, but you really must have a register,' I said, smiling at her innocence. 'Where are the letters accompanying the donations in cash and in kind? You will excuse me one small practical hint, Natalie, but it's essential to keep those letters. You should number each one and enter it in a special register, and you should do the same with your own letters. Anyway, I shall deal with all that myself.'

'All right then,' she said. 'Deal with it.'

I was very pleased with myself. Fascinated by this active, interesting job, by the small table, the unsophisticated exercise-books and the delightful prospect of doing the work in my wife's company, I feared lest she suddenly thwart me and spoil everything with some surprising outburst. So I hurried, striving to attach no meaning to her trembling lips and frightened, baffled, sidelong glances like those of a small trapped animal.

'Now then, Natalie,' I said without looking at her. 'Let me take all these papers and books upstairs. I'll see what they're like and let you know what I think tomorrow.

'Have you no more papers?' I asked, bundling the exercise-books and papers together.

'Take them, take the lot!' said my wife, helping me to put the papers together, and huge tears flowed down her cheeks. 'Take the lot! It's all I had left in life. Take away my last possessions.'

'Oh, Natalie, Natalie,' I sighed reproachfully.

Elbowing my chest and brushing my face with her hair, she pulled out the table drawer and started throwing me papers on to the table more or less at random, while small sums of money poured on to my knees and the floor.

'Take it all,' she said hoarsely.

After throwing out the papers, she moved away and collapsed on the sofa, clutching her head in both hands. I picked up the money, put it back in the drawer and locked it so as not to tempt the servants. Then I gathered all the papers in my arms and went to my rooms.

I paused as I passed my wife.

'You are such a baby, Natalie, dear me you are,' I said, looking at her back and quivering shoulders. 'Now, listen. When you see how serious and important this business is you will be the first to thank me, I give you my word.'

Reaching my quarters, I tackled the papers at my leisure. The exercise-books were not bound, the pages were not numbered and entries had been made in various hands. Obviously every chance comer had had a shot at keeping those books. In the lists of donations in kind there was no note of their cash value. But, with due respect, the rye which sells at one rouble fifteen copecks now . . . it can go up to two roubles fifteen copecks in two months' time, can't it? What a way to run things! Why were 'thirty-two roubles given to A. M. Sable'? When were they given? For what purpose? Where was the receipt? There was nothing, none of it made sense. In the event of legal proceedings these papers would only befog the issue.

'How naïve she is!' I marvelled. 'She's such a child.'

I was both annoyed and amused.

V

My wife had already collected eight thousand roubles. Add my five, and that made thirteen thousand all told. Not a bad start. At last I had come to grips with this business which so fascinated and troubled me, I was doing what others neither would nor could do, I was fulfilling my duty, I was organizing famine relief on a proper, serious basis.

Everything seemed to be working out as I intended and desired. Why, then, was I still a prey to uneasiness? I spent four hours going through my wife's papers, finding out what they meant and correcting mistakes, but derived no comfort, feeling instead as if a stranger stood behind me and was passing a rough hand over my back. What then did I lack? The relief work had fallen into reliable hands, the starving would be fed, so what else did I want?

This easy four-hour job so tired me for some reason that I couldn't bend forward in my chair or write. Occasional dull groans reached me from below: my wife's sobs. My Alexis, always so meek, sleepy and sanctimonious, kept coming to the desk to attend to the candles, giving me some rather odd looks.

'I really must go away,' I decided in the end, utterly exhausted. 'I must flee these scenes of grandeur, I'll leave tomorrow.'

I put the papers and books together and went down to see my wife. Dead beat, absolutely worn out, I pressed the papers and books to my chest with both arms, went through my bedroom, saw my suitcases, and as I did so the sound of weeping came to me from below.

'So you hold an official position, do you?' someone seemed to ask in my ear. 'Very nice too, but you're a swine all the same.'

'This is all such arrant nonsense,' I muttered as I went downstairs. 'It's nonsense. And it is also nonsense to say that I am actuated by selfishness or vanity. How petty! It's not as if I was going to get a medal for my famine work! Or be made departmental director! Stuff and nonsense! And, anyway, what scope does our local countryside offer for displays of ostentation?'

I was tired, so terribly tired.

'That's all very well,' something whispered in my ear. 'But you are still a swine.' For some reason I recalled a line from an old poem which I once knew as a child: 'Virtue brings its own reward.'

My wife was lying on the sofa in her former attitude: face downwards, head clutched in both hands. She was crying. Near by stood her maid, looking terrified and perplexed. I sent the maid away and put the papers together on the table.

'This is our office, Natalie,' I said, after a moment's thought. 'Everything is all right, everything's fine and I'm very glad. I leave tomorrow.'

She was still crying. I went into the drawing-room and sat there in the dark. My wife's sobs and sighs seemed to put me in the wrong, so by way of self-justification I recalled our whole quarrel, beginning with my unhappy notion of inviting her to a consultation, and ending with those exercise-books and these tears. This was a routine spasm of conjugal hatred, ugly and meaningless like so many others which had followed our marriage. But where did the famine victims fit in? How on earth had they fallen foul of us? It was as if we had happened to chase each other into a church, and had started fighting in front of the altar.

'Do give over, Natalie,' I said quietly from the drawing-room. 'That'll do.'

To stop her crying, to end this painful situation, I must go to her, comfort her, show her affection or say I was sorry. But how could I carry conviction? How could I persuade this wild duckling, this enslaved creature which loathed me, that I was fond of it, that I sympathized with its sufferings? Never having really known my wife, I have never known what to talk to her about or how to put it. I knew her appearance well and duly appreciated it. But her spiritual and moral world, her intelligence, her general outlook, her frequent changes of mood, her eyes so filled with hatred, her arrogance, the scope of her reading (which sometimes astonished me) or the nun-like expression, say, that she had worn yesterday . . . I found all those things a mystery and enigma. When we clashed I would try to define what she was like, but my psychology had not gone beyond such formulations as 'capricious', 'frivolous', 'unfortunate character' or 'typical female mentality', which had seemed an adequate explanation. But now, as she wept, I felt a tremendous urge to know more.

The tears stopped, and I went to my wife. She sat on the sofa, propping her head on both hands and staring pensively at the fire without moving.

'I leave tomorrow morning,' I said.

She said nothing. I walked across the room and sighed.

'Natalie,' I said, 'when you asked me to leave you told me you'd forgive me every single thing. So you must think I have treated you badly. Now, just what have I done wrong? Pray formulate it calmly and in brief terms.'

'I'm tired,' she said. 'Some time later——'

'Where have I gone wrong?' I went on. 'What have I done? You'll say you are young and beautiful, that you want a bit of excitement, whereas I am nearly twice your age and you can't stand me. But is that my fault? I didn't force you to marry me. All right then, if you want your freedom—go your own way, I won't stop you. Leave me, love anyone you like. You can have a divorce too.'

'I don't want that,' she said. 'You know I used to love you and always thought of myself as older than you. All that means very little. Your fault is not in being older while I'm younger, or in my being able to love someone else if I had my freedom, it's in your being a selfish, misanthropic bore.'

'Perhaps,' said I. 'I don't know.'

'Now, please leave me alone. You want to go on nagging me till day-break, but I warn you I feel completely feeble and I can't answer you. You promised to leave this place and I am extremely grateful, I ask nothing more.'

She wanted me to go upstairs, but it was not easy for me to do that. I felt weak, I dreaded my huge, uncomfortable, cheerless rooms. When I had a pain as a little boy I used to snuggle up to my mother or nanny. Hiding my face in the folds of a warm dress, I felt as if I was hiding from the hurt. Similarly, I now somehow felt that I could escape my troubles only in this little room, near my wife. I sat down, screening my eyes from the light with one hand. It was quiet.

'You ask what you've done wrong,' said my wife after a long silence, looking at me, her eyes red and gleaming with tears. 'You are highly educated and well-bred, you're extremely honest, you're fair, you're high-principled, but the general effect of it all is that you always carry round an aura of overwhelming stuffiness offensive and humiliating in the ultimate degree. You are a man of integrity, so you hate the whole world. You hate believers because their faith reflects immaturity and ignorance, yet you also hate unbelievers for having no faith or ideals. You hate old folk for being backward and conservative, you hate young people for free-thinking. You value the interests of Russia and the Russian peasant, so you hate the peasants because you suspect them all of being thieves and robbers. You hate everyone. You are a just man, you always take your stand on grounds of law and order, so you're involved in constant litigation with peasants and neighbours. You had twenty sacks of rye stolen, and such was your love of order that you reported the peasants to the Governor and all the authorities, after which you reported the local authorities to St. Petersburg. And that's what you call law and order!'

She laughed. 'On the basis of law, in the interests of morality, you refuse me a passport. A fine sort of morality and law this is, whereby a self-respecting, healthy young woman has spent her life in idleness, misery and constant fear, all in return for board and lodging from a man she doesn't love! You know the law inside out, you are extremely honest and fair, you respect marriage and the family principle, but the upshot is that you have never performed a single kind act in your life, that you're generally detested, that you're at odds with all and sundry, and that you haven't lived so much as seven months with your wife in seven years of marriage. You haven't *had* a wife, I haven't had a husband. One can't live with someone like you, I just can't cope. In the early years I feared you, now I'm ashamed of you. You have ruined the best years of my life! Fighting you has spoilt my temper, made me brusque, rude, scared and suspicious. Oh, why talk about it? As if you even wanted to understand! Just go away, bother you.'

My wife lay on the sofa, plunged in thought.

'And what a marvellous, enviable life we might have had,' she said quietly, looking dreamily at the fire. 'What a life! But there's no turning back now.'

All who have wintered in the country know those long, tedious, quiet evenings when even dogs are too bored to bark and when the very clock seems to languish, weary of ticking. If, on such evenings, you have been troubled by pangs of guilt, and have rushed feverishly about from pillar to post, trying now to lull your conscience, now to unravel its secrets, then you will understand what entertainment and pleasure I derived from the sound of a woman's voice in a snug little room as she told me what a bad man I was. I couldn't understand the promptings of my conscience, but my wife translated them, interpreting my disquiet in her feminine way, yet clearly. How often, at times of extreme uneasiness in the past, I had guessed that the clue to the whole secret was not starving peasants but my being the wrong kind of person.

My wife stood up with great effort and came towards me.

'I'm sorry, Paul, but I don't believe you,' she said with a sad smile. 'You won't leave. But I repeat my request.'

She pointed to her papers. 'Say I'm deceiving myself, call me a typical illogical female, say I am wrong, say whatever you like, but do leave me alone. This is all that's left of my life.'

She turned away and paused briefly. 'Before this I had nothing at all. I wasted my youth fighting you. Since I tackled this job I have come to life, I'm happy. I feel I have found a way of justifying my existence.'

'You are a fine woman, Natalie, an idealist,' I said, gazing at her rapturously. 'Whatever you do and say is so splendid and intelligent.'

I walked up and down the room to hide my emotion.

'Natalie,' I continued a minute later, 'before I leave I beg you one special favour: help me to do something for the starving peasants.'

'But how can I help?' she asked with a shrug. 'I suppose I could give you this subscription list.'

She rummaged in her papers and found it.

'Subscribe some money,' she said, her tone showing that she attached no serious importance to the list. 'There's no other way in which you can help the cause.'

I took the list and wrote:

'Five thousand roubles,
'AN ANONYMOUS DONOR'

That word anonymous had a wrong, false, selfish ring, but I only realized that when I saw my wife blush violently, rapidly thrusting her list into a heap of papers. We were both embarrassed. I felt I simply must redeem my clumsiness at once, at all costs, or else I should feel ashamed of myself afterwards, in the train and in St. Petersburg. But how? What could I say?

'I thoroughly approve of what you are doing, Natalie,' I said sincerely. 'I wish you every success. But permit me one parting word of advice, my dear. Do be careful with Sable and your helpers in general, don't confide in them. I don't say they are dishonest, but they aren't gentlemen. They have no ideas, these people, they lack ideals and faith, they're without any purpose in life or definite principles, and their whole lives revolve around money. Money, money, money!'

I sighed. 'They're spongers and parasites, which means that the better educated they are the more dangerous they become to the cause.'

She went to the sofa and lay down.

'Ideas, ideals,' she brought out half-heartedly and reluctantly. 'Ideals, ideas, purpose in life, principles . . . those are the words you have always used to humiliate and wound, or to make yourself disagreeable. Now, isn't this just you all over! With your outlook, with your approach to people . . . why, if one let you come anywhere near this business it would mean wrecking it at the start, and it's about time you realized that!'

She sighed and paused.

'It's your coarseness of fibre, Paul,' she said. 'You are a well-educated, well-bred man, but fundamentally you're an absolute . . . yahoo. It's because you live shut in on yourself, you're such a misanthrope, you never meet anyone, you read nothing but your engineering books. Yet there *are* such things as nice people, you know, and decent books too, oh yes there are. But I'm tired out and fed up with talking. It is time I went to bed.'

'All right, I will leave home, Natalie,' I said.

'Yes, do that. Thank you.'

I stood there for a moment, then went upstairs. An hour later, at half past one, I came back downstairs with a candle to talk to my wife. I didn't know what to say, yet I felt that what I had to convey was vitally important. She was not in her work-room and her bedroom door was closed.

'Natalie, are you asleep?' I asked softly.

There was no answer. I stood near the door, sighed and went into the drawing-room. There I sat on the sofa, put out my candle and stayed in the dark until dawn.

VI

At ten o'clock next morning I left for the station. It was not freezing, but dense sleet poured from the sky and a foul, damp wind blew.

We passed the pond, then the birch copse, and began climbing the hill path visible from my window. Turning for one last look at my home, I saw nothing for sleet. Soon afterwards dark huts loomed ahead, as through fog. This was Pyostrovo.

'If I ever go mad it will be Pyostrovo's fault,' I thought. 'I am hounded by the place.'

We came out in the village street. All the roofs were intact, not one had been stripped. So my manager had been lying. A boy was giving a toboggan ride to a little girl and a baby. Another boy of about three, wearing huge mittens, his head muffled like an old woman's, tried laughingly to catch flying snowflakes on his tongue. Then a waggon loaded with faggots came towards me. Beside it walked a peasant with a white beard—whether white by nature or from snow was not clear. Recognizing my coachman, he smiled, said something and automatically doffed his cap to me. The dogs ran out of the yards and stared inquisitively at my horses. Everything was quiet, normal and ordinary. The migrant peasants had come home, there was no food, in the huts 'some are roaring with laughter, others are going right round the bend', but it all seemed so very ordinary that you really couldn't believe any of these things. There were no distracted faces, no voices crying for help, nor was there weeping and cursing, but just quiet, orderly life all around: children, toboggans, dogs with their tails in the air. The children were not worrying, nor was the peasant whom we had met. Why, then, was I so upset?

Looking at the smiling peasant, at the little boy with the huge mittens, at the huts, and remembering my wife, I saw now that no disaster could crush these people. I seemed to scent victory in the air, I felt proud and I was ready to shout aloud that I too was with them. But my horses swept me out of the village into open country, snow whirled, wind bellowed and I was alone with my thoughts. From the millions who were working for the public weal, life had cast me out as an unwanted, useless, rotten member. I was a nuisance, I was one of the peasants' woes myself. Beaten and rejected, I was rushing to the station so that I could go and hide in a hotel on Great Morskoy Street in St. Petersburg.

We reached the station a hour later. A porter with a badge helped my coachman to carry the suitcases into the ladies' waiting-room. Felt-booted, drenched with sleet, his coat-tails tucked inside his belt, my coachman Nikanor was glad I was leaving.

'A pleasant journey, sir, and the best of luck to Your Excellency,' he said with a cordial smile.

Everyone calls me Your Excellency, by the way, though my civil service rank is only equivalent to a colonel's. The porter said that the train had not left the last station yet, and there would be a delay. I went outside and drifted aimlessly towards the water-pump, my head heavy after my sleepless night. I could hardly drag one foot after the other, I was so tired. There was no one about.

'Why am I going?' I wondered. 'What awaits me there? Friends that I have already run away from once, loneliness, restaurant meals, noise, electric light which hurts my eyes. Where am I going? Why? Why go?'

It was rather odd, too, to depart without a word to my wife. I felt as if I had left her in a state of uncertainty. I should have told her as I went that she was quite right, I really am a bad man.

Turning from the water-pump, I saw the station-master in the doorway—I had already reported the man to his superiors twice. He had turned up his frock-coat collar and approached me, cringing in wind and snow, laying two fingers on the peak of his cap. His face frantic with loathing and simulated respect, he said that my train would be twenty minutes late. Wouldn't I like to wait in the warm?

'No, thank you,' I replied. 'I'm probably not going, anyway. Tell my coachman to stay, I haven't made up my mind.'

I paced the platform, wondering: to go or not to go. When the train pulled in I decided to stay. At home I could expect my wife's amazement—perhaps her sneers—my dismal upper storey and my worries. But still, at my age all that was easier and somehow closer to one's heart than spending forty-eight hours travelling with strangers to St. Petersburg, where I should be perpetually conscious of a life utterly useless to anyone, a life that was drawing to its end. No, better go home whatever the cost.

I left the station.

To return by daylight to a house where everyone had so welcomed my departure . . . how awkward. I might spend the rest of the day until evening with one of the neighbours. But which? I was on bad terms with some, others I didn't know at all. After reflection I thought of Bragin.

'To Bragino,' I told my coachman, getting into the sledge.

'That's a fair distance,' Nikanor sighed. 'All of eighteen miles that'll be, I reckon, if not twenty.'

'Come along, old man,' I said in a tone which implied that Nikanor had the right to refuse. 'Come on, let's go, please.'

Nikanor shook his head dubiously and slowly stated that he should really have put Ploughboy or Goldfinch in the shafts instead of Circassian. Hesitant, as if expecting me to change my mind, he took the reins in his mittens, rose in his seat, pondered and then swung his whip.

'A whole chain of inconsistencies,' I thought, hiding my face from the snow. 'I must be mad. Ah well, never mind——'

At one point, as we descended a very high, steep slope, Nikanor carefully eased the horses half way down, but then they suddenly bolted and careered off at a fearful lick. He gave a start and raised his elbows.

'Hey, let's give the master a drive!' he bellowed in a wild, frenzied voice which I had never heard him use before. 'If the pace is too hot he'll buy new horses, my darlings! You there, watch out, we'll run you over!'

Only now, as our hurtling speed took my breath away, could I see that he was extremely drunk. He must have had something at the station. At the bottom of the dip ice cracked, and a lump of heavy, dung-encrusted snow flew up from the road and hit me painfully in the face. The bolting horses galloped full tilt up hill with no loss of speed, and before I could shout to Nikanor my three-horse team was already dashing along level ground in an old fir forest where tall trees stretched out their frizzy white paws towards me from all sides.

'I'm crazy, my coachman's drunk,' I thought. 'A fine state of affairs!'

I found Bragin at home. He laughed till he coughed, laid his head on my chest and greeted me with his usual remark.

'You look younger every day. I don't know what you dye your head and beard with, but you might give me some.'

'I'm returning your call, Bragin,' I lied. 'I hope you don't mind, but I have my fads, being from St. Petersburg, and I always keep count of visits.'

'Delighted, old boy. I'm half dotty in my old age and I like a bit of ceremony. Yes, indeed.'

From his voice and beatific smile I could tell that my visit greatly flattered him. Two peasant women helped me off with my coat in the hall and a red-shirted peasant hung it on a hook. Then Bragin and I went into his small study, where two barefooted little girls sat on the floor looking at a picture-book. Seeing us, they jumped up and ran out, immediately after which a tall, slim, bespectacled old woman entered, bowed gravely, picked a cushion from the sofa and the picture-book from the floor, and went out. From adjoining rooms constant whispering and barefoot shuffling were heard.

'I'm expecting the doctor for lunch,' said Bragin. 'He promised to look in from the clinic. Yes, indeed, he lunches here every Wednesday, more power to his elbow.'

He bent forward and kissed me on the neck.

'You can't be angry with me, old man, or you wouldn't be here,' he whispered wheezily. 'No need for anger, old boy. No, indeed. Never mind insults, just don't be angry. Before I die I ask God only this: to live the right way, in peace and harmony with one and all. Yes, indeed.'

'Excuse me, Bragin, I'll put my feet up on a chair,' I said, feeling so utterly exhausted that I couldn't be my usual self. I settled back in the sofa, putting my feet up on an arm-chair. My face glowed from snow and wind, and I felt as if my whole body was sucking up warmth and growing weaker from it.

'You are very snug here,' I went on. 'You're warm, soft, comfortable. You even have goose-quill pens.'

I laughed and looked at his desk. 'And a sand-box too.'

'Eh? Quite so. Yes, indeed. That desk and this little mahogany cupboard were made for my father by a self-taught cabinet-maker: Gleb Butyga, one of General Zhukov's serfs. Yes, indeed. A great artist in his own line.'

In the dreary tones of one dropping off to sleep, he began talking about Butyga the cabinet-maker, and I listened. Then he went into the next room to show me a remarkably handsome and inexpensive rosewood chest-of-drawers. He tapped it with a finger, then drew my attention to a stove of patterned tiles such as one doesn't see anywhere nowadays. That stove too he tapped with a finger. The chest-of-drawers, the tiled stove, the arm-chairs, the wool and silk samplers in their solid, ugly frames . . . these things breathed a cloyed complacency. When one remembers that all these objects had been standing in just the same places, in the very same order, when I was a little boy and used to come over to parties with my mother, it becomes quite inconceivable that they could ever cease to exist.

How terribly different Butyga and I were, thought I. As one who built—and made a great point of building—solidly and substantially, Butyga attached particular significance to human longevity, and never thought of death. He barely conceived it possible, very likely, whereas I built my iron and stone bridges to last thousands of years, yet just couldn't help thinking that they would not last all that long and that there was no point in them anyway.

In due course some competent art historian may light upon Butyga's cupboard and my bridge.

'These were two remarkable men in their own way,' he will say. 'Loving his fellow men, Butyga did not concede that they might die and decompose, so he made his furniture with an immortal man in mind, whereas Engineer Asorin did not love people—or life either. Even in blissful moments of creativity he was not repelled by thoughts of death, dissolution and the finite. So look how wretched, limited, timid and pitiful those lines are.'

'I only heat these rooms,' muttered Bragin, showing me round. 'Since my wife died, and my son was killed in the war, I've kept the best rooms shut up. Yes, er, as you see——'

He unlocked one door and I saw a large room with four columns, an old upright piano and a heap of peas on the floor. It smelt cold and damp.

'I keep garden benches in the next room,' muttered Bragin. 'We've no one to dance the mazurka any more, so I've locked it up.'

We heard the noise of Dr. Sable's arrival. While he rubbed his cold hands and tidied his wet beard I had time to notice: firstly, that he was bored with life, and therefore glad to see me and Bragin—and, secondly, that he was a bit of a simpleton and an innocent. He looked at me as if I must be overjoyed and fascinated to see him.

'I haven't slept for two nights,' he said, gazing at me innocently and combing his beard. 'Spent the first one on a confinement and the next at a peasant's where I had bed-bugs biting me all night. I'm as tired as hell, if you see what I mean.'

With the air of one who could not fail to purvey pleasure unalloyed, he took my arm and led me to the dining-room. His innocent eyes, crumpled frock-coat and cheap tie, the smell of iodoform . . . these things struck me disagreeably and made me think of him as a social inferior. We sat down to table and he poured me some vodka. I drank it, smiling helplessly. He put some ham on my plate. I ate it obediently.

'*Repetitio est mater studiorum*,' said Sable, swiftly tossing down his second glass. 'I'm so glad to see such nice people, you know, I don't even feel tired any more. I've turned into a peasant, I've gone to seed out here in the back of beyond—run wild, I have. But I am still an intellectual, gentlemen, and I can't stand the lack of social life, I tell you straight.'

As the cold dish, white sucking-pig was served with horse-radish and sour cream, followed by a rich, piping hot cabbage stew cooked with pork and buckwheat gruel, which sent up a column of steam. The doctor went on talking and I soon realized that this was a feeble, slovenly, unhappy creature. He grew tipsy on three glasses, became unnaturally excited, gorged himself with a grunting and smacking of lips and was now addressing me in Italian style: as *Eccelenza*. With the innocent look of one certain that I must be overjoyed to see and hear him, he notified me that he had been separated from his wife for some time, that he gave her three quarters of his salary, that she lived in town with his children (a boy and girl whom he adored), that he loved another woman—a squire's widow, an intellectual—but seldom saw her, being busy all day long and not having a moment free.

'I am in hospital all day or on my rounds,' he said, 'and I swear I haven't time to read a book, *Eccelenza*, let alone visit the woman I love. It's ten years since I read anything, *Eccelenza*, ten years. And as for things material, there are times when I can't afford tobacco, even—you ask Bragin here.'

'But you do have moral satisfaction,' I said.

'Eh?' he asked, screwing up an eye. 'Oh, do let's have another drink.'

As I listened to the doctor I followed my invariable practice and measured him by my routine criteria: 'materialist', 'idealist', 'filthy lucre', 'herd instinct' and so forth. But not one yardstick fitted even approximately. Moreover, while I was only listening and looking at him I could make complete sense of him, curiously enough, but as soon as I began trying to classify him he became extraordinarily complex, intricate and mysterious, for all his candour and frankness. Could this man, I wondered, embezzle money, abuse confidence, have a bent for scrounging? This question, once so serious and significant, now seemed naïve, trivial, crude.

A pie was served—followed, I remember (with long intervals of drinking home-made liqueurs), by a stew of pigeons, a tripe dish, roast sucking-pig, duck, partridge, cauliflower, fruit dumplings, curds and whey, jelly . . . and finally pancakes and jam. I started eating with relish, especially the cabbage stew and buckwheat, but then munched and swallowed like an automaton, smiling helplessly, tasting nothing. The hot stew and the heat of the room made my face burn. Bragin and Sable too were red in the face.

'To your wife's health!' said Sable. 'She likes me. Her personal physician sends his regards, tell her.'

'She has a knack, I must say,' Bragin sighed. 'Without fussing, worrying or bothering at all she has emerged as the key figure in our whole county. Most of this business is in her hands, she's the focus for everyone: doctor, local magistrates, ladies. People of the right sort can carry off such things without trying. Yes, indeed. Your apple-tree doesn't have to bother growing apples, they just come.'

'If you don't bother, it means you just don't care,' I said.

'Eh? Oh, quite,' muttered Bragin, not hearing me. 'Quite true. One should cultivate indifference. Quite, quite so. Precisely. Just you do your duty by God and your neighbour and let everything else go hang.'

'Look at nature around us, *Eccelenza*,' said Sable solemnly. 'If you poke your nose or ear outside your collar you get frost-bite, and if you spend an hour out in the fields you'll be buried by snow. The Russian countryside is just as it has been from time immemorial, it hasn't changed a scrap, it's still as primitive and savage as it was back in the dark ages. It's all burning and starving and fighting nature tooth and claw. Now, what was I on about? Yes, indeed. When you come to think of it, you know, when you scrutinize and sift all this muck, if you'll pardon my language, it's no sort of a life, this isn't, it's more like a fire in a theatre. Anyone falling over, shouting in panic or rushing to and fro . . . he's the worst enemy of good order. So mind you stand up straight, keep your wits about you and don't bat an eyelid. There's no time for snivelling and trivial fussing. When tackling the elements, set the other elements against them. Be firm, be unyielding, be rock-like.'

He turned to Bragin.

'What do you say, Granddad?' he laughed. 'I'm a real old woman, a miserable, maudlin sentimentalist, which is just why I can't stand sentimentality. I dislike petty feelings. One man mopes, another's a coward. A third will come in here right now. "Look at you," he'll say. "Going on about the starving with a ten-course meal inside your belly!" That's so petty and stupid. And yet another will blame you for being rich, *Eccelenza*.

'I'm sorry, *Eccelenza*,' he went on noisily, laying his hand over his heart, 'but the way you've bothered the detective and had him hunting your burglars morning noon and night . . . I'm sorry, but that's a pretty mean trick too. I'm a bit drunk, which is why I'm saying this. But a mean trick it is, if you see what I mean.'

'Who asked him to take all that trouble? That's what I don't see,' I said, standing up.

Feeling intolerable shame and mortification, I started walking round the table. 'Who asked him to go to all that trouble. Not me, I can tell you—blast the man!'

'He arrested three men and released them,' Sable laughed. 'They weren't the ones, it turned out, so now he's looking for some others. What a business!'

'I didn't ask him to take all that trouble,' I said, ready to weep with vexation. 'What, oh what, is the point of all this? Very well—let us say I was wrong, let's say I behaved badly. But why must people try to put me even more in the wrong?'

'Well, well, well, well!' Sable spoke soothingly. 'Come, now. I only said it because I've taken a drop or two. My tongue is my worst enemy.

'Ah, well,' he sighed, 'we have eaten, we've drunk wine and now it's good old bed-time.'

He got up from table, kissed Bragin on the head and left the dining-room, staggering and surfeited. Bragin and I silently lit cigarettes.

'I never sleep after dinner, my dear chap,' said Bragin, 'but you are welcome to go and lie down in the lounge.'

I accepted. By the walls of the dim, well-heated so-called lounge stood sofas. Long and broad, solid and heavy, they were cabinet-maker Butyga's work and carried high, soft, white bedding which had probably been made up by the bespectacled old woman. On one couch—coatless, bootless, facing the back of the sofa—Sable was already asleep. Another couch awaited me. Removing coat and boots, I yielded to fatigue, to the spirit of Butyga which presided over this quiet lounge, to Sable's gentle, caressing snore . . . and obediently lay down.

At once I began dreaming about my wife, her room, the station-master with his look of hatred, the heaps of snow and the theatre fire. I dreamt of the peasants who had stolen the twenty sacks of rye from my barn.

'Anyway, I'm glad the detective let them go,' I said.

Woken by my own voice, I stared for a minute in bewilderment at Sable's broad back, at his waistcoat buckle and thick heels, then lay down and went to sleep again.

It was quite dark when I awoke for the second time. Sable was asleep. Relaxed and eager to go home at once, I dressed and went out of the lounge. Bragin was sitting quite still in his large arm-chair. His face wore a fixed stare and he had obviously been in this petrified state all the while I had been sleeping.

'Very good,' I said yawning. 'I feel as if I had woken up on the morning after a carnival. I'm going to come here often from now on. Tell me, has my wife ever eaten here?'

'Yes, er, sometimes,' muttered Bragin, trying to bestir himself. 'She lunched last Saturday. Yes, indeed. She's fond of me.'

'Remember telling me I was a bad character, Bragin?' I asked after a short pause. 'And what a bore I was? Well now, how can I change myself?'

'I can't say, old man. I'm just a doddering old fogy, I can't advise you. No, indeed. But I told you that because I'm fond of you, and of your wife, as I was of your father too. Yes, indeed. I shall soon be dead, so why should I conceal anything from you or tell you lies? So that's what I say: I'm very fond of you, but I don't respect you. No, respect you I do not.'

He turned to me.

'One can't respect you, old man,' he whispered, gasping. 'From the look of you, you are a more or less real person. In appearance and bearing you're like President Carnot of France—I saw a picture of him the other day in the *Illustrated*. Yes, indeed. You speak impressively, you are clever, you're high up in the service, you've left us all standing, but you haven't really got a soul, old man. It has no strength to it. No, indeed.'

I laughed. 'In other words, I'm beyond the pale. But what of my wife? Tell me about her, you know her better.'

I wanted to talk about my wife, but Sable came in and prevented us.

'I've slept and washed,' he said, giving me his innocent glance. 'I'll have some tea and rum and be off home.'

VII

It was about half past seven. Bragin accompanied us from hall to porch, as also did incantations and miscellaneous good wishes from the female servants, the bespectacled old woman, the little girls, the peasant. Men with lanterns were standing and moving in the dark near our horses as they told our coachmen the best way home and wished us a pleasant journey. Horses, sledge and people . . . all were white.

'Where do all these people come from?' I asked as my three-horse team and the doctor's pair were ambling out of the yard.

'They're all his serfs,' said Sable. 'Emancipation hasn't reached him yet. Some of the old servants are living out their lives and, well, there are various orphans who have nowhere to go. Some of them forced themselves on him and he can't get rid of them. He is a funny old boy.'

Once again we sped swiftly along. Drunken Nikanor shouted his weird shouts, while wind and snow were everywhere, driving into eyes, mouth and every fold of one's furs.

'What a ride!' thought I as my sleigh-bells pealed in unison with the doctor's, wind whistled, coachmen whooped. While the frantic racket proceeded I called to mind every detail of this strange, wild day unique in my life, feeling as if I really had gone mad or become a different man: as if I was already a stranger to the person whom I had been until yesterday.

The doctor drove behind, keeping up loud converse with his coachman. From time to time he caught me up and drove alongside, always with the same innocent assurance of giving pleasure. He offered cigarettes and asked for matches. Then he drew level and suddenly rose full height in the sledge, waving coat sleeves nearly twice as long as his arms.

'Flay 'em, Vaska!' he yelled. 'You show those thoroughbreds! Gee up, you kittens!'

Sable and his Vaska gave loud, jeering laughs as the doctor's kittens flew ahead. Taking umbrage, my Nikanor held back our team. But when the doctor's sleigh-bells could be heard no more he raised his elbows with a whoop and off our outfit hurtled in pursuit as if berserk. We drove into some village. Lights and hut silhouettes flashed past.

'Damn and blast 'em!' someone yelled.

We must have raced for well over a mile, and still the road stretched ahead with no end in view. We caught the doctor up and drove at a slower pace. He asked for matches.

'How can you feed a street like that?' he asked. 'And this, dear sir, is only one of five such streets.'

'Stop! Stop!' he shouted. 'Turn off at the inn! We must have something warm and rest our horses.'

We stopped at the inn.

'I have plenty such villages in my "diocese",' said the doctor. Opening a heavy door with a squeaking block-and-pulley, he ushered me in first. 'When you look at these streets by daylight they seem to go on for ever, and there are side streets too. You can only scratch your head over it, more it's hard to do.'

We went into a saloon bar smelling strongly of table-cloths. A sleepy peasant, in waistcoat and shirt worn outside his trousers, jumped up from a bench at our appearance. Sable ordered beer, I tea.

'It's hard to do anything,' said Sable. 'Your wife has faith and I honour and respect her, but I'm a bit of a sceptic myself. So long as our dealings with the peasant smack of mere common charity—orphanages, old people's homes, that sort of thing—we shall just be cheating, shilly-shallying and deceiving ourselves, that's all. Our relations should be businesslike and based on self-interest, knowledge and fairness. My

Vaska always used to work for me as a labourer. Now his crops have failed, he's sick and starving. If I offer him fifteen copecks a day now I thereby seek to restore him to his former labourer's position—which means I'm looking after my own interests first and foremost, and yet for some reason I call the fifteen copecks "relief", "aid", "good works". Now, look at it this way. Reckoning seven copecks per head and five persons per family, it takes 350 roubles a day to feed a thousand families on the most modest estimate. This figure defines our essential business relations towards a thousand families. Yet we don't give them 350 roubles a day, we give them only ten and we term this "relief" and "assistance", we say it makes your wife and the rest of us perfectly splendid people, we give three cheers for philanthropy. That's the way of it, old boy. Oh, if only we talked less about how philanthropic we are, if we did more calculating and reasoning, if we took our duties conscientiously! How many humane, sensitive people we have among us who solemnly trot round the peasants' homesteads waving their subscription lists . . . yet don't pay their tailors and cooks. There's no logic in our lives, that's what it comes to. They don't make sense!'

We paused for a moment and I made a mental calculation.

'I'll feed a thousand families for two hundred days,' I said. 'Come and talk about it tomorrow.'

I was pleased to have put it so simply and was glad when Sable answered even more simply.

'Right.'

We paid what we owed and came out of the inn.

'I like these muddles,' said Sable, mounting his sledge. 'Let's have a match, *Eccelenza*, I left mine in the pub.'

Fifteen minutes later his pair had fallen behind and I no longer heard his sleigh-bells through the blizzard's roar. Arriving home, I walked up and down my rooms, trying to work out and define my position as precisely as possible. I hadn't one word or sentence ready for my wife. My brain was not working.

I had still hit on nothing when I went down to see her. She stood in her room, still in that same pink house-coat, still in the same pose of one shielding her papers from me. Her face expressed dismay and derision. She had obviously learnt of my arrival and had made up her mind not to cry, not to ask for anything, not to defend herself as yesterday—but to laugh at me, to answer me with contempt, to act decisively.

'If that's how things are there is no more to be said,' her expression conveyed.

'I haven't left home, Natalie,' I said, 'but it isn't a trick. I am crazy, old, ill, I'm a changed man—make of it what you like. I have recoiled from my former self with horror—yes, with horror, I tell you! I despise it, I'm ashamed of it, and my new self, born yesterday, won't let me leave. Don't make me go, Natalie.'

Staring into my face, she believed me and a worried look flashed in her eyes, while I was enchanted by her presence and warmed by the heat of her room.

'You're the only person I care for in the world, believe me,' I muttered deliriously, holding out my arms to her. 'I have missed you every minute of the day and only my stubborn pride has stopped me admitting it. We cannot, we need not restore the days when we lived as man and wife, but you must make me your servant. Take all my property, give it away to anyone you like. I am at peace, Natalie, I'm content. I'm at peace.'

She stared inquisitively into my face, then gave a sudden, low cry, burst into tears and ran into the next room. I went to my quarters upstairs.

An hour later I was at my desk writing my history of the railways, unhampered by thoughts of the starving. Now I no longer feel worried. The disorderly scenes which I saw the other day when touring the Pyostrovo huts with my wife and Sable, the malignant rumours, the mistakes of those around me, the approach of old age . . . none of these things bother me. Flying cannon-balls and bullets don't stop soldiers on active service talking of their affairs, eating and mending their boots, nor do the starving peasants stop me sleeping peacefully and dealing with my private affairs. In my house and yard and far around them work is in full swing: an 'orgy of charity', Doctor Sable calls it. My wife often visits me and looks nervously round my rooms as if seeking something else to give the starving so as to 'justify her existence', while I see that we shall soon have no property left, thanks to her. We shall be poor, but I don't mind and I give her a cheerful smile.

What will happen later I don't know.

THE TWO VOLODYAS

'LET GO of me, I want to drive, I'm going to sit by the driver,' shouted Sophia. 'Wait, driver, I'm coming on the box with you.'

She was standing in the sledge while her husband Volodya and her childhood friend, another Volodya, both held her arms to stop her falling. On rushed the troika.

'I told you not to give her brandy,' whispered her husband irritably to the other Volodya. 'It really was rather naughty of you.'

With women like his wife Sophia, rowdy and somewhat tipsy high spirits usually presaged hysterical laughter and then tears—the Colonel knew that from experience, and he dreaded having to fuss with compresses and medicines when they got home, instead of going to bed.

'Whoa there,' shouted Sophia. 'I want to drive.'

She was truly happy and jubilant. During the two months since her wedding she had been nagged by the thought of having married Colonel Yagich for his money and 'out of frustration'. But at the out-of-town restaurant this evening she had at last convinced herself that she loved him passionately. He was so trim, so spry, so lithe despite his fifty-four years, he was so charming when he joked and hummed an accompaniment to the gipsy girls' music. Older men are a thousand times more attractive than young ones nowadays, that's a fact, as if age and youth had exchanged roles. The Colonel was two years older than her father, but what did that matter when he was far, far more dynamic, high-spirited and vivacious, quite honestly, than she was herself? And she was only twenty-three.

'Oh my darling,' she thought. 'You splendid man.'

She had also decided at the restaurant that no spark of her old feelings for the other Volodya remained in her heart. To that childhood friend whom, only yesterday, she had loved to distraction and despair, she now felt utterly indifferent. He had seemed such an apathetic, drowsy, unattractive nonentity all evening. His casual habit of dodging payment in restaurants had outraged her this time, and she had nearly told him to stay at home if he was so poor. The Colonel had paid for everything.

Perhaps it was the trees, telegraph poles and snow-drifts flitting past her eyes which prompted such a variety of thoughts. The restaurant bill had come to a hundred and twenty roubles, she reflected, the gipsies had been paid a hundred, and she could throw away a whole thousand tomorrow if she liked, whereas before her wedding two months ago she had had less than three roubles to call her own. She had had to go to her father for every little thing. How her life had changed!

Her thoughts were muddled, and she remembered when she had been about ten—how Colonel Yagich, now her husband, had flirted with her aunt, how everyone at home had said that he had 'ruined' Aunt, how Aunt indeed had often come down to dinner with her eyes red from crying, how she was always going off somewhere, how people had said that the poor creature didn't know what to do with herself. He had been very handsome then, famous all over town for his fantastic success with women, and was said to visit his lady admirers daily like a doctor on his rounds. Even now, for all the grey hair, wrinkles and spectacles, his lean face sometimes looked very handsome, especially in profile.

Sophia's father was an army doctor who had once served in Yagich's regiment. The other Volodya's father was a medical officer, and had served in the same regiment too. Despite amorous adventures often highly complex and hectic, the younger Volodya had been a brilliant student. After graduating with honours he had chosen to specialize in foreign literature, and was said to be writing a thesis. He lived in barracks with his father the medical officer, and had no money of his own though he was now thirty. As children he and Sophia had lived in different flats in the same building, he had often come and played with her, they had been taught dancing and French together. But when he had grown into a slender, very handsome youth she had begun to feel shy with him, and had then fallen madly in love with him. And in love with him she had remained until her recent marriage. He too had had remarkable success with women, pretty well from the age of fourteen, and the ladies who deceived their husbands with him would excuse themselves by saying that Volodya was so 'little'. There was a recent account of him as a student living in rooms near the university—every time you knocked you'd hear his step on the other side of the door and the low-voiced apology, '*Pardon, je ne suis pas seul.*' He was a great joy to Yagich, who, like the old poet Derzhavin blessing the young Pushkin, expected great things of him, and was obviously devoted to him. They would play billiards or piquet for hours in silence. If Yagich went troika-riding he would take Volodya with him, and only Yagich was privy to the secrets of Volodya's thesis. Earlier, in the Colonel's younger days, they had often found themselves in competition, but without jealousy. When they were in company together Yagich was called 'Big Volodya' and his friend 'Small Volodya'.

Besides Big Volodya, Small Volodya and Sophia, the sledge had another occupant, Sophia Yagich's cousin Rita—a spinster in her thirties, very pale with black eyebrows and pince-nez, who chain-smoked even in the freezing cold. She always had ash on the front of her dress and on her lap. She spoke through her nose, she drawled, she was undemonstrative, she could put back as many liqueurs and brandies as she liked without getting drunk, and she told *risqué* stories in a dull, tasteless way. At home she read the intellectual reviews morning, noon and night, scattering ash over them, or ate crystallized apples.

'Do stop fooling, Sophia,' she drawled. 'Don't be so silly, really.'

When the city gates came in view the troika slowed down, there were glimpses of houses and people, and Sophia subsided, cuddling up to her husband, utterly lost in thought. Small Volodya sat opposite her. Now gloomy notions began to tinge her happy, light-hearted reveries. The man opposite knew she had been in love with him, she supposed, and he must have believed this talk about her marrying the Colonel 'out of frustration'. She had never told him she loved him, she had no wish for him to know about it, she had hidden her feelings, but his expression showed that he understood her perfectly—and her pride suffered. But most humiliating of all, given her situation, was that Small Volodya had suddenly started taking notice of her after her marriage, which had never happened before. He would sit with her for hours in silence or idly chatting, and now in the sledge he was gently pressing her leg and massaging her hand without talking to her. He had only been waiting for her to get married, obviously. No less obviously, he despised her. She aroused in him only interest of a certain kind, as if she was a loose woman. And it was this combination of jubilant love for her husband with humiliation and injured pride that made her feel so thoroughly mischievous, made her want to sit on the driver's box, shout and whistle.

They were just passing the convent when a great clanging came from the huge twenty-ton bell. Rita made the sign of the cross.

'That's where Olga is,' said Sophia, also crossing herself and shuddering.

'What made her take the veil?' the Colonel asked.

'Sheer frustration,' answered Rita angrily, with an obvious allusion to the marriage of Sophia and Yagich. 'That sort of thing is all the rage now. It's a challenge to society as a whole. A jolly girl she was, a terrific flirt who cared only for dances and dancing partners. And then, suddenly, this business! What a surprise.'

'That's not true,' said Small Volodya, lowering the collar of his fur coat and revealing his handsome face. 'It wasn't just frustration, I'm very sorry, it was something utterly horrible. Her brother Dmitry was sentenced to hard labour in Siberia, and now no one knows where he is. Her mother died of a broken heart.'

He raised his collar again.

'Olga did the right thing,' he added tonelessly. 'To be a foster-child, and in our precious Sophia's home at that—it's enough to give you pause.'

Sophia heard the sneer in his voice and wanted to pay him back in kind, but said nothing. Then, feeling that mischievous urge again, she stood up.

'I want to go to the service,' she shouted tearfully. 'Turn back, driver, I want to see Olga.'

They turned back. The tolling of the convent bell was deafening, and there was something in it reminiscent of Olga and her life, Sophia felt. Other church bells also started ringing. When the driver halted Sophia jumped from the sledge and rushed to the gate unescorted.

'Do please hurry,' shouted her husband. 'It's late.'

She went through the dark gate and along the path to the main church. Snow crunched under her feet and the tolling resounded right above her head, seeming to penetrate her whole being. She came to the church door, the three steps down and the porch with frescoes of saints on both sides. There was a smell of juniper and incense. Then came another door which a dark figure opened with a low bow.

In church the service had not yet started. One nun was attending to the icon screen and lighting the candles in their massive holders, another was lighting a chandelier. Here and there by the columns and side-altars stood unmoving black figures.

'They'll just stand where they are till morning,' thought Sophia. How dark, cold and depressing this was, she felt—worse than a graveyard. Feeling bored, she looked at the still, frozen figures, and suddenly her heart missed a beat. Somehow she had recognized one of the nuns—short, with thin shoulders and a black shawl on her head—as Olga, though Olga had been a buxom lass and rather taller when she had entered the convent. Hesitant and mightily agitated for some reason, Sophia went up to the novice, looked into her face over her shoulder and recognized Olga.

'Olga!' She threw up her arms, too moved to say more.

The nun knew her at once. She raised her eyebrows in amazement, and her pale, freshly washed, clean face glowed with pleasure—as did also, apparently, the white kerchief visible under her shawl.

'The Lord has wrought a miracle.' She too threw up her hands, which were thin and pale.

Sophia embraced her firmly and kissed her, afraid as she did so that she must smell of brandy.

'We were just driving past and thought of you,' she gasped, as if she had been walking too fast. 'Lord, how pale you are. I, er, I'm very glad to see you. Well, how are things, how are you, are you bored?'

Sophia looked round at the other nuns. 'We've had so many changes,' she went on quietly. 'I married Volodya Yagich, you know, I'm sure you remember him. I'm very happy with him.'

'The Lord be praised. And is your father well?'

'Yes, he often remembers you. But you should come and see us during the holiday, Olga. How about it?'

Olga laughed. 'Very well, I'll come the day after tomorrow.'

Without knowing why, Sophia burst into tears, wept silently for a minute, then wiped her eyes.

'Rita will be so sorry to have missed you,' she said. 'She's with us too. Small Volodya's here as well. They're at the gate. They'd be so pleased to see you. Let's go out to them—the service hasn't begun, has it?'

'All right then,' agreed Olga. She crossed herself three times and went out with Sophia.

'You're happy then, are you, Sophia?' Olga asked when they were outside the gate.

'Yes, very.'

'Thank God.'

When Big Volodya and Small Volodya saw the nun they got off the sledge and greeted her respectfully, both obviously touched by the pallor of her face and her black habit, both pleased that she remembered them and had come to greet them. To shield her from the cold Sophia wrapped her in a rug and covered her with a flap of her fur coat. Her recent tears had relieved and purged her spirits, and she was glad that this rowdy, turbulent and essentially sullied night had unexpectedly come to so pure and gentle an end. To keep Olga near her longer she suggested taking her for a ride.

'Get in, Olga, we'll go for a bit of a spin.'

The men expected the nun to refuse since the religious don't gad around in troikas, but to their surprise she assented and mounted the sledge. As the three-horse team whisked them off towards the city gates all were silent, concerned only for her comfort and warmth, each comparing her former with her present state. Her expression was neutral, rather impassive, frigid, pale and transparent as though she had water rather than blood flowing through her veins. Two or three years ago she had been a buxom, rosy-cheeked girl, always talking about young men and laughing uproariously at the slightest pretext.

The sledge turned back at the town gate. About ten minutes later they halted at the convent and Olga got out. A medley of peals now rang from the belfry.

'May the Lord preserve you.' Olga gave a low nun-like bow.

'You will visit us, won't you, Olga?'

'Yes, yes, of course.'

She moved off quickly and soon disappeared through the dark gateway. Then the sledge bowled off again, and they all somehow felt terribly sad. Nobody spoke. Sophia felt weak all over and her spirits fell. To have got a nun into a sledge and taken her for a troika ride in tipsy company—it now struck her as silly, tactless and rather sacrilegious. The desire for self-deception had left her along with her intoxication. She neither did nor could love her husband, she now realized, all that was arrant nonsense. She had married him for his money because he was what her schoolfriends had called 'madly rich', because she was terrified of being left on the shelf like Rita, because she was fed up with her doctor father, because she wanted to spite Small Volodya. Could she have imagined, when contemplating the marriage, that it would prove so ugly and unnerving an ordeal, nothing in the world would have induced her to consent to it. But things were past praying for now, she must put up with them.

They arrived home. Climbing into her warm, soft bed, pulling the quilt over her, Sophia remembered the dark porch, the smell of incense, the figures by the columns, and was aghast to think that those figures would stand there without moving all the time she would be asleep. Early mass would last a very long time, then there would be the Hours, then another mass and a prayer service.

'But God does exist, He certainly does, and I shall most certainly die, so sooner or later I must think about my soul and eternal life, as Olga does. Olga is saved now, she has solved all her problems. But what if there is no God? Then her life has been wasted. But what do I mean, "wasted"? Wasted how?'

A minute later another thought occurred.

'God exists, death will come without fail and one must think about one's soul. Should Olga face death this instant she would be unafraid, she is prepared. But the main thing is, she has made her own decision about life's problems. God exists, indeed. But is entering a convent really the only answer? To take the veil—why, that means renouncing life, destroying it.'

Sophia felt rather terrified and hid her head beneath her pillow. 'I mustn't, mustn't think about that,' she whispered.

Yagich was pacing the carpet in the next room, his spurs gently jingling. He was pondering.

It struck Sophia that the man was near and dear to her only in this, that he too was called Volodya. She sat up in bed.

'Volodya,' she called tenderly.

'What do you want?' her husband responded.

'Oh, nothing.'

She lay down again. There was a tolling, perhaps from that same convent bell, and she again remembered the porch and the dark figures. Thoughts about God and the inevitability of death drifted through her mind, and she pulled the quilt over her head to shut out the bells. She reckoned that she had a long, long life ahead of her before old age and death. Day in day out she would have to cope with the proximity of this man whom she didn't love, who had just come into the bedroom and was getting into bed, and she would have to suppress her hopeless love of another man—young, charming, somehow special. She looked at her husband and wanted to say good night, but suddenly burst into tears instead. She was annoyed with herself.

'Here we go again,' said Yagich.

She did calm down, but later—towards ten in the morning. She had stopped crying and shivering all over, but had acquired an acute headache instead. Yagich was hurrying off to late mass and was in the next room grumbling at the batman who was helping him dress. He came into the bedroom once, his spurs faintly jingling, and fetched something, then came in a second time—now wearing his epaulettes and decorations, limping a bit because of his rheumatism. He vaguely impressed Sophia as prowling and lurking like a beast of prey.

Then she heard him on the telephone.

'Put me through to the Vasilyevsky Barracks, please.' There was a short pause. 'Vasilyevsky Barracks? Kindly call Dr. Salimovich to the telephone.' Another short pause. 'Who's that speaking? Volodya? Good. Then ask your father to call round here straight away, there's a good fellow. Fact is, my lady wife has come considerably unstuck after last night's business. He's out, eh? Ah, well. Many thanks, that's fine—I'll be most obliged. *Merci*.'

Yagich came into the bedroom for the third time, bent over his wife, made the sign of the cross over her, gave her his hand to kiss—the women who loved him used to kiss his hand, and he expected it—and said he would be back for dinner. He left.

Towards noon the maid announced Small Volodya. Swaying with fatigue and her headache, Sophia swiftly donned her splendid new lilac-coloured négligé with the fur trimmings and hurriedly did something to her hair. She felt inexpressibly tender, trembling both with joy and the fear that he might leave. She only wanted to look at him.

Small Volodya had arrived in formal visiting style—tail-coat and white tie. When Sophia came into the drawing-room he kissed her hand and said how truly sorry he was that she was unwell. When they had sat down he praised her négligé.

'I was put out by meeting Olga last night,' she said. 'It rather unnerved me at first, but I envy her now. She's as firm as a rock, there's no budging her. But was there really no other resort, Volodya? Can you really solve life's problems by burying yourself alive? That's death, isn't it—not life?'

At the mention of Olga, Small Volodya's face expressed tender concern.

'Now you're a clever man, Volodya,' said Sophia. 'So show me how I can best follow her example. I'm not a believer, of course, and couldn't take the veil, but I could do something equivalent, couldn't I? My life isn't easy,' she went on after a short pause. 'You teach me, then. Tell me something that will convince me. Say but one word.'

'One word? All right then. Ta-ra-ra-boomdeay.'

'Why do you despise me, Volodya?' she asked impetuously. 'You talk to me in some special—forgive me—caddish language. No one talks to their friends or to decent women like that. You're a successful scholar, you love academic work, but why, oh why do you never speak to me of that? Am I unworthy?'

'Whence this sudden yearning for scholarship?' Small Volodya frowned irritatedly. 'Perhaps you yearn for constitutional government? Or perhaps you'd prefer sturgeon with horseradish?'

'Oh, all right, I'm an insignificant, worthless, immoral, half-witted woman. I've made masses and masses of mistakes, I'm a nervous wreck, I'm corrupt and so I deserve contempt. But you're ten years older than me, Volodya, aren't you? And my husband's thirty years older. You watched me grow up, and if you'd wanted you could have made anything of me you liked—an angel, even. But you'—her voice trembled—'you treat me terribly. Yagich married me in his old age, and you——'

'Oh really, do give over.' Volodya moved nearer to her and kissed both her hands. 'Let us permit the Schopenhauers to philosophize and argue to their hearts' content, while we just kiss these dear little hands.'

'You despise me—oh, if you only knew what suffering that causes me,' she faltered, knowing in advance that he would not believe her. 'But I so much want to change, to turn over a new leaf, did you but know. I think of it with such joy,' she added, and tears of joy actually came to her eyes. 'To be a good, honourable, decent person, not to lie, to have a purpose in life——'

'Oh, for heaven's sake drop the play-acting, I dislike it.' Volodya's face assumed a petulant expression. 'It's so melodramatic, honestly. Let's behave like real people.'

To prevent him from leaving in a huff she began justifying herself, forcing a smile to please him, and again spoke of Olga, and of wanting to solve her problems in life and become a real person.

'Ta-ra-ra-boomdeay, ta-ra-ra-boomdeay,' he sang softly, spacing out the syllables.

Then he suddenly seized her waist. She, not knowing what she was doing, put her hands on his shoulders and for a minute gazed enraptured and entranced at his clever, ironical face, his forehead, his eyes, his handsome beard.

'As you have known for some time, I love you,' she confessed, blushing painfully and feeling her very lips twisted in a spasm of embarrassment. 'I love you. So why torture me?'

She closed her eyes and kissed him firmly on the lips. For a long time, perhaps a whole minute, she could not bring the kiss to an end, though she knew that it was improper, that he himself might think badly of her, that one of the servants might come in.

'Oh, how you torture me,' she said.

Half an hour later, when he had had what he wanted, he was eating a snack in the dining-room while she knelt before him, gazing passionately into his face, and he said that she was like a little dog waiting to be thrown a piece of ham. Then he sat her on one knee, rocked her like a child and sang.

'Ta-ra-ra-boomdeay.'

When he was ready to leave she asked him in a voice choked with passion when they could meet next. 'Later today? Where?'

She held out both hands to his mouth, as if wanting to catch the answer in them.

'I don't think today's convenient,' he said after some thought. 'We might manage tomorrow.'

They parted. Before lunch Sophia went to see Olga at the convent, but was told that she was reading the Psalter in memory of someone who had died. From the convent she went to see her father, but he was out too. Then she took a different cab and drove aimlessly up and down streets broad and narrow, continuing thus until evening fell. Meanwhile she somehow kept remembering the aunt with the eyes red from crying and without a place in life.

That night they went troika-riding again and heard the gipsy singers at the out-of-town restaurant. As they were driving past the convent again Sophia remembered Olga, and was aghast to think that girls and women of her class had no resort but non-stop troika rides and living a lie, or taking the veil and mortifying the flesh.

Next day she had a rendezvous with her lover, after which she took another lonely cab drive and again remembered her aunt.

A week later he dropped her, and then life resumed its former routine, being just as dull, painful—just as agonizing, sometimes—as ever. The Colonel and Small Volodya played billiards and piquet for hours, Rita limply told insipid anecdotes, Sophia kept going for cab drives and asking her husband to take her on troika trips.

Calling at the convent almost daily, she bored Olga with complaints about her unbearable sufferings. And she wept, feeling as if she had brought something soiled, pathetic, worn-out into the cell with her. But Olga told her in the wooden voice of one repeating a lesson that none of it mattered, it would all pass, God would forgive her.

THE BLACK MONK

I

ANDREW KOVRIN M.A. was exhausted and distraught, but instead of seeking regular medical treatment he had a casual word over a bottle of wine with a doctor friend who advised him to spend spring and summer in the country. This coincided with a long letter from Tanya Pesotsky inviting him to stay at Borisovka. So he decided that he really did need the trip.

First he went to his own family estate, Kovrinka, in April and spent three weeks there on his own. Then, after waiting till the roads were passable, he set off by carriage to see his former guardian and mentor Pesotsky, a horticulturalist of national repute. From Kovrinka to the Pesotskys' place at Borisovka was reckoned about fifty miles, and it was sheer joy, that spring day, to drive on the soft surface in a well-sprung carriage.

Pesotsky's house was huge, with its columns, its peeling plaster lions, its frock-coated footman at the front door. The old-fashioned park, bleak and forbidding, was laid out in English style, extending nearly a thousand yards from house to river and ending in a precipitous clay cliff sprouting pines with exposed roots like hairy paws. Down below the water gleamed uninvitingly, sandpipers swooped and squeaked piteously. The atmosphere was always positively elegiac. But near the house—in the gardens, orchards and nursery beds occupying some eighty acres altogether—it was bright and cheerful even in bad weather. Nowhere had Kovrin seen such superb roses, lilies, camellias and tulips in all conceivable hues from snow-white to soot-black, such a general profusion of blooms, as at Pesotsky's. Spring was only beginning, and the true glory of the flower-beds still lurked in hot-houses. But what was already in bloom along the paths, and here and there in the beds—it sufficed to transport you, as you strolled about, to a realm of delectable colours, especially in the early morning when dew gleamed on every petal.

This ornamental part of the garden, which Pesotsky himself dismissed as mere frippery, had been sheer magic to Kovrin as a boy. What curiosities, what grotesque freaks, what travesties of nature were here! There were espaliered fruit trees, a pear formed like a Lombardy poplar, globose oaks and limes, an umbrella-shaped apple-tree, arches, letter designs, candelabra, and even an '1862'—the year of Pesotsky's horticultural début—in plums. There were also fine, graceful saplings with firm, straight stems like palms, and only a close look showed that these saplings were gooseberries or currants. But the most exhilarating and stimulating aspect of the garden was the constant bustle. From dawn to dusk near trees and shrubs, on paths and flower-beds, gardeners swarmed ant-like with their barrows, mattocks, watering cans.

Reaching the Pesotskys' house towards ten in the evening, Kovrin found Tanya and her father Yegor in a great pother. The clear, starry sky and the thermometer presaged frost by morning, but the head gardener Ivan Karlych had gone to town and there was no one dependable left. They talked of nothing but this frost over supper, and it was decided that Tanya would patrol the orchard after midnight instead of going to bed, to keep an eye on things, and that her father would rise at three or even earlier.

Kovrin sat with Tanya all evening and went into the garden with her after midnight. It was cold outside, there was a strong smell of burning. In the large 'commercial' orchard—it earned Pesotsky several thousand roubles' annual profit—thick, black, acrid smoke was settling on the ground and enveloping the trees, protecting all that money from frost. The trees stood like pieces on a draughts board, their rows as straight and even as soldiers on parade. This strict, meticulous precision, combined with the trees' identical height and their absolutely uniform crowns and trunks—it made a monotonous, depressing picture. Walking down the files, where bonfires of dung, straw and mixed rubbish smouldered, Kovrin and Tanya met occasional labourers drifting wraith-like through the smoke. The only trees in bloom were cherries, plums and certain varieties of apple, but the whole orchard swam in smoke. Not till they reached the nursery beds did Kovrin draw a deep breath.

'The smoke used to make me sneeze as a boy.' He shrugged. 'But I still don't see how smoke protects from frost.'

'It replaces the clouds when the sky's clear,' Tanya answered.

'But what do the clouds do?'

'You don't get frost in dull, cloudy weather.'

'So that's it.'

He laughed and took her arm. Her broad, very serious-looking, chilled face, her thin black eyebrows, the raised overcoat collar impeding the movements of her head, her whole slender, graceful presence, her dress hitched up because of the dew—it all moved him.

'Heavens, how we have grown up,' he said. 'When I last left here five years ago you were still a child. You were thin, long-legged, bare-headed in your short little dress. I used to tease you—called you "the heron". How time changes things!'

'Yes, it's five years.' Tanya sighed. 'A lot of water has flowed under the bridge since then. Tell me honestly, Andrew.' She spoke vivaciously, looking into his face. 'Have you grown away from us? Why do I ask, though? You're a man, you live your own fascinating life, you're a somebody. It's only natural we should feel strangers. Still, I'd like you to think of us as family, Andrew—we've earned that.'

'And so I do, Tanya.'

'Word of honour?'

'Yes indeed.'

'Yesterday you were surprised that we had so many photographs of you. But Father idolizes you, you know. Sometimes I think he's fonder of you than me. He's so proud of you. You're a scholar, a distinguished man, you've made a brilliant career, and he's certain you turned out that way only because he brought you up. I don't try to stop him thinking that, why shouldn't he?'

Dawn was breaking, as was particularly evident from the clarity with which smoke puffs and tree-tops were outlined in the air. Nightingales sang, the quails' call wafted in from the fields.

'Well, it's time for bed—it's cold too.' Tanya took his arm. 'Thanks for coming, Andrew. The people we know are dull and there are so few of them. With us it's garden, garden, garden and nothing else.' She laughed. 'Standard, half-standard, pippins, rennets, codlings, budding, grafting. Our whole life's gone into this garden. All I dream of is apples and pears. It's all very well of course, it's useful, but you do want a change sometimes. I remember you coming over for the holidays or just on a visit, and how the house felt fresher and brighter, as if the dustcovers had been taken off the chandelier and furniture. I was only a child, but I understood.'

She spoke at length, ardently, and it suddenly struck him that he might grow fond of this small, frail, voluble creature during the summer—be attracted, fall in love. Given their situation it would be so possible and natural. The idea moved and amused him. Bending down to that dear, worried face, he sang softly.

'Onegin, I cannot deny
I'll love my Tanya till I die.'

When they returned to the house Pesotsky was already out of bed. Not feeling sleepy, Kovrin got talking to the old man, and went back to the garden with him. Pesotsky was tall, broad-shouldered, large-paunched and short-winded, but always walked so fast that it was hard to keep up with him. He had a most preoccupied look, and was for ever hurrying as if expecting total disaster should he ever be one minute late.

'Now, here's an odd thing, dear boy.' He paused for breath. 'It's below zero at ground level, as you see. But you put a thermometer on a stick and lift it a dozen feet in the air, and it's warm. Now, why?'

'I really don't know.' Kovrin laughed.

'Humph. One can't know everything of course. However capacious the brain, it can't hold everything. You're more on the philosophical side, aren't you?'

'Yes. I lecture in psychology, but I study general philosophy.'

'And don't you get bored?'

'Far from it, it's all I live for.'

'Then may God bless you.' Pesotsky thoughtfully stroked his grey side-whiskers. 'Good luck to you. I'm delighted for you, delighted, dear boy——'

But then he suddenly cocked his ears, grimaced horribly, ran to one side, swiftly disappeared behind the trees in clouds of smoke.

'Who tied a horse to that apple-tree?' the desperate, blood-curdling shout was heard. 'What bastard, what swine dared tie a horse to an apple-tree? God, God, they've ruined, frozen, befouled and mucked everything up! The garden's ruined—ye gods, it's wrecked!'

When Pesotsky returned he had a worn-out, aggrieved look.

'What in hell can one do with these bloody yokels?' he asked tearfully, waving his arms. 'Stepka was carting dung last night and tied his horse to an apple-tree. He twisted the reins as tight as could be, the blackguard, and so the bark has been chafed in three places. What do you say to that? I spoke to him and he just stood there blinking, the imbecile. Hanging's too good for him.'

Calming down, he embraced Kovrin and kissed his cheek.

'Ah well, God bless you,' he muttered. 'I'm so glad you came—more than I can say. Thanks.'

Then, with that same swift gait and preoccupied look, he toured the whole garden, showing his former ward all the greenhouses, conservatories, cold houses and two rows of beehives which he called the wonder of the age.

As they walked the sun rose and brightly lit the garden. It grew warm. Foreseeing a fine, happy, long day, Kovrin recalled that this was only early May after all, and that the whole summer lay ahead—a summer which would be just as bright, happy and long, and there suddenly stirred within him a joyous, youthful feeling such as he had experienced when running about this orchard as a boy. He embraced the old man, kissed him tenderly. Much moved, both went into the house and drank tea out of old-fashioned porcelain cups with cream and rich, plump pastries. These small details again reminded Kovrin of his childhood and youth. The marvellous present, the newly-awakened impressions of the past—they blended together, making him feel fine, yet hemmed in.

He waited for Tanya to wake, had coffee with her, took a stroll, then went to his room and sat down to work. He read attentively, he made notes, occasionally raising his eyes to glance at the open windows or fresh flowers which stood, still wet with dew, in vases on the table, then again lowered his eyes to his book, feeling all his veins throbbing and vibrating with pleasure.

II

In the country he continued to lead a life no less febrile and restless than in town. He read a lot, he wrote, he studied Italian. When strolling he enjoyed thinking that he would soon be back at his desk again. Everyone was surprised that he slept so little. If he chanced to doze for half an hour during the day he would lie awake all that night, and this sleepless vigil would leave him as buoyant and cheerful as ever.

He talked a lot, drank wine, smoked expensive cigars.

The Pesotskys were visited almost daily by young ladies of the locality who played the piano and sang with Tanya. A young man, a neighbour and an excellent violinist, sometimes came over too. Kovrin listened to the playing and singing so avidly that he became exhausted, the symptoms being eyes that seemed glued shut and a head lolling to one side.

One afternoon he was sitting reading on the balcony after tea. Meanwhile Tanya, a soprano, with one of the young ladies, a contralto, and the young violinist were practising Braga's famous *Serenade* in the drawing-room. Kovrin hung on the words—it was in Russian—but just couldn't understand them. At last, putting his book aside and concentrating, he did understand. In a garden at night a morbidly imaginative girl hears mysterious sounds so weird and wondrous that she is compelled to acknowledge them as divine harmony which soars back aloft to the heavens, being incomprehensible to us mortals. Kovrin's eyelids grew heavy. He rose, he wearily paced the drawing-room and then the ballroom. When the singing ended he took Tanya's arm and they went out on the balcony.

'I've been obsessed with a certain legend since this morning,' said he. 'I don't know whether I read it or heard it somewhere, but it's an odd, incongruous sort of story. It's not remarkably lucid, for a start. A thousand years ago a black-garbed monk was walking through some Syrian or Arabian desert. A few miles away fishermen saw another black monk moving slowly over the surface of a lake. This second monk was a mirage. Now forget all the laws of optics seemingly ignored by the legend, and hear the next bit. The mirage generates another mirage. The second generates a third, and so the black monk's image is endlessly transmitted from one atmospheric stratum to another. He is seen, now in Africa, now in Spain, now in India, now in the far north. Having left the earth's atmosphere behind at last, he now wanders through the entire universe, never encountering conditions which would enable him to fade away. Perhaps he's to be seen on Mars somewhere, now, or on some star of the Southern Cross. But the legend's very kernel and essence is this, my dear. Exactly a thousand years after that monk walked in the desert the mirage will return to the earth's atmosphere and manifest itself to men. The thousand years is said to be just about up, so we can expect the black monk any day now according to the legend.'

'An odd sort of mirage.' Tanya disliked the legend.

'But I just can't remember where I got it all from, that's what baffles me.' Kovrin laughed. 'Did I read it somewhere? Was I told it? Can I have dreamt of the black monk? I swear to God I don't remember. But the tale obsesses me, I've thought of it all day.'

Leaving Tanya to her guests, he went out and strolled pensively near the flower-beds. The sun was setting, and the newly watered flowers gave off a tantalizing damp scent. Singing had started in the house again, the distant fiddle sounding like a human voice. Where had he heard or read the legend? Racking his brains, Kovrin wandered into the park and found himself by the river.

Descending the path down a steep bank past bare roots to the water, he disturbed the sandpipers and put up a brace of ducks. The last rays of the setting sun still gleamed here and there on the grim pines, but on the river's surface evening had fully set in. Kovrin crossed the footbridge to the other side. Before him lay a broad field of young rye not yet in ear. No abode of man, no living soul was out there, and the path looked as if it led to that unknown, mysterious spot where the sun had just gone down, and where its setting rays flamed so broadly and majestically.

'What a sense of space, of peace, of freedom,' Kovrin thought as he walked along the path. 'The whole world seems to gaze at me, holding its breath, waiting for me to grasp its meaning.'

But then the rye rippled and a gentle evening breeze softly brushed his bare head. Soon afterwards came another more powerful gust, the rye rustled and he heard the pines' muffled murmur behind him. Kovrin halted in amazement. On the horizon a tall, black column like a whirlwind or sand-storm had risen from earth to sky. Though the outlines were blurred it was not standing still, but moving with awesome speed—that was immediately obvious. It was coming straight at Kovrin, growing smaller and clearer the nearer it came. Plunging into the rye on one side to make way, he was only just in time.

Arms crossed on chest, bare feet not touching the ground, the black-garbed, grey-haired, black-browed monk hurtled past.

Rushing on another half dozen yards, he looked back at Kovrin, nodded, gave a friendly yet knowing grin. Oh, what a white, a ghastly white, thin face. Swelling again, he skimmed the river, crashed soundlessly into clay cliff and pines, went straight through them and vanished into thin air.

'Well, well,' muttered Kovrin. 'So the legend was true.'

Without trying to explain this weird apparition, satisfied just to have got such a near, clear view, not only of the black robes but even of the monk's face and eyes, Kovrin returned home agreeably excited.

There were people strolling calmly in the park and garden, there was piano-playing in the house—only he had seen the monk, then. He longed to tell Tanya and Pesotsky all about it, but realized that they would certainly think he was raving and panic. Better say nothing. He laughed aloud, he sang, he danced a mazurka, he was in great form. Everyone—Tanya, her guests—found that he had a special, somehow radiantly inspired look about him this evening, and that he was quite fascinating.

III

When the guests had left after supper he went to his room and lay on the sofa, wanting to think about the monk. But soon afterwards Tanya came in.

'Here, Andrew, have a look at Father's articles.' She handed him a bundle of pamphlets and offprints. 'They're very good, he does write beautifully.'

'Now, that's going too far.' Pesotsky had followed her in with a forced laugh, feeling embarrassed. 'Don't listen to her please, and don't read them. Oh, all right, do read them if you need something to send you to sleep. They're an excellent soporific.'

'I think they're superb.' Tanya spoke with deep conviction. 'You read them, Andrew, and persuade Father to write more often. He could produce an entire course in horticulture.'

Pesotsky gave a forced guffaw, blushed and uttered the phrases commonly spoken by bashful authors. In the end he yielded.

'Then you must read Gaucher's piece first, and these articles in Russian,' he muttered, running his trembling fingers through the pamphlets. 'Otherwise you won't understand. Before reading my objections you must know what I'm objecting to. But it's all such nonsense, so boring. Besides, I think it's bedtime.'

Tanya went out. Sitting on the sofa beside Kovrin, Pesotsky sighed deeply.

'Yes, dear boy,' he said after a short pause. 'Yes indeed, my academic friend. Here am I writing my articles, exhibiting at shows, winning medals. "Pesotsky's apples are big as your head," they'll tell you. "Pesotsky has made his fortune with his orchard," say they. Pesotsky's king of his own little castle, in other words. What's it all for, though, that's the problem? The garden really is splendid, it's a show-piece. It's less a garden than an institution vital to the state—one which marks, as it were, a step towards a new era in Russian economics and industry. But to what purpose, what's it all in aid of?'

'It speaks for itself.'

'That's not my point. What will become of the garden when I die, that's what I want to know. Without me it won't last one month as you now see it. The key to its success isn't that it's a big garden with lots of gardeners, it's my love of the work, don't you see? Perhaps I love it more than I love myself. See here, I do everything myself. I work from dawn to dusk. All the grafting, all the pruning, all the planting—I do it, the whole lot. When anyone helps I grow so jealous and annoyed that I'm rude. The key to it all is love. I mean the keen eye and hands of a man handling his own property. I mean how you feel when you're away visiting someone for an hour, and you sit down but you aren't really there. You're not yourself because you're afraid of something happening to your garden. But who'll look after it when I die? Who'll do the work? My head gardener? My under-gardeners? What do you think? Now, I'll tell you something, friend. The worst enemy isn't hares, cockchafers or frost in this business, it's man—the man whose heart's not in it.'

'But what about Tanya?' Kovrin laughed. 'She can't possibly do more damage than the hares. She loves gardening, she understands it.'

'Indeed she does. If the garden goes to her after I'm dead, if she runs it, then that's ideal of course. But what if she marries, God forbid?' Pesotsky whispered with a scared glance at Kovrin. 'That's just the point. If she marries and has children she'll have no time to think of the garden. What I most fear is her marrying some greedy young coxcomb who'll let the place out to market-women, and it will go to rack and ruin in a year. Women—they're all hell let loose in this business.'

Sighing, Pesotsky paused for a while.

'I may be selfish, but I don't want Tanya to marry, quite honestly. There's that popinjay with the fiddle who visits us. I know Tanya won't marry him, I'm sure of that. But I can't stand the sight of him. Altogether I'm rather a crank, dear boy, I confess it.'

Pesotsky stood up and paced the room excitedly, obviously wanting to say something crucial but not venturing.

'I'm very fond of you indeed and I'm going to be frank.' He had steeled himself at last, thrusting his hands into his pockets. 'On certain ticklish questions I'm quite blunt, I don't beat about the bush. And I can't stand what's called minding one's own business. So I tell you straight, you're the one man I wouldn't fear marrying my daughter to. You're intelligent, you're good-hearted, you wouldn't let my labour of love perish. But above all I love you as a son, I'm proud of you. If you and Tanya should hit it off together, well, I'd be all for it. I'd be glad. I'd be happy, even. I tell you straight with no trimmings, as an honest man.'

Kovrin laughed. Pesotsky opened the door to go out, paused on the threshold.

'If you and Tanya had a son I'd make him a gardener,' he said thoughtfully. 'Anyway, that's all idle dreaming. Good night.'

Left to himself, Kovrin settled down more comfortably and tackled the articles. One was entitled 'Catch-Cropping', another 'Observations on Mr. Z's Remarks on Double Trenching the Soil of a New Garden'. A third was 'Grafting with Dormant Buds, Continued'. It was all like that. But what a neurotic, uneasy tone. What frenzied, almost clinical zeal. One article had what seemed a most inoffensive title and uncontroversial subject, being about the golden rennet apple. But Pesotsky began and ended it with *audiatur altera pars* and *sapienti sat*, sandwiching between these tags a spate of mixed venomous adjurations on 'the ignorant pedantry of our high and mighty horticultural pundits who gaze down on nature from their ivory towers', or on M. Gaucher, 'whose reputation has been created by ignoramuses and amateurs'. At this point there was an out-of-context, strained, bogus-sounding expression of regret that peasants could no longer be birched for damaging trees while stealing fruit.

'Gardening's a fine, nice, healthy pursuit,' thought Kovrin. 'Yet even here passions rage. It must be because intellectuals are neurotic and hyper-sensitive in every walk of life. Perhaps it can't be helped.'

He remembered how keen Tanya was on her father's articles. Short, pale, so thin that her shoulder-blades stuck out, with dilated, dark, intelligent eyes, she was always peering and questing. She walked like her father, with short, brisk steps. She spoke a lot, she liked arguing, and when doing so would mimic and gesticulate an accompaniment to every sentence, even the least important. She must be excessively sensitive.

Kovrin read on, but could take nothing in and gave it up. A pleasant excitement, the feeling with which he had just danced the mazurka and listened to the music, now weighed him down, evoking a host of thoughts. He stood up and paced the room, thinking of the black monk. It struck him that if no one else had seen that strange phantom, then he himself must be ill and had reached the stage of seeing things. The idea frightened him, but not for long.

'But I feel all right, don't I? I'm not hurting anyone. So there's no harm in my hallucinations,' he thought, and was reassured.

He sat on the sofa, clutching his head to contain the joy passing understanding which filled his whole being, then paced the room again and sat down to work. But the ideas which he found in his book did not satisfy him. He wanted something colossal, vast, shattering. Towards dawn he undressed and went reluctantly to bed. He must get some sleep, after all.

Hearing Pesotsky walk out into the garden, Kovrin rang for a servant and ordered wine. He enjoyed several glasses of claret and then covered himself up. His consciousness became dimmed, he fell asleep.

IV

Pesotsky and Tanya often quarrelled and abused each other.

One morning Tanya burst into tears after some squabble and went to her room. She did not come out for lunch or tea. At first Pesotsky walked around looking pompous and sulky, as if trying to show that justice and order were the most important things in life, but he soon flagged and lost heart. He drifted sadly through the park, sighing 'Oh, God, God, God', he ate not a crumb for dinner. At last, guilty and remorseful, he knocked on her locked door and timidly called her name.

The response from behind the door was a faint voice, exhausted by crying, yet resolute. 'Kindly leave me alone.'

The master's and mistress's distress was reflected by the whole household, even the gardeners. Kovrin too, deep in some fascinating work, felt depressed and embarrassed in the end. Hoping somehow to dispel the general low spirits, he decided to intervene, and knocked on Tanya's door in the late afternoon. He was admitted.

'Come, come, you should be ashamed,' he joked, looking in amazement at Tanya's tear-stained, grief-stricken face covered with red blotches. 'Is it really so serious? Come, now.'

'How he torments me, did you but know.' Tears, hot and profuse, spurted from her large eyes. 'He's made my life a misery.' She wrung her hands. 'I didn't say anything to him, not a thing. All I said was that there's no need to keep extra gardeners if—if you can hire them by the day when you need them. Why, our—our gardeners have been idle all this week. That's all I—I said, but he yelled at me and made a lot of insulting, deeply offensive remarks. What for?'

'That's quite enough of that.' Kovrin patted her hair. 'You've had your quarrel and your little cry, and that will do. You mustn't be angry any more. It won't do, especially as he loves you so very, very much.'

'He has ruined my—my whole life,' sobbed Tanya. 'All I hear from him is taunts and—and insults. He thinks I don't belong in this house. Very well then, he's right. I'll leave here tomorrow and get a job as a telegraph clerk. I don't care.'

'Come, come. Don't cry, Tanya. Don't, dear. Both of you are

quick-tempered and highly-strung, and you're both in the wrong. Come along, I'll help heal the breach.'

Kovrin spoke kindly and persuasively, but she still cried, her shoulders quivering, her fists clenched as if she had been genuinely overtaken by some dire calamity. He pitied her all the more because, though her grief was not serious, she yet suffered deeply. How little was needed to make this creature unhappy for a whole day, perhaps for a whole lifetime. While soothing her, Kovrin reflected that he could search the entire face of the globe in vain without finding anyone who loved him as dearly as this girl and her father. He had lost his own father and mother in early childhood, and but for these two would perhaps never have known true affection until his dying day—never have known that innocent, selfless love only possible with someone very dear and close. This weeping, trembling girl's nerves responded, he felt, to his own half-sick, overwrought nerves as iron to a magnet. He, who could never have loved a healthy, strong, rosy-cheeked girl, was attracted by pale, frail, unhappy Tanya.

He gladly stroked her hair and shoulders, pressed her hands, wiped her tears.

Then she at last stopped crying. She went on complaining for some time—about her father and her intolerably hard life in that house, begging Kovrin to see things her way. Then she gradually began to smile, sighing that God had given her such a bad character. In the end she laughed aloud, called herself an idiot and ran from the room.

A little later, when Kovrin went into the garden, Pesotsky and Tanya were walking side by side down a path just as if nothing had happened, eating rye bread and salt because they were both famished.

V

Pleased to have proved so successful a peacemaker, Kovrin went into the park. He sat on a bench pondering, and heard the rattle of carriages and women's laughter as guests arrived. While evening's shadows fell across the garden he vaguely heard a fiddle and singers' voices, which reminded him of the black monk. Where, in what clime, on what planet was that optical incongruity now floating?

Barely had he recalled the legend, conjuring up in fancy the dark phantom seen in the rye field, when without the faintest rustle there silently emerged from behind the pine tree exactly opposite a man of medium height, his grey head uncovered, garbed all in black, barefoot, like a beggar. On his deathly white face black eyebrows stood out sharply. With a friendly nod the beggar or pilgrim silently approached the bench and sat down. Kovrin recognized the black monk. For a moment each gazed at the other—Kovrin with amazement, the monk amiably and with his old, rather sly, knowing look.

'But you're a mirage, you know,' Kovrin said. 'So why are you here, why are you sitting still? It doesn't fit the legend.'

'No matter,' the monk answered quietly after a short pause, turning to face Kovrin. 'Legend, mirage, I myself—these are all figments of your overheated imagination. I am an apparition.'

'So you don't exist then?' Kovrin asked.

'Think as you choose.' The monk gave a slight smile. 'I exist in your imagination, and your imagination is part of nature. Therefore I exist in nature too.'

'You have a very mature, intelligent, highly expressive face, as if you really had lived more than a thousand years,' said Kovrin. 'I had no idea that my imagination could create such phenomena. But why do you look at me so delightedly? Do you like me?'

'Yes. You are one of those few justly called the Elect of God. You serve Eternal Truth. Your ideas, your purposes, your outstanding scholarship, your whole life—all bear the divine, celestial stamp, being dedicated to the Rational and the Beautiful, that is to the Eternal.'

'You speak of Eternal Truth. But can men attain that, do they need it, if there is no life after death?'

'But there is,' said the monk.

'You believe in eternal life, then?'

'Of course. You human beings have a great and glorious future. And the more men there are like you on earth the quicker will that future be attained. Without you—you who serve the highest principles, who live consciously and freely—humanity would be nothing. In the normal course of events it would have had to wait a long time for the consummation of its terrestrial evolution. But you will lead it to the Kingdom of Eternal Truth several thousand years ahead of time. Herein lies your high merit. You are the incarnation of God's blessing immanent in mankind.'

'But what purpose has eternal life?' Kovrin asked.

'The same as any other life. Pleasure. True pleasure is knowledge, and eternal life will offer sources of knowledge infinite and inexhaustible. That's what "in my Father's house are many mansions" means.'

'It's so nice hearing you talk, did you but know.' Kovrin rubbed his hands delightedly.

'I'm so glad.'

'But when you've gone I know I shall worry about whether you exist or not. You're a ghost, a hallucination. Does that mean I'm mentally ill, insane?'

'Suppose you are. Why let it bother you? You're sick because you're overworked, you've worn yourself out. You have sacrificed your health to the Ideal, in other words, and ere long you'll sacrifice your very life to it. What could be better? Such is the goal of all lofty natures endowed with superior gifts.'

'But if I know I'm insane how can I have faith in myself?'

'Now, why assume that men of genius, those in whom all mankind has faith, haven't also seen visions? Genius is akin to madness, scientists now tell us. Only mediocrities, only the common herd are healthy and normal, my friend. Talk about the neurosis of the age, overwork, degeneracy and so on can seriously disturb only those who see life's goal in the present—the common herd, that is.'

'The Romans spoke of *mens sana in corpore sano*.'

'Not everything the Romans and Greeks said is true. Heightened consciousness, excitement, ecstasy, all that distinguishes prophets, poets and martyrs to the Ideal from common folk—it's all inimical to man's animal nature, that is to his physical health. I repeat, if you want to be healthy and normal, join the herd.'

'It's funny how you say things that often occur to me independently,' said Kovrin. 'It's as if you had spied and eavesdropped on my secret thoughts. But let's not talk about me. What do you mean by eternal truth?'

The monk gave no answer. Kovrin glanced at him, but could not make out his face, the features being hazy and blurred. Then the monk's head and hands began to disappear. His body merged with the bench and the evening twilight until he had vanished entirely.

'The hallucination is over.' Kovrin laughed. 'What a pity.'

He went back to the house in the best of spirits. It had not been his vanity, it had been the very core of his being which the monk's few words had flattered. To be one of the Elect, to serve Eternal Truth, to join ranks with those who will make man worthy of God's Kingdom several thousand years ahead of time, saving him from several millennia of unnecessary struggle, sin and suffering, to sacrifice youth, strength, health and all else to the Ideal, to be ready to die for the common weal

—how lofty, how beatific a destiny! His own past—so pure, so chaste, so industrious—flashed through his mind. He remembered what he had learnt, what he had taught others, and decided that the monk had not exaggerated.

Tanya was coming towards him through the park. She had changed her dress.

'So you're here,' she said. 'We've been looking for you everywhere. But what's the matter?' she wondered, glancing at his radiant, beaming face and tear-filled eyes. 'Andrew, how strange you seem.'

'I am contented, Tanya.' Kovrin put his hands on her shoulders. 'More than that, I am happy. Tanya, dear Tanya, you're such a nice creature. Dear Tanya, I am so very, very glad.' He fervently kissed both her hands. 'I have just experienced such wonderful, bright, celestial moments. But I can't tell you all of it because you'd say I was mad or disbelieve me. Let's talk about you. Lovely, marvellous Tanya! I love you and that love is now part of me. To have you near me, to meet you a dozen times a day—it has become a spiritual necessity. I don't know how I'll do without you when I go home.'

'Oh, really.' Tanya laughed. 'You'll forget us in a couple of days. We're nobodies and you're a great man.'

'No, we must be serious,' he said. 'I'll take you with me, Tanya. How about it—will you come. Will you be mine?'

'Oh, really.' Tanya tried to laugh again, but the laugh would not come and red blotches appeared on her face.

She was breathing fast and walked quicker and quicker, not towards the house but further into the park.

'I never thought of that, never.' She clenched her hands as if in despair.

Kovrin followed her, talking and still wearing that radiant, beatific expression.

'I want a love to possess me entirely, and only you can give me such love, Tanya. Oh, I'm so happy.'

Dumbfounded, she stooped—shivering, seeming ten years older. But he found her beautiful, loudly and joyfully exclaiming how lovely she was.

VI

Having learnt from Kovrin that the two had not only 'hit it off together', but that there was even to be a wedding, Pesotsky paced his room for a while, trying to hide his excitement. His hands shook, his neck swelled and turned crimson, he gave orders for his trap to be harnessed and he drove off. Tanya, seeing him whip the horses and pull his cap hard down almost on to his ears, understood his mood, locked herself in her room and spent the day crying.

Peaches and plums were already ripe in the greenhouses. The packing and despatch to Moscow of this delicate, sensitive freight required much care, labour and fuss. So hot and dry had the summer been that every tree had needed watering, a very time-consuming procedure for the gardeners. And swarms of caterpillars had appeared, which the gardeners and even—to Kovrin's great disgust—Pesotsky and Tanya would squash with their fingers. Meanwhile they also had to take orders for fruit and trees in the autumn, and to conduct a large correspondence.

Then, just at crisis point, when no one seemed to have a free moment, harvesting began and robbed the garden of more than half the labour force. Very sunburnt, dead tired, bad-tempered, Pesotsky kept dashing off into garden or fields, shouting that he was being torn limb from limb and would put a bullet in his brain.

Then came fuss over the trousseau, to which the Pesotskys attached no small importance. The snipping of scissors, the rattle of sewing-machines, the fume of flat-irons, the tantrums of the dressmaker, a neurotic, touchy lady—these things had everyone in the house in a daze. As if to make things worse, guests came every day and had to be amused, fed and even put up for the night. But all this drudgery was as nothing, it passed unnoticed. Tanya felt as if love and happiness had caught her unawares, though she had been certain, somehow, since the age of fourteen that Kovrin would marry her and no one else. She was stunned and bewildered, she could not believe it all.

Now such joy would suddenly overwhelm her that she felt like soaring into the clouds and giving thanks to God, now she would suddenly remember that she would have to leave her beloved home and part from her father in August. Or the idea would strike her from God knows where that she was a trivial nonentity unworthy of a great man like Kovrin, and off to her room she would go, lock herself in and weep bitterly for several hours. When they had guests Kovrin would suddenly impress her as strikingly handsome—she thought all the women were in love with him and jealous of her. Her heart would swell with exultant pride as if she had vanquished the whole world. But let him so much as smile a welcome to some young lady and she would shake with jealousy. Off to her room she would go, and there would be more tears. These new emotions obsessed her, she helped her father like an automaton, not noticing the peaches, the caterpillars, the workmen or the swift passage of time.

Pesotsky's evolution was much the same. He worked from dawn to dusk, he was always dashing off somewhere, flaring up, losing his temper, but all in an enchanted daze. There might have been two of him. One was the real Pesotsky listening to the head gardener Ivan Karlych reporting mishaps, waxing indignant, clutching his head in despair. The other was an impostor, a semi-intoxicated creature who suddenly broke off business conversations in mid-sentence and patted the head gardener's shoulder.

'Say what you like, but breeding does count,' he would mutter. 'His mother was a marvellous, admirable, brilliant woman. To look at her kind, clear, pure, angelic face—it was a real joy. She drew beautifully, wrote verse, spoke five foreign languages, sang. The poor woman died of consumption, may she rest in peace.'

'When he was a little boy and grew up in my house,' Unreal Pesotsky would sigh a little later, 'he had just such an angelic, clean-cut kind face. His glance, his movements, his conversation were gentle and elegant like his mother's. As for brains, he always astounded us with his intelligence. He wasn't, incidentally, made an M.A. for nothing, indeed he was not! But you just wait and see what he'll be like in ten years' time, Ivan Karlych. There will be no touching him.'

But then Real Pesotsky would take over, grimace fearfully, clutch his head, shout.

'Bastards! They've messed it, mucked it, frozen it all to hell! The garden's gone to rack and ruin!'

Meanwhile Kovrin was working with his former zeal, not noticing all the fuss. Love only added fuel to the flames. After every meeting with Tanya he would go to his room happy and elated, would take up book or manuscript as passionately as he had just kissed Tanya and told her that he loved her. What the black monk had said about the Elect of God, Eternal Truth, the brilliant future of mankind and the rest of it—all that conferred outstanding significance on his work, filling his heart with pride and a consciousness of his own superiority. He met the black monk once or twice a week in the park or at home, and had a long conversation. But this did not so much frighten as delight him, for he was absolutely convinced by now that such visions visit only the élite of distinguished men consecrated to the service of the Ideal.

The monk once appeared at dinner time and sat by the dining-room window. Overjoyed, Kovrin most adroitly struck up a conversation with Pesotsky and Tanya on a subject likely to interest the black guest, who listened, nodding affably. Pesotsky and Tanya also listened—merrily smiling and without suspecting that Kovrin was speaking to a figment of his imagination, not to them.

The Fast of the Assumption arrived unnoticed, and soon after that came the wedding—celebrated 'with a splash' at Pesotsky's insistence, that is, with senseless revels lasting forty-eight hours. Some three thousand roubles' eating and drinking were done, but what with the wretched hired band, the rowdy toasts and the waiters' bustle, what with the din and the crowd, the expensive wines and remarkable viands ordered from Moscow went unappreciated.

VII

On a long winter's night Kovrin lay in bed reading a French novel. Poor Tanya, whose head ached in the evenings because she wasn't used to town life, had long been asleep and was uttering occasional incoherent sentences.

It struck three. Kovrin put out his candle and lay down. He lay with eyes closed for a while but could not sleep, probably because the bedroom was too hot and Tanya was talking in her sleep. At half-past four he relit his candle and saw the black monk sitting in the armchair by his bed.

'Greetings.' The monk paused. 'What are you thinking about now?'

'Fame,' Kovrin answered. 'I've just been reading a French novel about a young scholar who behaves foolishly and pines away because he yearns to be famous. I don't understand that yearning.'

'That's because you have too much sense. You don't care for fame, it's a toy which doesn't interest you.'

'True enough.'

'Repute does not attract you. What's flattering, amusing or edifying about having your name carved on your tombstone only to be erased, gilt and all, by the passage of time? Anyway, there are too many of you, luckily, for mankind's feeble memory to retain your names.'

'Quite so,' Kovrin agreed. 'Besides, what need to remember them? But let's discuss something else. Happiness, for instance. What is happiness?'

When five o'clock struck he was sitting on the bed, feet dangling on the carpet. He addressed the monk.

'In ancient times there was a happy man who ended up scared of his own happiness, so great was it. So he sacrificed his favourite ring to the gods in order to appease them. Now, do you know, I'm getting a bit worried about my own happiness, just as Polycrates was. I find it odd to experience bliss unalloyed from dawn to dusk. It obsesses me, it swamps all other feelings. Sadness, grief, boredom—I don't know what they are. Here I am unable to sleep, I have insomnia, but I'm not bored. It's beginning to puzzle me, quite seriously.'

'Now, why?' the monk was astonished. 'Is joy so unnatural a feeling? Shouldn't it be man's normal lot? The loftier his intellectual and moral development, the freer he is, the more pleasure does life afford him. Socrates, Diogenes and Marcus Aurelius felt joy, not grief. And the Apostle says "Rejoice evermore". So do rejoice, then, and be happy.'

Kovrin laughed. 'But what if the gods wax angry?' he jested. 'If they remove my comforts, make me cold and famished, I doubt if that will suit me.'

Meanwhile Tanya had woken up and was staring at her husband in horror and amazement. There he was talking, addressing the armchair, gesticulating and laughing. His eyes gleamed, and there was something odd about that laugh.

'Who are you talking to, Andrew?' She clutched the hand which he had stretched towards the monk. 'Who is it, dear?'

'Eh?' Kovrin was taken aback. 'Who, you ask? Why, with him sitting over there.' He pointed at the black monk.

'There's no one there, no one at all. You're ill, Andrew.'

Tanya embraced her husband. She clung to him as if she was protecting him from apparitions, covering his eyes with her hand.

'You're ill,' she sobbed, trembling all over. 'Forgive me, my dearest darling, but I've noticed something amiss with you for some time. Your mind is sick, my dear.'

Infected by her trembling, he again glanced at the armchair, now empty, felt a sudden weakness of the arms and legs. Scared, he started dressing.

'It's nothing, Tanya, nothing,' he muttered, quivering. 'Actually, I am a bit unwell, it's time to admit it.'

'I noticed it ages ago, and so did Father.' She tried to force back her sobs. 'You talk to yourself, you smile oddly, you don't sleep. God,

God, save us,' she said in horror. 'But don't be afraid, dear. Never fear, for God's sake don't be afraid.'

She started dressing too. Only as he looked at her now did Kovrin take in the full danger of his position—the meaning of the black monk and the conversations with him. Now he knew that he had lost his reason.

Not understanding why, both dressed and went into the ballroom—she leading, he following. And there, woken by the sobbing, in his dressing-gown, candle in hand, stood Pesotsky, who was staying with them.

'Never fear, my dear,' said Tanya, shaking like one in fever. 'Don't be afraid. This will all pass, Father, it will be all right.'

Kovrin was too upset to speak. He wanted to make a jocular remark to his father-in-law. 'You must congratulate me, I think I've gone off my head.' But he only moved his lips, smiling bitterly.

At nine o'clock that morning they put on his greatcoat and his furs, wrapped a shawl round him, and took him to the doctor by carriage. He began to receive treatment.

VIII

It was summer again, and the doctor had ordered him to go to the country. Kovrin was better now, he no longer saw the black monk, he needed only to get fit. Living with his father-in-law in the country, he drank a lot of milk, worked only two hours a day, took no wine, did not smoke.

On St. Elias' Eve at the end of July a service was held in the house. When the clerk handed the priest the censer the huge old ballroom smelt like a graveyard. Kovrin was bored. He went into the garden. Ignoring the gorgeous flowers, he drifted about, sat on a bench, strolled through the park. Reaching the river, he climbed down and stood there, pensively contemplating the water. Those grim pines with their matted roots which had seen him here so young, so merry, so high-spirited last year—they no longer whispered, but stood still and dumb as if not recognizing him. And in fact his head was cropped, he no longer had his beautiful long hair, his walk was listless, he was fuller in the face and paler than last summer.

He crossed the footbridge to the far bank. Rows of cut oats stood where rye had grown last year. The sun had set, and a broad red glow burned on the horizon, presaging wind next day. It was quiet. Gazing towards where the black monk had first appeared last year, Kovrin stood for about twenty minutes until the sunset had faded.

When he reached home again, weary and discontented, the service was over. Pesotsky and Tanya were having tea on the terrace steps. They were talking, but when they saw Kovrin they stopped abruptly and he concluded from their expressions that they had been discussing him.

'It must be time for your milk,' Tanya told her husband.

'No it's not.' He sat on the lowest step. 'Drink it yourself, I don't want it.'

Tanya exchanged an alarmed glance with her father. 'You yourself say the milk does you good,' she said apologetically.

'Oh yes, lots and lots of good,' Kovrin sneered. 'I congratulate you. Since Friday I have put on another pound.' He clutched his head tightly in his hands and spoke in anguish. 'Why, oh why did you try to cure me? Bromides, idleness, warm baths, being watched, this craven fear of every mouthful, every step—it will turn me into a downright imbecile in the end. I was losing my mind, I had delusions of grandeur, but I was elated, I was even happy, I was attractive and original. Now I've become more reasonable and stable, but I'm just like everyone else—I'm a mediocrity, and I'm bored with life. Oh, how cruelly you have treated me! I saw visions, but what harm did they do anyone, I'd like to know?'

Pesotsky sighed. 'God knows what you're on about, it makes tedious listening.'

'Then don't listen.'

Other people's presence, Pesotsky's in particular, now riled Kovrin, who would answer drily and coldly—rudely, even—never looking at the other without a sneer of hatred, much to Pesotsky's distress as he coughed, apologetically but not feeling in the least to blame. Not understanding why their affectionate, friendly relations had so abruptly changed, Tanya would cling to her father and gaze anxiously into his eyes. She wanted to understand but could not. All she knew was that relations were deteriorating daily, that her father looked much older of late, while her husband had become irritable, moody, cantankerous, unattractive. No longer could she laugh and sing, she left her meals untouched, she lay awake all night with terrible forebodings. Such were her torments that she once spent the time from lunch till evening in a dead faint. Her father had seemed to be weeping during the service, and now, as the three of them sat on the terrace, she strove to put it from her mind.

'How lucky Buddha, Mahomet and Shakespeare were that their kind relatives and doctors did not treat them for ecstasy and inspiration,' said Kovrin. 'Had Mahomet taken potassium bromide for his nerves, worked only two hours a day and drunk milk, that remarkable man would have left as little trace behind him as his dog. It's the doctors and the well-meaning relatives who will cretinize mankind in the end. Mediocrity will rate as genius, civilization will perish. I'm so, so grateful to you, did you but know it,' Kovrin added irritably.

He felt so exasperated that he stood up quickly and went indoors to stop himself saying more. It was quiet, the smell of tobacco flowers and jalap drifted in from the garden through the open windows. In the huge, dark ballroom flecks of green moonlight lay on the floor and the grand piano. Kovrin remembered the ecstasies of the previous summer with this same scent of jalap and the moon shining in through the windows. To recreate his previous year's mood, he hurried to his study, lit a strong cigar and told a servant to bring wine. But the cigar left a disgustingly bitter taste in his mouth, and the wine too had a different taste from last year's. And such were the effects of abstinence that the cigar and two gulps of wine made his head spin and his heart pound so that he had to take potassium bromide.

'Father idolizes you,' Tanya told him before going to bed. 'You have some grudge against him, and it's killing him—one sees him ageing by the hour. I implore you, Andrew, for God's sake, for your own dead father's sake, for the sake of my peace of mind—do be nice to him.'

'I neither can nor will.'

'But why not, why ever not?' Tanya trembled all over.

'Because I dislike him and that's that,' said Kovrin casually, shrugging his shoulders. 'But don't let's talk about him, he's *your* father.'

'I simply fail to understand.' Tanya clutched her temples and stared fixedly. 'Something mysterious and horrible is happening in this house. You've changed, you're not yourself. You, a rational, distinguished man, lose your temper over trifles, involve yourself in squabbles. Such little things upset you—one's so amazed sometimes, one can't believe it's you. All right, all right, don't be angry, please,' she went on, fearing her own words and kissing his hands. 'You're an intelligent, amiable, decent man. You'll be fair to my father, he's so kind-hearted.'

'He's not kind-hearted, he's just complacent. These farcical buffoons like your father, with their smug, fat faces, these dear old hail-fellow-well-met cranks—I once found them touching and amusing in fiction, in music-hall turns and in life too. But now they just disgust me. All they think of is self, self, self. And what disgusts me most is their smugness. They're like oxen or pigs, complacent down to their very guts.'

Tanya sat on the bed, laid her head on the pillow.

'This is sheer torture.' Her voice betrayed her utter exhaustion and difficulty in speaking. 'Not a moment's peace since winter. God, it's so dreadful, it's agony.'

'Oh yes, we all know I'm the wicked ogre, and you and daddy dear are the babes in the wood. Naturally!'

Tanya found his face ugly and disagreeable. The hatred, the sneering did not suit him. She had, indeed, noticed previously that there was something missing from his face, as if that too had changed since he had had his hair cut short. She wanted to say something wounding but, at once detecting this hostile impulse, took fright and left the bedroom.

IX

Kovrin was appointed to a university chair. His inaugural lecture was scheduled for the second of December and a notice to that effect had been posted in the university corridor, but on the date in question he wired the registrar that he was too ill to lecture.

He was bringing up blood. He would spit blood, and had sizeable haemorrhages twice a month, when he would feel exceptionally weak and drowsy. The illness did not particularly alarm him because he knew that his mother, now dead, had survived ten or more years of the same disease. His doctors told him there was no danger, only advising him not to get excited, to lead a regular life and talk less.

In January the lecture was again cancelled for the same reason, and by February it was too late to start the course. He had to postpone it until the following year.

He no longer lived with Tanya, but with another woman two years older than himself, who looked after him like a baby. His mood was calm and submissive. He readily yielded, and when Barbara—such was his companion's name—proposed taking him to the Crimea, he agreed, though foreseeing no good outcome to the trip.

They reached Sevastopol one evening and put up at an hotel to rest before going on to Yalta next day. Both were tired after their journey. Barbara had some tea, went to bed and was soon asleep. But Kovrin stayed up. Before leaving home—an hour before driving to the station—he had received from Tanya a letter which he had not dared open and which was now in his coat pocket. The thought of it worried him. In his heart of hearts he now believed that his marriage to Tanya had been a mistake, he was glad to have broken with her finally. The memory of this woman who had ended as a walking skeleton, in whom everything seemed to have died but those large, staring, intelligent eyes—that memory evoked in him only pity and annoyance with himself. The handwriting on the envelope reminded him how unfair and cruel he had been two years ago, how he had taken revenge on completely innocent people for his own spiritual emptiness, boredom, loneliness and discontent. He also, incidentally, remembered tearing his thesis, and all the articles written during his illness, into small pieces, throwing them out of the window, and seeing the scraps of paper fluttering in the breeze and lodging in trees and flowers. In every line he saw strange, utterly unfounded pretensions, militant frivolity, impudence and delusions of grandeur. It had made him feel as if he was reading a description of his own vices. But when the last notebook had been torn up and thrown out of the window he had suddenly felt bitterly distressed, had gone to his wife and made a lot of disagreeable remarks. God, how he had tormented her. He had once said, wanting to hurt her, that her father had played an invidious role in their relationship by asking him to marry her. Chancing to overhear, Pesotsky had burst into the room in speechless despair, capable only of stamping his feet and uttering a sort of bellow like a man without a tongue, while Tanya had looked at her father, given a heart-rending shriek and fainted. It had been an ugly scene.

All this came to mind when Kovrin looked at the familiar handwriting. He went out on to the balcony. The weather was fine and warm, he could smell the sea. The glorious bay reflected the moon and the lights, and had an indefinable colour—a delicate, soft medley of dark blue and green. Here the water had the dark blue tint of vitriol, there the moonbeams seemed to have congealed and filled the bay in place of water. The general impression was a symphony of hues, an atmosphere peaceful, calm and elevating.

The ground-floor windows under the balcony must have been open because women's voices and laughter were clearly heard. Someone must be giving a party.

Kovrin forced himself to open the letter. He went back into his room and read as follows.

'My father has just died. I have you to thank for that, for you killed him. Our garden is going to ruin, strangers have the run of it—just what poor Father feared. For that too I have you to thank. I hate you from the bottom of my heart, I hope you'll soon be dead. Oh, how I do suffer—an unbearable pain is burning inside me. I curse you. I thought you were an outstanding man, a genius. I loved you, but you turned out to be a maniac.'

Unable to read on, Kovrin tore up the letter and threw it away. Anxiety—panic, almost—seized him. Barbara was asleep behind a screen, he could hear her breathing. Women's voices and laughter came up from the floor below, yet he felt as if there was no living soul in the hotel besides himself. That the unhappy, broken-hearted Tanya had cursed him in her letter, that she wanted him dead—it unnerved him. He glanced briefly at the door, as if fearing that the unknown force, that force which had wrought such havoc in his own life and in the lives of those dear to him in the last two years, might enter the room and possess him again.

That the best cure for jangled nerves is work he knew from experience. You must sit at your desk and at all costs make yourself concentrate on a single idea. From his red briefcase he took a notebook containing a draft scheme for a short work which he had thought of compiling if he got bored doing nothing in the Crimea. Sitting at the table, he tackled this plan, and felt as if his calm, resigned, detached mood was returning. The notebook and the project even made him think of the vanity of things earthly. How much life does exact in return for those insignificant or very ordinary benefits which it can bestow on man, he thought. To be given a university chair in one's late thirties, to be a conventional professor, expounding in listless, bored, ponderous language commonplace thoughts not even your own —to attain, in short, the status of a second-rate scholar—he, Kovrin, had had to study fifteen years, to work day and night, to suffer serious mental disorder, to experience a broken marriage and to commit various stupid, unjust acts better forgotten. That he was a mediocrity he now clearly realized, accepting the fact gladly since everyone ought, in his view, to be satisfied with what he is.

The draft project would have soothed him, but the torn letter, gleaming white on the floor, prevented him from concentrating. He got up from the table, collected the scraps of paper and threw them out of the window, but a light breeze blew in from the sea and scattered the bits of the paper about the window-sill. Once again anxiety akin to panic seized him, and he felt as if he was the only living soul in the whole hotel.

He went out on the balcony. The bay gazed at him like a living thing with its masses of azure, dark blue, turquoise and red eyes. It seemed to beckon him. Indeed, as it was hot and stuffy, a bathe might be a good idea.

On the ground floor beneath the balcony a violin suddenly struck up, and two female voices sweetly sang something familiar. That song from down below—it was about a deranged girl who heard mysterious sounds one night in a garden and decided that this was sacred harmony incomprehensible to us mortals.

Kovrin caught his breath, sadness seemed to make his heart miss a beat, and a wondrous, sweet, long-forgotten joy quivered in his breast.

On the far shore of the bay appeared a tall black column like a whirlwind or sand-storm. It swooped over the bay towards the hotel with terrifying speed, becoming ever smaller and darker. Barely had Kovrin time to make way.

The grey-haired, bareheaded, black-browed monk, barefooted, arms crossed on his breast, swept past and stopped in the middle of the room.

'Why did you not trust me?' he reproached Kovrin, gazing at him affectionately. 'Had you only trusted me when I told you you were a genius, you would not have spent two such miserable and sterile years.'

Now believing himself the Elect of God and a genius, Kovrin vividly recalled all his previous conversations with the black monk, and tried to speak, but blood was spurting straight out of his throat on to his chest. Not knowing what to do, he moved his hands over his chest, and his cuffs became soaked with blood. Wanting to call Barbara, who was asleep behind the screen, he made an effort.

'Tanya,' he called.

He fell on the ground and raised himself on his arms.

'Tanya,' he called again.

He called on Tanya, he called on the great garden with its gorgeous, dew-sprinkled flowers, he called on the park, he called on the pines with their matted roots, the rye field, his brilliant research work, his youth, his daring, his joy, he called on life which had been so beautiful. Seeing a great pool of blood on the floor near his face, he was too weak, now, to utter a word, but bliss, boundless and ineffable, suffused his whole being. While a serenade was played beneath the balcony the black monk whispered to him that he was a genius—that he was dying only because his weak human body had lost its equilibrium and could no longer serve as the frame for a genius.

When Barbara woke and emerged from behind the screen Kovrin was dead with a frozen smile of ecstasy on his face.

A WOMAN'S KINGDOM

I

On the Eve

THERE was a thick wad of banknotes from the manager of Anne's timber plantations who had written enclosing fifteen hundred roubles, the proceeds of winning a court case on appeal. She disliked and feared such words as 'proceeds', 'winning' and 'case'. That legal proceedings were necessary she knew, but whenever her works manager Nazarych or her timber bailiff—great litigants, those two—won her a case, she always felt abashed and rather guilty. Now too she was embarrassed and ill at ease, wanting to put these fifteen hundred roubles away from her and not see them.

Other women of her age—twenty-five—were busy looking after homes, she wistfully reflected. They were tired, they would sleep soundly, they would wake up in the best of holiday spirits tomorrow. Many were long since married and had children. She alone was somehow obliged to pore over these letters like some old crone, to jot notes on them, to write answers, and then to do nothing all evening until midnight but wait until she felt sleepy. Tomorrow people would be wishing her happy Christmas and asking favours of her all day, and the day after tomorrow there was bound to be trouble at the works—someone beaten up, someone who had drunk himself to death—which would somehow make her suffer pangs of conscience. After the holidays Nazarych would dismiss a score of workers for absenteeism, and all twenty would huddle, bare-headed, at her porch. She would be too embarrassed to go out to them, and they would be driven off like dogs. Then everyone she knew would tittle-tattle behind her back and write anonymous letters about her being a millionairess—an exploiter who ruined people's lives and trod the workers into the dust.

Here, on one side, was a bundle of letters which she had read and set apart—begging letters. They were hungry, drunken people, these, burdened with large families, ill, humiliated, unrecognized.

Anne had already noted on each letter that three roubles were to go to one man and five to another. These letters would go to the office today, and tomorrow the distribution of relief—what her clerks called 'feeding time at the zoo'—would take place there.

They would also distribute four hundred and seventy roubles in dribs and drabs—interest on the capital willed to the poor and needy by her late father. There would be ugly jostling. A queue, a long line of people of a sort—alien, with bestial faces, ragged, cold, hungry, already drunk—would stretch from works gates to office door, hoarsely invoking their mother, their patroness Miss Glagolev and her parents. Those at the back would shove those in front, those in front would curse and swear. Tiring of the noise, the oaths, the keenings, the office clerk would leap out and cuff someone's ear to the general satisfaction. But her own people—the workers who had received nothing for the holiday beyond their wages, and had already spent the last copeck of those—would stand in the middle of the yard, look and laugh, some enviously, others ironically.

'Factory owners, especially women, prefer their beggars to their workpeople,' thought Anne. 'That's always the way.'

Her glance fell on the wad of money. It would be a good idea to distribute this unneeded, odious lucre to the workers tomorrow, but you couldn't give a worker something for nothing, or else he would ask you for more later. And what did these fifteen hundred roubles add up to anyway seeing that there were over eighteen hundred workers at the factory, not counting wives and children? Perhaps one might single out the author of one of these begging letters, some miserable creature who had long lost hope of a better life, and give him the whole lot. The poor fellow would be thunderstruck at getting the money, he might feel happy for the first time in his life. The idea struck Anne as original, amusing, entertaining. She pulled one letter out of the pile at random and read it. Some clerk called Chalikov had been out of work for a long time. He was ill, and he was living in the house belonging to one Gushchin. He had a consumptive wife and five young daughters. This four-storey tenement where he lived—Gushchin's—was well known to Anne. And a nasty, rotten, unhealthy building it was too.

'I'll give this Chalikov the money,' she decided. 'But I won't send it, I'd better take it myself to avoid unnecessary fuss. Yes,' she reasoned, putting the fifteen hundred in her pocket, 'I'll have a look, and perhaps fix up something for the little girls too.'

She cheered up, rang the bell and asked for her sledge to be brought round.

It was nearly seven in the evening when she got into her sledge. The windows of all the works buildings were brightly lit, which made it seem very dark in the huge compound. By the gate and in the far part of the yard, near the stores and the workers' barracks, electric lights glowed.

Anne disliked and feared these dark, grim blocks, these store-sheds and the barracks where the workers lived. She had only been inside the main factory building once since her father's death. High ceilings with iron girders, masses of huge, swiftly turning wheels, transmission belts and levers, the piercing hiss, the shriek of steel, the clattering of trollies, the harsh breath of steam, the faces pale, crimson or black with coal dust, the shirts wet with sweat, the gleam of steel, copper and fire, the smell of oil and coal, and the wind, now very hot, now cold—it all seemed sheer hell. She felt as if the wheels, the levers, the hot, hissing cylinders were striving to break loose from their couplings and annihilate people, while worried-looking men ran about, not hearing each other, bustling round the machines, trying to halt their terrible movement. They had shown Anne some object, explained it respectfully. She remembered them drawing a piece of white-hot iron out of the furnace in the forging shop, and how an old man with a strap on his head and another—young, in a dark-blue blouse with a chain on his chest, angry-looking, presumably a charge-hand—struck a piece of iron with hammers, how golden sparks scattered in all directions, how a little later they clattered a huge piece of sheet iron in front of her. The old man stood to attention, smiling, while the young one wiped his wet face with his sleeve and explained something to her. She still remembered, too, a one-eyed old man sawing a piece of iron in another workshop with a scatter of filings, and a red-haired man in dark glasses with holes in his shirt working a lathe, making something out of a piece of steel. The lathe roared, shrieked, whistled—a noise which made Anne feel sick, she felt as if something was boring into her ears. She looked, listened, understood nothing, smiled condescendingly, felt ashamed. To live off work you don't understand and can't like, to receive hundreds of thousands of roubles from it—how odd.

Not once had she visited the workers' barracks, reputedly an abode of bed-bugs, damp, debauchery and chaos. Astonishingly enough, thousands of roubles were spent yearly on the amenities of those barracks, but the workers' plight worsened every year, to judge from the anonymous letters.

'There was more system in Father's time,' thought Anne, driving out of the yard. 'That was because he'd been a worker himself, and knew what was needed. But I know nothing and get everything wrong.'

She again felt depressed, no longer glad to have embarked on this excursion. No longer was she intrigued and amused to think of the lucky creature on whose head the fifteen hundred roubles would suddenly alight like manna from heaven. To visit this Chalikov person while a business worth millions gradually disintegrated at home, while the workers in their barracks lived worse than convicts—that was stupid behaviour, it meant trying to cheat one's conscience.

Along the metalled road and across the field beside it workers from the neighbouring cotton and paper mills were thronging towards the lights of the city. Laughter and cheerful conversation hung in the frosty air. Looking at the women and youngsters, Anne suddenly felt a need for their simplicity, the crudeness, the jostling. She clearly pictured the distant past when she had been little Annie sharing a blanket with her mother—while their tenant, a washerwoman, was laundering in the next room. From adjoining apartments the sound of laughter, swearing, children's crying, an accordion, the buzz of lathes and sewing-machines had penetrated the thin walls, while her father Akim, that jack-of-all-trades, would ignore the cramped conditions and the noise as he soldered away at the stove, drew plans, used his plane. And she longed to wash and iron clothes, and run errands to shop and tavern, as she had every day when living with her mother. She would rather be a worker than an owner. Her huge house with its chandeliers and pictures, her butler Misha complete with tail-coat and velvety moustache, the imposing Barbara, the sycophantic Agatha, the young persons of both sexes who came begging for money almost daily and who always made her feel rather guilty, the officials, the doctors, the ladies who dispensed charity on her behalf, flattering her while secretly despising her lowly origins—how it all bored her, how alien it was.

She reached the level-crossing and barrier. Houses alternated with allotments. And here at last was the wide street where the legendary Gushchin tenement stood. As it was Christmas Eve there was a lot of coming and going in this usually quiet street. The taverns and alehouses were rowdy. If someone not of the locality, some resident of the town centre, had driven past, he would have noticed only dirty, drunken, swearing people. But Anne, having lived in these regions since childhood, seemed to see her late father, her mother, her uncle in the crowd.

Her father had been an easy-going, vague character. Carefree and frivolous, a bit of a dreamer, he had had no hankering for money, status or power. He would say that a working man had no time to bother with holidays and church-going. But for his wife he might never have kept the fasts, he would have eaten forbidden food in Lent. Now, her uncle Ivan, by contrast, had been hard as nails. In matters religious, political and moral he had been stern and inflexible, not only keeping himself up to the mark, but all his servants and acquaintances as well. God help anyone who had entered his room without making the sign of the cross. The sumptuous chambers where Anne now lived —he had kept them locked up, opening them only on special occasions for important guests, while living in the small icon-festooned room which was his office. He had leaned to the Old Religion, constantly receiving bishops and priests of that persuasion, though he had been christened and married, and had buried his wife, by Reformed Orthodox rites. He had disliked his brother Akim, his only heir, for his easy-going attitude, which he called simple-minded and foolish, and for his indifference to religion. He had treated Akim shabbily, like one of his workers, paying him sixteen roubles a month. Always addressing his brother rather formally, Akim would take his whole family and do obeisance to him at Shrovetide. But then, three years before his death, Ivan had made himself more approachable. He had forgiven Akim and told him to hire a governess for Anne.

The gates to the Gushchin tenement were dark, deep-set and stinking, there was the sound of men coughing by the walls. Leaving her sledge in the street, Anne went into the yard and asked the way to the clerk Chalikov's flat, Number Forty-Six. She was directed to the last door on the right on the second floor. Near that last door, in the yard, and even on the stairway, there was the same foul smell as at the gate. Anne had lived in houses like this as a child, when her father had been an ordinary worker. Then, after her circumstances had changed, she had often visited them on charitable errands. The narrow stone staircase with its high steps, dirty, with its landing on each floor, the greasy lamp in the well, the stink, the bins by the doors on the landings, pots, rags—she had known it all from time immemorial.

Through one door, which was open, she saw some Jewish tailors sitting on a table wearing their caps and sewing. She passed people on the staircase, but it did not occur to her that they might harm her. She feared workers and peasants, sober or drunk, as little as she feared her intellectual friends.

Flat Forty-Six had no hall, but opened straight into the kitchen. In factory-hands' and craftsmen's quarters there is usually a smell of varnish, tar, leather or smoke, depending on the occupant's job, but the quarters of impoverished gentlefolk and clerks are distinguished by a dank, rather acrid stench. No sooner had Anne crossed the threshold than this disgusting stink enveloped her. In one corner a man in a black frock-coat sat at a table, his back to the door. That must be Chalikov himself, and there were five little girls with him. The eldest, broad-faced and thin, with a comb in her hair, looked about fifteen, while the youngest was a plump little thing with hair like a hedgehog, no more than three years old. All six were eating. Near the stove, cooking tongs in hand, stood a small, very thin, yellow-faced woman in a skirt and white blouse. She was pregnant.

'I never thought you'd be so disobedient, Liza,' said the man reproachfully. 'You should be ashamed, dear me you should. So you want Daddy to whip you, do you?'

Seeing an unknown lady on the threshold, the emaciated woman quivered and put down her tongs.

'Vasily,' she called after a while in a hollow voice, as if not believing her eyes.

The man looked round and jumped up. He was a bony, narrow-shouldered person with sunken temples and a flat chest. His eyes were small, deep-set and dark-rimmed, his nose was long, beaky and somewhat twisted to the right, his mouth was wide. With his forked beard and clean-shaven upper lip he looked more like a footman than an official.

'Does Mr. Chalikov live here?' Anne asked.

'Yes indeed, ma'am,' Chalikov answered sternly, but then recognized Anne.

'Miss Glagolev, Miss Anne!' he shouted, then suddenly choked and threw up his arms as if scared out of his wits. 'My guardian angel!'

He ran towards her, groaning like one suffering a stroke. There was cabbage in his beard, he smelt of vodka. Laying his forehead on her muff, he appeared to swoon.

'Your hand, your precious hand!' he gasped. 'This must be a dream, a wonderful dream. Wake me up, children.'

He turned to the table. 'Providence has hearkened to us,' he sobbed, waving his fists. 'Our rescuer, our angel is here. We're saved! On your knees, children, on your knees.'

For some reason Mrs. Chalikov and all the girls except the youngest began tidying the table.

'You wrote that your wife was very ill.' Anne felt ashamed and annoyed. 'I shan't give him that fifteen hundred,' she thought.

'Here my wife is.' Chalikov spoke in a thin little voice like a woman's, sounding as if he was fighting back his tears. 'Here she is, poor creature, with her one foot in the grave. But we don't complain, ma'am. Better death than such a life. Die, poor woman, die!'

Why was the man so affected wondered Anne with annoyance. 'He's been used to dealing with merchants, that's obvious.'

'Please talk to me sensibly,' she said. 'I don't like play-acting.'

'Yes, ma'am. Five orphan children by their mother's coffin with the funeral candles burning, and you call that play-acting. Ah me!' said Chalikov bitterly, and turned away.

'You shut up,' whispered his wife, pulling him by his sleeve and turning to Anne. 'The place is untidy, ma'am. You must excuse us, you know how it is with families. Cramped we may be, but our hearts are in the right place.'

'I shan't give them that fifteen hundred,' thought Anne again.

To be quickly rid of these people and the sour smell, she took out her purse, deciding to leave twenty-five roubles, no more, but then suddenly felt ashamed at having driven so far and troubled them for nothing.

'If you'll give me paper and ink I'll write to a doctor now, one I know well, and ask him to call.' She blushed. 'He's a very good doctor. And I'll leave money for medicine.'

Mrs. Chalikov rushed to wipe the table.

'It's dirty here, what do you think you're doing?' hissed Chalikov, looking at her angrily. 'Take her to the lodger's room.' He addressed Anne. 'Come into the lodger's room, ma'am, I venture to request. It's clean there.'

'Mr. Pimenov asked us not to go into his room,' said one of the little girls sternly.

But they had already taken Anne out of the kitchen through a narrow corridor-room, between two beds. From the way the beds were placed it was clear that two people slept lengthways on one, and three crossways on the other. The next room, the lodger's, really was clean. There was a neat bed with a red woollen quilt, a pillow in a white pillow-case, and even a special watch-holder. On a table covered with a linen tablecloth were a cream inkwell, pens, paper, framed photographs, all tidily arranged, and there was a second, black table with watch-making instruments and dismantled watches in orderly array. About the walls hung hammers, pincers, augers, chisels, pliers and so on, and three wall clocks, all ticking, hung there too—one of them huge with fat pendulum weights such as you see in taverns.

As she started writing the letter Anne saw on the table before her a portrait of her father and one of herself. Surprised, she asked who the room's occupant was.

'The lodger, ma'am—Pimenov. He works at your factory.'

'Oh? I thought it must be a watch-maker.'

'He works on watches privately, in his spare time. It's his hobby, ma'am.'

After a pause, during which only the clocks' ticking and the squeaking of pen on paper could be heard, Chalikov sighed and spoke with sardonic resentment.

'Being a gentleman, a white-collar worker—these things don't make your fortune, that's sure enough. For all your badges of office and status you may still have nothing to eat. If one of the lower orders helps the poor he's a much finer gentleman, say I, than one of your Chalikovs sunk in poverty and vice.'

To flatter Anne he added one or two more sentences disparaging his social position, obviously demeaning himself because he thought himself above her. Meanwhile she had finished the letter and sealed it. Her letter would be thrown away, the money would not be used for medical treatment—that she knew, but she still left twenty-five roubles on the table and then, after some thought, added two more red, ten-rouble notes. Mrs. Chalikov's thin yellow hand flashed before her eyes like a hen's claw and clutched the money.

'You've graciously given us money for medicines,' Chalikov quavered. 'But now hold out a helping hand to me too, and to my children.' He sobbed. 'My unhappy children—it's not myself I fear for, it's my daughters. I fear the Hydra of Debauchery!'

Trying to open her purse, which had jammed shut, Anne felt embarrassed, and blushed. She was ashamed to have people standing before her looking at her hands, waiting and probably laughing at her to themselves. Meanwhile someone had come into the kitchen and stamped his feet to shake off the snow.

'It's the lodger,' said Mrs. Chalikov.

Anne felt still more embarrassed, not wanting any of her work-people to find her in this ludicrous position. And then of course the lodger had to enter his room just as she had finally broken open the catch of her purse and was handing some banknotes to Chalikov, while that same Chalikov bellowed like one suffering a stroke, working his lips as if looking for a part of her to kiss. In the lodger she recognized the workman who had once banged that iron sheet in front of her in the foundry and given her those explanations. He had come straight from work, obviously. His face was black with smoke and near his nose one cheek had a smear of soot. His hands were quite black, his unbelted shirt shone with greasy dirt. He was a black-haired, broad-shouldered man of about thirty, of medium height, obviously very strong. One glance told her that he was a charge-hand on at least thirty-five roubles a month. Here was a tough, loud-mouthed fellow, one to bash his men's teeth in—you could tell that from the way he stood, from the posture which he suddenly and automatically assumed on seeing a lady in his room, and above all from his wearing his trousers outside his boots, from the pockets on his shirt, from the well-groomed pointed beard. Her late father Akim, brother to the owner though he had been, had yet feared charge-hands like this lodger, and had tried to keep on the right side of them.

'I'm sorry, we've rather taken over here while you were out,' said Anne.

The workman looked at her with surprise and an embarrassed smile, but said nothing.

'Speak a little louder, ma'am,' said Chalikov quietly. 'Mr. Pimenov's a bit hard of hearing when he gets home from work of an evening.'

But Anne, relieved to have nothing more to do here, nodded and quickly left. Pimenov saw her out.

'Have you been with us long?' she asked in a loud voice, not facing him.

'Since I was nine. I got my job in your uncle's day.'

'That's quite some time ago. Uncle and Father knew all the workers, but I know hardly any. I've seen you before, but I didn't know your name was Pimenov.'

Anne felt an urge to justify herself by pretending that she hadn't been serious, that she had been joking, when giving them that money just now.

'What a thing poverty is,' she sighed. 'We do our good deeds day in day out, but it makes no sense. I see no point in helping the Chalikovs of this world.'

'Of course not,' Pimenov agreed. 'What you give him will all go on drink. Now husband and wife will spend all night quarrelling and trying to get that money off each other,' he added with a laugh.

'Yes, our charity's useless, boring and ridiculous, admittedly. But then, one can't just ignore things either, can one? One must do something. What, for instance, can one do about the Chalikovs?'

She turned towards Pimenov and halted, waiting for his answer. He halted too, slowly and silently shrugging his shoulders. He obviously did know what to do about the Chalikovs, but it was something so crude and inhumane that he did not even venture to say it. So dull and unimportant were the Chalikovs to him that he had forgotten all about them a second later. Gazing into Anne's eyes, he smiled his pleasure, looking like someone who has had a delightful dream. Only now that she stood near to him could Anne see from his face, especially the eyes, how worn out and tired he was.

'This is the one I should give the fifteen hundred to,' she thought, but found the idea vaguely out of place and insulting to Pimenov.

'You must be aching all over after your day's work, but you insist on seeing me out,' she said on the way downstairs. 'Do go back.'

But he heard nothing. When they emerged in the street he ran ahead, unbuttoned the apron of the sledge and wished Anne a happy Christmas as he helped her into her seat.

II

Morning

'The bells stopped long ago. Everyone will be leaving church by the time you arrive, Lord help us. Do get up.'

'Two horses running, running,' said Anne as she woke up. Her maid, red-haired Masha, stood before her carrying a candle. 'What is it? What do you want?'

'The service is already over,' said Masha desperately. 'This is the third time I've tried to wake you. Sleep till evening for all I care, but it was you told me you wanted to be called.'

Anne raised herself on an elbow and looked out of the window. It was still quite dark outside, except that the bottom edge of the window frame was white with snow. The low, full-toned tolling of bells was heard, but that was some way off in another parish. The clock on the small table showed three minutes past six.

'All right, Masha, just a couple of minutes,' entreated Anne, pulling the quilt over her head.

She pictured the snow by the porch, the sledge, the dark sky, the congregation in church and the smell of juniper, which was all rather forbidding, but she was still determined to get up straight away and go to early service. Enjoying the warm bed, fighting off sleep—it has a way of being most delightful just when one is told to wake up—and picturing, now a huge garden on a hill, now the Gushchin place, she was irked all the time at having to get up that instant and drive to church.

When Anne did get up it was quite light and the clock said half-past nine. Masses of new snow had piled up overnight, the trees were robed in white, the air was extraordinarily bright, transparent and limpid, so that when she looked through the window she at first felt like giving a huge sigh. But, as she was washing herself, a residual childhood memory of joy that it was Christmas Day suddenly stirred within her, after which she felt relaxed, free and pure-hearted as if her very soul had been washed or plunged in white snow. In came Masha—tightly corseted, in her best clothes—and wished Anne Happy Christmas before doing her hair and helping her to dress, which took some time. The smell, the feel of her gorgeous, splendid new dress, its slight rustle and the whiff of fresh scent—all excited Anne.

'So Christmas has come,' she cheerfully remarked to Masha. 'Now we'll tell our fortunes.'

'Last year it came out as I was to marry an old man. Three times it came out that way.'

'Never mind, God is merciful.'

'I don't know, though, ma'am. Rather than be at sixes and sevens all the time I might do better marrying an old man, it seems to me.' Masha sighed sadly. 'I'm gone twenty, it's no laughing matter.'

Everyone in the house knew that red-haired Masha loved the butler Misha with a deep yet hopeless passion which had now lasted three years.

'Oh, don't talk such nonsense,' said Anne, attempting to console her. 'I'll soon be thirty and I still mean to marry a young man.'

While the mistress was dressing, Misha paced the ballroom and drawing-room in his new tail-coat and lacquered boots, waiting for her to come out so that he could offer her the compliments of the season. He had a special walk, always treading softly and delicately. Looking at his legs, his arms and the tilt of his head, you might have thought that he wasn't just walking but learning to dance the first figure of the quadrille. Despite his thin, velvety moustache, despite his handsome, not to say caddish exterior, he was as dignified, judicious and pious as an old man. He always bowed low when praying, and liked burning incense in his room. Respecting and venerating the rich and well-connected, he scorned the poor and suppliants of any kind with the full force of his chaste flunkey's soul. Under his starched shirt he wore a flannel vest, winter and summer, setting great store by his health. He kept his ears plugged with cotton-wool.

When Anne and Masha crossed the ballroom he inclined his head downwards, slightly to one side, and spoke in his pleasant, honeyed voice. 'Madam, I have the honour to wish you all happiness on the solemn occasion of Our Lord's Nativity.'

Anne gave him five roubles and poor Masha nearly fainted. His festive air, his posture, his voice, his words pierced her with their beauty and elegance. She continued to follow her mistress, her mind a blank, seeing nothing, only smiling—now blissfully, now bitterly.

The upper storey of the house was called 'the best rooms', 'above stairs' or 'the chambers', while the lower floor, where Aunt Tatyana officiated, was 'the tradesmen's', 'the old folks' ' or simply 'the women's' quarters. In the former they received the quality and educated persons, in the latter humbler folk and Aunt's own friends.

Beautiful, buxom, healthy, young, fresh, radiantly conscious of her gorgeous dress, Anne went down to the ground floor. There she met reproaches. 'Here are you, an educated woman, forgetting God, sleeping through morning service, and not coming down to break your fast.' They all threw up their hands and fervently told her that she was a remarkably good-looking woman. Not doubting that they meant what they said, she laughed, kissed them, and gave them one, three or—as the case might be—five roubles. She liked it down here. On all sides were icon-cases, icons, icon-lamps, portraits of men of the cloth. It smelt of monks. There was a clattering of knives in the kitchen, a whiff of something rich and succulent swept through the place. The yellow-stained floors shone, and from the doors to the corners with their icons were narrow carpet runners with bright blue stripes. The sun's rays slashed through the windows.

In the dining-room sat some old women—strangers. There were old women in Barbara's room too, and a deaf-and-dumb girl who seemed vaguely embarrassed and kept mumbling incoherently. Two thin little girls, invited over from the children's home for the holidays, came up to kiss Anne's hand, but stopped in front of her, stunned by the richness of her dress. One girl was a bit cross-eyed, Anne noticed, feeling a sudden pang, for all the relaxed Christmassy mood, to think that the child would be neglected by suitors and never get married. In Agatha's, the cook's, room half a dozen enormous peasants in new shirts were sitting over the samovar—not factory-hands, these, but relatives of the kitchen staff. Seeing Anne, they jumped up and stopped chewing out of politeness though all had their mouths full. Her chef Stephen came in from the kitchen in his white hat, carrying a knife, and wished her happy Christmas. Felt-booted yardmen came in and did the same. A water-hauler peered in with icicles on his beard, but dared not enter.

Anne walked from room to room with the whole lot tagging behind —her Aunt, Barbara, Nikandrovna, the seamstress Martha, 'Downstairs' Masha. Barbara—a thin, slim, tall woman, the tallest person in the house—was all in black, smelling of cypress-wood and coffee. She crossed herself and bowed to the icons in each room. The sight somehow reminded one that she had prepared a shroud for her own funeral, and also that she kept her lottery certificates in a trunk along with that shroud.

'Now, let's see some Christmas spirit, Annie dear.' Barbara opened the kitchen door. 'Do forgive the wretch—such nuisances these people are.'

In the middle of the kitchen knelt the coachman Panteley, dismissed for drunkenness back in November. Though a kindly man, he was prone to violence in his cups, when he couldn't sleep but haunted the works, shouting menacingly that he knew 'all the goings-on'. That he had been drinking non-stop between November and Christmas was obvious from his jowly, puffy face and bloodshot eyes.

'Forgive me, Miss Anne,' he wheezed, banging his head on the ground and displaying a neck like a bull's.

'My aunt it was dismissed you, so you'd better ask her.'

'What's this about your aunt?' asked her aunt, puffing her way into the kitchen. She was so fat that you could have rested a samovar and tray of cups on her bust. 'What's this aunt business? You're mistress here, so you deal with it. These scallywags can all go to blazes for all I care. Oh, stand up, you great ox!' she shouted at Panteley, losing her temper. 'Get out of my sight! This is the last time I'll forgive you—if it happens again you can expect no mercy.'

They went to the dining-room for coffee. But hardly were they seated at table when Downstairs Masha hurtled in, uttered the horror-struck announcement 'carol singers', and ran out again. There was a noise of people blowing their noses, of a deep bass cough and of foot-steps, as if shod horses were being brought into the vestibule by the ballroom. Then, after half a minute's silence, the singers suddenly emitted so loud a shriek that everyone jumped. While they were singing the almshouse priest arrived with his verger and sexton. Donning his stole, the priest slowly averred that it had snowed that night while the bells were ringing for early service, but it had not been cold, whereas a sharp frost had come on by morning, dash it, and it must now be about twenty degrees below.

'There are, however, those who claim that winter is healthier than summer,' said the verger, but at once assumed a stern expression and sang after the priest: 'Thy Nativity, O Christ, our God——'

Soon afterwards the priest from the works hospital arrived with his sexton, followed by nuns from the Red Cross and children from the local home. Singing went on almost without a break. They sang, they ate, they departed.

Members of the works staff, about a score of them, came to offer the compliments of the season. These were all senior people—engineers, their assistants, pattern-makers, the accountant and so on—all respectable in their new black frock-coats. They were a fine body of men, an élite, and each knew his worth—if he lost his job today he'd be gladly taken on at another factory tomorrow. That they liked Anne's aunt was obvious because they relaxed with her and even smoked, and the accountant put his arm round her broad waist as they all crowded over to the buffet. One reason why they felt so much at ease was perhaps that Barbara—the all-powerful supervisor of staff morals in the old man's day—now counted for nothing in the house. And perhaps another reason was that many of them still remembered the days when Aunt Tatyana, treated strictly by the brothers, had dressed like an ordinary peasant such as Agatha, and when Miss Anne herself had run round the yard near the works buildings and everyone had called her little Annie.

The staff ate, smoked and gazed dumbfounded at Anne. How she had grown up, how pretty she had become. Yet this elegant girl, reared by governesses and tutors, was to them a stranger and an enigma, and so they involuntarily gravitated to her aunt, who spoke to them more intimately, who kept pressing them to eat and drink, who clinked glasses with them and had already drunk two rowanberry gins. Anne was always scared of being thought proud, an upstart, a crow decked in peacock's feathers. Now, as the staff crowded round the food, she stayed in the dining-room and joined in the talk. She asked Pimenov, whom she had met on the previous day, why he had so many watches and clocks in his room.

'I do repairs,' he answered. 'I do them in my spare time, on holidays, or when I can't sleep.'

Anne laughed. 'So if my watch goes wrong I can bring it to you for repair?'

'Certainly, I'll be glad to,' said Pimenov. And when, not knowing why, she unhooked the magnificent watch from her corsage and gave it to him, he looked quite overcome with emotion. He examined it silently and gave it back. 'Certainly, I'll be glad to,' he repeated. 'I don't mend pocket watches any more. I have bad eyesight, and the doctor has told me not to do close work. But I can make an exception for you.'

'All doctors are liars,' said the accountant, and everyone laughed. 'Don't you believe them,' he went on, flattered by the laughter. 'In Lent last year a cog flew out of a drum and caught old Kalmykov on the head. You could actually see his brains, and the doctor said he was going to die. He's still alive and working, though, only he now has a stutter through this business.'

'Doctors do talk nonsense, indeed they do, but not all that much,' sighed Aunt. 'Peter Andreyevich lost his sight, God rest his soul. He worked all day in the factory near a hot furnace like you, and he went blind. Heat's bad for the eyes. Anyway, why talk about it?' She shook herself. 'Let's go and have a drink. Happy Christmas to you all, dears. I don't usually drink, but I'll have one with you, may I be forgiven. Cheers!'

Anne sensed that Pimenov despised her as a dispenser of charity after yesterday's business, but was entranced by her as a woman. She noticed that he was really behaving quite nicely, and was presentably dressed. True, his frock-coat sleeves were a bit short, the waist seemed too high, and the trousers were not of the fashionable broad cut, but his cravat was tied with tasteful nonchalance, nor was it as loud as the others'. And he must be good-natured, for he submissively ate everything that her aunt put on his plate. She remembered how black, how sleepy he had been yesterday—a rather touching recollection.

When the staff were ready to leave, Anne held out her hand to Pimenov and felt like asking him to call on her some time, but was unable to. Somehow her tongue would not obey her. And, in case anyone might suppose that she found Pimenov attractive, she shook hands with his colleagues too.

The next arrivals were boys from the school where she was Visitor. All had short hair and wore grey smocks in uniform style. Their schoolmaster—a tall, whiskerless, obviously nervous youth with red blotches on his face—paraded them in rows. The boys started singing in harmony, but with harsh, disagreeable voices. The works manager Nazarych—a bald, sharp-eyed Nonconformist—never had got on with schoolteachers, but this one with his fussy arm-waving he despised and hated without even knowing why. He treated him arrogantly and rudely, he withheld his salary, he interfered with the teaching. In order to get rid of the man once and for all, Nazarych had, a fortnight before Christmas, appointed a distant relative by marriage to the post of school caretaker, a drunken oaf who disobeyed the teacher and was impertinent to him in his pupils' presence.

Anne knew all this, but could not help, being scared of Nazarych herself. Now she at least wanted to be kind to the schoolteacher and tell him that she was very satisfied with him, but when the singing was over and he embarked on some highly embarrassed apology, and after her aunt, speaking to him as one of the family, had casually dragged him off to the table, she felt depressed and ill at ease. Ordering that the children should be given presents, she went upstairs to her own quarters.

'There's a lot of cruelty about these Christmas arrangements really,' she said aloud a little later, looking out of the window at the boys flocking from the house to the gate and putting on their furs and overcoats as they went, shivering from cold. 'On holidays you want to rest and stay at home with your family, but the poor boys, the master and the staff are somehow obliged to go out in the cold, wish you happy Christmas, convey their respects, suffer embarrassment.'

Misha, standing just by the ballroom door, heard all this.

'We didn't start it and it won't end with us. Of course, I'm not an educated man, madam, but to my way of thinking the poor must always respect the rich. God puts his mark on a scoundrel, 'tis said. Gaols, doss-houses, taverns—they're always full of the poor, while decent people are always rich, mark my words. Deep calls to deep, that's what they say of the rich.'

'You're rather given to such boring, incomprehensible talk, Misha.' Anne crossed to the other side of the room.

It was just turned eleven o'clock. The calm of the vast rooms, broken only now and then by singing wafted up from the ground floor, was enough to make you yawn. The bronzes, the albums, the pictures on the wall—seascapes with little boats, a meadow with cows, views of the River Rhine—were so unoriginal that one's eyes slid over them seeing nothing. The Christmas spirit had already begun to pall. Anne still felt beautiful, kind, admirable, but now sensed that these qualities were of no use to anyone. For whom had she put on this expensive dress? Why? She had no idea. As always on festive occasions, she began to suffer from loneliness, obsessed with the thought that her beauty, her health, her riches were only a sham, that she was a misfit on this earth, that no one needed or loved her. She walked through all her rooms, humming and glancing through the windows. Pausing in the ballroom, she could not help addressing Misha.

'I don't know who you think you are, Misha.' She sighed. 'Truly, God will punish you for this.'

'For what, madam?'

'You know perfectly well. I'm sorry to meddle in your private affairs, but I think you're ruining your life out of sheer obstinacy. You're just the age to marry, now, aren't you? And she's a fine, a most deserving girl. You'll never find a better, she's beautiful, clever, gentle, devoted. And her looks! If she was one of our set, or in high society, men would love her for her marvellous red hair alone. Look how her hair sets off her complexion. Oh God, you understand nothing, you don't know what you need yourself,' Anne added bitterly, and tears came to her eyes. 'Poor child, I'm so sorry for her. I know you want to marry someone with money, but I've told you I'll give Masha a dowry.'

Misha could picture his future wife only as a tall, buxom, stately, respectable-looking woman, strutting like a peahen, always wearing a long shawl on her shoulders for some reason, whereas Masha was thin, slight, corseted, and walked with a modest gait. Above all she was too seductive, and sometimes strongly attracted Misha. But he thought that sort of thing went with impropriety, and not at all with marriage. When Anne has promised the dowry he had weakened for a time. But then a poor student, with a brown top-coat over his uniform, had brought Anne a letter, and had been so taken with Masha that he couldn't resist embracing her near the coat-hooks downstairs, and she had given a little cry. Misha had seen this from the staircase above them, and had been rather put off by Masha ever since. A poor student! Had she been kissed by a rich student or an officer the result might have been different, who knows?

'Why don't you?' Anne asked. 'What more could you want?'

Eyebrows raised, Misha stared silently at an armchair.

'Do you love anyone else?'

No answer. Masha of the red hair came in with letters and visiting cards on a tray. Guessing that they had been talking about her, she blushed till she nearly cried.

'The postmen are here,' she muttered. 'And a clerk, a Chalikov or something, has come and is waiting downstairs. He says you asked him here today for some reason.'

'What impudence.' Anne was angry. 'I never asked him at all. Say he's to clear out, I'm not at home.'

There was a ring at the door. This was their own parish priests, who were always received in the best rooms—upstairs, that is. After the priests the works manager Nazarych and then the works doctor called. Then Misha announced the inspector of elementary schools. The reception of visitors had begun.

Whenever she had a free moment Anne sat in a deep armchair in the drawing-room, closed her eyes and reflected that her loneliness was entirely natural since she had not married and never would. But it was not her fault. From ordinary working-class surroundings—where, if memory served, she had been so comfortable, so much at ease—fate itself had cast her into these huge rooms. What was she to do with herself? She couldn't think. Why did all these people keep coming and going? She hadn't the faintest idea. The present proceedings seemed trivial and otiose since they neither did not could give her a minute's happiness.

'Oh, to fall in love.' She stretched herself, and the mere idea warmed her heart. 'And I should get rid of the factory,' she mused, imagining all those ponderous buildings, those barracks and that school being lifted from her conscience.

Then she remembered her father, reflecting that he would surely have married her to some working man like Pimenov if he had lived longer. He would have told her to marry, and that would have been that. It would have been all right too, for then the factory would have fallen into the right hands.

She pictured the curly head, the bold profile, the thin, mocking lips, the strength, the terrible strength of his shoulders, arms and chest, and the rapture with which he had examined her watch today.

'Why not?' she said. 'It would be all right, I'd marry him.'

'Miss Anne,' called Misha, coming silently into the dining-room.

'How you did frighten me.' She trembled all over. 'What do you want?'

'Miss Anne,' he repeated, laying his hand on his heart and raising his eyebrows. 'You are my employer and benefactress, no one but you can tell me who to marry, seeing that you are a mother to me. But do ask them not to laugh at me and tease me below stairs. They won't let me alone.'

'And what form does this teasing take?'

'Masha's Misha, they call me.'

'Ugh, how idiotic.' Anne was outraged. 'You're all so stupid—you too, Misha. Oh, you do bore me so, I can't bear the sight of you.'

III

Dinner

As in the previous year, Anne's last visitors to arrive were Krylin, a senior civil servant, and the well-known lawyer Lysevich. They came as dusk was falling.

Old Krylin, in his sixties, wide-mouthed and lynx-faced with white dundrearies round his ears, wore uniform, a St. Anne ribbon and white trousers. He held Anne's hand in both his own for some time, staring into her face, moving his lips.

'I respected your uncle and your father, and they were favourably disposed towards me,' he brought out at last, all on one note, carefully articulating each syllable. 'Now, as you see, I consider it my pleasant duty to convey the compliments of the season to their respected lady successor, despite my infirmity and the considerable distance. And very glad I am to see you in good health.'

The barrister Lysevich—tall, handsome, fair-haired, with a touch of grey about temples and beard—was notable for extreme elegance of manner. He would waltz into the room, bow with apparent reluctance, wriggle his shoulders as he spoke—all with the lazy grace of a spoilt horse in need of exercise. He was sleek, rich, remarkably healthy. Once he had even won forty thousand roubles in a lottery, but had concealed this from his friends. He liked good food, especially cheese, truffles, shredded horse-radish in hempseed oil, and claimed to have eaten uncleaned giblets, fried, in Paris. He spoke smoothly, evenly, without hesitation, permitting himself the occasional coy pause and flick of the fingers as if at a loss for a word. He had long ceased believing what he had to say in court. Or perhaps he did believe it, but attached no value to it. All that stuff was so old hat, out-of-date, trite.

He believed only in the unusual and the recondite. Hackneyed moralizing could move him to tears, if expressed with originality. His two notebooks were bescribbled with out-of-the-way expressions culled from various authors, and when at a loss for a phrase he would nervously rummage in both books and usually fail to find it. Old Akim had once light-heartedly taken him on as works lawyer to lend tone to the place, at a retainer of twelve thousand roubles. But the factory's entire legal activity consisted only of a few minor suits which Lysevich left to his assistants.

Anne knew that there was no work for him at the factory. But she could not bring herself to dismiss him, lacking the courage and liking him. He called himself her 'legal adviser', referring to his retainer, for which he applied regularly on the first of the month, as 'this boring necessity'. When Anne's woods had been sold for railway sleepers after her father's death, Lysevich had fiddled more than fifteen thousand on the deal and shared it with Nazarych, as she knew. She had wept bitterly on learning of the fraud, but had then come to accept it.

Having wished her a happy Christmas and kissed both her hands, Lysevich looked her up and down, and frowned.

'Don't!' he said with sincere regret. 'I've told you not to, dear lady.'

'Don't what, Victor?'

'I've told you not to put on weight. Your family all have this unfortunate tendency to stoutness. Don't do it,' he pleaded, kissing her hand. 'You're such a fine, splendid woman.' He turned to Krylin. 'Here she is, my dear sir. Permit me to present—the only woman in the world I have ever really loved.'

'That doesn't surprise me. To know Miss Glagolev at your age and not love her would be impossible.'

'I adore her,' the lawyer went on with complete sincerity but with his usual lazy grace. 'I love her, but not because I'm a man and she's a woman. When I'm with her I feel as if she belonged to some third sex and I to a fourth, as if we were soaring off together to a domain of the most subtle hues, and there blending into a spectrum. Such relationships are defined best of all by Leconte de Lisle. He has one marvellous passage, truly remarkable.'

Rummaging in one notebook and then in the other, Lysevich calmed down on failing to find the dictum. They talked of the weather, of the opera, of Duse's imminent tour. Anne recalled Lysevich and, she thought, Krylin dining with her on the previous Christmas Day, and as they were about to leave she urgently submitted that they must stay to dinner as they had no more visits to make. After some hesitation the guests agreed.

Besides the ordinary meal of cabbage stew, sucking pig, goose with apples and so on, a 'French' or 'chef's' dinner would be prepared in the kitchen on major festive occasions in case any first-floor guests should wish to partake. When the clattering of crockery began in the dining-room Lysevich evinced obvious excitement. He rubbed his hands, wriggled his shoulders, frowned, movingly described the dinners that the old men had once given, and said what a superb turbot soup Anne's chef made—more of a divine inspiration than a *bouillabaisse*. He was looking forward to the meal, he was already eating and enjoying it in his imagination. When Anne took his arm and led him to the dining-room, when he had at last drunk a glass of vodka and put a piece of salmon in his mouth, he was actually purring with pleasure. He chewed loudly and revoltingly, making noises through his nose, his eyes greasy and voracious.

The *hors-d'œuvre* were lavish, including fresh mushrooms in sour cream and *sauce provençale* with fried oysters and crayfish tails well primed with sour pickles. The main part of the meal consisted of exquisite dishes specially cooked for the festivities, and the wines were excellent. Misha served like one in a trance. Placing a new dish on the table, removing the lid of a gleaming tureen, pouring the wine, he was solemn as a professor of the black art. From his face, from his walk like the first figure in the quadrille, the lawyer several times concluded that the man was a fool.

After the third course Lysevich turned to Anne.

'A *fin de siècle* woman—I mean a young one and, of course, a rich one—must be independent, clever, elegant, intelligent, bold. And a shade immoral. I say a shade immoral, immoral within limits, because you'll agree that everything is exhausting in excess. You mustn't vegetate, dear lady, you mustn't live like all the rest, you must savour life, and a touch of immorality is the very spice of existence. Plunge into flowers with a reek that drugs the senses, choke in musk, eat hashish. Above all love, love, love. If I were you I'd start off with seven men, one for each day of the week, and I'd call one Monday, the next Tuesday, the third Wednesday and so on. Let each know his own day.'

His talk unnerved Anne. She ate nothing, drank only one glass of wine, and told him that he must for goodness' sake let her speak.

'To me personally love makes no sense without a family,' she said. 'I'm lonely—lonely as the moon in the sky, and the waning moon at that. Say what you like, but I know, I feel that this void can only be filled by love in its ordinary sense. Such a love will define my duties, my work, enlighten my view of life, I feel. From love I want peace of mind, calmness. I want to get as far as possible from musk and all your *fin de siècle* mumbo-jumbo. In other words,' she said with embarrassment, 'I want a husband and children.'

'You want to marry? Why not? That too is possible,' agreed Lysevich. 'You should try everything—marriage, jealousy, the sweetness of your first adultery, children even. But hurry up and enjoy life, dear lady, hurry—time's passing, it won't wait.'

'All right, I jolly well will marry.' She looked angrily at his sleek, complacent face. 'I'll marry in the most conventional, commonplace way, I'll radiate happiness. And, believe it or not, I'll marry an ordinary working man, a mechanic, a draughtsman or something.'

'Not a bad idea either. Princess falls in love with swineherd. That's all right, seeing that she's a princess. It's all right for you too because you're exceptional. If you want to love some Negro or blackamoor, dear lady, go ahead and send for a Negro. Deny yourself nothing. Be bold as your own desires, don't tag along behind them.'

'Am I really so hard to understand?' Anne was outraged, tears gleamed in her eyes. 'Can't you see I have a huge business on my hands, two thousand workers for whom I must answer before God? Men go blind and deaf working for me. Life frightens me, scares me stiff. And, while I suffer, you have the cruelty to bring up these wretched Negroes. And—and you grin.' Anne banged her fist on the table. 'To go on living as I am now, to marry someone as idle and incompetent as myself—that would just be a crime. I can't go on like this,' she said fiercely. 'I can't cope.'

'How pretty she is!' Lysevich was entranced. 'What a devilish handsome woman. But why so angry, dear lady? I may be quite wrong, but what if you do make yourself miserable and renounce the joys of life in the name of ideals which I, incidentally, deeply respect? What good will that do the workers? None. No, it's immorality for you, debauchery,' he said decisively. 'Be corrupt, it's your duty—get that well and truly into your head, dear lady.'

Glad to have had her say, Anne cheered up. She was pleased to have spoken so well, pleased to be reasoning so honestly and stylishly. She was also certain that if Pimenov, say, should fall in love with her she would be delighted to marry him.

Misha poured champagne.

'You provoke me, Victor.' She clinked glasses with the lawyer. 'You annoy me by giving advice when you know nothing of life yourself. A mechanic or draughtsman—to you he's a country bumpkin. But they're such clever people, they're quite outstanding.'

'I knew and respected, er, your father and uncle,' Krylin enunciated. He was stretched out like an effigy, and had been eating non-stop. 'Those were men of considerable intellect and, er, high spiritual qualities.'

'Oh, we've heard quite enough about those qualities,' muttered the lawyer, and asked permission to smoke.

After dinner Krylin was led off for his nap. Lysevich finished his cigar and followed Anne to her study, waddling because he had eaten too much. Disliking secluded nooks full of photographs, fans on the wall, the inevitable pink or blue lamp in the middle of the ceiling, he thought them expressions of a feeble, unoriginal mind. Moreover, memories of certain romantic affairs, of which he was now ashamed, were associated with such a lamp. But he much liked Anne's study with its bare walls and characterless furniture. He felt easy and relaxed on the sofa, glancing at Anne who usually sat on the carpet in front of the hearth, knees clasped in her hands as she gazed meditatively at the flames while giving him the impression that her Nonconformist peasant instincts were aroused.

When coffee and liqueurs were served after dinner he would perk up and tell her bits of literary news. He spoke in the flamboyant, exalted style of one transported by his own rhetoric, while she listened, reflecting as ever that such enjoyment was worth his twelve thousand roubles three times over, and forgave all she disliked in him. Sometimes he described the plots of short stories or even novels, and a couple of hours would pass unnoticed like so many minutes. Now he began in a rather sentimental, feeble voice, eyes closed.

'It's ages since I read anything, dear lady,' he said when she asked him to talk. 'Though I do sometimes read Jules Verne.'

'And I thought you were going to tell me something new.'

'Humph. Something new,' Lysevich muttered sleepily and settled back still further into the corner of the sofa. 'Modern literature doesn't suit the likes of you and me, dear lady. It can't help being what it is, of course, and to reject it would be to reject the natural order of things, so I do accept it, but——'

Lysevich seemed to have fallen asleep, but a little later his voice was heard again. 'Modern literature's all like the autumn wind in the chimney, for ever groaning and moaning. "Oh, oh, oh, you're so unhappy, your life is like prison, and a dark, damp prison at that. Alas, you're doomed, there's no hope for you." That's all very well, but I'd rather have a literature which teaches you to escape from prison. Maupassant is the only modern writer I occasionally read.' Lysevich opened his eyes. 'He's a good writer, a fine writer.' Lysevich stirred on the sofa. 'He's a remarkable artist, a terrifying, monstrous, supernatural artist.' Lysevich got up from the sofa, raised his right hand. 'Maupassant!' said he in ecstasy. 'Read Maupassant, dear lady. One page will give you more than all the riches of this earth. Every line contains a new horizon. The most delicate and tender spiritual motions alternate with mighty tempestuous sensations, your soul seems subjected to a forty-thousandfold atmospheric pressure, and turns into an insignificant speck of an indeterminate pinkish substance—if you could put it on your tongue it would have a bitter, sensuous taste, I think. What a frenzy of transitions, motifs, melodies. You are resting on lilies-of-the-valley and roses when suddenly an idea—awful, wonderful, irresistible—unexpectedly swoops on you like a railway train, swamps you with hot steam, deafens you with its whistle. Read, read, read Maupassant. I demand it, dear lady.'

Lysevich brandished his arms and paced the room in a great pother.

'No, it cannot be,' he said, as if in despair. 'His last work exhausted, intoxicated me. But I'm afraid you won't react to it at all. If it is to sweep you off your feet you must savour it, slowly squeeze the juice out of each line and drink it. Yes, drink it!'

After a long exordium containing many expressions like 'demoniac passion', 'tissue of nervous ganglia', 'sand-storm', 'crystal' and so on, he at last began to explain the plot. Now speaking in less high-flown style and in great detail, he quoted by heart whole descriptions and conversations. The characters enchanted him, and as he retailed them he assumed poses, changing his voice and facial expression like a real actor. He gave exulting cachinnations—now low-pitched, now thin and reedy—he threw up his hands, he clutched his head as if it was about to burst. Anne had read the book, yet listened with fascination, finding the lawyer's account far finer and more complex than the original. He directed her attention to the various subtleties, he emphasized the felicitous expressions and profound ideas, while she saw it all as if it was actually happening, with herself as one of the characters. She cheered up, she too laughed aloud and threw up her hands, reflecting that an existence like hers was impossible—why live badly when one could live well? She remembered what she had said and thought at dinner, gloried in it. And when Pimenov suddenly came to mind she felt happy and wanted him to love her.

His recital concluded, Lysevich sank exhausted on the sofa.

'You're a wonderful, splendid woman,' he said a little later in a feeble, sick voice. 'I'm so happy with you, dear lady. But why must I be forty-two and not thirty? My tastes and yours don't coincide. You need immorality, whereas I went through that phase ages ago and want a most subtle love, insubstantial as a sunbeam—to a woman of your age, in other words, I'm no damn use.'

He reckoned to like Turgenev, that bard of first love, purity, youth and melancholy Russian landscapes. Yet there was nothing that touched him closely in this passion for 'virgin' love, it was just something he had heard of, something abstract and divorced from reality. He was now telling himself that his love for Anne was platonic and idealistic. What that meant he didn't know, but he felt relaxed, at ease, warm. Anne seemed enchantingly eccentric, and he mistook the euphoria aroused in him by this ambience for his 'platonic' love.

He pressed his cheek to her hand. 'Why have you punished me, dearest?' he asked in the voice with which people coax infants.

'How? When?'

'You haven't sent me my Christmas bonus.'

Never having heard of lawyers receiving Christmas bonuses, Anne was embarrassed at not knowing how much to give him. And something she must give him because he obviously expected it even as he gazed at her with love-lorn eyes.

'Nazarych must have forgotten, but it's not too late to be mended,' she said.

Then she suddenly remembered yesterday's fifteen hundred roubles, now on her bedroom dressing-table. Fetching that distasteful sum, she gave it to the lawyer, who stuck it in his coat pocket with his lazy elegance. It all went off rather charmingly and naturally. The unexpected reminder of the bonus, the fifteen hundred roubles—it was pure Lysevich, all this.

'*Merci.*' He kissed her finger.

In came Krylin with a beatific, sleepy air, having taken off his decorations.

He and Lysevich sat on a bit longer, drank their glass of tea, prepared to leave. Anne was rather put out, having quite forgotten where Krylin worked. Should she give him money too? And, if so, should she give it now or send it in an envelope?

'Where does he work?' she whispered to Lysevich.

'Damned if I know,' muttered the yawning lawyer.

She reflected that Krylin would not have paid his respects to her uncle and father for no return. He had obviously been their agent in good works, serving in some charitable institution, so she thrust three hundred roubles in his hand as she said good-bye. He seemed astounded. For a time he looked at her silently, eyes glazed, but then seemed to understand.

'But you can't have a receipt before the new year, dear madam.'

Now completely limp, Lysevich slumped and tottered as Misha helped him into his furs. On his way downstairs he looked utterly debilitated, and would obviously fall fast asleep the moment he got into his sledge.

'Have you, sir, ever felt,' he languidly asked Krylin, pausing on the staircase, 'as if some invisible force was stretching you out until you got longer and longer and ended up as a length of the finest wire? The feeling is, subjectively speaking, peculiarly and quite incomparably sensual.'

Standing on the upper level, Anne saw both give Misha a banknote.

'Good-bye, don't forget me,' she shouted, and ran to her bedroom.

She quickly threw off her dress, which now bored her, put on her négligé and ran downstairs, laughing and clattering her feet like an urchin. She felt very skittish.

IV

Evening

Aunt in her loose cotton blouse, Barbara and a couple of old women were having supper in the dining-room. Before them on the table was a hunk of salt-beef, a ham and various salted foods, and from the very fat, tasty-looking salt-beef steam rose to the ceiling. They did not drink wine down here, but had a great variety of spirits and cordials. The cook Agatha—buxom, fair-haired, stocky—stood by the door, arms crossed, talking to the old women while the dishes were taken and served by Downstairs Masha with a crimson ribbon in her dark hair. The old women had been stuffing themselves since morning, and had had tea with a rich pie only an hour before supper, so they were now forcing themselves to eat as if it were a duty.

'Oh dear,' gasped Anne's aunt when Anne suddenly ran into the dining-room and sat on the chair next to her. 'You nearly scared me to death.'

The household liked Anne being cheerful and frolicsome, which always reminded them that the old men had died, that the old women no longer held sway in the house, and that they could all do as they liked without fear of being kept up to the mark. Only the two old women unknown to Anne looked askance at her, amazed that she was singing to herself, for singing at table is a sin.

'She's pretty as a picture, is Madam,' drooled Agatha in her sing-song voice. 'A pearl beyond price she is. And oh what a lot of nice people came to see our princess today, Lord love us. Generals, officers, fine gentlemen. I kept a-looking through the window and a-counting of 'em, and then I gave up.'

'Let them stay at home, the scallywags,' said Aunt. She looked sadly at her niece, adding that they had only 'wasted the poor child's time'.

Having eaten nothing since morning, Anne was famished. They poured her a very dry cordial which she drank, eating salt-beef and mustard and finding it all most tasty. Then Downstairs Masha served turkey, soused apples and gooseberries, which Anne also liked. Only one thing irked her—waves of heat came from the tiled stove, it was stuffy and everyone's cheeks glowed. After supper they took off the tablecloth and served bowls of mint cakes, nuts and raisins.

'Now, you sit with us too, come on,' Aunt told the cook.

Agatha sighed and sat down at table. Masha set a cordial glass before her too, and Anne felt as if the heat proceeded equally from the stove and Agatha's white neck. They all said how hard it was to get married these days. At one time men had at least been attracted by money if not by beauty, whereas there was no telling what they wanted now. Once only the lame and the hunchbacks had been left on the shelf, but even beauty and riches were spurned nowadays. It was all because they were immoral and didn't fear the Lord, Aunt began saying, but then suddenly remembered that her brother Ivan and Barbara had both been righteous-living, God-fearing people, yet had had children on the wrong side of the blanket and sent them to a home. So she pulled herself up and changed the conversation to a former suitor of hers, a factory employee, and how she had loved him. But her brothers had made her marry a widowed icon-painter who had died two years later, thank God. Downstairs Masha also sat at table and enigmatically averred that a strange man—black-moustached, in an overcoat with an astrakhan collar—had taken to appearing in their yard every morning this week. He would come into the yard, look up at the mansion windows, then go on to the factory. He wasn't bad either—quite good-looking.

All this talk somehow made Anne suddenly long for marriage. She was seized by an urge akin to anguish, feeling ready to give half her life and all her possessions just to know that there was a man upstairs dearer to her than anyone on earth, one who really loved her and yearned for her. The idea of intimacy so inexpressibly entrancing moved her. Her healthy young woman's instincts flattered her with the lie that true romance lay ahead, even though it had not yet arrived. Convinced, she threw herself back in her chair, which made her hair fall down. She began laughing, and that set the others laughing too. For some time this spontaneous laughter rang through the dining-room.

It was announced that 'the Beetle' had arrived, and would stay the night—a small, thin, pious woman of about fifty called Pasha or Spiridonovna, in black dress and white kerchief, sharp-eyed, sharp-nosed, sharp-chinned. She had a sly, venomous look, and stared at you as if she could see through you. Her lips were heart-shaped, and her poisonous, misanthropic character had earned her the nickname Beetle in business people's houses.

She entered the dining-room, looking at no one, faced the icons and sang in an alto voice 'Thy Birth', 'A Maid This Day' and 'Christ is Born'. Then she turned and riveted them all with a glance.

'Happy Christmas.' She kissed Anne's shoulder. 'Such a trouble I did have getting here, kind ladies.' She kissed Aunt's shoulder too. 'I started off this morning, but on my way I called on some folk for a bit of a rest. "Do stay, do stay, Spiridonovna," said they. Aye, and evening came on before I noticed.'

As she did not eat meat they gave her caviare and salmon, which she ate while scowling at everyone, and she drank three glasses of spirits. Having had her fill, she said grace and bowed low to Anne.

As they had done last year and the year before that, they played Kings, while all the servants from both floors crowded at the door to watch the game. Anne seemed to notice Misha, complete with condescending smile, flash past a couple of times amid the thronging lower orders. The first to be King was the Beetle, and Anne—a Soldier—paid her a forfeit. Then Aunt became King and Anne was a Peasant or Bumpkin, much to everyone's delight, while Agatha became a Prince and felt positively guilty, she was so pleased. At the other end of the table a second game was made up by the two Mashas, Barbara and the seamstress Martha, whom they had woken up specially to play, and who looked sleepy and bad-tempered.

During the game their talk touched on men, on how hard it was to find a good husband these days, on whether it was better to be a spinster or a widow.

'You're a fine, healthy, strapping wench,' the Beetle told Anne. 'But who are you saving yourself for, girl? That's what I don't see.'

'But suppose no one will have me?'

'Happen you've sworn to stay unwed?' the Beetle went on as if she hadn't heard. 'All right then, don't you wed. Don't,' she repeated, looking attentively and venomously at her cards. 'Have it your own way, friend. But they come in different shapes and sizes, do spinsters—bless 'em.' She sighed and led a King. 'They ain't all the same, dear. There's some keeps themselves like nuns, as pure as pure can be, or if one of them does sin now and then the poor thing suffers such agonies you wouldn't have the heart to blame her. Then there's others that wears black and makes their own shrouds while secretly loving some rich old fellow. Yes, my pets, there's witches that puts spells on an old man. They enslaves the man, my poppets, that they do, they turns him this way and that, and once they've snaffled lots of his money and securities, then they bewitches him to death.'

To these hints Barbara responded only by sighing and looking at the icon, her face a picture of Christian humility.

'There's one girl I know what's my worst enemy,' continued the Beetle, looking exultantly at everyone. 'Oh yes, she'm always a-sighing and a-looking at the icons, the she-devil. When she had a certain old fellow under her thumb you'd visit her, belike, and she'd give you a bite to eat and order you to bow to the ground while she recited her "A virgin did give birth". She'd give you a bite of food on holidays, but on working days she'd give you a telling off. Well, I'm going to make fun of her now as much as I want, my darlings.'

Barbara again looked at the icon and crossed herself.

'But no one will have me, Spiridonovna.' Anne wanted to change the subject. 'It can't be helped.'

'It's your fault, girl. You expect a gentleman, someone educated like, when you should marry among businessfolk like yourself.'

'We want none of them, heaven forbid.' Aunt was much alarmed. 'A gentleman will squander your money, but at least he'll be nice to you, silly girl. But a merchant—he'll be so strict you'll never feel at home in your own house. While you want to cuddle up to him he'll be claiming the interest on your investments, and if you sit down to a meal with him the lout will blame you for eating him out of *your* house and home. You marry a gentleman.'

They all spoke at once, loudly interrupting each other, while Aunt banged the nutcrackers on the table.

'We don't want your merchants here, that we don't.' She was angry and red-faced. 'If you bring a merchant to this house I shall enter a nunnery.'

'Shush! Be quiet!' shouted the Beetle. When all were silent she screwed up one eye. 'Know what, Anne, my pet? There ain't no sense in your getting wed proper like other folks. You're rich, you're free, you're your own mistress. But it ain't quite right for you to stay an old maid either, child. Now, I'll find you—you know—some miserable little half-wit what you can marry for appearance' sake, and then you'll have the time of your life. Oh yes, you'll toss your husband his five or ten thousand and let him go back where he came from, and then you'll be your own mistress. Love whom you like, no one can say a thing. That way you can love your gentlemen, your educated men. You'll be on top of the world.' Beetle clicked her fingers and whistled. 'A high old time you'll have.'

'But that would be a sin,' said Aunt.

'Never mind the sinning,' laughed the Beetle. 'She's educated, she understands. To cut someone's throat, to put spells on an old man—that's a sin, no doubt of it. But to love your sweetheart—that ain't no sin, far from it. Oh, really, what *ever* next! There's no sin in that, it was all invented by pious old women to cheat simple folks. I'm always on about sinning myself, but I don't even know what I means by it.' The Beetle drank some cordial and cleared her throat. 'You really let yourself go,' she said, now evidently addressing herself. 'Thirty years I spent brooding on sin, girls, being scared of it, but now I see I missed me chance, let it pass me by. Oh, I'm a fool, such a fool.' She sighed.

'It's a short life a woman's is, and she should make the most of each little day. You're beautiful, Anne dear, very beautiful and you're rich, but when you're thirty-five or forty you'll be finished, that'll be the end. Don't you listen to anyone, my girl. You enjoy yourself, you have your fling until you're forty—plenty of time to pray about it after, plenty of time for doing penance and sewing your shroud. Give the devil his due, say I. You really let yourself go. Well, how about it—will you make some little man happy?'

'I will,' laughed Anne. 'I don't care now, I'd marry an ordinary worker.'

'That's right, and a good idea too. And you could have the pick of the bunch, by golly!' The Beetle frowned and shook her head. 'Not half you couldn't.'

'That's what *I* tell her,' said Aunt. 'If you can't find a gentleman, says I, then don't marry a merchant, but someone more common. At least we'd have a man about the house. And there's no lack of good folk. Take our own factory workers—sober, respectable lads, they are.'

'Not half they ain't,' agreed the Beetle. 'Fine fellers, they are. How about me marrying her to Basil Lebedinsky, Auntie?'

'But Basil's legs are too long,' said Aunt seriously. 'He's a dry stick and there's not much to his looks.'

The crowd near the door laughed.

'Well, there's Pimenov. Want to marry Pimenov?' the Beetle asked Anne.

'All right. Marry me to Pimenov.'

'You really mean it?'

'Yes I do,' said Anne resolutely, and banged the table. 'I'll marry him, I promise.'

'You mean it?'

Anne suddenly felt ashamed of her burning cheeks, of everyone staring at her. She jumbled the cards on the table, rushed from the room. Dashing upstairs, reaching the upper floor, sitting by the grand piano in the drawing-room, she heard a roar like the crashing of the sea from below. They were talking about her and Pimenov, probably, and perhaps the Beetle was exploiting her absence to insult Barbara, without of course scrupling to mince her words any longer.

On the whole upper floor there was only one lamp lit, in the ballroom, and its feeble light filtered through the door into the dark drawing-room. It was ten o'clock, no more. Anne played a waltz, then a second and a third without a pause. She looked into the dark corner behind the piano, she smiled, she felt as if she was appealing to someone, and it occurred to her to go to town and pay a visit—to Lysevich, say—and tell him about her feelings. She wanted to talk non-stop, to laugh, to play the fool, but the dark corner behind the grand piano was grimly silent, and all around her the entire upper storey was quiet and deserted.

She loved sentimental ballads, but as her voice was rough and untrained she only played accompaniments and sang barely audibly, under her breath. She sang in a whisper one song after another, all mostly about love, parting, hopes dashed. And she imagined herself stretching out her hands to him. 'Pimenov, take this burden from me,' she would beg him in tears. And then, as though her sins were forgiven, she would feel joy and peace of mind. A free and perhaps happy life would begin. Yearning and expectant, she bent over the keys. She fervently wanted a change to take place in her life there and then, straight away, and was scared to think that her present existence would still continue for a while. Then she again played the piano and sang under her breath, while all around was silence. No longer was the roar heard from below, they must all be asleep down there. It had struck ten some time ago. The long, lonely, boring night was upon her.

Anne paced all the rooms, lay on the sofa for a while, read some letters, delivered that evening, in her study. There were twelve letters wishing her a happy Christmas, and three anonymous unsigned ones. In one an ordinary worker complained in an atrocious, hardly legible hand that workers were sold rancid vegetable oil smelling of paraffin in her factory shop. In another someone respectfully denounced Nazarych for taking a thousand-rouble bribe when buying iron at the last auction. In a third she was abused for callousness.

Anne's excited, festive mood was now passing, and she tried to maintain it by sitting at the piano again and quietly playing one of the latest waltzes. Then she remembered how intelligently and straightforwardly she had reasoned and talked at dinner this evening. She looked around at the dark windows, at the walls with their pictures, at the feeble light which came from the ballroom—and then suddenly and unexpectedly burst into tears. She was distressed to feel so lonely, to have no one to talk to or consult. She tried to keep up her spirits by picturing Pimenov in her imagination, but nothing came of it.

The clock struck twelve. In came Misha in a jacket instead of his tail-coat, and silently lit two candles. Then he went out and came back a minute later with a cup of tea on a tray.

'Why do you laugh?' She had noticed a smile on his face.

'I heard you make that joke about Pimenov when I was downstairs.' He covered his laughing face with his hand. 'You should have asked him to dinner with Mr. Lysevich and Mr. Krylin just now. He'd have had the fright of his life.' Misha's shoulders shook with laughter. 'I bet he doesn't even know how to hold a fork.'

The flunkey's laughter, his words, his jacket and his little whiskers impressed Anne as unclean. To avoid seeing him, she covered her eyes and involuntarily imagined Pimenov dining with Lysevich and Krylin. And Pimenov's figure—so diffident, so unlike a professional man's—seemed pathetic and helpless, arousing her disgust. Only now did she clearly see for the first time that day that all her thoughts and words about Pimenov and marriage to an ordinary working man were foolish, unreasonable, wrong-headed. To prove the opposite, to conquer this disgust, she wanted to remember what she had said at dinner, but could not call it to mind. She was ashamed of her thoughts and deeds, scared that she might have spoken foolishly during the day, disgusted at her own feebleness. How very distressing it all was. She took a candle, rushed downstairs as if someone was chasing her, woke up Spiridonovna and assured her that it had all been a joke. Then she went to her bedroom. Red-haired Masha, who had been dozing in the armchair near the bed, jumped up to adjust the pillows. Her face was exhausted and sleepy, and her splendid hair was all over on one side.

'That clerk Chalikov was here again this evening,' she yawned. 'But I didn't dare tell you. He was very drunk, says he'll be back tomorrow.'

'What does he want with me?' Anne angrily flung her comb on the floor. 'I don't want to see him, I won't!'

There was nothing left to her in life but this Chalikov, she concluded, and he would never stop persecuting her—reminding her daily how dull and inane her existence was. What else was she capable of but helping the poor? Oh, how stupid it all was.

She lay down without taking off her clothes, and burst out sobbing from shame and boredom. The most aggravating and stupid thing seemed to her that today's thoughts about Pimenov had been decent, fine, honourable. Yet she felt at the same time that Lysevich and even Krylin were nearer to her than Pimenov and all her workers put together. Were it possible to portray the long day, now ended, in a picture, then everything rotten and cheap—the dinner, say, the lawyer's words, the game of Kings—would have been the truth, she now felt, while her dreams and the talk about Pimenov would have stood apart from it all as striking a false, jarring note. She also reflected that it was too late, now, for her to dream of happiness. Her whole life was in ruins, and it was impossible for her either to return to the days of sharing a bed with her mother or to devise some new, special mode of existence.

Red-haired Masha knelt in front of the bed looking at Anne sadly, with amazement. Then she too burst into tears and leant her face against Anne's hands. No words were needed to explain why the girl was so upset.

'We're such idiots, you and I,' said Anne, laughing and crying. 'Idiots, that's what we are.'

AT A COUNTRY HOUSE

PAUL RASHEVICH paced up and down, stepping softly on the floor covered with Ukrainian rugs, throwing a long, narrow shadow on wall and ceiling. His guest Meyer, an acting coroner, sat on the ottoman, one leg tucked under him, smoking and listening. The clock said eleven, and they could hear someone laying the table in the room next to the study.

'From the standpoint of brotherhood, equality and all that, Mike the pigman may be as good as Goethe or Frederick the Great, I grant you that,' said Rashevich. But take the scientific view, have the courage to face the facts, and you'll see that breeding is no illusion or old wives' tale. Breeding, dear boy, has its biological validity, and to deny it is as odd, to my mind, as denying that a stag has horns. Just face up to things. As a lawyer you've confined your studies to the arts field—*you* can flatter yourself with illusions about equality, fraternity and all that. But I'm an incorrigible Darwinist. For me such terms as breeding, aristocracy, pedigree are more than empty sounds.'

Rashevich was excited, and spoke with emotion. His eyes gleamed, his pince-nez kept slipping down his nose, he nervously twitched his shoulders, he winked, and at the word 'Darwinist' he had cast a jaunty glance at the mirror, smoothing his grey beard with both hands. He wore a very short, shabby jacket and narrow trousers. His rapid movements, jauntiness, short jacket—they were not really his style, and it was as if his large, handsome head—complete with flowing locks and suggesting some bishop or venerable poet—had been stuck on the body of a tall, thin, affected youth. When he straddled his legs his long shadow was scissor-shaped.

Fond of a chat, he always felt he was saying something fresh and original, and in Meyer's presence he felt on top of his form—simply bursting with ideas. He liked the coroner. His youth, his health, his excellent manners, his reliability, and above all his affectionate attitude to Rashevich and his family—what a tonic they all were. Most of Rashevich's acquaintances disliked him, gave him a clear berth. As he was aware, they said he had talked his wife to death, and behind his back they called him Old Misery. Meyer alone, that go-ahead, open-minded man, was glad to be a frequent visitor, and had even remarked somewhere that Rashevich and his daughters were the only people in the county who made him feel really at home. Rashevich also liked him as a young man who might make a good husband for his elder daughter Zhenya.

Savouring his thoughts and the sound of his own voice, glancing with pleasure at the somewhat portly, elegantly barbered, respectable Meyer, Rashevich yearned to find his Zhenya such a husband, after which all the troubles with his estate would devolve on the son-in-law. And irksome troubles those were. His last two interest payments had not been made to the bank, and his various arrears and forfeitures came to over two thousand roubles.

Rashevich warmed to his theme. 'If some Richard Cœur de Lion, say, or Frederick Barbarossa, is brave and noble, these qualities are transmitted by heredity to his son along with his cranial convolutions and bumps, you take it from me. Now, if this courage and generous spirit are preserved in the son by education and cultivation, and if he marries a princess who is also noble and brave, then these qualities are transmitted to the grandson and so on, thus becoming a characteristic of the species and being, so to speak, organically transmuted into flesh and blood. Thanks to strict sexual selection, thanks to noble families instinctively shunning unions beneath their station, thanks to well-connected youngsters not marrying hell knows who, exalted mental characteristics have passed, all unalloyed, from generation to generation. They have been preserved, their cultivation has been perfected and refined in course of time. It is to nature—to nature, sir—that we owe mankind's assets, and that ordered, efficacious biological process which has over the centuries so sedulously set men of breeding apart from the common herd. Depend on it, dear boy—it wasn't your lower orders, your working-class lads, that gave us literature, learning, the arts, law, concepts of honour and duty.

'Humanity owes all that exclusively to its upper crust, in the light of which your most churlish backwoods squire belongs, biologically speaking—simply because he comes out of the top drawer—to a higher and more useful order of being than your finest businessman, one who has built fifteen museums. Say what you like, but if I refuse to shake hands with some common lout, if I don't invite him to my table, I am thereby conserving the finest fruits of the earth, and am implementing one of Mother Nature's loftiest designs for perfecting the species.'

Rashevich paused, stroking his beard with both hands, his scissor-shaped shadow projected on to the wall.

'Now, take good old Mother Russia,' he went on, thrusting his hands in his pockets and standing, now on his heels, now on his toes. 'Who are her élite? Take our first-class artists, writers, composers. Who are they? They all came straight out of the top drawer, dear boy. Pushkin, Gogol, Lermontov, Turgenev, Goncharov, Tolstoy—those were no sextons' sons.'

'The Goncharovs were in trade,' said Meyer.

'Aha! But exceptions only prove the rule. And Goncharov's talents are highly disputable anyway. But never mind the individuals. Back to the facts. Now, what of this fact, sir—one which speaks volumes? No sooner has your underdog invaded fields previously barred to him —high society, the academic world, literature, local government, the courts—than Nature herself has stepped forward to champion mankind's loftiest perquisites, she has been first to declare war on this rabble. No sooner, indeed, has your Mister Average Man quitted his proper station in life than he has begun to waste away, go off his head, wither on the bough, run to seed. Nowhere will you find so many neurotics, consumptives, mental cripples and miscellaneous ninnies as among these birds. They die like flies in autumn. But for this salutary degeneracy our civilization would have gone to rack and ruin long ago, your *hoi* bloody *polloi* would have gobbled it all up. Now, tell me, pray—what has this intrusion given us so far? What contribution have these scum made?'

Rashevich adopted an enigmatic, frightened air.

'Never have our literary and academic achievements sunk as low as they are now. People have no ideas or ideals nowadays, dear old boy. Whatever they're up to they have only one thing in mind—how to feather their own nests while beggaring their neighbours. Those who try to pass as progressive, "decent" men nowadays, they can all be bought for one rouble apiece, and the hallmark of your modern intellectual is just this—that you must keep hold of your pocket when talking to him, or you'll find yourself minus a wallet.'

Rashevich winked and roared with laughter. 'He'll have your wallet, believe you me,' he gleefully pronounced in a reedy little voice.

'Then there's morality. What price morality?' Rashevich looked round at the door. 'No one's surprised any more when a wife robs and deserts her husband—it's nothing, nothing. These days, old chap, a girl of twelve is already looking for a lover, and all these amateur theatricals and literary evenings have been invented solely to make it easier to hook some well-heeled bumpkin and become a kept woman.

'Mothers sell their daughters, and husbands are asked straight out how much they want for their wives. They'll even come down a bit if you bargain, dear boy.'

Meyer, who had sat still all this time saying nothing, suddenly rose from the sofa and looked at his watch. 'Excuse me, Mr. Rashevich, but it's time I went home.'

Rashevich had not finished, though. He put his arm round Meyer, sat him forcibly back on the sofa, swore he should not leave without supper. So Meyer once more sat listening, but was now giving Rashevich baffled and perturbed glances as if he was just beginning to take the man's measure. Red blotches appeared on his face. And when at last the maid entered and said that the young ladies would like them to come to supper, he gave a faint sigh and was first to leave the study.

At table in the next room sat Rashevich's daughters Zhenya and Iraida—twenty-four and twenty-two years old, both black-eyed, very pale, of the same height. Zhenya had her hair down, Iraida wore hers piled up. Before eating they both drank a glass of home-made spirits, looking as if they did so by accident, for the first time in their lives. Both were embarrassed and laughed.

'Now, don't you be such naughty children,' said Rashevich.

Zhenya and Iraida talked French to each other, but Russian to their father and his guest. Interrupting one another, mixing Russian with French, they rapidly explained how they had always gone off to their boarding school in the old days at exactly this time of year, August. What fun it had been! But now there was nowhere to go, and they had to live in the country all year round, summer and winter. And that was no fun at all.

'Now, don't you be such naughty children,' Rashevich repeated.

He wanted to do the talking. If others spoke in his presence he felt something akin to jealousy.

'Well, that's the way of it, dear boy.' He was off again, looking fondly at the coroner. 'In our kindness and simplicity, and because we fear to be thought retrograde, we fraternize with all sorts of scum, if you'll pardon the term. We preach brotherhood and equality with jumped up yokels and bartenders. But if we put our minds to it we'd see how criminal such kindness is. We've brought civilization to the edge of the abyss, dear boy. Our ancestors' age-old achievements will be desecrated and wrecked tomorrow by these latter-day vandals.'

After supper all went to the drawing-room. Zhenya and Iraida lit candles on the piano and prepared the music.

Rashevich was still at it, though, there was no knowing when he would be done. It was in agonized irritation that they looked at the selfish father for whom the pleasure of chattering and displaying his intellect was patently so much more precious and important than his daughters' happiness. Meyer, the only young man to visit their home, did so, they knew, for their charming feminine company. But the incorrigible old man had taken him over and gave him no inch of leeway.

'Just as the Western Knights flung back the Mongol invasion, so we too must unite before it's too late and strike a collective blow at our enemy,' Rashevich continued in prophetic tones, raising his right hand. 'Let me confront the common herd, not as Paul Rashevich, but as the dread and mighty Richard Cœur de Lion. And an end to the kid-glove treatment. Enough is enough. Let's all agree that as soon as one of these plebeians approaches us we'll at once fling our scorn right in his ugly mug. "Be off with you, sir! Know your place, insect!"

'We'll let him have it straight between the eyes!' continued Rashevich gleefully, stabbing a bent finger in front of him. 'Plumb in the centre of his great fat face!'

Meyer turned away. 'I can't do that.'

'But why ever not?' Rashevich spoke forcefully, anticipating a long and interesting argument.

'Because I'm working class myself.'

With this Meyer blushed. His neck swelled, even, and actual tears appeared in his eyes.

'My father was a working man,' Meyer added in a harsh, abrupt voice. 'And I see nothing wrong in that.'

Rashevich was frightfully put out. He was shattered, as if caught committing a crime, and he stared at Meyer baffled, at a loss for words. Zhenya and Iraida blushed and bent over their music, ashamed of their tactless father. A minute had passed in silence and unbearable embarrassment when suddenly a voice—a neurotic, tense, jarring voice—rang in the air.

'Aye, I'm working class and proud of it.'

Then Meyer took his farewell, awkwardly bumping into furniture—and went quickly into the hall though his carriage had not yet been brought round.

'You'll find it a bit dark on the road tonight,' muttered Rashevich, following him. 'The moon doesn't rise till later.'

Both stood in the dark porch waiting for the carriage to be fetched. It was cool.

'There's a shooting star,' said Meyer, huddling in his overcoat. 'There are lots of those in August.'

When the carriage appeared Rashevich looked keenly at the sky.

'A phenomenon worthy of a Flammarion's pen,' he sighed.

Having seen his guest off he paced the garden, gesticulating in the dark, not wanting to believe that such an odd, such a silly misunderstanding had just occurred. He was ashamed, vexed with himself. First, it had been highly imprudent and tactless of him to raise this blasted question of breeding without finding out in advance who he was dealing with. Something similar had happened before. He had once started running down Germans in a railway compartment, whereupon his travelling companions had all turned out to be German. Secondly, he sensed that Meyer would never call again. They're so pathologically conceited, so stubborn, so rancorous, are these intelligent artisans.

'Bad, bad, very bad indeed,' muttered Rashevich, spitting. He felt put out and queasy, as if he had been eating soap.

From the garden he could see Zhenya through the drawing-room window—with her hair down, very pale and scared-looking, she was talking away at high speed by the piano.

Iraida faced the room, deep in thought. But then she too started speaking rapidly, looking highly indignant. Both were talking at once. Though no word was audible Rashevich guessed what they were saying. Zhenya was probably complaining that her father had driven all decent people from the house with his talk, talk, talk, and had today deprived them of their one friend—a prospective husband, perhaps—and now the poor young man had nowhere in the whole county where he could feel at home. Iraida, from the way she had raised her hands in despair, was probably saying how boring things were and how her young life had been ruined.

Rashevich went to his room, sat on his bed, slowly undressed. He felt dejected, still haunted by that sensation of having eaten soap. He was ashamed. After undressing he looked at his long, sinewy, old man's legs and remembered how he'd been nicknamed Old Misery in the county, and how every long conversation left him with this feeling of shame. Somehow or other, as if foredoomed, he would begin so gently, so kindly, with such good intentions, calling himself a former university man, an idealist, a tilter at windmills. But then, all unawares, he would gradually descend to abuse and slander. Oddest thing of all, he would criticize learning, the arts and morals in all sincerity, though he hadn't read a single book for twenty years, had never travelled farther than the local county town, and had no real idea of what went on in the world at large. If he sat down to write anything, be it a mere congratulatory letter, that too turned out full of abuse. And this was odd because he was a sensitive man, really, always on the verge of tears. Could there be some evil spirit inside him, spreading hate and slander against his will?

'A bad, bad business,' he sighed, lying under his quilt.

His daughters could not sleep either. There was loud laughter and a shout as if they were chasing someone—that was Zhenya having hysterics. A bit later Iraida too burst out sobbing. A barefoot maid ran up and down the corridor several times.

'Lord, what a business,' muttered Rashevich, sighing and tossing from side to side. 'Bad.'

He had a nightmare, dreaming that he, naked and tall as a giraffe, stood in the middle of a room talking and stabbing his finger in front of him.

'Fling it straight into their great fat faces!'

He awoke in terror, and the first thing he remembered was yesterday's misunderstanding—Meyer would never come back, of course. He remembered too that he must pay interest to the bank, marry off his daughters, eat, drink. Then there was old age, there were illnesses, there were other nuisances, and soon it would be winter and he had no firewood.

It was past nine a.m. Rashevich slowly dressed, drank his tea, and ate two large slices of bread and butter. His daughters did not come down to breakfast. They were avoiding him, and this offended him. He lay on his study sofa, then sat at his desk and started writing his daughters a letter. His hand quaked, his eyes itched. He wrote that he was old, unwanted and unloved, he asked his daughters to forget him and, when he died, to bury him in a simple pine coffin without ceremony, or to send the corpse to the medical research people at Kharkov. He felt that every line breathed malice and buffoonery, but he couldn't stop writing, writing, writing.

Then, from the next room, his elder daughter's voice—outraged, hissing—suddenly rang out. 'Old Misery, Old Misery!'

'Old Misery, Old Misery!' the younger echoed.

MURDER

I

THEY were holding a church service—vespers—at Progonnaya station. Before the great icon, brightly painted on a gold background, stood a crowd of railwaymen, their wives and children, and lumbermen and sawyers who worked near by along the line. They stood silent, entranced by the glittering lights and the howling blizzard outside—it had blown up without warning, though this was the eve of Lady Day. The old priest from Vedenyapino was taking the service and the singers were the precentor and Matthew Terekhov.

Matthew's face glowed with pleasure. He craned his neck as he sang, as if he wanted to take wing, chanting and reciting the canon in his bland, persuasive tenor. While the 'Song of Archangels' was being sung he waved his hand like a choirmaster, and did some highly complex tenor flourishes as he tried to harmonize with the old parish clerk's hollow bass. You only had to look at him to see how much he was enjoying himself.

The service ended, the congregation quietly dispersed and the place was dark and empty again. A great calm descended, such as is found only at lonely stations in open country or in a forest where there is no sound but the soughing of the wind. You seem cut off from everything and the slow pace of life makes you thoroughly wretched.

Matthew lived near the station at his cousin's inn, but he did not feel like going home and sat at the counter in the station buffet talking in a low voice.

'Up at the tile-works we had our own choir. And fine singers we were too, I must say—a real choir, even if we were only ordinary workmen. We were often invited to the town and when Bishop John, the Suffragan, took the service at Trinity Church, the cathedral choir sang in the stalls on the right, and we on the left. In town, though, they complained that we went on too long. "Those tile-works people do drag things out," they said. True, our St. Andrew's Vigil and Te Deum service did start before seven and end after eleven, so it would sometimes be midnight before you were back home at the works.'

Matthew sighed. 'Wonderful it was, Sergey, really wonderful. But I can't enjoy myself here in the old home. It's three miles to the nearest church, I can't even go that far in my state of health and they don't have any choir. And there's no peace in our family, what with the swearing and hullabaloo going on morning, noon and night, and their filthy ways, everyone eating out of one bowl like peasants and cockroaches in the stew.... If God had given me health, I'd have been off long ago, Sergey.'

Matthew Terekhov was not old—he was about forty-five—but he looked ill, his face was a mass of wrinkles, his sparse, straggly beard was quite white and that made him seem a lot older. He spoke diffidently, in a feeble voice, clutched at his chest when he coughed, with a worried, troubled look—like all very neurotic people. He never said what was wrong with him in so many words, but liked spinning a long yarn about lifting a heavy box at the works once and straining himself. That had given him a 'ructure', so he had left his job at the tile-works and come back home. What a 'ructure' was he could not explain.

'I don't like that cousin of mine, I must say,' he went on, pouring himself some tea. 'He's older than me and I shouldn't say a word against him—and me a God-fearing man—but I can't abide him. He's very high and mighty—and surly. He's always cursing and he ill-treats his relatives and workmen. Never goes to confession either. "Cousin Jacob," I asked him nice and politely last Sunday, "let's go to the service at Pakhomo." "No fear," said he. "Their priest plays cards." He didn't come here today either. Says the Vedenyapino priest smokes and drinks vodka. Can't stand the clergy. Says his own offices, matins and vespers with his sister doing the responses. While he's at his "We beseech thee, Lord God", she's cackling away like an old turkey at her "Lord, have mercy". Proper sinful, I call it. "Come to your senses, Cousin Jacob," I tell him every day. "Repent, Cousin." But he takes no notice.'

Sergey the buffet-attendant poured out five glasses of tea and took them to the ladies' waiting-room on a tray.

A moment later a bellow was heard. 'Call that serving tea, you dirty little swine! You don't know your job!'

That was the stationmaster. There was a timorous mumble, followed by another shout, angry and brusque.

'Clear out!'

The attendant came back looking very crestfallen.

'Time was I gave satisfaction to counts and princes,' he said quietly. 'But now I don't know how to serve tea, see...? Swears at me in front of the priest and the ladies!'

Sergey the attendant had been rather well off at one time and had managed the refreshment-room at a main-line station, a junction in a county town. He had worn a tail-coat and a gold watch, but then fell on evil days after spending all his money on luxurious equipment and being robbed by his staff. Things went from bad to worse, and he moved to a less busy station. Then his wife ran away with all the silver and he moved to a third station, worse still, where hot meals were not served. Then to a fourth. After all these changes and sinking lower and lower, he had landed up at Progonnaya, where he just sold tea and cheap vodka and served no snacks except hard-boiled eggs and tough salami smelling of tar that he sneered at himself and said was fit only for bandsmen. The top of his head was quite bald, and he had bulging blue eyes and thick, bushy whiskers which he was always combing, looking at himself in a little hand-mirror. He was forever haunted by memories and could not get used to 'bandsman's sausage', the stationmaster's rudeness, and peasants arguing about his prices, for he thought it as unseemly to haggle at a snack-bar as in a chemist's shop. He was ashamed to be so poor and downtrodden, and nowadays his disgrace was his main concern in life.

'Spring's late this year,' said Matthew, cocking an ear. 'A good job too. I don't like spring. A very muddy season is spring, Sergey. Books are written about spring and birds singing and the sun going down, but what's so nice about that? A bird is a bird and what of it? I like good company so I can hear folks talking. I like a bit of a chat about religion, or singing a nice chorus. All them nightingales and pretty little flowers, I've no use for them!'

He started off about the tile-works and choir again, but Sergey was aggrieved and just could not relax—kept shrugging his shoulders and muttering. Matthew said good night and went home. It was not freezing and water was dripping from the roofs, yet it was snowing hard. Snow whirled swiftly through the air, white clouds of it chasing each other along the railway track. Faintly lit by the moon lurking high in the clouds, the oak forest on both sides of the line kept up a grim roar. Trees shaken by a great storm can be terrifying. Matthew walked down the road by the railway, covering his face and hands. The wind thrust him in the back. Suddenly he saw a pony plastered with snow, a sledge scraped the bare stones of the road, and a peasant with head muffled, as white as his horse, cracked a whip. Matthew looked round, but sledge and peasant were gone and it might all have been a dream. He quickened his pace, suddenly scared—of what he did not know.

He came to the level-crossing and the dark hut where the crossing-keeper lived. The barrier was raised. All around were huge snow-drifts and clouds of snow whirling like a coven of witches. At this point the line was crossed by an old road, once a main thoroughfare and still called the highway. To the right, near the level-crossing and on the edge of the road, stood Terekhov's Inn, an old coaching-house where there was always a glimmer of light at night.

When Matthew reached home the whole place, even the hall, smelt strongly of incense. His cousin Jacob was still celebrating vespers in the prayer-room or 'chapel'. In the corner facing the door was an icon-case with old-fashioned, gilt-mounted family icons. The walls to the right and left were covered with icons in old and new style, some in cases and some not. On the table, draped with a cloth that reached the ground, was an icon of the Annunciation, together with a cypress-wood cross and a censer. Candles were burning and there was a lectern near the table.

Matthew paused on his way past the chapel to look through the door. Jacob was reading at the lectern and Jacob's sister Aglaya, a tall, scraggy old woman in navy-blue dress and white kerchief, was at worship with him. Jacob's daughter Dashutka was there too, a girl of about eighteen, ugly, with a lot of freckles. She was barefoot as usual, and wore the dress in which she watered the cattle of an evening.

'Glory to Thee, Who has shown us the light,' proclaimed Jacob in a booming voice, bowing low.

Aglaya propped her chin on her hand and chanted in a thin, shrill whine.

From above the ceiling came vague voices like threats and forebodings. There had been a fire in the house a long time ago, since when no one had lived on the upper storey, the windows were boarded up and empty bottles were strewn about on the floor between the joists. The wind banged and howled up there and it sounded as if someone was running around and stumbling over the joists.

Half the ground floor was given over to the tavern and the Terekhov family lived in the other half, so when drunken rowdies visited the inn every word could be heard in their living-quarters. Matthew's room was next to the kitchen and contained a large stove in which bread had been baked every day when the place was a coaching-inn. Having no room of her own, Dashutka bunked in there as well, behind the stove. At nights there was the chirping of crickets and the scurrying of mice.

Matthew lit a candle and began reading a book that the railway policeman had lent him. While he sat reading, the service ended and everyone, Dashutka included, went to bed. She started snoring at once, but soon woke up.

'You shouldn't waste candles, Uncle Matthew,' she yawned.

'It's my own candle,' answered Matthew. 'I bought it myself.'

Dashutka tossed about for a while and fell asleep again. Matthew sat up for a long time, not feeling sleepy, finished the last page, and took a pencil from a trunk. 'I, Matthew Terekhov,' he wrote in the book, 'have read this book and find it the best of all books heretofore read by me, of which I appress my expreciation to Kuzma Zhukov, senior constable of railway police, owner of the said pressious volume.'

He thought it was only good manners to write things like this in other people's books.

II

On the next day—Lady Day itself—Matthew sat in the station refreshment-room, after the mail train had been seen off, talking and drinking tea with lemon.

The buffet-attendant and Constable Zhukov were his audience.

'Always one for religion I was, and that's a fact,' said Matthew. 'Even as a child. When I was a boy of twelve I used to read the Acts and the Epistles in church. A great comfort to my parents it was. And I used to go on pilgrimage every summer with my mother, God rest her. Other kids sang songs or caught crayfish, but I spent my time with Mother. Older people thought a lot of me and as for me, well, I enjoyed being so well behaved. When I left Mother and went to the works with her blessing, I spent my spare time singing tenor in our choir there. Never enjoyed anything so much.

'I didn't drink spirits or smoke of course and I was a clean-living man. Of course the Devil doesn't like it when you live like that, and he decided to destroy me and began to confuse my mind, same as he has Cousin Jacob's.

'First thing, I took a vow to fast on Mondays and not to eat meat on any day. Before long, in fact, I went a bit barmy. The Holy Fathers prescribe dry cold food up to the Saturday in the first week of Lent, but it's no sin for them that toil or are weak to drink a spot of tea even. But not one crumb passed my lips till the Sunday. Not a drop of fat did I allow myself all Lent, and on Wednesdays and Fridays I just ate nothing. Same thing during the lesser fasts. At the Fast of St. Peter the lads at the works had their fish stew, but I kept off it and just had a dry crust to suck.

'Some men are stronger than others of course, but I didn't suffer all that much on fast-days, I'll say that for myself. In fact the harder you try, the easier it is. You only feel hungry on the first few days of your fast. When you get the hang of things it comes easier and easier and by the end of the week, why there's nothing to it and your legs have that numb feeling as if you were walking on air. What's more, I made myself do all sorts of penances—getting up at night and doing prostrations, dragging heavy stones about and going barefoot in the snow. Wearing irons too.

'But then after a bit I happened to go to confession and the idea suddenly struck me—why, this priest's married, I thought to myself. He eats meat and smokes. So why should he hear my confession? What right had he to forgive my sins, and him a worse sinner than me? I even kept off vegetable oil—when he'd been eating sturgeon, like as not.

'I went to another priest, but by sheer bad luck hit on a fat-bellied creature in a silk cassock that rustled like a lady's dress. Smelt of tobacco too. I went to a monastery to prepare for communion, but didn't feel easy there either. The monks didn't seem to keep their rule. Then I couldn't find a church service to suit me. They either got through it too quickly or sang the wrong anthem, or else the parish clerk spoke through his nose.

'Time was—God forgive me, sinner that I am—when I'd stand in church fair gibbering with rage, and what good's that sort of worship? The people didn't seem to cross themselves properly. Or listen properly. Wherever I looked they were all drunkards, smokers, fornicators and card players. And they didn't keep their fasts. No one lived by the Commandments except me.

'But Satan never slept and things went from bad to worse. I left the choir and stopped going to church, my idea being that church wasn't good enough for a righteous man like me. I was like the fallen angel in fact, proud and puffed up past belief.

'Then I took steps to set up my own church. I rented a little box of a room from a deaf woman a long way out of town near the cemetery and set up a little chapel like my cousin's, though I did have real church candlesticks—and a proper censer too. I kept the Mount Athos rule in my chapel, so my matins always started at midnight and vespers on the eve of the twelve big festivals lasted ten or even twelve hours. Monks' rules at least let them sit when the Psalms and Prophets are read, but I wanted to do better than them and stood up all the time. I read and sang with tears and sighs, dragging it all out and lifting up my arms. I went straight from prayers to work without sleep and always prayed at work too.

'Well, the news went round town—Matthew's a saint, Matthew heals the sick and the mad. I never healed anyone of course, but we all know that when any schism and heresy like that crops up, the women are on to it like wasps round a honeypot. Various old women and old maids took to visiting me, bowing down to the ground, kissing my hands and shouting that I was a saint and all that. One of them even saw a halo round my head.

'My chapel got crowded, so I took a bigger room and all hell broke loose. The Devil had me in his clutches good and proper and his accursed hooves stood between my eyes and the light. We all seemed to have the Devil in us. I read and the grannies and old maids sang, and this way we went without food and drink for long stretches, standing twenty-four hours or more on end. They'd suddenly start shaking as if they'd caught a fever, and then one shouts out, and then another. Gave me the creeps, it did. I was jumping like a cat on hot bricks myself, I didn't know why. Fair prancing about we were. A queer business, I must say, when you can't help skipping about and waggling yours arms. Then there was this shouting and shrieking, and we all danced and chased each other round and round till we dropped. This was how—in one of these crazy fits—I committed fornication.'

The policeman guffawed, but seeing that no one else was laughing, grew serious.

'It's like the Molokans,' he said. 'They're all that way down in the Caucasus, I've read.'

'But no lightning struck me down,' Matthew went on, crossing himself before the icon and moving his lips. 'All I can think is, my old mother must have put in a prayer for me in heaven. When everyone in town thought me a saint and even the ladies and the nobs were sneaking off to me for comfort, I happened to go and see the boss, Mr. Osip, to ask his forgiveness, it being Forgiveness Day.

'Well, he puts the latch on the door and us two are alone together. And he gives me a real dressing down. Mr. Osip hasn't any education, but he's pretty fly, believe you me. Everyone thought well of him and feared him, seeing as how he led a strict and godly life and wasn't afraid of hard work. Been mayor and churchwarden, he had, for twenty years maybe, and done a power of good. Put gravel down on the New Moscow Road and had our church painted—the pillars was done to look like malachite.

'Well, he fastens the door. "I've had my eye on you for some time, you ruddy so-and-so . . ." says he. "Call yourself a saint, do you?" he says. "You're no saint, you're just a godless heretic, you villain. . . ."

'He goes on and on and on. . . . I can't put it like he did, all smooth and clever like—oh, he made a lovely job of it, fit to make you cry. Two hours he kept on at me. His words went home all right and my eyes were opened. I listened and listened till I was crying fit to bust. "Just be an ordinary man," said he. "Eat, drink, dress and pray like everyone else. Overdoing things is devil's work. Them irons are from the Devil," he said. "Your fasts are devil's fasts and your chapel's a devil's chapel. It's all pride," said he.

'Next day—the first Monday of Lent—I fell ill by God's will. I'd strained myself and they took me to hospital. Suffering a great deal I was, crying like anything and trembling. I thought I was going straight from that hospital to hell and it nearly did for me. Six months or so I suffered on my bed of pain and when I was let out, first thing I did was confess and take communion properly and that made a human being of me again.

'Mr. Osip let me go home. "And just you remember, Matthew," he lectured me, "overdoing things is devil's work." Now I eat and drink—*and* worship—same as everyone else. . . . Nowadays if our old priest should smell of tobacco or spirits, I don't make so bold as to condemn him—the priest's human too, isn't he? But when I'm told some holy man's set himself up in town or country who doesn't eat for weeks on end and has his own rites, then I know whose work that is and no mistake. Well, good sirs, that's the story of something that happened to me in my time. I'm like Mr. Osip these days—keep telling dear Cousin Jacob and his sister what to do. I heap reproaches on them, but I'm a voice crying in the wilderness. God never gave me the gift.'

Matthew's story produced no apparent impression. Sergey said nothing and started clearing the food from the counter and the policeman said how rich Matthew's cousin Jacob was. 'Thirty thousand he must have, at least.'

Constable Zhukov was red-haired and full-faced and his cheeks quivered as he walked. He was sturdy and well fed. When not in the presence of superiors he usually lolled in his chair with his legs crossed. When he spoke he always rocked to and fro, whistling casually, looking smug and sleek as if he had just had dinner. He was well off and always spoke of money as if he knew what he was talking about. He sold things on commission and when people had an estate, horse or second-hand carriage to dispose of, they applied to him.

'Yes, he must be worth thirty thousand, I reckon,' agreed Sergey. 'Your granddad had a sizeable fortune,' he said, turning to Matthew. 'A proper man of property, he was. Then it all went to your father and uncle. Your father died young and your uncle got it, and then it went to your cousin Jacob. While you and your mother were visiting monasteries and singing in the factory choir, Cousin Jacob wasn't letting the grass grow under his feet.'

'Your share's about fifteen thousand,' said the policeman, rocking to and fro. 'The inn's your joint property, so the same goes for the capital too. Aye. In your place I'd have sued them long ago. I'd have gone to court, stands to reason, but in the meantime I'd have taken him on one side and bashed his face in good and proper. . . .'

Jacob Terekhov was unpopular—religious cranks always do seem to upset people, even the irreligious—and the policeman did not like him anyway because he too dealt in horses and second-hand carriages.

'You can't bother to sue your cousin because you've plenty of money of your own,' the buffet-attendant said to Matthew, looking at him enviously. 'It's all right for them that has means. But I'll be stuck as I am till my dying day, bound to be. . . .'

Matthew tried to tell them that he had no money, but Sergey was not listening. A flood of memories came over him—of his past life and the insults that he suffered daily. His bald head sweated, he blushed and started blinking.

'Oh, damn this life!' he said wretchedly and threw a stick of salami on the floor.

III

The old coaching-inn was said to have been put up in Alexander I's time by a widow called Avdotya Terekhov who had settled there with her son. If you went past by mail-coach, especially on a moonlit night, one glance at the dark yard, with its gates always bolted and the open shed inside it, was enough to put you off—it made your flesh creep as if it was a sorcerer's or highwayman's den. Once past the place, drivers would look back and whip up their horses. No one was keen on stopping, for the management was surly and the charges were high.

The yard was muddy even in summer, with great fat pigs wallowing in the mire. Horses, the Terekhovs' stock-in-trade, wandered round untethered and often grew restive, ran out of the yard and bolted down the road, frightening women who were passing through on pilgrimage. There was plenty of traffic in those days. Long trains of loaded wagons went through and there had been incidents like the one about thirty years ago when some carters lost their temper, picked a fight and killed a passing merchant. About a quarter of a mile from the inn a twisted cross still stands. Mail troikas with bells and country gentlemen's heavy dormeuses drove by and herds of cattle passed, bellowing in clouds of dust.

When the railway was first built, there had only been a wayside halt here, called the 'passing-point'. Then about ten years later the present Progonnaya station was built. Traffic had almost disappeared from the old post-road, now used only by local squires and peasants and gangs of workmen who came through on foot in spring and autumn.

The coaching-house became an ordinary inn. The top storey was damaged by fire, the roof rusted yellow, and the open shed gradually collapsed, but great fat pigs still wallowed, pink and loathsome, in the mire outside. As of old, horses were still known to career out of the place and bolt down the road with their tails flying. Tea, hay, oats and flour were sold at the inn as well as vodka and beer for consumption on or off the premises, but they were rather cagey about the spirits that they sold, never having had a licence.

The Terekhovs had always been known as a pious lot and had even been nicknamed 'their Reverences'. They kept themselves to themselves, each as unsociable as a bear in his den. They kept their own counsel too, which is perhaps why they were so given to doubts and religious aberrations, almost every generation having its own slant on the faith.

Grandma Avdotya, who built the coaching-inn, was an Old Believer, but her son and two grandsons—fathers of Matthew and Jacob—attended the Orthodox Church, invited the clergy to their home and prayed to the new icons as fervently as to the old. Her son gave up meat in his old age and took a vow of silence, believing it a sin to talk at all. And the grandsons were peculiar in not taking the Scriptures simply, but always looking for a hidden meaning. Every holy word must contain a mystery, they claimed.

Avdotya's great-grandson Matthew had wrestled with doubts since boyhood and nearly come to grief. The other great-grandson, Jacob, was Orthodox, but when his wife died he suddenly stopped going to church and began worshipping at home. Seduced by his example, his sister Aglaya did not go to church herself and would not let Dashutka go either. In youth Aglaya had attended Flagellant meetings in Vedenyapino, it was said, and was still a secret Flagellant, which was supposed to be why she wore a white kerchief.

Jacob Terekhov was ten years older than Matthew, a fine-looking old man, tall, with a broad white beard nearly down to his waist and bushy eyebrows that made his face look stern—ill-natured even. He wore a long jerkin of good cloth or a black, fleece-lined jacket and always tried to be neatly and decently dressed. He wore galoshes even on fine days. The churches did not observe their rites correctly according to him, and priests drank at the wrong times and smoked, which was why he never went to church. He and Aglaya read and sang the service together at home every day. At matins in Vedenyapino the canon was not read and even important festivals went by without vespers, whereas he read through each day's prescribed stint at home, neither hurrying nor leaving out a single line. And in his spare time he read aloud from the Lives of the Saints. He kept strictly to the book in his everyday life too. Thus, if the regulations permitted wine on a certain day during Lent 'because of the long vigil', he made a point of drinking some even if he did not feel like it.

Why did he read, sing, burn incense and fast? Not in the hope of benefits to be received from God, but for form's sake. Without faith man cannot live. And faith must be correctly expressed from year to year and day to day according to a certain system whereby man addresses God each morning and evening with the precise words and thoughts appropriate to that day and hour. His life—and thus his worship too—must be pleasing to God, so he must read and sing each day only what pleases God, in other words what is laid down. Thus the first chapter of St. John may be read only on Easter Sunday, and certain anthems may not be sung between Easter Sunday and Holy Thursday and so on. Awareness of this procedure and its importance gave Jacob Terekhov much pleasure during worship. Forced to break routine—by fetching goods from town, say, or going to the bank—he felt guilty and miserable.

When Cousin Matthew suddenly turned up from the factory and made his home at the inn, he began breaking the rules from the start. He would not join the others in worship, had his meals and his tea at the wrong time, got up late in the morning and drank milk on Wednesdays and Fridays because of the 'state of his health'. Almost every day during service he went into the chapel and shouted, 'Come to your senses, Cousin! Repent, Cousin!' At this Jacob always flared up and Aglaya lost her temper and started cursing. Or Matthew would steal into the chapel at night. 'Cousin,' he would say quietly, 'your prayer is not acceptable to God. For it is said, "first be reconciled to thy brother, and then come and offer thy gift." And here are you—a usurer and vodka-pedlar. Repent!'

All Jacob could see in Matthew's words was the usual special pleading of futile, sloppy people who go on about 'loving thy neighbour', 'being reconciled to thy brother' and that sort of stuff only as a substitute for praying, fasting and reading holy books, and who sneer at profit and interest only because they dislike hard work. After all, it is easy enough to be poor and put nothing by—a lot easier than being rich.

Still, he was upset. He could not worship in the old way. As soon as he was inside his chapel with the book open he would start worrying—any moment his cousin might come in and disturb him. And sure enough before long Matthew would appear, shouting 'Come to your senses, Cousin! Repent, Cousin!' in quavering tones, while Aglaya cursed and Jacob lost his temper too.

'Clear out of my house!' he would yell.

'This house belongs to all of us,' Matthew told him.

Jacob would go back to his reading and singing, but could never settle down and would suddenly find himself day-dreaming over his book. He set no store by his cousin's words, but why had he recently taken to thinking how hard it is for a rich man to enter the Kingdom of Heaven? Then there was the stolen horse that he had bought about two years ago and done pretty well out of, and the drunk who had died of a surfeit of vodka at the inn in his wife's time. . . .

He slept badly at nights—very lightly. He heard Matthew, who could not sleep either, sighing as he pined for his tile-works. And at nights as he tossed from side to side, Jacob thought of that stolen horse, of the drunkard, and of what the Gospels say about camels and needles' eyes.

Could his 'doubts' be starting again?

March was nearly over, but there was this damned snow every day, the forest roared as if it was still winter and it looked as if spring would never come. It was just the weather to breed boredom, quarrels and bad feeling, and when the wind howled above the ceiling at night, it seemed that there was someone living up in that empty storey. Doubts gradually swamped his brain, his head seemed on fire and he did not feel like sleeping.

IV

In the morning of the Monday of Passion Week, Matthew was in his room and heard Dashutka talking to Aglaya.

'The other day,' she said, 'Uncle Matthew was telling me there's no need to fast.'

Remembering the conversation that he had had with Dashutka on the previous day, Matthew suddenly felt insulted.

'That's sinful talk, girl,' he said in a sick man's moaning voice. 'Fasts there must be. Our Lord himself fasted for forty days. I was only trying to say that even fasting ain't no good to the wicked.'

'Hark at his tile-works talk! Quite a lesson in behaviour, ain't it!' sneered Aglaya, mopping the floor. She usually cleaned the floors on week-days, losing her temper with all and sundry.

'Oh, we know how they keep their fasts up at the tile-works!' she went on. 'You just ask your uncle about his lady friend, about him and that dirty bitch swigging their milk in Lent. Gives the rest of us lessons in behaviour and conveniently forgets that trollop. Go on, ask him who he left that money with—go on.'

Matthew had a secret—a sort of skeleton in the cupboard. At the time of his high jinks and cavortings with those old women and young girls at prayer-meetings, he had formed a liaison with a local woman who bore him a child. On leaving for home he had given her all the savings that he had put by at the works and had borrowed his fare home from the boss. So now he had only a few roubles to spend on tea and candles. This 'lady friend' later told him that the child had died and wrote to ask what she should do with the money. The hired man brought the letter from the station, but Aglaya intercepted it and read it, after which she was on to Matthew about his 'lady friend' every day.

'Just fancy, only nine hundred roubles!' Aglaya continued. 'Gives nine hundred roubles to that tile-works cow, a slut what hasn't got nothing to do with us! Blast you!' She was quite beside herself, shouting and screeching. 'Lost your tongue, eh? Oh, I could tear you in pieces! Damned weakling! Nine hundred roubles down the drain! You could have made it over to Dashutka, she is your own flesh and blood. Or sent it to them poor orphans at the Home in Belyov. Oh, why didn't it choke her? Cow! Damn her, damn her, damn her! Hellish bitch! Damn her eyes!'

Jacob called her, for it was time to begin the offices. She washed, put on a white kerchief and joined her dear brother in the chapel, now quiet and meek. Speaking to Matthew or serving tea to peasants in the inn, she was a scraggy, sharp-eyed old harridan, but in chapel she looked blissful and serene. She seemed so much younger as she did her fancy curtsies and even demurely pursed her lips.

Jacob began reading the offices with quiet gloom, as always in Lent. He read for a while and then stopped to enjoy the calm that filled the whole house. Then he started reading again, enjoying himself. He clasped his hands in prayer, turned up his eyes, shook his head and sighed.

Suddenly voices were heard. Sergey and the policeman had come to see Matthew. Jacob disliked reading aloud and singing with strangers in the house, so on hearing voices he started reading in a whisper, slowly. In the chapel they could hear what the buffet-attendant was saying.

'The Tartar at Shchepovo's letting his business go for fifteen hundred. He'll take five hundred on account and the rest on credit, so be a friend in need, Mr. Terekhov sir, and lend me the five hundred roubles. I'll pay you two per cent a month.'

Matthew was aghast. 'But I haven't any money! What makes you think I have?'

'Two per cent a month—money for old rope,' the policeman explained. 'Your money will only feed the moths lying round here, and what good's that?'

The visitors left and silence fell, but Jacob had hardly gone back to his reading and singing before a voice was heard through the door.

'Cousin, let's have a horse to go to Vedenyapino.'

It was Matthew.

Jacob's ill humour returned. 'But which horse?' he asked after a moment's thought. 'The man's using the bay to cart a pig and I'm taking the stallion to Shuteykino, soon as I'm through here.'

Matthew was annoyed. 'Cousin,' he asked, 'why can you say what's to be done with the horses, when I can't?'

'Because I don't want them to amuse myself, I want them for a job.'

'Our property belongs to all of us, so the horses belong to us all too. You must see that, Cousin.'

A pause followed. Jacob did not go back to his worship, but waited for Matthew to move away from the door.

'I'm a sick man, Cousin,' said Matthew. 'I don't want the estate. You hang on to it, I don't mind. Just give me a bit to keep me going while I'm poorly, then I'll leave.'

Jacob said nothing. He very much wanted to be rid of Matthew, but could not give him money, all his own being tied up in the business. Anyway, there had never been a case of brothers or cousins sharing in the Terekhov family. Going shares means going bust.

Jacob said nothing, waiting for Matthew to leave and looking at his sister, afraid of her chipping in and starting another row like the one they had had that morning. Matthew left at last and Jacob went on reading, but there was no pleasure in it. His head felt heavy from his prostrations, his eyes were dim, and he found the sound of his own quiet, gloomy voice tedious. When this depression came over him at nights he put it down to lack of sleep, but by day it scared him and he felt that there were devils perched on his head and shoulders.

Disgusted, peevish, he somehow got through the offices and left for Shuteykino. Some navvies had dug a boundary ditch near Progonnaya in the autumn, and had run up a bill for eighteen roubles at the inn. He must catch their boss in Shuteykino and get the money from him. The thaw and the snow-storms between them had ruined the road. It was dark and bumpy and breaking up in places. The snow had settled below road level on each side, so that it was like driving on a narrow causeway and it was quite a business giving way when you met someone coming in the other direction. The sky had been overcast since morning and there was a damp wind. . . .

A long line of sledges came towards him—some women with a consignment of bricks—and Jacob had to turn off the road. His horse sank up to its belly in snow, his one-man sledge lurched to the right, while he twisted to the left to save himself falling out and sat like that while the sledges slowly moved past. Through the wind he heard the sledges creaking, the scraggy horses panting, and the women talking about him. ('There goes his Reverence!') One gave his horse a pitying glance.

'The snow will lie till St. George's Day, I'll be bound,' she said quickly. 'What a time we've had.'

Jacob sat hunched awkwardly, his eyes screwed up in the wind while horses and red bricks passed by. He was uncomfortable and had a pain in his side, which is perhaps why he suddenly felt annoyed. His errand seemed unimportant, and he reckoned that he could send his hired man to Shuteykino tomorrow.

Again for some reason, as on his last sleepless night, he remembered the words about the camel. Then various memories came to mind—the peasant who sold him the stolen horse, that drunkard and the women who pawned their samovars with him. All traders are out to make money of course, but Jacob was tired of trading. He felt he must get right away from the whole business and was depressed to think that there were vespers to be read that evening. The wind, beating straight in his face and rustling in his collar, seemed to be whispering all these thoughts to him, bringing them from the open white fields.

Looking at the countryside that he had known from boyhood, Jacob remembered having just the same worried thoughts when he was young and was assailed by doubts that shook his faith.

He was alone in open country—an eerie feeling. He turned back and drove slowly behind the sledge-train.

'His Reverence has turned back,' laughed the women.

It was Lent, so they were not cooking or using the samovar at home, which made the day drag. Jacob had long ago stabled his horse and sent some flour to the station. He had started reading the Psalms once or twice, but evening was still a long way off. Aglaya had already mopped all the floors and was tidying her trunk for something to do. It had bottle labels stuck all over the inside of the lid. Matthew, hungry and miserable, sat reading or went over to the dutch stove and spent some time examining the tiles—they put him in mind of the works. Dashutka slept, but woke up a little later and went to water the cows. She was drawing water from the well when the rope broke and the bucket fell in. The hired man started looking for a hook to fish the bucket out, and Dashutka pursued him over the muddy snow, her feet bare and red as a goose's. She kept saying it was 'a bit dippy', meaning the well water was too deep for the hook, but the man did not understand and showed his annoyance by turning round suddenly and swearing at her.

Just then Jacob came out of the house and heard Dashutka reply by gabbling out a stream of prime filth that she could only have picked up from drunken peasants at the inn.

He was quite frightened. 'What's that, you hussy!' he shouted. 'What sort of language is that?'

She gave her father a dumb, baffled look, having no idea why she should not use such words. He wanted to tell her off, but she struck him as so barbarous, so primitive. For the first time in their life together he realized that she believed in nothing. His way of life—woods, snow, drunken peasants, swearing and all—struck him as being barbarous and primitive like the girl, so instead of telling her off he just waved his arm and went back to his room.

Just then Sergey and the policeman came back to see Matthew again. Jacob remembered that these people did not believe in anything either —which bothered them not one whit. 'Life's a funny thing,' he thought. 'It's mad, it's hopeless—oh, it's a dog's life all right!' He paced the yard bareheaded, then went out in the road and walked up and down, his fists clenched, while snow fell in big flakes and his beard streamed in the wind. He kept tossing his head, for he seemed to feel a weight on head and shoulders as though there were devils perched there. He felt as if it was not he, but some enormous, terrifying monster that was stalking about. He had only to shout, he felt, for his voice to roar through fields and woods and strike fear into one and all. . . .

V

When he went back into the house the policeman had gone and the buffet-attendant was sitting in Matthew's room, busy with his abacus. There had been a time when he was in and out of the place almost every day. Then it had been Jacob whom he came to see, but lately it was Matthew. He was always at his abacus, his face tense and sweaty, or asking for money, or stroking his whiskers and telling how he had once mixed champagne-cup for officers at a main-line station. He personally had served the sturgeon soup at banquets. Catering was his only interest in life. Food, cutlery, china and wines—they were all he could talk about.

'Mother's breast is baby's snack-bar,' he had once remarked while serving tea to a young mother who was feeding a baby. It was his idea of a compliment.

He was working his abacus in Matthew's room and asking for money, saying that he could not live at Progonnaya any longer.

'Where oh where can I go now?' he asked several times, as if on the point of tears. 'Kindly tell me that.'

Then Matthew went into the kitchen and started peeling some boiled potatoes that he must have put aside the day before. It was quiet and Jacob thought that the buffet-attendant had left. And it was high time to start vespers. Jacob called Aglaya and, thinking the house was empty, began singing in a loud, uninhibited voice. He sang and read, but his mind was pronouncing quite different words—'Lord, forgive me! Lord, save me!' He did a series of low bows in succession, as if to exhaust himself and kept tossing his head, which made Aglaya look puzzled. He was afraid of Matthew coming in, in fact he was quite sure that he was going to come in, and neither prayers nor frequent self-prostrations could quell his rage.

As quietly as could be Matthew opened the door and entered the chapel.

'Oh, what a grievous sin!' he sighed reproachfully. 'Repent! Come to your senses, Cousin!'

Fists clenched, Jacob rushed out of the chapel, not looking at Matthew for fear of hitting him. Feeling as he had felt just now on the road, like some great monster, he crossed the hall into the dirty, grey rooms, thick with haze and smoke, where peasants drank their tea. There he stalked about for a while, treading so heavily that the crockery jingled on the shelves and the tables shook. He saw now that his religion was no use to him any more and that he could no longer worship as before. He must repent, come to his senses, pull himself together, live and worship differently. But how should he worship? Or was all this just the Devil trying to confuse him? Should he do none of those things?

What would happen? What should he do? Who could tell him? How helpless he felt! He stopped, clutched his head and started to think, but could not collect his thoughts in peace because Matthew was somewhere about. He went quickly back into the living quarters.

Matthew was sitting in the kitchen with a bowl of potatoes in front of him, eating. Aglaya and Dashutka were there too, sitting facing each other near the stove and winding yarn. An ironing-board had been put up between the stove and the table where Matthew sat and there was a cold flat-iron on it.

'Cousin Aglaya,' said Matthew, 'may I have some oil, please?'

'What! Oil in Lent!' said Aglaya.

'I'm no monk, Cousin Aglaya, I'm an ordinary man. I'm even allowed milk, let alone oil, in my state of health.'

'Quite a law unto yourselves, you tile-works people are!'

Aglaya took a bottle of vegetable oil from the shelf and dumped it irritably in front of Matthew, grinning maliciously, only too pleased to see him so deep in sin.

'Now look here, you can't have oil!' shouted Jacob.

Aglaya and Dashutka gave a start, but Matthew poured some oil in his bowl and went on eating as if he had not heard.

'No oil, I say!' shouted Jacob even louder. He turned red, snatched up the bowl, raised it above his head and smashed it on the floor as hard as he could. Splinters flew into the air.

'How dare you speak!' he shouted furiously, though not a word had Matthew said. 'How dare you!' repeated Jacob, banging his fist on the table.

Matthew went very white and stood up.

'Cousin!' he said, still chewing. 'Pull yourself together, Cousin!'

'Out of my house this instant!' Jacob shouted. He was sick of Matthew's wrinkled face and voice, the crumbs of food in his moustache and his chewing. 'Get out, I say!'

'Calm yourself, Cousin! This pride is devil's work.'

'Shut up!' Jacob stamped his feet. 'Out of here, you fiend of hell!'

'You're a godless heretic, in case you want to know,' Matthew went on in a loud voice, also growing angry. 'Accursed devils have come between you and the true light, and your prayers are not acceptable to God. Repent while there is yet time. It's a fearful thing, the death of a sinner is. Repent, Cousin!'

Jacob seized Matthew by the shoulders and dragged him from the table. Matthew turned paler still.

'Whatever next!' he muttered, scared out of his wits. 'Whatever next!'

Tugging and fighting to free himself from Jacob's grip, Matthew happened to grasp his shirt near the neck and tore the collar. Aglaya thought that this detested cousin was trying to hit Jacob. Shrieking, she snatched the bottle of oil and slammed it down as hard as she could on top of his head.

Matthew staggered. Quite suddenly he looked calm and unconcerned.

Jacob was breathing heavily. He was very worked up. Connecting with Matthew's head, the bottle had grunted like a living thing and that he really had enjoyed. He held Matthew up and several times, as he clearly remembered afterwards, pointed to direct Aglaya's attention to the flat-iron. A stream of blood flowed through his hands, he heard Dashutka sobbing, and the ironing-board crashed to the ground with Matthew slumped over it.

Only then did Jacob's fury subside and he knew what had happened.

'Let him die! The ruddy ram, him and his tile-works!' said Aglaya with loathing, still holding the iron in both hands. Her white, blood-stained kerchief had slipped down to her shoulders and her grey hair was all over the place. 'Serves him right!'

It was horrible. Dashutka sat on the floor near the stove with yarn in her hands, sobbing. She kept prostrating herself and made a sort of champing noise every time she did it. But what scared Jacob most were the bloodstained boiled potatoes. He was afraid of stepping in them.

Then came another horror, a sheer nightmare that plunged him deeper in despair, and seemed the direst threat of all. At first he just could not take it in. Sergey the buffet-attendant stood in the doorway holding his abacus. Very pale, he was watching proceedings in the kitchen with horror. He turned and rushed through the hall and out of the house. Only then did Jacob realize who it was. He went after him.

Jacob rubbed snow on his hands as he went and thought things over. It flashed through his mind that the hired man had asked for a night off and left for his village some time ago. They had killed a pig the day before and there were great smears of blood in the snow and on the sledge—and even blood splashes on one side of the well-head, so Jacob's whole family could be knee deep in blood without arousing suspicion. It pained Jacob to think of concealing the murder, but more painful still was the prospect of the policeman turning up from the railway station with his whistling, sneering and grinning—and of peasants coming, binding Jacob's and Aglaya's hands and leading them off in triumph to the nearest big village and thence to the town. Everyone would point at them on the way and gloat. ('Their Reverences have been run in!') He wanted to put off the evil day. It seemed better to suffer this disgrace at some time in the future rather than now.

He caught Sergey up. 'I'll lend you a thousand roubles . . .' he said. 'Why tell anyone? It won't do any good . . . won't bring him back to life anyway.'

Jacob could hardly keep up with the buffet-attendant, who did not look round and was doing his best to walk faster.

'I could make it fifteen hundred . . .' went on Jacob.

He paused, being out of breath, but Sergey walked on at the same speed, probably scared of becoming the next victim. Only when he was past the level-crossing and half way along the road to the station did he cast a glance over his shoulder and slacken his pace. In the station and along the line the red and green lights were already shining. The wind had dropped, but thick snow was still falling and the road was white again. Then, almost by the station, Sergey stopped, thought a minute and turned resolutely back. It was growing dark.

'Let's have your fifteen hundred roubles, Mr. Jacob,' he said quietly, trembling all over. 'I'll take it.'

VI

Jacob Terekhov's money was in the town bank or loaned out on mortgage and he did not keep much in the house—no more than he needed to trade with. He went to the kitchen and felt for his tin of matches. The sulphurous, dark blue flame flared up and he managed to have a good look at Matthew, who still lay on the floor near the table with a white sheet over him now, so that only his boots showed. A cricket chirped. Aglaya and Dashutka were not in the living-quarters, but sat behind the counter in the tea-room, silently winding yarn. Jacob took a lamp, went to his room, and pulled out from under his bed the small chest where he kept the ready cash. It amounted to four hundred and twenty roubles in small notes, and thirty-five in silver. The notes had an evil, oppressive smell. Putting the money in his cap, Jacob went into the yard and out of the gate. He looked from side to side as he went, but there was no sign of the buffet-attendant.

'Hallo there!' Jacob shouted.

Right by the level-crossing a dark figure detached itself from the barrier and moved hesitantly towards him.

Jacob saw who it was. 'Why can't you stay put?' he asked the buffet-attendant irritably. 'Here you are. It's a bit short of five hundred . . . but I've no more in the house.'

'All right . . . most grateful,' muttered Sergey, greedily clutching the money and stuffing it in his pockets. Even in the dark it was obvious that he was shaking all over. 'Don't you worry, Mr. Jacob. . . . No reason for me to open my big mouth. I came here and I went away again. And that's all I did. Like they say, hear no evil, see no evil. . . . Damn awful life, this!' he added with a sigh.

They stood silent for a minute, not looking at each other.

'All blew up from nothing, it did, God knows how . . .' said the buffet-attendant, shivering. 'I'm sitting there doing my sums and suddenly I hear a noise. . . . I look through the door and see you're all on about some oil. . . . Where is he now?'

'In the kitchen.'

'You should get rid of him somewhere. . . . Don't leave it.'

Jacob escorted him to the station without a word, then went back home and harnessed the horse to convey Matthew to Limarovo, having decided to take him to the forest there and leave him on the road. He would tell everyone that Matthew had left for Vedenyapino and not come back, then they would think that he had been killed by wayfarers. No one would really be taken in, Jacob knew that, but it was less of an ordeal to be on the move, doing something and making arrangements, than just to sit and wait. He called Dashutka and they took Matthew away together while Aglaya stayed behind to clean up the kitchen.

Jacob and Dashutka were held up on their way back because the barrier was down at the level-crossing. A long goods train passed, pulled by two panting engines that belched shafts of crimson flame from their funnels. At the crossing, in full view of the station, the front engine gave a piercing whistle.

'Hear that whistle . . . !' said Dashutka.

The train passed through at last and the crossing-keeper slowly raised the barrier.

'That you, Jacob?' he asked. 'Well, they say it's a lucky sign, not recognizing people.'

Then they got home and had to go to bed. Aglaya and Dashutka made up a bed on the tea-room floor and lay down together, while Jacob stretched out on the counter. They did not pray before turning in or light the icon-lamps. All three stayed awake till morning, but not a word did they utter and they had the feeling all night that someone was moving about in the empty storey above them.

Two days later a police inspector and examining magistrate came from town and searched Matthew's room and then the whole premises. They first questioned Jacob, who testified that Matthew had left for Vedenyapino late on Monday afternoon to go to church, so he must have been killed on the way by sawyers employed on the line. But the magistrate pointed out that Matthew had been found on the road, yet his cap had turned up at home. How could that be? Had he really gone to Vedenyapino without his cap? And why had they found not a single drop of blood near him in the snow on the road, when his skull was smashed in and his face and chest were black with blood? Jacob was shaken.

'Don't know, sir,' he answered, completely at his wits' end.

Jacob's worst fears came true. The railway policeman did arrive. And a local police sergeant smoked in the chapel. Aglaya pitched into him, swore at him and was rude to the inspector. Afterwards, as Jacob and Aglaya were being taken away, peasants milled round the gate. 'They've run in his Reverence!' they said.

One and all seemed delighted.

Under cross-examination the railway policeman stated positively that Jacob and Aglaya had murdered Matthew to avoid sharing the property with him, and Matthew had money of his own—if it had not turned up in the search, that was only because Jacob and Aglaya had done something with it. They also questioned Dashutka. Uncle Matthew and Aunt Aglaya had rows every day, she said, and almost came to blows over money. And Uncle must have been rich to have given as much as nine hundred roubles to some 'lady friend'.

Dashutka stayed on at the inn, alone. No one came in for tea or vodka and she either did housework or drank mead and ate buns. But a few days later the crossing-keeper was questioned and said that he had seen Jacob and Dashutka driving back from Limarovo late on Monday evening, so Dashutka too was arrested, taken to town and put in prison.

From what Aglaya said it soon became clear that Sergey had been present during the murder, so they searched his things and found money in an odd place—a felt boot under the stove. It was all in small change and there were three hundred roubles in one-rouble notes alone. He swore that he had made it by trading and had not been to the inn for over a year, but witnesses stated that he was poor and had been particularly hard up lately. They said he had been going to the inn every day to try and borrow from Matthew, and the policeman described how, on the day of the murder, he himself had twice been to the inn with the buffet-attendant to help him raise a loan. It was remembered in this connection that Sergey had been missing on the Monday evening and had not met the mixed goods and passenger train, so they arrested him as well and sent him to town.

The trial took place eleven months later.

Jacob looked much older. He was thinner and spoke in a low voice like a sick man, feeling pathetic and feeble, as if he was shorter than everyone else. Doubts and a bad conscience—his constant prison companions—seemed to have aged and enfeebled his spirits as much as his body.

It came out that he did not go to church.

'Are you a dissenter?' the judge asked him.

'Don't know, sir.'

By now he did not believe in anything. He knew nothing, understood nothing, and his former religion disgusted him—it seemed irrational and primitive.

Aglaya was still up in arms—still swore at poor Matthew and blamed him for all that had gone wrong.

Sergey had a beard now instead of his former whiskers. He sweated and blushed in court, looking ashamed of his grey prison coat and of being in the dock with ordinary peasants. He defended himself clumsily and argued with all the witnesses, trying to prove that he had not been at the inn for a whole year. There was laughter in court.

Dashutka had filled out in prison. She did not understand the questions put to her at the trial and just said that she had been scared out of her wits while Uncle Matthew was being killed, but felt all right afterwards.

All four were found guilty of murder for gain. Jacob was sentenced to twenty years' hard labour, Aglaya to thirteen and a half, Sergey to ten and Dashutka to six.

VII

In the Dué Roads off Sakhalin a foreign steamship anchored late one evening and demanded coal. Asked to wait till morning, the captain refused to delay even an hour and said that if the weather broke in the night he risked having to leave without any coal at all. The weather in the Straits of Tartary can change violently in half an hour or so, making the shores of Sakhalin perilous. And it was freshening up already, with a fair sea running.

At Voyevoda Gaol, the grimmest and most forbidding prison on Sakhalin, a gang of convicts was ordered out to the pits. They were to load coal onto barges for towing by steam-launch to the ship anchored half a mile from shore, where they would transfer the load—an appalling job, what with the launch crashing into the ship and the men so seasick that they could hardly stand.

The convicts had just been turned out of bed and walked along the shore, half asleep, stumbling in the dark and clanking their leg-irons. To the left a high, indescribably gloomy cliff loomed dimly, while on the right was solid blackness without a glint of light, where the sea gave out long, monotonous groanings. Now and then a warder lit his pipe and threw a flash of light on an armed guard and two or three rough-looking convicts near by, or he took his lantern near to the water, and only then could the white crests of the nearest waves be seen.

The party included Jacob, whose long beard had earned him his prison nickname of 'Old Tufty'. It was a long time since he had been Mr. Jacob to anyone. He was plain Jake now. He was in disgrace too. Feeling violently, unbearably homesick about three months after reaching Siberia, he had run away—the temptation was too much for him. He was soon caught and given a life sentence and forty lashes, since when he had been flogged twice again for losing prison clothing though it had been stolen from him on each occasion.

Jacob had started feeling homesick on the way to Odessa. The convict train had stopped at Progonnaya for the night and he had pressed against the window, trying to make out the old home, but could not see anything in the darkness.

There was no one to talk to about home. His sister Aglaya had been sent to a prison on the other side of Siberia and her whereabouts were unknown. Dashutka was in Sakhalin, but had been given to some ex-convict to live with, away in a distant settlement. There was no news of her at all, except that a settler who turned up in Voyevoda Gaol told Jacob that she now had three children. Sergey was in service with an official here in Dué, quite near by, but you couldn't bank on meeting him, for he turned up his nose at the common run of convict.

The gang reached the pits and the men took their places on the wharf. The weather was said to be getting too bad for loading and the ship was supposed to be about to weigh anchor. Three lights could be seen. One was moving—the steam-launch, which had been to the ship and was now apparently coming back to say whether the job was on or not.

Shivering in the autumn cold and the damp sea air, huddled in his short, torn fleece jacket, Jacob stared unblinking in the direction of his homeland. He had been in prison with people from here, there and everywhere—Russians, Ukrainians, Tartars, Georgians, Chinese, Finns, gipsies and Jews. Hearing their talk and seeing so much of their sufferings, he had begun to turn to God once more. At last, he felt, he had come to know the true faith for which his whole family from Grandma Avdotya onwards had thirsted, seeking it so long in vain. Where God was, how to serve Him—all that he knew and understood now. What he could not see was why one man's lot should be so different from another's. This simple faith that God gives to some men as their birthright—why had it cost him so dear? Why all these horrible sufferings that made his arms and legs twitch like a drunkard's and would clearly go on and on till his dying day?

He stared intently into the darkness. Through thousands of miles of blackness he seemed to see his homeland, his native province, his own district, Progonnaya itself. He saw darkness, barbarity, callousness and the dumb, harsh, cowlike indifference of those he had left behind there. His eyes were dim with tears, but still he gazed into the distance where the pale lights of the steamer glinted faintly. His heart ached with longing for his home. He wanted to live. He wanted to go back there and tell them all about his new faith. If he could only save one person from disaster and live but one day free from suffering!

The launch arrived and the warder loudly announced that loading was off.

'Back with you!' he commanded. 'Attention there!'

They heard the anchor-chain being dragged up on the steamship. A strong, piercing wind blew and somewhere on the cliff-top trees were creaking.

A storm must be getting up.

MY LIFE

A PROVINCIAL'S STORY

I

'I ONLY keep you here out of respect for your esteemed father,' the director told me. 'Otherwise you'd have been sent flying long ago.'

'Sir,' I replied, 'you flatter me unduly if you think I can defy the laws of gravity.' Then I heard him say, 'Take this character away, he gets on my nerves.'

I was dismissed two days later, and that made nine jobs I had had since reaching man's estate, to the great grief of my father, the city architect. I had worked in various government offices, but all nine jobs had been exactly alike and involved sitting down, copying, listening to stupid, insensitive remarks and waiting to be sacked.

Father was sitting back in his armchair with his eyes closed when I went to see him. His gaunt, emaciated face, with a bluish-grey shadow where he shaved, was the picture of meekness and resignation and he looked like an elderly Catholic organist. He did not answer my greeting or open his eyes.

'If my dear wife, your mother, were still alive,' he said, 'your way of life would be a constant thorn in her flesh. I see the workings of Providence in her premature death. Tell me, wretched youth,' he went on, opening his eyes, 'what, pray, am I to do with you?'

When I was younger my friends and relations had known what to do with me, some advising me to volunteer for the army, while others wanted me to work in a chemist's shop or a telegraph office. But now I was turned twenty-five and even a bit grey at the temples, now I had actually been a volunteer, a chemist's assistant and a telegraph operator, I had used up my chances in life, it seemed, so they stopped advising me and just sighed or shook their heads.

'Who do you think you are?' Father went on. 'By your age most young men have a position in life, but look at you, you penniless lout, living on your father.'

He made his usual speech about young men nowadays being doomed—doomed by atheism, materialism and inordinate conceit—and about how amateur theatricals should be banned for distracting them from religion and duty.

'You'll come with me tomorrow, you'll tell the director you're sorry and you'll promise to work properly,' he ended. 'You must regularize your position in society before another day has passed.'

'Do you mind if I say something?' I asked sullenly, expecting nothing good from this conversation. 'What does your "position in society" come to? Simply the privileges conferred by capital and education. Poor, uneducated people earn their living by manual labour. Why should I be different? That's what I don't see.'

'When you talk about manual labour you sound stupid and vulgar,' said Father irritably. 'Look here, you nit-wit, can't you get it into your thick skull that there's more to it than brute strength? You also have the divine spirit within you—the sacred flame that sets you quite apart from an ass or a reptile and gives you an affinity with the sublime. And what produced this flame? Thousands of years' effort by the best of mankind. Your great-grandfather, General Poloznev, fought at Borodino. Your great-uncle was a poet, public speaker and marshal of the nobility, your uncle's a teacher, and lastly I, your father, am an architect. Don't tell me we Poloznevs have all handed on this sacred flame just for you to put it out!'

'Be fair,' I said. 'Millions of people do work with their hands.'

'Let them! That's all they're fit for! Anyone—a complete idiot or criminal even—can work with his hands. Such work is the hallmark of slaves and barbarians, while the sacred flame is granted only to the few.'

There was no point in going on. Father worshipped himself and no words could sway him unless they came out of his own mouth. Besides, I was pretty sure that these high-handed references to manual labour were prompted less by any notion about sacred flames than by a secret dread that I might become a labourer and set the whole town talking about me. But the main thing was that other men of my age had all graduated long ago and were doing well—the son of the manager of the State Bank was an established civil servant already—while I, my father's only son, was a nobody.

There was no point in going on with this unpleasant conversation, but I sat there feebly protesting and hoping to make my point in the end. The problem was simple and straightforward enough, goodness knows—how was I to earn my living? That's all. But this simplicity went unnoticed as the mellifluous sentences rolled on, all about Borodino, sacred flames and my father's uncle, a forgotten poet whose verse had been wretched, bogus stuff. And rude remarks about nit-wits and their thick skulls were made at my expense.

But I did so much want to be understood. In spite of everything I loved my father and sister. I had been asking them for advice ever since I was a child and by now the habit was so ingrained that it was with me for life. Right or wrong, I was always afraid of annoying them —and afraid because Father was now so upset that his stringy neck had turned red and he might have a stroke.

'Sitting in a stuffy room, copying and competing with a typewriter,' I pronounced. 'What a disgrace and humiliation for a man of my age! There's no sacred flame about that.'

'It is brain work all the same,' Father said. 'But enough! This conversation must cease. In any case I warn you that if you won't go back to the office and if you follow your own contemptible inclinations, my daughter and I will banish you from our hearts. I'll cut you out of my will too, and by God I mean it!'

'Your will doesn't matter to me,' I said in all sincerity, to show the absolute purity of the motives which I wished to rule my life. 'I renounce my inheritance in advance.'

Somehow, to my astonishment, these words hurt Father terribly. He turned crimson.

'How dare you talk to me like that, you idiot!' he shouted in a thin, shrill voice. 'You good-for-nothing!' And with a practised hand, quickly and deftly, he slapped my face twice. 'You forget yourself!'

When Father beat me as a child I was made to stand to attention and look him in the face. And I was so flabbergasted when he struck me nowadays that I always drew myself up and tried to look him in the eye as if I were still in the nursery. My father was old and very thin, but those slender muscles must have been tough as whip-cord because the blows really hurt.

I reeled back into the hall and he snatched up his umbrella and struck me several blows on the head and shoulders. Then my sister opened the drawing-room door to see what the noise was about, but turned away at once with a look of pity and terror, not saying a word in my defence.

I did not intend to go back to the office and I did mean to start a new life as a worker. And nothing was going to stop me. I only had to choose a job, and that did not seem so very difficult, for I felt I had plenty of strength and stamina to tackle the toughest work. I was going to live as a worker with all the monotony, hunger and smells. I should have to rough it. I should always be worried about earning enough to make ends meet, and coming home from work along

Great Dvoryansky Street I might well find myself envying Dolzhikov the engineer, who worked with his brain. Who could tell? At the moment I enjoyed thinking about these future tribulations.

At one time intellectual activity had fired my imagination and I had seen myself as a teacher, doctor or writer, but those dreams had never come true. I was passionately addicted to such intellectual pleasures as reading and the theatre. But could I do brain work? I don't know. At school I had an absolute aversion to Greek and had to be taken away in the fourth form. For a long time I had private tutors trying to get me into the fifth form. Then I worked in various offices, doing absolutely nothing most of the day, and was told that was brain work.

Nothing I did as pupil or clerk needed any mental effort, talent, special ability or creative drive. It was all mechanical. I regard that kind of brain work as lower than manual labour, I despise it and do not think it can justify an idle, carefree life for one moment, being simply a sham—another form of idleness in fact. Very likely I just don't know what real brain work is.

Evening came on. We lived in Great Dvoryansky Street, the city's main thoroughfare, where the local smart set paraded in the evening for want of a decent municipal park. And a splendid street it was, almost as good as a park. On both sides grew poplars, especially sweet-scented after rain. Acacias, lilac bushes, wild cherries and apple-trees hung out over fences and railings. Twilight in May, the young, green leaves and the shadows, the scent of lilac, the humming of insects, the stillness and the warmth—spring comes round every year, it's true, but it seems so fresh and wonderful each time. I stood at the garden gate watching people stroll by. I had grown up with most of them and we had played together as children. But they might be a bit put off by me now in my cheap, unfashionable clothes with narrow trousers tucked into large, clumsy boots—people called me 'drain-pipes'. Besides, I had a bad name in town because I lacked social standing and was always playing billiards in low dives. Having twice been hauled off to the local police station probably didn't help much either, though I had done absolutely nothing to deserve it.

Someone was playing the piano in Mr. Dolzhikov's flat in the large house opposite. It was growing dark and stars twinkled in the sky. I saw Father walk slowly past with my sister on his arm, returning the bows of passers-by. He wore an old top-hat with a broad upturned brim.

'Just look,' he said to my sister, pointing at the sky with the umbrella that he had been hitting me with. 'Look at the sky. Even the tiniest star is a world of its own. Man is indeed insignificant compared with the universe.'

He sounded as if he enjoyed being insignificant and found it most flattering. What a mediocrity! He was the only architect we had, I am sorry to say, and not one decent house had been built in our town in the fifteen or twenty years I could remember.

When he was asked to plan a house, he usually drew the ballroom and drawing-room first. In the old days boarding-school girls couldn't dance at all unless they started at the stove, and in the same way his creative thinking could not develop unless he started with ballroom and drawing-room. He would tack on dining-room, nursery and study, all linked by doors which inevitably turned them into corridors, each room with two, even three, doors too many. His imagination must have been muddled, chaotic and stunted. He always seemed to feel that something was missing and resorted to various kinds of annexes which he planted on top of each other. I can still see those narrow entrance halls, poky little passages and crooked little staircases leading to mezzanines where you could not stand upright, with three huge steps instead of a floor—like the shelves in a Russian bathhouse. The kitchens must always be in the basement with vaulted ceilings and brick floors, the façades had a stubborn, crusty expression, their lines stiff and timid, and the roofs were low and squashed, while the plump, hefty-looking chimneys were incomplete without wire caps and squeaky black cowls.

Somehow all these houses built by Father, each so like the next, vaguely evoked his top-hat and the austere, stiff lines of the back of his neck. The town became accustomed to Father's incompetence in time. It took root and became the local style.

Father also brought this style into my sister's life. To start with he gave her the name Cleopatra, just as he had named me Misail. When she was a child he would scare her with talk about the stars, the wise men of old and our ancestors, and would explain at some length the nature of life and duty. Now that she was twenty-six he was still at it. No one might take her arm except himself, and he somehow imagined that an eligible young man must come along sooner or later to seek her hand out of respect for his moral calibre. She adored Father, feared him, and thought him highly intelligent.

It grew quite dark and the street gradually emptied. The music stopped in the house opposite us and the gates were flung wide open. A troika bowled off down our street with a dashing air, its bells softly jingling. The engineer and his daughter had gone for a spin. Time for bed.

I had my own room in our house, but lived in a shed tacked onto a brick outbuilding. Very likely it had been put up as a harness room originally, for there were huge pegs driven into the walls, but it was no longer needed as such. For thirty years Father had been stacking newspapers there. He had them bound, heaven knows why, in half-yearly batches and let no one touch them. Living there, I ran into Father and his guests less often. I felt that not having a proper room and not going into the house for dinner every day took some of the sting out of Father's talk about my being a burden to him.

My sister was waiting for me. Without telling Father, she had brought me some supper, a small piece of cold veal and a slice of bread. They were always on about 'counting your copecks' in our house—'taking care of your roubles' and that sort of stuff. These clichés rather got my sister down and she thought only of economizing, so we ate badly. She put the plate on the table, sat on my bed and burst into tears.

'Oh Misail,' she said, 'what are you doing to us?'

She did not cover her face. The tears fell onto her breast and hands and she looked miserable. She threw herself down on the pillow and let the tears come, shaking all over and sobbing.

'That's another job you've walked out of . . .' she said. 'Oh, how dreadful.'

'But my dear sister, you must see . . .' I said. Her tears filled me with despair.

Then of course my lamp had to run out of paraffin. It had started smoking, and was about to go out. The old pegs on the walls looked grim and their shadows flickered.

'Don't be too hard on us,' said my sister, getting up. 'Father's terribly upset and I'm ill, nearly out of my mind. What will become of you?' she asked, sobbing and holding out her hands. 'Please, I beg you for our dear mother's sake, go back to the office.'

'I can't, Cleopatra,' I said, on the verge of giving in. 'I can't.'

'Why not?' my sister went on. 'Why not? Look, if you didn't get on with your boss, find another job. For instance, why not go and work on the railway? I've just been talking to Anyuta Blagovo and she says they're sure to take you on there. She's even promised to put in a word for you. For God's sake, Misail, do think about it. Give it some thought, please.'

After a little more talk I gave in. I said I had never thought of a job on the new railway and didn't mind having a go.

She smiled happily through her tears and pressed my hand, and then went on crying, unable to stop. I fetched some paraffin from the kitchen.

II

No one in town was more addicted to amateur theatricals, concerts and *tableaux vivants* for charity than the Azhogins, who owned a house in Great Dvoryansky Street. They provided the premises, did the organizing, and bore the expense. The family was rich and owned land, having about eight thousand acres in the district with a magnificent manor-house and garden, but they disliked the country and lived in town all year round.

There was the mother—a tall, lean, genteel woman with short hair, short blouse and narrow skirt in the English fashion—and three daughters who were called not by name, but simply 'Eldest', 'Middle' and 'Youngest'. Short-sighted and round-shouldered, they all had hideous sharp chins and dressed like their mother. They lisped unattractively. But despite all this they needs must be in every show and were always doing something for charity—acting, reciting, singing. They were very earnest, never smiled, and even acted in musical comedies without a spark of life, looking as businesslike as if they were auditing accounts.

I liked our theatricals, especially the numerous rehearsals—somewhat chaotic, but great fun and always followed by supper. I had no hand in choosing plays or casting, for my job was off stage, painting scenery, copying parts, prompting and doing the make-up. I was also put in charge of sound effects—thunder, nightingale song and all that. Having neither social standing nor respectable clothes, I always kept to myself at rehearsals, lurking in the wings, too shy to speak.

I painted scenery in the Azhogins' shed or yard, helped by a house-painter or, as he called himself, 'decorating contractor', one Andrew Ivanov. He was about fifty, tall, very thin and pale, with a sunken chest, sunken temples and dark blue rings under his eyes. He looked slightly frightening. He suffered from some wasting disease and every autumn and spring people said he was fading away, but he would have a spell in bed and then get up again.

'Still alive, you see,' he would say with an air of surprise.

In town he was called Radish, which was said to be his real surname. He was as fond of the theatre as I was, and would drop everything when he heard that a show was in the air, and go to the Azhogins' to paint scenery.

The day after my talk with my sister I worked all day at the Azhogins'. The rehearsal was to start at 7 p.m. All the company met in the ballroom an hour before that, and the three sisters—Eldest, Middle and Youngest—were walking up and down the stage reading from notebooks. Radish, in a long reddish-brown overcoat with a scarf round his neck, stood leaning his head against a wall, reverently watching the stage. Mrs. Azhogin went up to each guest in turn and made polite remarks. She had a trick of staring you in the face and speaking quietly as though revealing a secret.

'It must be hard work painting scenery,' she said quietly, coming up to me. 'I was just talking to Mrs. Mufke about superstitions when you came in. God knows, my whole life has been one long fight against superstition. Just to show the servants how silly such fears are, I always light three candles in my room and begin any important venture on the thirteenth of the month.'

Mr. Dolzhikov's daughter came in—a beautiful, buxom, fair-haired girl, 'dressed Paris fashion', as people put it locally. She did not act, but they put a chair on the stage for her at rehearsals, and performances never started till she appeared in the front row, dazzling and breathtaking in her fine clothes. Coming from the metropolis, she was allowed to pass remarks at rehearsal and did so with a smile of charming condescension, obviously thinking our shows a sort of child's game. She had studied singing at the St. Petersburg Conservatoire, it was said, and had even sung for a whole winter in a private opera house. I found her very attractive and could hardly take my eyes off her at rehearsals and performances.

I had already picked up a notebook to prompt from when my sister suddenly appeared. She came up without taking off her hat and coat and asked if I would please go with her.

I went. Anyuta Blagovo stood in the doorway back-stage. She also had her hat on, and wore a dark veil. She was the daughter of a Deputy Judge who had served in our town for some time, pretty well since the local court was first set up. Tall and well-built, Anyuta was thought essential for *tableaux vivants* and when she represented a fairy or 'Glory' her face burnt with shame. But she took no part in theatricals.

She did sometimes drop in at rehearsals for a moment on some errand, but never came into the hall and it was obvious now that she had looked in only for a moment.

'My father's been talking about you,' she said dryly, blushing and not looking at me. 'Dolzhikov says he'll give you a job on the railway. Will you see him tomorrow? He'll be at home.'

I bowed and thanked her for her trouble.

'You can leave that,' she said, pointing to my notebook.

Anyuta and my sister went up to Mrs. Azhogin and they all whispered for a minute or two with an occasional glance at me. This was some sort of consultation.

'Yes indeed,' said Mrs. Azhogin quietly, coming up to me and staring me in the face. 'Yes indeed, if this is keeping you from serious work,'—she took the notebook from my hands—'you can hand over to someone else. It's all right, my dear man. Be off, and good luck to you.'

I said goodbye and went out feeling awkward. On my way downstairs I saw Anyuta Blagovo and my sister leaving in a hurry and talking excitedly—no doubt about my railway job. My sister had never been at a rehearsal before and very likely felt guilty, scared of Father finding out that she had been at the Azhogins' without his permission.

About half-past twelve next day I went to see Dolzhikov. A manservant showed me into a very fine room which served the engineer as both drawing-room and office. It was all so soft, elegant and—to someone as unused to it as I was—even a bit strange. There were expensive carpets, huge armchairs, bronzes, pictures, gilt and plush frames. The walls were covered with photographs of very beautiful women and people with fine, intelligent faces in relaxed poses. A door from the drawing-room led straight to a balcony facing the garden. There were lilac-bushes, a table laid for lunch, lots of bottles and a bunch of roses. It smelt of spring and expensive cigars—the very smell of happiness. 'Here's a man who really has lived,' everything seemed to say. 'He has worked hard and earned such happiness as this world can offer.'

The engineer's daughter was sitting at the desk reading a newspaper.

'You want Father?' she asked. 'He's having a shower, but he'll be here in a minute. Won't you sit down?'

I did.

'I believe you live opposite?' she said after a short pause.

'Yes.'

'I watch you every day from the window for something to do. I hope you don't mind,' she went on, looking at her paper. 'I often see you and your sister. She looks so kind and seems to be so intent on what she's doing.'

Dolzhikov came in, rubbing his neck with a towel.

'It's Mr. Poloznev, Daddy,' his daughter said.

'Yes, yes, Blagovo told me.' He turned to me briskly, but did not offer to shake hands. 'Now look here, what do you want out of me? What are these "jobs" I keep hearing about? You're a funny lot,' he went on in a loud voice as if telling me off. 'A score of you come here every day. Think I'm running an office? I'm running a railway, my dear sirs. It's a tough job of work and I need mechanics, fitters, navvies, carpenters, tunnellers. All you people can do is sit on your backsides and write! Oh, you're all great writers!'

He had an air of well-being like his carpets and armchairs. Plump, healthy, rosy-cheeked, broad-chested, well-scrubbed, he looked like a china figure of a coachman in his cotton print shirt and wide trousers tucked inside his boots. He had not a grey hair on his head. He had a full, curly beard, a hooked nose and dark, clear, innocent eyes.

'What good are you?' he went on. 'You're no damn good at all. Oh yes, I'm an engineer. I've made my way in life. But before I ran the railway I sweated my guts out for years. I've been an engine-driver and I worked two years in Belgium as a common greaser. Judge for yourself, man—what work can I give you?'

'You're right of course . . .' I muttered, greatly put out. Those clear, innocent eyes were too much for me.

'Can you at least work a telegraph?' he asked after a moment's thought.

'Yes, I've been a telegraph clerk.'

'Well, we'll see. You'd better go to Dubechnya for the moment. I have someone there, but he's no damn good.'

'What will my duties be?' I asked.

'We'll see. You run along there for the moment and I'll fix things up. But I won't have you going on the booze, mind. And don't come bothering me or I'll boot you out.'

He moved off without even a nod. I bowed to him and his daughter, who was reading the paper, and went out. I was so fed up that when my sister asked how I had got on with Dolzhikov I just could not speak.

I rose at sunrise to walk to Dubechnya. There was no one in our street—everyone was still in bed—and my footsteps sounded lonely and hollow. The dew-drenched poplars filled the air with soft fragrance. I was sad and did not feel like leaving town. I loved my native town—it was a place of warmth and beauty to me. I loved the green leaves, the quiet sunny mornings, the bells ringing. But the people bored me. I lived with them, but we had nothing in common and at times they made me feel sick. I disliked them, couldn't make them out at all.

What kept these sixty-five thousand people going? That's what I couldn't see. Kimry got its living by boots, I knew. Tula made samovars and guns, Odessa was a port. But what our town was and what it did, I had no idea. Great Dvoryansky Street and a couple of the smarter streets were kept going on capital and civil servants' salaries paid by the government. But what of the other eight streets that ran parallel for a couple of miles and vanished behind the hill? What did they live on? That's what baffled me.

The way these people lived was shameful beyond words. There was no park, no theatre, no decent orchestra. No one went inside the town library or club reading-room except for a few Jewish youths, so magazines and new books lay around uncut for months. Well-off professional people slept in cramped, stuffy bedrooms on wooden, bug-infested beds. They kept their children in revoltingly dirty rooms called nurseries, and servants, even old and respected ones, slept on the kitchen floor under rags. On fast days their houses smelled of sturgeon fried in sunflower oil and on other days of *borshch*. Their food tasted awful and their drinking-water was unwholesome. At the town hall, governor's office, bishop's palace and all over town they had been going on for years about how we had no good, cheap water and must borrow two hundred thousand roubles from the government to lay on a proper supply. Very rich people—our town had about three dozen, who were known to gamble away whole estates at cards—also drank tainted water and talked excitedly about this loan, in fact they never stopped. It made no sense to me. I should have thought they would have found it easier to go ahead and put up the two hundred thousand out of their own pockets.

I did not know one honest man in the whole town.

My father took bribes, thinking they were offered out of respect for his moral calibre. And if boys wanted to be moved into a higher form at school they boarded out with their teachers and paid through the nose. At recruiting time the military commander's wife took bribes from the young men. She was not above accepting a few drinks either, and was once too drunk to get off her knees in church. The doctors also took bribes at call-up time. The town medical officer and the vet levied a regular tax on butchers' shops and restaurants, and there was a brisk trade in exemption certificates at the local college. The higher clergy took bribes from the lower and from churchwardens. If you applied to the municipal offices, the citizens' bureau, the health centre or any other institution, they would shout after you, 'Remember to say thank you', and you would go back and hand over thirty or forty copecks.

Those who took no bribes—high officials of the law-courts, say—were arrogant and held out two fingers instead of shaking hands. They were callous and narrow-minded, played cards, drank a lot and married rich girls. And they had an evil, corrupting influence on their surroundings, there was no doubt about that.

Only the young women had an air of integrity, being mostly honourable, decent, high-minded girls. But they knew nothing of life and thought bribes were offered out of respect for people's moral calibre. After marriage they let themselves go and aged quickly, hopelessly swamped in the morass of this vulgar, commonplace existence.

III

They were building a railway in our district and on Saturday nights hordes of riff-raff loafed about the town. People called them navvies and were afraid of them.

I have often seen one of these toughs hauled off to the police station with no cap on and blood all over his face, while the *corpus delicti*—a samovar or wet underwear fresh from the washing-line—was carried behind. The navvies usually swarmed round the taverns and markets. They ate, drank and swore, and when a woman of easy virtue went past they pursued her with piercing whistles.

Our shop-assistants tried to amuse this starving rabble by giving dogs and cats vodka or tying an empty paraffin can to a dog's tail and whistling, whereupon the dog bolted down the street as if it had a fiend from hell at its heels. Squealing with terror with the can clattering after it, it would run far out into the country till it dropped. There were some dogs in our town that shook all the time and kept their tails between their legs. These, it was said, hadn't quite seen the joke. They had gone mad.

They were building the station about three miles from town. The engineers had wanted a fifty thousand rouble bribe, it was said, to bring the line right up to town, but the town council would not go above forty and they had fallen out over the odd ten thousand roubles. Now the townsfolk were sorry, as they had to build a road to the station and the estimate for that came to a lot more.

Sleepers and rails had been laid along the whole line and service trains ran, carrying building material and workers. Now they were just waiting for the bridges which Dolzhikov was building and one or two uncompleted stations.

Dubechnya, as our first station was called, was a dozen miles from town. I walked there. Caught by the morning sun, the cornfields shone bright green. It was cheerful, flat country, with the station, hillocks and far-away farms clearly outlined in the distance.

It was so pleasant to be out in the country. I longed for this feeling of freedom to soak into me, if only for one morning, to save me from thinking about events in town, or about how hard life was and how hungry I felt. I have never known anything so frustrating as those moments of acute hunger, when thoughts of higher things become strangely mixed with thoughts of porridge, rissoles and fried fish. And here was I standing alone in the fields, looking up at a lark which floated motionless in the air trilling away as if it had hysterics, while I thought, 'I wouldn't mind a bit of bread and butter'. Or I would sit by the wayside and close my eyes so that I could rest and listen to the magical sounds of May, and would suddenly remember the smell of hot potatoes. I did not usually have enough to eat for someone as tall and hefty as I was, so my main feeling during the day was hunger. Perhaps that is why I understood so well how many people work only to get their daily bread and can talk of nothing but food.

At Dubechnya they were plastering the inside of the station and putting a wooden upper storey on the pumping shed. It was hot and smelt of quicklime. Workmen were loafing about among piles of shavings and rubble, and a signalman was asleep near his little hut with the sun beating down on his face. There were no trees. A faint hum came from the telegraph wires on which a few hawks were perched here and there. Not knowing what to do, I strolled among the piles of rubble like everyone else. I remembered asking the engineer about my duties and being told, 'We'll see'. But how could you 'see' about anything in this dump? The plasterers spoke of a foreman and one Fedot Vasilyev, but that meant nothing to me and I became more and more fed up—physically depressed, as when you are conscious of your arms, legs and great hulking body, but do not know what to do with them or where to put them.

I walked about for two hours at least and then noticed a row of telegraph poles leading off to the right from the station and ending by a white stone wall a mile or so away. That was the office, some of the men told me, and, as I finally worked out, it was where I should be heading.

It was an old estate long abandoned. The wall was of spongy white stone, thoroughly weathered and broken in places. There was a lodge with a blank wall facing outwards and a rusty roof with shiny tin patches dotted about on it. The gates opened onto a wide yard—a mass of weeds—and onto an old manor-house with sunblinds in the windows and a high roof red with rust. Twin lodges stood one on each side of the house. One was boarded up, but the windows of the other one were open, washing hung on the line and calves were wandering about. The last telegraph pole stood in the yard, and a wire led to the window of the lodge with the blank wall facing outwards. The door was open and I went in.

There was some character sitting at a table by a telegraph apparatus. He had dark, curly hair and wore a canvas jacket. He gave me a sullen scowl, but immediately smiled.

'Hallo, Better-than-nothing,' he said.

This was Ivan Cheprakov, an old school friend of mine who had been expelled for smoking when he was in the second form. We used to catch goldfinches, greenfinches and linnets together in autumn and sell them in the market in the early morning while our parents were still in bed. We ambushed flocks of migrating starlings, firing small shot at them and picking up the wounded, some of which died in dreadful agony—I still remember them squeaking in the cage at night. When any recovered we put them up for sale and swore blind that they were males. At market once I had only one starling left which I kept trying to sell and eventually let go for a copeck. 'Better than nothing, anyway,' I said to console myself, putting the copeck in my pocket. It was then that urchins and schoolchildren nicknamed me Better-than-nothing. Urchins and shopkeepers still used the name to jeer at me, though no one except me remembered where it came from.

Cheprakov was not very strongly built. He was narrow-chested, round-shouldered, long-legged. His tie looked like a piece of string, he wore no waistcoat and his boots were in poorer shape and more down-at-heel than my own. He had an unblinking stare and always looked ready to pounce. He was always fussing.

'Hold on a moment,' he would say in his fidgety way. 'Now just you listen to me. Er, what was it I was saying just now?'

We had a talk and I learnt that not long ago the Cheprakovs had owned the estate on which I now was. It was only in the previous autumn that Mr. Dolzhikov had got hold of it. He thought it better to put money into land than to keep it in cash and had already bought three sizeable mortgaged estates in our district. When she sold the place, Cheprakov's mother had reserved the right to live in one of the lodges for two years and had secured a job in the office for her son.

'Buying this place was nothing.' Cheprakov was referring to the engineer. 'If you knew how much money he makes out of the contractors alone! Nobody's safe.'

Then he took me to dinner, having decided after a lot of fuss that I should share the lodge with him and board with his mother.

'She's a bit stingy,' he said. 'But she won't charge you much.'

His mother's quarters were very cramped and tiny. The whole place, hall and entrance-lobby included, was cluttered up with furniture brought from the big house after the sale, all old-fashioned mahogany stuff. Mrs. Cheprakov, a very stout middle-aged woman with slanting Chinese eyes, sat in a large armchair by the window, knitting a stocking. She greeted me ceremoniously.

Cheprakov introduced me. 'This is Mr. Poloznev, Mother. He's going to work here.'

'Are you a gentleman?' she asked in a strange, disagreeable voice. It sounded as if there was fat gurgling in her throat.

'Yes.'

'Then please sit down.'

It was a poor sort of dinner—only sour curd pie and milk soup. Our hostess kept winking in a curious way, first one eye, then the other. She spoke and ate, but she was somehow dead all over and even seemed to smell like a corpse. There was only a faint flicker of life, a dim feeling that she was the lady of the manor, had owned serfs and been a general's wife—'my lady' to the servants. When these pitiful embers flared up for a second she would say to her son, 'Now Ivan, that's no way to hold your knife'.

Or she took a deep breath and addressed me in the affected style of a society hostess trying to amuse a guest.

'We sold the estate, you know. A pity of course, we're so fond of it, but Dolzhikov has promised to make Ivan stationmaster at Dubechnya, so we shan't be leaving. We shall live at the station, which is as good as living on our estate. The engineer's so kind. He's very good-looking too, don't you think?'

Not long ago the Chepraklovs had lived in style, but all that changed when the general died. Mrs. Cheprakov quarrelled with the neighbours, became involved in lawsuits, stopped paying her managers and work-people, and was terrified of being robbed. In ten years or so Dubechnya had changed out of all recognition.

Behind the big house was an old garden, gone to seed and choked with weeds and bushes. I strolled along the terrace, which was still firm and beautiful, and saw through a french window a room with a parquet floor, probably the drawing-room. There was an old-fashioned upright piano and there were engravings in broad mahogany frames—that was all. Nothing was left of the old flower-beds except peonies and poppies that raised their white and crimson heads above the grass. Young maples and elms, nibbled by cows, grew over the paths, reaching out and crowding each other. The garden was densely overgrown and seemed impenetrable, but this was only near the house, where poplars and pines still stood with old lime-trees all of an age, sole relics of former avenues. Farther out the garden was cleared for mowing and was less dank, one's eyes and mouth were not assailed by cobwebs, and now and then a breeze stirred. The farther you went, the more it opened up. Here cherries and plums grew wild. There were spreading apple-trees disfigured by props and canker, and pear-trees too spindly, it seemed, to be pear-trees at all. This part of the garden was let to women who sold fruit in town and was guarded from thieves and starlings by a sort of village idiot who lived there in a shack.

The garden opened up into a real meadow sloping down to a river overgrown with green reeds and willow. There was a milldam with a deep millpond full of fish. An angry roar came from the small thatched mill and there was a furious croaking of frogs. An occasional ripple ruffled water smooth as glass, and water-lilies quivered, stirred by playful fish. Beyond the stream was the small village of Dubechnya. The still, blue millpond was inviting with its cool, quiet promise.

And now all this—millpond, mill, delightful riverside—belonged to the engineer.

So I started my new job. I received and forwarded telegrams, filled in returns and made fair copies of indents, complaints and statements sent to the office by foremen and workmen who could hardly write their own names. Most of the time I did nothing but walk up and down waiting for telegrams or got a boy to sit in the lodge and strolled in the garden till he ran to tell me that the machine was clicking. I ate at Mrs. Cheprakov's. Meat was seldom served, we had nothing but milk dishes, and Wednesdays and Fridays were fast days when special pink 'lenten' plates were used. Mrs. Cheprakov had this trick of always winking and I felt uneasy in her presence.

There was little enough work in the lodge for one, so Cheprakov just dozed or went duck-shooting by the millpond. He got drunk every evening in the village or at the station and before going to bed stared in the mirror and shouted, 'Hallo, Ivan Cheprakov'.

When drunk he turned very pale and kept rubbing his hands and giving a neighing laugh. He used to strip and run round the fields naked for a lark. He ate flies and said that they had quite a nice tang to them.

IV

One day after dinner he dashed breathlessly into the lodge.

'You'd better run along,' he said. 'Your sister's here.'

I went out. And there by the porch of the big house was a hired cab from town. My sister had arrived with Anyuta Blagovo and a man in a military tunic, whom I recognized when I came nearer as Anyuta's brother, an army doctor.

'We've come out for a picnic,' he said. 'Hope you don't mind.'

Anyuta and my sister wanted to ask how I was getting on, but neither spoke. They just looked at me and I said nothing too. They saw that I disliked the place and tears came into my sister's eyes. Anyuta Blagovo blushed. We went into the garden with the doctor leading the way.

'What air!' he said ecstatically. 'Goodness me, what air!'

He still looked like a student. He walked and talked like a student and his grey eyes—like the best type of student's—had a lively, frank, open look. Beside his tall, good-looking sister he seemed frail and thin. His beard was thin, as was his voice—a thin, but quite pleasant tenor. He had been with his regiment, but was home on leave now and said he was going to St. Petersburg in the autumn to take a higher degree. He was a family man with a wife and three children, having married young, as a second-year student. It was said in town that his family life was unhappy and that he was separated from his wife.

'What's the time?' My sister was worried. 'We'd better go back early. Daddy said I could come to see my brother on condition that I was back by six.'

'Oh, confound Daddy!' sighed the doctor.

I put on the samovar and we sat and had tea on a rug in front of the terrace of the big house. The doctor knelt down and drank out of his saucer and said he called this sheer bliss. Then Cheprakov fetched a key and opened the french windows and we all went inside. The house was gloomy and mysterious and smelt of fungus. Our footsteps sounded hollow, as if there was a cellar beneath the floor. The doctor stood by the piano and touched the keys, which gave back a faint, quavering chord, a bit fuzzy, but melodious. He tried his voice and sang a song, frowning and tapping his foot impatiently whenever he hit a dead key. My sister forgot about going home and walked up and down excitedly.

'Oh, I'm so happy,' she said. 'So very, very happy.'

She sounded surprised, not believing, it seemed, that she could be gay like other people. I had never seen her so happy in all my life. She even looked prettier. She was not much to look at in profile because her nose and mouth seemed to jut out, and she always looked as if she was blowing. But she had lovely dark eyes, a pale, very delicate complexion and a kind, sad look that was most appealing. When she spoke she seemed attractive, even beautiful. We both took after our mother, being broad-shouldered, strong and tough. But her pallor came from ill health. She was always coughing and I sometimes caught in her eyes the look of a person who is seriously ill, but for some reason doesn't want you to know it.

There was something childlike and naïve in her gaiety now, as if childhood's joys, suppressed and stifled by our strict upbringing, had suddenly awoken inside her and found an outlet.

When evening came on and the horses were brought round, my sister grew quiet and seemed to shrivel up. She got into the carriage and sat down looking like a prisoner in the dock.

When they had all gone and the place was quiet, it struck me that Anyuta Blagovo had not said a word to me all day.

'A wonderful girl,' I thought. 'Wonderful!'

St. Peter's Fast began and we ate only lenten food. My idleness and the uncertainty of my position had brought on a physical depression. Dissatisfied with myself, listless and hungry, I drifted round the estate. I was only waiting till I was in the right mood to leave.

Late one afternoon when Radish was with us in the lodge, Dolzhikov unexpectedly came in, very sunburnt and covered with grey dust. Having spent three days on his section of the line, he had just come to Dubechnya by rail and walked over from the station to see us. A cab was coming from town to fetch him, and while waiting for it he went round the grounds with his manager, giving orders in a loud voice. Then he sat in our lodge for a whole hour writing letters. While he was there some telegrams came for him and he tapped out the answers himself. We three stood to attention and said nothing.

'What a mess!' he said with a scornful glance at the records. 'I'm moving the office to the station in a fortnight, but what to do with you lot I really don't know.'

'I do try, sir,' said Cheprakov.

'So I've noticed.'

The engineer looked at me.

'All you're good for,' he went on, 'is drawing your salary. You think because you have friends in the right places you can hope for a quick shove up the ladder. Well, no one gets a leg up from me. No one ever put himself out on my account. Before I ran the railway I was an engine-driver and I worked in Belgium as a common greaser. Hey, you there, what are you doing here?' he asked, turning to Radish. 'Boozing with this lot, I suppose.'

For some reason he called all working men 'You there'. As for me and Cheprakov, he despised our sort and called us a lot of drunken swine behind our backs. He was harsh with all his low-grade clerks, fining them and coolly giving them notice without saying why.

In the end his carriage arrived. As he left he said that he was going to sack the lot of us in a fortnight and called his manager an oaf, then sprawled back in his carriage and bowled off to town.

'Look here, Andrew, why don't you give me a job?' I asked Radish.

'All right.'

So we set off for town together. When we had left the station and manor-house some way behind, I asked why he had just been to Dubechnya.

'Firstly, some of my lads are working on the railway, and secondly, I went to pay the general's widow her interest. I borrowed fifty roubles off her last year and now I pay her a rouble a month.'

The painter stopped and seized me by a button.

'The way I look at it is this, mate,' he went on. 'Anyone, worker or gent, who lends money at interest, is a bad man and the truth is not in him.'

Gaunt, pale, terrifying, Radish closed his eyes and shook his head.

'Grass doth wither,' he proclaimed with a sagacious air, 'iron doth rust and lies do rot the soul. Lord, save us sinners.'

V

Radish was an impractical man. He hadn't much sense. He took on more jobs than he could handle, then lost his head when it came to settling up and so was almost always out of pocket. He did painting, glazing, wall-papering and even took on roof work, and I remember him running round for three days looking for roofers—all for the sake of some twopenny-halfpenny job. He was a first-class workman and had been known to earn as much as ten roubles a day. He might have been pretty well off but for this urge to be a boss at all costs and call himself a contractor.

He was paid by the job, but he paid me and the other men daily—between seventy copecks and one rouble. In hot, dry weather we did outside jobs, mainly roof-painting. I was new to this and my feet burnt as if I was walking on hot bricks, but if I put on felt boots they got even hotter. That was only at the start. Later on I became used to it and it all went like a dream. I was living among people who had to work. They could not avoid it. They slaved away like cart-horses, often without seeing the moral purpose of work and never once bringing the word 'work' into their conversation. Among them I felt a bit of a cart-horse myself. What I was doing had to be done, I felt, and there was no getting out of it. This feeling obsessed me more and more, making life easier and removing all my doubts.

At the start everything was fresh and absorbing, as if I had been reborn. I could sleep on the ground or go barefoot, a most pleasant sensation. I could stand in an ordinary crowd without anyone minding, and when a cab horse fell down in the street I ran and helped to pull it up without caring if my clothes got dirty. Above all, I was earning my own living and was not a burden to anyone else.

Painting roofs, especially with our own materials, was thought a very rewarding job, so even skilled men like Radish did not turn up their noses at this rough, boring work. Walking on a roof in shorts, he looked like a stork with his scraggy purple legs. I often heard him heave a sigh as he plied the brush and said, 'Woe, woe unto us sinners!'

He was as much at home on a roof as on the ground, being wonderfully nimble, though ill and white as a corpse. He painted the dome and cupolas of a church just like a young man, using no scaffolding—

only ladders and rope. It was rather frightening to see him standing up there so far from the ground, stretching himself to his full height and declaring for the benefit of some person unknown, 'Grass doth wither, iron doth rust and lies do rot the soul.'

Sometimes he ruminated and answered his thoughts aloud. 'Anything's possible. Yes, anything's possible.'

When I went home from work, everyone sitting about on benches near gateways—shop assistants, errand-boys and their masters—pursued me with jeers and abuse. This upset me at first and seemed quite monstrous.

'Better-than-nothing!' I heard on all sides. 'Where's yer paint-brush, mister?'

No one treated me more unkindly than those who not so long ago had themselves been working men, earning their living by unskilled labour. Among the shops I might have water thrown over me accidentally on purpose when I went past the ironmonger's, and someone once actually hurled a stick at me. One time a white-haired old fish merchant barred my way.

'I don't care about you, you idiot,' he said with a dirty look. 'It's your father I'm sorry for.'

For some reason my friends were embarrassed to meet me. Some thought me a freak or clown. Others felt sorry for me. Others again did not know how to treat me, and it was hard to make them out.

One afternoon I ran across Anyuta Blagovo in a side road near Great Dvoryansky Street. I was on my way to work, carrying two long brushes and a bucket of paint. Anyuta flared up when she saw me.

'Pray don't bow to me in the street . . .' she said in an edgy, severe, quavering voice without offering to shake hands, her eyes suddenly bright with tears. 'If you must go in for this sort of thing, you must . . . I don't care. But kindly keep out of my way.'

I had left Great Dvoryansky Street now and was boarding in the suburb of Makarikha with my old nanny Karpovna, a kind-hearted but lugubrious old woman who always thought that something awful was going to happen, feared all dreams without exception, and even saw bad omens in the bees and wasps that flew into her room. The fact that I had become a worker boded no good, or so she thought.

'You're finished,' she used to say, shaking her head sadly. 'Done for.'

She shared her cottage with her adopted son, the butcher Prokofy, a hulking, clumsy fellow of about thirty with red hair and a bristly moustache. If we met in the hall he never spoke, but moved aside respectfully, and when he was drunk he gave me a military salute. When he had supper in the evening I could hear him grunting and sighing through the board partition as he downed glass after glass of vodka.

'Ma,' he would call in a low voice.

'Well?' Karpovna would answer. Her love for her adopted son knew no bounds. 'What is it, sonny?'

'I'll do the decent thing by you, Ma. All this earthly life I'll keep you in your old age in this here vale of tears and when you die I'll pay for your funeral, honest I will.'

I was up before dawn each day and went to bed early. We decorators ate heartily and slept soundly. But for some reason my heart used to beat loudly at night. I did not quarrel with my mates. Swear words, foul oaths and things like 'damn your eyes!' or 'rot your guts!' were all in the day's work. Still, we got on well together. The lads thought I was some sort of religious crank and pulled my leg good-humouredly. They declared that even my own father had disowned me, and then told me that they rarely put their nose inside a church and that many of them had not been to confession in ten years. They tried to justify such slackness by saying that painters were the black sheep of the human flock.

The men thought highly of me and respected me. What they obviously liked was that I neither smoked nor drank, and led a quiet, orderly life, but they were a little shocked when I would not steal linseed oil with them or join them in wheedling tips from the people that we worked for. Stealing employers' oil and paint was common practice among house-painters—to them it was not really stealing at all. Funnily enough, even someone as upright as Radish always took some whiting and oil when he finished work, and even respectable old men, with houses of their own in Makarikha, thought nothing of asking for a tip. It was a sorry, shameful business when the boys were starting or finishing a job and all rushed off to crawl to some little worm and thank him humbly for the ten copecks that he handed them.

They behaved like sly courtiers with the people whose houses they painted and almost every day I was reminded of Shakespeare's Polonius.

'Looks like rain,' a client would say with a glance at the sky.

'Oh yes sir, definitely,' the painters would agree.

'I don't know though, those aren't rain clouds. Perhaps it won't rain after all.'

'Oh no sir. Definitely not.'

Behind their clients' backs the attitude was usually ironical. For instance, if they saw a gentleman sitting on his balcony with a newspaper, they would say, 'Sits reading the paper, but I bet he's got nothing to eat.'

I never visited my family. When I returned from work I often found short, anxious notes from my sister about Father. One day he had been unusually thoughtful at dinner and had eaten nothing. Or he had fallen over. Or had locked himself in his room and not come out for a long time. This sort of news disturbed me and stopped me sleeping. Sometimes I even walked past our house in Great Dvoryansky Street at night, peering into the dark windows and trying to make out whether all was well at home. My sister came to see me on Sundays, but furtively, pretending to be visiting Nanny instead of me. If she came into my room she was always very pale, with tear-stained eyes, and began crying at once.

'Father will never get over it,' she said. 'If, God forbid, anything happens to him, you'll have it on your conscience all your life. It's terrible, Misail. For our mother's sake, mend your ways, I beg you.'

'My dear good sister,' I said. 'How can I mend my ways when I know I'm obeying my conscience? Try and understand.'

'I know you're obeying your conscience. But couldn't you do it a bit differently so as not to annoy people?'

'Oh dearie me!' the old woman would sigh in the other room. 'You're done for. Bad times are coming, my dears, bad times indeed.

VI

One Sunday Dr. Blagovo suddenly visited me. He was wearing a military tunic over a silk shirt, and patent leather top-boots.

'I've come to see you,' he began, pumping my hand like a student. 'I hear of you every day and I've kept meaning to come over for a "heart to heart". This town is no end of a bore. They're all half dead and there's no one to talk to. My God, isn't it hot!' he went on, taking off his tunic and standing there in his silk shirt. 'Let's have a talk about things, old man.'

I felt bored myself. For a long while I had wanted to pass the time of day with someone other than a house-painter and I was really glad to see him.

'To start with, I'm completely on your side,' he said, sitting on my bed. 'I thoroughly respect your way of life. No one appreciates you in this town. But what else can you expect? As you know yourself, they're a prize collection of gargoyles here, with very few exceptions. But I saw what you were like at once, at that picnic. You're a thoroughly honest, decent, high-minded person.

'I respect you,' he went on ecstatically, 'and I'm greatly honoured to shake your hand. No one makes a sharp break like you without first going through a complex emotional experience. If you are to carry on as you do, trying to live up to your beliefs all the time, you have to put your heart and soul into the thing day after day. Now tell me this for a start. If you devoted all this will-power, effort and potential to something else—turning yourself into a great scholar or artist, for instance—don't you think that would give your life greater depth and scope and make it more productive in every way?'

We talked, and when the subject of manual work cropped up I expressed myself as follows. 'The strong must not enslave the weak and the minority must not be parasites on the majority or vampires forever sucking their blood. In fact everyone without exception—strong and weak, rich and poor—should do his bit equally in the struggle for existence.' This brought me to the point that manual work is the greatest leveller of all if everyone is made to do his bit.

'So your idea is that every single person should do manual work?' asked the doctor.

'Yes.'

'Well, let's suppose all of us, including the élite—the thinkers and great scholars—play our part in the struggle for existence and spend our time breaking stones or painting roofs. Don't you think that might be a serious threat to progress?'

'Where's the threat?' I asked. 'Surely progress consists in good works and obeying the moral law. If you don't enslave anyone, if you aren't a burden to anyone, what more progress do you need?'

'But look here!' Blagovo exploded, jumping to his feet. 'Just look here! If a snail in its shell spends its time trying to lead a better life, fiddling around with moral laws—is that what you call progress?'

'Why "fiddling around"?' I was offended. 'If you stop making your neighbour feed you, clothe you, carry you about and defend you from your enemies, surely that *is* progress in the context of a life built entirely on slavery. I think that's real progress, perhaps the only kind man can have or needs.'

'Mankind has infinite scope for progress in this world. To talk about the sort of progress which we "can have"—progress limited by our needs or by short-term theories—well, that's odd to say the least.'

'If, as you make out, the bounds of progress are infinite, its aims must be vague,' I said. 'Fancy living without knowing definitely what you're living for!'

'Have it your own way. But my ignorance is less of a bore than your knowledge. I'm climbing a ladder called progress, civilization, culture. I'm going higher and higher and I don't know exactly where I'm heading, but really, this wonderful ladder alone makes life worth living. Now you know what you're living for. You want one lot of people to stop enslaving another, you want the artist and the man who mixes his colours to eat the same food. But that side of life's so dim, grey and commonplace, can't you see? Can't you see it's disgusting to live for that alone? If one lot of insects enslaves another, to hell with them! They can eat each other alive for all I care. We shouldn't be thinking about them at all—they'll all die and rot, won't they, however hard you try to save them from slavery? We should be thinking about the great Unknown that awaits man in the distant future.'

Blagovo argued hotly, but had something quite different on his mind, I could see that.

'Your sister can't be coming,' he said, with a look at his watch. 'She was at our place yesterday and said she was coming out here. You keep on and on about slavery,' he continued. 'But that's a special problem and mankind always solves such problems gradually, in due course.'

So we got on to the gradual approach. I said that every man decided for himself whether to do good or evil without waiting for mankind to evolve a solution gradually.

'What's more,' I said, 'your gradual approach cuts both ways. The gradual evolution of humane ideas has gone hand in hand with the gradual growth of other ideas of quite a different kind. Serfdom has gone, but capitalism is spreading. Ideas of freedom are enjoying a great vogue, but now, as in the days of the Mongols, the majority still feeds, clothes and protects the minority, while remaining hungry, unclothed and unprotected itself.

'The system fits in beautifully with any trend or current you like, because the art of enslavement is being gradually perfected as well. True, we don't flog our servants in the stables any more, but we do evolve new refinements of slavery—or at least we're pretty good at finding justifications for it in individual instances. Ideas are all very well, but if now, at the end of the nineteenth century, it should become possible to foist our more unpleasant bodily functions onto the workers as well, then foist away we would. After which of course we should defend ourselves by saying that if "the élite of thinkers and great scholars" were to waste their precious time on these functions, progress might be seriously threatened.'

At this point my sister arrived. She seemed agitated and alarmed at seeing the doctor and said at once that she must go home to Father.

'Look here, Cleopatra,' urged Blagovo, pressing both hands to his heart, 'your dear Daddy won't burst if you spend half an hour or so with me and your brother.'

He was completely natural with us and his high spirits were infectious. After a moment's thought my sister laughed and suddenly cheered up as on the day of the picnic. We went into the fields and lay down on the grass to go on with our talk, looking at the town, where all the west-facing windows seemed bright gold because the sun was setting.

After this Blagovo always appeared when my sister came to see me and they greeted each other as if they had met in my room by accident. While I argued with the doctor, my sister listened with a happy, enthralled, interested look and seemed greatly affected. I felt that a new world was gradually opening up before her, a world that she had never even dreamt of and was now trying to fathom. When the doctor was not there she was always quiet and sad, and when she sat and cried on my bed these days she never told me why.

In August Radish told us to prepare to leave for the railway line. A couple of days before we received our 'marching orders', Father came to see me. He sat down, without looking at me, and slowly wiped his red face. Then he took a copy of the local *Herald* out of his pocket. Slowly, emphasizing each word, he read out an item about the son of the manager of the State Bank who was the same age as me and had been made a head of department in the treasury office.

'And look at you,' he said, folding the newspaper. 'Pauper! Tramp! Scoundrel! Even working men and farm labourers get an education so they can make their way in life. And you, a Poloznev, despite your distinguished, illustrious ancestors, are heading for the rubbish dump. But I didn't come here to talk to you, I've washed my hands of you,' he went on in a strangled voice, standing up. 'I've come to ask where your sister is, you scoundrel. She went out after dinner, but it's nearly eight and she still isn't back. She goes out quite often now without a word to me. She's less respectful than she was, and I put that down to your vicious, evil influence. Where is she?'

He was carrying the umbrella that I knew so well. I was at my wits' end and jumped to attention, feeling like a schoolboy and expecting Father to hit me, but he saw me looking at the umbrella and that probably stopped him.

'Live as you please,' he said. 'I shall not give you my blessing.'

'Oh dearie dearie me,' my old nanny muttered behind the door. 'You poor unhappy boy! No good will come of this, I feel it in my bones.'

I worked on the railway line. It rained non-stop all through August and it was damp and cold. They could not get the crops in, and on the large farms which used reaping machines the wheat was not in stooks, but just lay about in heaps. I remember those miserable heaps growing darker and darker every day and the grain sprouting in them. It was hard work. The torrential rain ruined everything that we managed to do. They would not let us eat or sleep in the station buildings, so we sheltered in filthy, damp dugouts, where the navvies had lived earlier in the summer. At night I could not sleep for the cold and the woodlice crawling over my face and arms. When we worked near the bridges a whole gang of navvies would visit us in the evenings, just to beat up the painters, which was their idea of fun. They beat us up and stole our brushes. They tried to provoke us to fight by ruining our work, for instance by daubing the signal-boxes with green paint.

To make matters worse, Radish took to paying us very irregularly. All the painting work on this sector had been put in the hands of a contractor. That contractor sub-contracted to someone else, who subcontracted further to Radish for a consideration of about twenty per cent. The work paid badly anyway, quite apart from the rain. Time was wasted and we could not get on with the job, but Radish had undertaken to pay the men daily. The hungry painters nearly beat him up. They called him a bloodsucking swindler, a regular Judas, while he, poor fellow, just sighed, lifted up his hands in despair and kept going to Mrs. Cheprakov for more money.

VII

Autumn came—dark, wet and muddy. Work was hard to come by and I sometimes sat at home doing nothing for three days on end, or took on odd jobs outside the decorating line like shifting earth for ballast at twenty copecks a day. Dr. Blagovo had gone off to St. Petersburg and my sister had stopped coming to see me. Radish was at home, ill in bed and thinking that every day would be his last.

The general mood was autumnal too. As a worker I saw only the seamy side of town life, and perhaps that is why I could not help making discoveries nearly every day that drove me quite frantic. It turned out that fellow citizens of mine who had never impressed me one way or the other before, or who had seemed quite decent folk, were mean and cruel and up to all kinds of dirty tricks. We working men were duped, swindled, made to wait for hours in cold vestibules or kitchens, insulted and treated with the utmost rudeness.

That autumn I papered the reading-room and two other rooms at the club. I was paid seven copecks a piece, but was told to sign for twelve and refused.

'No more of your lip, you blackguard, or I'll bash your dirty face in,' said a distinguished-looking gentleman with gold-rimmed spectacles, who must have been on the committee.

A servant whispered that I was the son of Poloznev the architect and he looked ashamed of himself and blushed, but regained his composure at once.

'Oh, to hell with him!' he said.

The shops palmed off their rotten meat on us workers—and their stale flour and used tea-leaves. We were shoved around by the police in church. In hospital the nurses and junior medical staff sponged on us, and if we could not afford to bribe them they got their own back by dishing up our food on filthy plates. Feeling entitled to treat us like dirt, the most junior post-office clerk shouted roughly and rudely at us. ('You! Just you wait! Where do you think you're going?') Even the yard-dogs were hostile and rushed at us with extra viciousness. But what really shocked me in my new situation was the blatant unfairness of everything—what the common people mean when they say that someone is 'lost to shame'. Few days passed without some piece of sharp practice. The tradesmen who sold us linseed-oil, our bosses, the other workmen and even our clients—all were on the fiddle. We had no rights—there was no question of that, needless to say—and always had to ask for our wages like beggars, standing cap in hand at the back door.

One evening I was papering a room next to the reading-room in the club and was about to knock off when Mr. Dolzhikov's daughter came in carrying a bundle of books.

I bowed.

'Oh, good evening,' she said, recognizing me at once and holding out her hand. 'How nice to see you.'

She smiled and stared, fascinated and puzzled, at my smock, paste-bucket, and wallpaper spread on the floor. I was a little taken aback and she was rather ill at ease too.

'Excuse me staring like this,' she said. 'I've heard so much about you, especially from Dr. Blagovo—he's quite crazy about you. I've met your sister too—such a dear, sweet girl, but I just couldn't make her see that there's nothing dreadful about you leading the simple life. Far from it, you've become the most interesting man in town.'

She took another look at the paste-bucket and wallpaper and went on.

'I asked Dr. Blagovo to put me in touch with you, but he must have forgotten or been too busy. Anyway, we have met before. Why not look me up some time? I'd be most obliged if you would, I'd so much like to talk to you. I'm not hard to get on with,' she said, holding out her hand, 'and I hope you'll feel at home with me. Father's away in St. Petersburg.'

She went into the reading-room, her dress rustling. I went home and could not sleep for a long time.

That cheerless autumn some good soul, obviously wanting to help me out a bit, sent me tea, lemons, cakes and roast grouse from time to time. Karpovna said that these things were always brought by a soldier, but who sent them she didn't know. The soldier would ask if I was well. Did I have a proper meal every day? Had I warm clothing? Then again, when the frosts came the soldier brought a soft knitted scarf while I was out. The scarf had a faint, delicate scent and I guessed who my good fairy was. It was lily-of-the-valley, Anyuta Blagovo's favourite scent.

As winter approached there was more work to be had and things were looking up. Radish revived and we did a job together in the cemetery chapel, preparing the icon-stand for gilding. It was a clean, quiet job—'a piece of cake', the men called it. You could get through plenty of work in a day and time sped past unnoticed. There was no swearing, laughter or loud talk. The place itself made us want to be quiet and well-behaved, and inspired calm, serious thoughts. We stood or sat, absorbed in our work, still as statues. There was a deathly hush, as befits a cemetery, and a dropped tool or sputtering icon-lamp gave out a harsh, hollow sound that made us look round. After a long silence there might be a sound like buzzing bees—the slow, soft chanting of the requiem for a dead baby at the back of the church. The artist—he was painting a dove with stars round it on a cupola—

would start whistling softly and then suddenly stop, remembering where he was. 'Anything's possible, anything at all,' Radish would sigh in answer to his thoughts. Or bells tolled slowly and lugubriously above our heads and the painters said that it must be for a rich man's funeral.

I spent my days in this stillness in the twilight of the church, and during the long evenings I played billiards or went to the theatre and sat in the gallery, wearing the new woollen suit that I had bought with my earnings. Concerts and performances had already begun at the Azhogins', and now Radish painted scenery on his own. He told me all about the plays and *tableaux vivants* that he saw there and I listened enviously. I longed to attend rehearsals, but could not bring myself to go to the Azhogins'.

A week before Christmas Dr. Blagovo came round. Again we argued and spent the evenings playing billiards. He took his coat off to play, unbuttoning his shirt at the front and somehow generally trying to look like a thoroughgoing rake. He did not drink much, but made a great to-do about it, contriving to spend twenty roubles an evening in a cheap dive like the 'Volga'.

My sister took to visiting me again. She and the doctor both seemed surprised to run across each other, but her happy, apologetic air showed that these meetings were no accident.

'Look here, why do you never go and see Masha Dolzhikov?' the doctor asked me as we were playing billiards one evening. 'You've no idea what a clever girl she is—so charming, natural, kind-hearted.'

I described the reception that I had had from her father in the spring.

'Don't be silly,' the doctor laughed. 'She's quite unlike her father, you know. Really, old boy, you mustn't hurt her feelings. Do call on her some time. How about us going along together tomorrow evening? What do you say?'

I let him talk me into it. Next evening I put on my new suit and set off with some trepidation to see Miss Dolzhikov. The footman no longer struck me as quite so high and mighty, nor did the furniture look so splendid as on the morning when I had come asking for a job. Miss Dolzhikov was expecting me and greeted me like an old friend with a firm, friendly handclasp. She was wearing a grey woollen dress with full sleeves. Her hair—we called the style 'dog's ears' when it came into vogue in our town a year later—was combed back from the temples onto her ears. It made her face seem broader, and this time

I thought that she looked very much like her father, who had a broad, ruddy face and an expression rather like a coachman's. She looked beautiful and elegant, but not particularly young—she seemed about thirty, though in fact she was no more than twenty-five.

'How nice of the doctor, I am grateful to him,' she said as she asked me to sit down. 'You wouldn't have come but for him. I'm bored to death. Father's gone away and left me on my own and I don't know what to do with myself in this town.'

Then she asked where I was working, how much I earned and where I lived.

'You manage on your wages then?' she asked.

'Yes.'

'Lucky man,' she sighed. 'I think all the evil in this world comes from idleness, boredom and having nothing to fill your mind. What else can you expect if you're used to sponging on other people? Don't think I'm just saying this for effect. Being rich is a dull, disagreeable business, I really mean it. "Make to yourselves friends of the mammon of unrighteousness,"—they say that because there's no such thing as righteous wealth and never can be.'

She gave the furniture a cold, solemn look, as if wanting to count it, and went on.

'Comfort and luxury can cast a magic spell. They gradually drag you down, even if you're strong-willed. Father and I once led ordinary, humble lives, but look at us now! Isn't it fantastic!' She shrugged her shoulders. 'We run through twenty thousand a year. In the provinces!'

'One's forced to look on comfort and luxury as the privilege of capital and education,' I said. 'Now I think that decent amenities could go with any kind of work, even the hardest and dirtiest. Your father's rich, but as he says himself, he had to put in time as an engine-driver and a common greaser.'

She smiled and shook her head doubtfully.

'Father sometimes eats bread dipped in kvass,' she said. 'It's a fad of his.'

The door-bell rang and she stood up.

'Rich and educated people should work like everyone else,' she went on. 'And any comforts should be shared out equally. We should do away with privilege. Oh well, that's quite enough clever talk. Tell me something amusing. Tell me about your decorators. What are they like? Funny?'

The doctor came in and I started telling them about the decorators, but lack of practice cramped my style and I spoke earnestly and lifelessly, like an ethnographer. The doctor also told a few funny stories of his own about working-class life—staggering, weeping, kneeling and even lying on the floor to imitate a drunk. It was as good as a play. Masha watched him and laughed till she cried. Then he played the piano and sang in his pleasant, light tenor while Masha stood by and chose the songs, putting him right when he made a mistake.

'You sing too, I hear,' I said to her.

' "Sing too"!' The doctor was horrified. 'She's a wonderful singer—a real artist—and you talk about her "singing too". Dear me, we *have* put our foot in it!'

'I did study seriously once,' she answered me. 'But I've given it up now.'

Sitting on a low stool, she spoke of her life in St. Petersburg and impersonated some well-known singers, mimicking their voices and styles. She did a sketch of the doctor in her album and then one of me. She drew rather badly, but both came out good likenesses. She laughed, joked and grimaced charmingly. This suited her better than talking about the mammon of unrighteousness and I felt that there had been something second-hand and not quite sincere in her recent remarks about riches and comfort. She was a superb comic actress. I found myself comparing her with our local young women. Even Anyuta Blagovo, though beautiful and stately, was not in the same class. There was a big gap between them—one might have been a fine garden rose and the other a wild briar.

The three of us had supper together. Masha and the doctor drank red wine and champagne, then went on to coffee and brandy. They clinked glasses and drank to friendship, intelligence, progress and freedom, without getting drunk. They only became red in the face and kept laughing over nothing till the tears ran down their cheeks. Not wanting to seem a killjoy, I had some wine too.

'Really brilliant, gifted people know how to live,' said Masha. 'They go their own way. But average people—people like me—don't know anything and can't do anything on their own. All they can do is spot some significant social movement and float with the stream.'

'Don't tell me you can spot something non-existent,' said the doctor.

'Non-existent? When we're just too blind to see!'

'You think so, do you? Trends are an invention of modern literature. We haven't any.'

They began arguing.

'We haven't any significant social trends and never have had,' shouted the doctor. 'There's no end to the things modern literature has invented. It's even dreamt up certain mysterious intellectuals who toil away in our countryside, though you can search our villages high and low without finding more than the occasional clodhopper in a jacket or black frock-coat who can't write a three-letter word without making four spelling mistakes. Cultural life in Russia hasn't even begun. Things are no better than they were five hundred years ago, for we're still savages and louts, all of us—nonentities! Trends and movements there may be, but what tenth-rate, dismal stuff—all tied up with some dirty little racket! Don't tell me you take that sort of thing seriously! If you feel you've spotted a significant trend and mean to follow it by devoting your life to the latest crazes, such as freeing insects from slavery or abstaining from beef rissoles, then I can only congratulate you, madam. What we need is study, study and yet more study. And significant social trends can wait a bit. We're not really up to that sort of thing yet and quite honestly we're out of our depth with it.'

'You may be, but I'm not,' said Masha. 'God, you are a bore this evening!'

'Our job is to study, I tell you. We must try to amass as much knowledge as we can because important social trends and knowledge go together. And man's future happiness can come only from knowledge. Here's to learning!'

'One thing's quite clear—we must somehow change our lives,' said Masha after a moment's thought. 'Life hasn't been worth living so far. Let's not talk about it.'

The cathedral clock struck two as we left.

'Do you like her?' asked the doctor. 'She's splendid, isn't she?'

On Christmas Day we had dinner with Masha and then went to see her almost every day during the holidays. We were her only visitors —she was right when she said that the doctor and I were the only people she knew in town. We talked most of the time. Sometimes the doctor brought a book or magazine and read to us. Actually he was the first educated man I had ever met. How well informed he was I cannot judge, but he was always bringing out things he knew, wanting others to share them. On medical subjects he was quite different from any of the local doctors. It was his freshness and originality that struck one somehow and I felt he had it in him to become a real scholar if he wanted. He was probably the only person with any real influence on me at that time. Meeting him and reading the books that he lent me, I felt more and more the need for knowledge to inspire my cheerless labours. I found it odd that I had once not known, say, that the world was made up of sixty elements, or what oil and paint consisted of—odd too that I had somehow managed without this knowledge. The doctor's friendship was good for my character as well. We were always arguing. I usually stuck to my guns, but thanks to him I came to see that I didn't know everything, and tried to work out principles of the utmost strictness so that the voice of my conscience should be clear and save me from woolly-mindedness.

The doctor may have been the best and most cultivated man in town, but he was far from perfect all the same. There was something a little crude and brash about his manners, his argumentativeness, his bland tenor voice and even his general friendliness. When he took off his coat and went about in his silk shirt or threw the waiter a tip in a restaurant, it always struck me that there was something pretty barbarous about him, culture or no culture.

Early in the new year, he left one morning to go back to St. Petersburg. After dinner my sister called on me. She did not take off her fur coat and cap, and just sat there not saying anything, very pale, staring fixedly before her. She was feeling the cold and was clearly overwrought.

'You must have caught a chill,' I said.

Her eyes filled with tears and she stood up and went to see Karpovna without a word to me, as if I had offended her. A little later I heard her voice raised in bitter complaint.

'What have I lived for all this time, Nanny? What's the point? I've wasted my youth, haven't I? I've spent my best years keeping accounts, pouring tea, counting pennies and entertaining visitors. And I thought these were the most important things in life. Do understand, Nanny. I have needs like any other person, I want a bit of real life—and they've made me into a sort of housekeeper. Can't you see how awful it is!'

She hurled the keys into my room and they fell jingling to the floor. They were the keys of the sideboard, the kitchen cupboard, the cellar and the tea-caddy—keys my mother used to carry.

'Oh goodness gracious me!' The old woman was horrified. 'Holy saints above!'

On her way out my sister came into my room to pick up the keys. 'I'm sorry,' she said. 'I don't know what's come over me lately.'

VIII

Late one evening I came home from Masha's to find a young police inspector in my room. He wore a new uniform and was sitting at my table looking through a book.

'Ah, at last!' he said, standing up and stretching. 'This makes the third time I've been here. The Governor orders you to report to him tomorrow at 9 a.m. precisely. Without fail.'

He made me sign an undertaking to obey the Governor's order and left.

The inspector's late visit and this unexpected summons to the Governor thoroughly depressed me. Since early childhood I have been terrified of policemen, officers of the law and court officials, and I was as worried now as if I had really done something wrong. And I just could not sleep. Nanny and Prokofy could not sleep either—they were too upset. Nanny had earache too. She kept groaning and several times started to cry with pain. Hearing that I was awake, Prokofy came cautiously into my room with a lamp and sat down by the table.

'You need a spot of pepper vodka,' he said after a moment's thought. 'A drink never comes amiss in this vale of tears. A drop of that vodka in her ear would do Ma a power of good too.'

At about half-past two he got ready to fetch meat from the slaughter-house. I knew I should have no sleep before daybreak now, and joined him so as to kill time till nine o'clock. We walked with a lantern. His assistant Nikolka—a lad of thirteen with blue blotches on his face from frostbite, a fearful young tough from the look of him—drove after us in the sledge, urging on the horse in a husky voice.

'You'll be punished at the Governor's, bound to be,' Prokofy told me on the way. 'Governors, bishops, officers, doctors—they all have their own rules. To every trade its own tricks. But you don't toe your line at all and you won't get away with that.'

The slaughter-house was beyond the cemetery and so far I had seen it only from a distance. There were three gloomy sheds with a grey fence round them and when the wind came from that quarter on a hot summer day the stench was enough to choke you. We went into the yard, but it was too dark to see the sheds. I kept meeting horses and sledges, some empty, some loaded with meat. Men walked about with lanterns, swearing like troopers. Oaths no less foul came from Prokofy and Nikolka and the air rang with continuous swearing, coughing and the neighing of horses.

There was a smell of dung and carcasses. It was thawing and the snow was mixed up with mud and in the dark I felt I was walking in pools of blood.

We piled our sledge full of meat and made for the butcher's stall in the market. Dawn was breaking. Cooks with baskets and elderly women in cloaks passed by one after the other. Cleaver in hand, wearing a bloodstained white apron, Prokofy swore fearful oaths, crossed himself in the direction of the church, and bellowed for the whole market to hear that he was letting his meat go at cost price, or even at a loss. He gave short weight and short change, as the cooks could well see, but, deafened by his yells, they raised no objection beyond calling him a shark. He assumed picturesque poses, brandishing his terrible cleaver and giving a ferocious yell each time he crashed it down. I was afraid that he might really chop off someone's head or hand.

I spent the morning at the butcher's. When at last I went to the Governor's, my fur coat smelt of meat and blood and I felt as if someone had given me a spear and told me to go and kill a bear. I remember a tall staircase with a striped carpet and a young official in a tail-coat with shiny buttons silently motioning me towards a door with both hands and running to announce me. I went into a large reception-room. It was luxuriously appointed, but cold and tasteless. The bright yellow window-curtains and tall, narrow mirrors on the walls were particular eyesores. Governors might come and governors might go, but the furnishings clearly went on for ever.

The young official again motioned me to a door with both hands and I made my way towards a large green table. Behind it stood a general with the Order of St. Vladimir at his throat.

'I've asked you to come here, Mr. Poloznev . . .' he began, holding a letter and opening his mouth wide like the letter O. 'I've asked you to come here to give you the following information. Your worthy father has made written and oral application to the provincial marshal of nobility, asking him to send for you and point out the discrepancy between your behaviour and the rank of gentleman which you are privileged to hold. His Excellency Alexander Pavlovich rightly supposed that your behaviour might be a bad example. He was also aware that mere exhortation on his part might be inadequate and that serious official action was called for. He has therefore put before me his views about you in this letter. Those views I share.'

He said all this quietly and deferentially, holding himself erect as if I was his superior officer and looking at me with no trace of severity. His face was flabby, worn and wrinkled, there were bags under his eyes and his hair was dyed. From the look of him he might have been any age from forty to sixty.

'I trust,' he went on, 'that you will appreciate the tact of our worthy Alexander Pavlovich in consulting me privately and unofficially. I have also invited you here unofficially and am speaking to you not as Governor, but as one who sincerely respects your father. So pray change your way of life and return to the duties proper to your rank. Or else keep out of mischief by moving to some part of the country where you're unknown and can do what you like. Otherwise I shall have to take extreme measures.'

He stood there for half a minute in silence, looking at me open-mouthed.

'Are you a vegetarian?' he asked.

'No sir, I eat meat.'

He sat down and drew a document towards him. I bowed and left.

There was no point in going to work before dinner, so I went home to bed, but was unable to sleep because of a disagreeable, painful feeling brought on by the slaughter-house and my talk with the Governor. I waited till evening and went, gloomy and distraught, to see Masha. I told her about my visit to the Governor. She looked as if she could not believe her ears and suddenly gave a loud, happy, ringing laugh as only good-natured people can—people who see the funny side of things.

'What a story!' she said, laughing so much that she could hardly stand up and leaning over her table. 'If one could only tell it in St. Petersburg!'

IX

We often met these days—twice daily. She came to the cemetery almost every afternoon and read the inscriptions on crosses and tombs while she waited for me. Sometimes she came inside the church and stood by me watching me work. The silence, the painters' and gilders' simple craft, Radish's grave disquisitions and the fact that I looked just like the other men, worked like them in waistcoat and worn shoes, and was treated as one of them—she found all this new and appealing. Once when she was there the artist, up aloft painting a dove, shouted, 'Misail, let's have some of the white.'

I took him some white paint and as I climbed back down the rickety scaffolding she looked at me, smiling and moved to tears.

'What a sweet person you are,' she said.

I have a childhood memory of a green parrot belonging to a rich man who lived in our town, a beautiful bird that escaped from its cage and was about the town for a whole month, flying lazily from garden to garden, lonely and homeless. Masha reminded me of that bird.

'I've nowhere to go these days except the cemetery,' she told me with a laugh. 'I'm sick to death of this town. There's all that reciting, singing and childish prattle at the Azhogins'—I can't stand that stuff these days. Your sister keeps herself to herself, Miss Blagovo dislikes me for some reason and I don't like the theatre. So where else can I go?'

I visited her with my hands black, and smelling of paint and turpentine. That she liked. She also wanted me to wear my ordinary working kit whenever I went to see her. But those clothes cramped my drawing-room style and I felt as awkward as if I was in uniform, so I always put on my new suit when I was going to see her. That she disliked.

'You must admit you're not quite happy in your new role,' she said to me once. 'You feel awkward and ill at ease in workman's clothes. Tell me, isn't that because you're not sure of yourself—not satisfied? And the kind of work you've picked on, this painting bug you've got, does that really satisfy you either? I know paint makes things look nicer and last longer,' she laughed. 'But these things do belong to our local plutocrats, don't they? And they are luxuries, let's face it. Besides, you've often said yourself that everyone should earn his bread with his own hands. But you don't earn bread. You earn money. Why don't you stick to the literal meaning of what you say? Bread is what you should be earning—in fact you should be ploughing, sowing, reaping, threshing or doing something directly connected with farm work like looking after cows, digging or building log huts. . . .'

She opened a pretty little cupboard which stood near her desk.

'I want to tell you my secret,' she said. 'That's what all this has been leading up to. Look—here's my agricultural library, all about field-work, vegetable plots, orchards, cattle-yards and bee-keeping. I find it terribly interesting and I know the whole theory of it already. It's my dearest wish, my great dream, to go over to Dubechnya at the beginning of March. It's marvellous there! Fabulous! Don't you think so? The first year I'll just have a look round and get the feel of things, but the year after that I'm going to do a job of work myself

—going to "put my back into it". Father's promised to give me Dubechnya and I shall do just what I like there.'

Blushing, laughing and nearly crying with excitement, she mused aloud about her future life in Dubechnya and how interesting it would be. I envied her. March was near, the days were drawing out, and melting snow dripped from the roofs in the bright noon sun. There was a smell of spring and I longed to be in the country myself.

When she told me that she was moving to Dubechnya I saw myself being left alone in town and felt jealous of her book-cupboard and farming. I knew nothing about farming and I disliked it. I nearly told her that tilling the soil was a form of slavery, but I remembered that Father often said something of the sort and held my peace.

Lent began. Victor Dolzhikov the engineer, whose existence I had almost forgotten, turned up unexpectedly from St. Petersburg without so much as a warning telegram. When I arrived as usual that evening, he was walking up and down the drawing-room telling some story. With his well-scrubbed look and his hair cut short, he seemed ten years younger. Kneeling down, his daughter was taking boxes, scent-bottles and books out of suitcases and handing them to Paul, the man-servant. When I saw the engineer I couldn't help taking a step backward, but he held out both hands.

'Well, well, well! Look who's here!' he said, baring his firm, white, coachman's teeth in a smile. 'Glad to see you, Mr. Painter. Masha's told me all about it—she certainly has been singing your praises.'

He took my arm. 'I see your point and I'm all for it,' he went on. 'It's a sight more sensible and honest to be a decent workman than to churn out red tape by the yard and wear a ribbon in your hat. I worked in Belgium myself with these two hands and then spent two years as an engine-driver. . . .'

He wore a short jacket and had slippers on and walked about, rubbing his hands, with a slight roll as if he had gout. He hummed and purred to himself, and kept hugging himself with pleasure at being back home at last and having had a shower-bath, a thing he much enjoyed.

'Oh, I don't deny it,' he said to me at supper. 'You're all charming, delightful people, I don't deny it at all. But why is it, my dear sirs, that the moment you take up manual work or peasant welfare, somehow all it really boils down to is being some sort of religious crank? Don't tell me you don't belong to some such movement. You don't drink vodka for instance. That can only mean one thing—you're a nonconformist.'

I had a vodka to please him, and some wine too. We sampled cheeses, salami, pâté, pickles and sundry delicatessen brought by the engineer, and the wines that had arrived from abroad in his absence. The wine was excellent. The engineer managed to get his wine and cigars from abroad duty free and someone sent him caviare and dried sturgeon for nothing. His flat was rent free because the owner supplied paraffin to the railway. From their general air, he and his daughter had all the best things in life for the asking—free, gratis and for nothing.

I still went to see them, though I was less keen on going now. The engineer put me off—I never felt at ease with him. Those clear, innocent eyes were altogether too much and his tiresome remarks sickened me. And I was depressed to think that this well-fed, ruddy-cheeked person had been my boss not so long ago and had been outrageously rude to me. True, he now put his arm round me, slapped me heartily on the shoulder, and was in favour of my way of life, but I felt that he still thought me a worm and only put up with me to please his daughter. Since I could not laugh or say what I liked, I more or less kept my mouth shut, expecting him to call me 'You there' any moment, as he did his servant Paul.

My petty provincial pride was hurt. I, a proletarian, a house-painter, now visited the rich every day, though we had nothing in common and the whole town looked on them as foreigners. I drank expensive wine there and ate outlandish food. All this was more than my conscience could stomach. On my way there I pulled a long face and avoided people in the street, scowling at them as though I really was some sort of religious crank. When I went home from the engineer's I used to feel ashamed of having done myself so well.

But I chiefly feared falling in love. Walking down the street, working or talking to my mates, I could only think of going to see Masha that evening. I thought of her voice, her laughter, her way of walking. Before visiting her I always spent a long time tying my tie in front of Nanny's crooked looking-glass and thinking how repulsive my new suit was. I really suffered, despising myself at the same time for worrying about such trifles. When she shouted from another room that she wasn't dressed and asked me to wait, I could hear her putting on her clothes and felt panicky, as if the ground was giving way beneath me. When I saw a woman in the street, even far away, I could not help comparing, and I found all our girls and women vulgar, absurdly dressed and lacking in poise. These comparisons made me feel proud, for Masha was the pick of the bunch! At night I dreamt of the two of us.

One evening at supper we polished off a whole lobster with the engineer's help. On my way home afterwards I remembered the engineer twice calling me 'my dear fellow' over supper. They were kind to me there, but they would have been just as kind, I decided, to some miserable big dog that had lost its master. They found me amusing, but the moment they tired of me they would kick me out like a stray dog. I was ashamed and felt so hurt that I was ready to cry. I felt insulted. Looking up at the sky, I swore to end all this.

I did not go to Dolzhikov's next day. Late in the evening—it was raining and already quite dark—I took a walk along Great Dvoryansky Street and looked at the windows. At the Azhogins' everyone seemed to have gone to bed, though a light shone in a window at the end. That would be old Mrs. Azhogin embroidering by the light of three candles and thinking that she was carrying on the fight against superstition. Our house was in darkness, but at the Dolzhikovs' opposite us the windows were bright, though nothing could be seen inside for flowers and curtains.

I went on patrolling the street, drenched by the cold March rain, and heard Father come home from his club. He knocked on the gate. A minute later a light showed in a window and I saw my sister hurry along with a lamp, patting her thick hair with one hand as she went. Then Father stalked up and down the drawing-room, talking and rubbing his hands, while my sister sat quite still in an armchair thinking and not listening.

Then they went away. The lights went out.

I looked round at the engineer's house. That too was dark now. In the rain and darkness I felt utterly lonely and abandoned to the whim of fate. All I had ever done or desired, all I had ever thought and said—how trivial it seemed compared with this loneliness, compared with my sufferings now and those which lay ahead. Alas, the deeds and thoughts of living creatures are of far less consequence than their miseries.

Without being quite clear what I was doing, I gave a frantic tug at the bell on Dolzhikov's gate. It broke and I dashed down the street like a naughty boy, terrified. I was sure that they would come straight out to see who it was, but when I paused for breath at the end of the street I heard only the rain and a watchman banging his sheet of iron somewhere far away.

For a whole week I stayed away from the Dolzhikovs. I sold my new suit. There was no painting work to be had and I was living from hand to mouth again, earning ten or twenty copecks a day doing odd jobs—heavy, irksome work. Floundering knee deep in cold mud, straining every muscle, I tried to stifle my memories, as if in revenge for all the cheeses and tinned delicacies that they had regaled me with at the engineer's. But as soon as I was in bed, hungry and wet, my sinful imagination would begin to conjure up marvellous, seductive scenes. I would realize to my astonishment that I was in love—passionately—and fall into a sound, healthy sleep, feeling that all this penal servitude only made my body younger and stronger.

One evening there was an unseasonable fall of snow and the north wind blew as if winter was about to return. Coming back from work, I found Masha sitting in my room in her fur coat, with both hands in her muff.

'Why have you stopped coming?' she asked, raising her clear, intelligent eyes. A thrill of joy went through me and I stood stiffly to attention, as when Father was about to hit me. She looked into my face and her eyes showed that she understood why I was so moved.

'Why have you stopped coming?' she said again. 'Since you won't come to me I've come to you.'

She stood up and came close to me.

'Don't desert me,' she said, and her eyes filled with tears. 'I'm lonely, so utterly lonely.'

She burst into tears and hid her face in her muff.

'I'm so lonely!' she said. 'Things have got me down, they really have. I've no one except you. Don't desert me.'

She looked for a handkerchief to wipe her eyes and smiled. For a time we said nothing. Then I put my arms round her and kissed her, scratching my cheek on her hat-pin.

We started talking as if we had been close friends for a long, long time.

X

A few days later, to my utter delight, she sent me to Dubechnya. Walking to the station, and later in the train, I kept laughing for no reason and people stared at me as if I was drunk. It was snowing and there were morning frosts, but the roads were no longer white and rooks hovered overhead, cawing.

My first idea was to fix up quarters for Masha and myself in one of the lodges at the side of the house, the one opposite Mrs. Cheprakov's, but it turned out that pigeons and ducks had moved in some time ago and it would have meant destroying a lot of nests to clean the place out. Like it or not, we had to move into the cheerless rooms of the large house with their venetian blinds. The villagers called it 'the big house'. It had over twenty rooms, but no furniture except an upright piano and a child's armchair in the attic. Even if Masha brought all her furniture from town we should never get rid of the grim, empty, cold feeling.

I chose three small rooms with windows facing the garden and worked from early morning to night, clearing them out, putting in new glass, papering the walls and filling in cracks and holes in the floors. It was pleasant, easy work. Now and then I would run down to the river to see if the ice was shifting and I kept fancying that the starlings had arrived. At night I thought about Masha and listened, enraptured and enthralled, to the rats scurrying and the wind soughing and banging above the ceiling. It sounded as if there was an old ghost coughing in the attic.

The snow was deep. A lot more fell at the end of March, but swiftly melted as if by magic. The spring floods swirled past and by the beginning of April starlings were chattering and yellow butterflies flew about the garden. The weather was wonderful. Every afternoon I went to meet Masha in town. And how I enjoyed treading barefoot on the road, which was drying out and still soft. When I was half way there I used to sit down and look at the town, not venturing nearer, for the sight of it upset me. I kept wondering what my friends would think when they heard of my love. What would Father say? What troubled me most was the thought of life having grown so complex that I had lost control over it. It was like a balloon sweeping me off God knows where. I no longer thought about how to earn my keep and how to live. I thought about—well I honestly can't remember what.

When Masha's carriage arrived, I got in with her and we drove off to Dubechnya, happy and carefree. Or I waited for the sun to set and went home, fed up, bored, wondering why she hadn't come. Then unexpectedly, at the gate or in the garden, a charming apparition would greet me—Masha, who, it turned out, had come by rail after all and walked from the station. That was always a great occasion. She wore a simple woollen dress and a scarf round her head, and carried an ordinary umbrella, but she was laced in and slender, and wore expensive foreign boots. She was a clever actress playing the part of a provincial housewife.

We would inspect our establishment and try to allot the rooms and plan the paths, vegetable plot and beehives. We already had our hens, ducks and geese which we loved because they were ours. Everything was ready for sowing—oats, clover, timothy grass, buckwheat and vegetables. We always spent a long time inspecting all this and discussing the harvest prospects. Masha's every word seemed extremely clever and delightful.

These were the happiest days of my life.

A few weeks after Easter we were married in our parish church at Kurilovka, the village about two miles from Dubechnya. Masha wanted a quiet wedding. At her wish the ushers were village lads, the parish clerk managed the singing, and she drove us back from the church in a jolting trap.

We only had one guest from town, my sister Cleopatra—Masha had sent her a note two or three days before the wedding. My sister wore a white dress and gloves. During the ceremony she was greatly moved and quietly wept tears of joy. Her expression was motherly and infinitely kind. Our happiness excited her and she smiled as if she was inhaling sweet, intoxicating fumes. Looking at her during the ceremony, I realized that to her love, yes love, was the most important thing in the world. It was what she always secretly longed for—timidly, but with all her heart. She put her arms round Masha and kissed her. Not knowing how to express her emotions, she said I was 'good, so very good'.

She changed into her ordinary clothes before leaving and took me into the garden to talk to me alone.

'Father's hurt because you didn't write,' she said. 'You should have asked for his blessing. But he's really very pleased—says this marriage will raise your standing in society and Masha's influence will make you take things more seriously. We talk only of you in the evenings these days and last night he even called you "our Misail". It gave me so much pleasure. He seems to have some plan in mind. I think he wants to set an example of generosity by being the first to propose a reconciliation. He'll be out to see you in a day or two, very likely.'

She quickly made the sign of the cross over me several times.

'Well, God be with you,' she said. 'Be happy. Anyuta Blagovo's a very clever girl and she says this marriage of yours is another ordeal sent by God. Well, so it may be. Family life can't all be happiness. There's bound to be suffering as well, you can't help that.'

Masha and I saw her off and walked a couple of miles with her. Then we turned back, walking slowly and saying nothing, as if we were resting. Masha held my arm. We felt relaxed and didn't want to talk about love any more. After the wedding we had become closer and dearer to each other than ever and we felt as if nothing could separate us.

'Your sister's very nice,' said Masha. 'But she looks as if her life has been one long agony. Your father must be an awful man.'

I started telling her how my sister and I had been brought up and how our childhood really had been meaningless and painful. When she heard about Father hitting me not so long ago she shuddered and pressed closer to me.

'Don't tell me any more,' she said. 'It's too horrible.'

We were inseparable now. We lived in the three rooms of the big house and bolted the door to the empty rooms in the evenings, as if they housed a stranger whom we feared. I rose at crack of dawn each day and got down to a job at once—mending carts, making garden paths, digging flower-beds or painting the roof of the house. When the time came to sow oats I tried my hand at double-ploughing, harrowing and sowing. I made a good job of it and kept up with our labourer. I used to get so tired. The biting cold wind and rain made my face and feet burn for hours and I dreamt of ploughland at nights. But working in the fields was not my idea of fun. I knew nothing about farming. I disliked it, perhaps because townsmen's blood flows in my veins and my ancestors have never tilled the soil.

Nature—fields, meadows, vegetable-plots—I loved dearly. But the peasant, turning the sod with his plough and urging on his miserable horse—the ragged, damp peasant, craning his neck—that was my idea of brute strength at its crudest and most barbarous. Watching his clumsy movements, I found myself thinking of that legendary life long ago before man knew the use of fire. The grim bull, moving among the peasants' cows, horses careering through the village with thundering hooves—they scared me stiff. Everything at all large, strong and angry—a horned ram, a gander or a watch-dog—seemed a symbol of this same barbarous, brute force. This prejudice affected me most in bad weather when heavy clouds lowered over the black plough-land. Above all, when I was ploughing or sowing and two or three people stood watching me work, I could not feel that what I was doing really mattered all that much. I felt that I was just amusing myself. I preferred jobs round the yard and liked painting the roof most.

I used to walk through the garden and meadow to our mill. It was rented to Stephen, a dark, handsome, sturdy-looking peasant from Kurilovka with a thick black beard. He disliked running a mill—said it bored him and there was no money in it. He only lived there so that he need not live at home. He was a saddler and carried a pleasant smell of tar and leather round with him. He was no great talker, but a listless, sluggish person, always sitting on the river bank or in his doorway and humming to himself. His wife and mother-in-law—pale, droopy, meek creatures—sometimes came over from Kurilovka to see him. They made him low bows and addressed him with great respect. In reply he neither moved nor spoke, but sat to one side on the bank, quietly humming. An hour or two would pass without a word spoken, then mother-in-law and wife would whisper together, stand up and look at him for some time, expecting him to turn round. They would bow low and say 'goodbye, Stephen' in honeyed, sing-song tones.

Then they would go. Stephen used to make off with the bundle of rolls or shirt that they had brought him, sighing.

'Women!' he would remark with a wink in their direction.

The mill had two sets of mill-stones and worked all day and night. I used to help Stephen. I liked the work and was glad to take over when he was away.

XI

A wet spell followed the warm, fine weather and May was rainy and cold. The noise of the mill-wheels and rain made one lazy and sleepy. The vibrating floor and the smell of flour made for drowsiness too. My wife came over twice a day, wearing a short fur-lined jacket and a pair of wellington boots, and always said the same thing.

'Call this summer! It's worse than October.'

We drank tea or made some porridge or sat for hours without speaking, waiting for the rain to stop. Once when Stephen was away at a fair, Masha spent the night at the mill. We had no idea what time it was when we got up because the whole sky was shrouded in rain-clouds, but sleepy cocks were crowing in Dubechnya and corncrakes were calling in the meadow. It was very early indeed.

I went down to the mill-pond with my wife and pulled out the fish-trap that we had seen Stephen throw in the night before. A large perch was floundering in it and a crayfish writhed about, clawing upwards with its pincers.

'Let them go,' said Masha. 'Let them be happy too.'

The day seemed very long because we had got up so early and then done nothing—it seemed the longest day of my life. Late in the afternoon Stephen came back and I went home to the manor-house.

'Your father was here today,' Masha told me.

'Then where is he now?'

'Gone. I wouldn't see him.'

I stood there without speaking. She saw that I was sorry for Father.

'One must be consistent,' she said. 'I wouldn't see him and sent him a message not to bother coming again.'

A moment later I was through the gate and on my way to town to straighten things out with Father. It was muddy, slippery, cold. Suddenly, for the first time since the wedding, I felt sad, and the thought that perhaps something was wrong with my life flashed through my brain, which was exhausted by this long, grey day. I was worn out and gradually gave way to indolence and faint-heartedness till I did not want to move or think. After walking a bit farther, I decided not to bother and turned back.

The engineer was standing in the middle of the yard in a leather coat with a hood.

'Where's the furniture?' he shouted. 'There was some splendid Empire stuff here. There were pictures, vases. But the place has been picked clean. I bought the estate with the furniture, damn her!'

Mrs. Cheprakov's odd-job-man Moses, a young fellow of about twenty-five, thin, with a pock-marked face and insolent little eyes, stood near him crumpling his cap. One of his cheeks was bigger than the other as though he had been lying on it too long.

'I'm afraid, sir, you did purchase it without the furniture, sir,' he said feebly. 'I happen to remember.'

'Shut up, you!' shouted the engineer, turning crimson and shaking with anger. The echo of his shout reverberated from the garden.

XII

When I did a job in the garden or yard, Moses always stood near by, his hands behind his back, watching me with a lazy, insolent look in his little eyes. It annoyed me so much that I used to stop work and go away.

This Moses was Mrs. Cheprakov's lover according to Stephen. I had noticed that anyone who came to borrow money always applied to him first. I once saw some fellow, black all over—he must have been a coal-heaver—prostrate himself in front of Moses. After some whispering he would sometimes hand over money on his own initiative, without telling his mistress, which made me think he must do occasional business on the side.

He went shooting in our garden under our very windows, helped himself to stuff from our larder and took our horses without so much as by your leave. We were furious and felt that we couldn't call the place our own. Masha would go white.

'Don't tell me we have to put up with these swine for another eighteen months,' she would say.

Mrs. Cheprakov's son Ivan was a guard on our railway. He had grown very thin and weak that winter. One drink was enough to make him tipsy these days and he felt the cold when out of the sun. He was ashamed of his guard's uniform and loathed wearing it, but thought his job worth while as he could steal candles and sell them. He viewed my new status with mixed feelings—wonder, envy and a vague hope that something of the sort might come his way. He pursued Masha with admiring glances and asked what I had for dinner these days. A sad, sickly look showed on his ugly, emaciated face and he moved his fingers as though he was testing the feel of my luck.

'Tell you what, Better-than-nothing,' he said in his fidgety way, forever relighting his cigarette—there was always a mess where he stood because it took him dozens of matches to light up once. 'I'm in a pretty poor way these days, you know. Worst of all, any jumped-up little second lieutenant can shout, "Hey, you! Guard! You there!" I've heard a thing or two in trains, old boy, I can tell you! I know one thing, though—life's a rotten business. Mother's been the ruin of me. A doctor in the train once told me immoral parents always have drunken or criminal children. And that's about the size of it.'

Once he staggered into our yard, breathing heavily, with a blank look, his eyes rolling. He laughed and cried and raved as if delirious. All I could make of this rigmarole was, 'My mother! Where's my mother?' which he brought out tearfully—like a child that has lost its mother in a crowd. I brought him into our garden and laid him under a tree, and Masha and I took turns to sit with him all day and night. He was in a bad way and the sight of his pale, damp face made Masha feel sick.

'Have we really got these swine round the place for another eighteen months?' she asked. 'Oh, how ghastly! Ghastly!'

What a trial the peasants were! And how badly they let us down at the very start, in those spring months when we so longed to be happy! My wife was building them a school, so I sketched out the plan of a school for sixty boys. The council passed it, but advised us to build at Kurilovka, the large village only two miles away. It so happened that the Kurilovka school—attended by children from four villages of which Dubechnya was one—was old and overcrowded and the floor was so rotten that you had to watch your step.

At the end of March, Masha was made trustee of the Kurilovka school at her own wish and in early April we held three meetings to persuade the peasants that their school was old and overcrowded and a new one should be put up. A local councillor and an inspector of state schools came along and put the same point. After each meeting the peasants crowded round us and asked us to stand them a keg of vodka. We felt hot in the crowd. Soon we grew tired and went home, annoyed and somewhat embarrassed.

In the end the peasants did set aside land for the school and undertook to cart all building material from town with their own horses. On the first Sunday after the spring sowing, carts left Kurilovka and Dubechnya to fetch bricks for the foundations. The men left at crack of dawn and came back late at night, drunk and talking about what an awful time they had had.

Needless to say the rain and cold went on all through May with the roads a shocking mess and mud everywhere. The carts usually turned into our yard when they came back from town, and quite an ordeal that was! A pot-bellied nag would appear in the gateway, splaying its front legs. Before coming into the yard it seemed to bow, after which a wet, slimy-looking thirty-foot beam would slither in on a long, low trailer. A peasant, muffled up against the rain, with his coat-tails tucked inside his belt, would walk alongside, not looking where he was going and stepping in all the puddles. A second cart would appear, carrying planks, then a third one with a beam and a fourth.

Bit by bit the space in front of the house became jammed with horses, beams and planks. Peasants and their women, heads muffled, skirts tucked up, stared balefully at our windows, making a great hullabaloo and demanding to see the missus. Their language was atrocious. Moses stood by, looking as if our discomfiture was all great fun.

'No more carting for us!' yelled the men. 'We're dead beat! She can get the stuff herself!'

Pale-faced and terrified, Masha thought that they were going to break into the house. She would send them the money for half a keg of vodka, whereupon the noise always died down and one after another the long beams crawled back out of the yard again.

My wife always worried when I left for the site.

'The men are in an ugly mood,' she would say. 'They might do you an injury. Wait a moment, I'm coming with you.'

We would drive off to Kurilovka together and the carpenters would ask us for a tip. The framework was ready and it was time the foundations were laid, but the bricklayers had not come and the carpenters grumbled at the delay. When at last bricklayers did appear, it turned out that there was no sand—we had somehow forgotten it would be needed. The peasants made the most of our predicament, demanding thirty copecks a load, though it was only a few hundred yards from the site to the river where they fetched the stuff. And we needed over five hundred loads.

There was no end to the muddling, swearing and cadging, and my wife was furious. The foreman-bricklayer, an old fellow of seventy called Titus Petrov, took her by the arm.

'Now look'ee here, I tell you!' said he. 'Just you get me that sand and I'll have a dozen of the lads here in a jiffy and the job'll be done in a couple of days. Look'ee here, I say!'

Well, they did bring the sand. And a couple of days did pass. Then four days, then a week. But there was still a yawning hole in place of those promised foundations.

'This is driving me crazy!' said my wife in great distress. 'What frightful, frightful people!'

In the middle of this chaos Victor Dolzhikov came to see us, bringing hampers of wine and delicatessen. He ate a leisurely meal and took a nap on the terrace. The workmen shook their heads at his snores and said, 'How do you like that!'

Masha was never pleased to see him. She distrusted him, yet took his advice. He would get up from his after-dinner nap in a bad mood and make nasty remarks about our way of running things or say how sorry he was to have bought Dubechnya and lost so much money on it. At such times poor Masha looked agonized. While she complained, he yawned and said the peasants needed a good thrashing.

He called our married life a farce—a piece of childish self-indulgence.

'She's done this sort of thing before,' he told me. 'She once saw herself as an opera singer and ran away from home. I was two months hunting for her. Spent a thousand roubles on telegrams alone, my dear man.'

He no longer called me a nonconformist or 'Mr. Painter'. And he no longer approved of my living as a workman.

'You're a funny chap,' he said. 'There's something wrong with you. I don't venture to prophesy, but you'll come to a bad end.'

At night Masha slept badly and was always sitting brooding by our bedroom window. There was no more laughter at supper, no more charming grimaces. I was miserable. When it rained, every drop seemed to go right through me and I felt like falling on my knees and apologizing to Masha for the weather. I felt equally guilty when the peasants kicked up a row in the yard.

For hours on end I sat in one place, thinking what a marvellous, splendid woman Masha was. I loved her passionately. Everything she did or said fascinated me. She was given to quiet, studious pursuits and liked reading or studying for hours on end. Though she knew farming only from books, her knowledge amazed us all. The advice that she gave was always to the point and helped to improve our methods. And with all this went such a generous nature, such good taste and good humour—the kind of good humour only found in well-educated people.

To a woman like Masha with her sound, practical brain, the chaos of our lives and all these petty cares and squabbles were sheer agony. I saw this and I could not sleep at night either. My mind was active, a lump came into my throat, and I would toss about, not knowing what to do.

Sometimes I galloped off to town and brought Masha books, newspapers, chocolates or flowers. Or I went fishing with Stephen and spent hours in the rain, wading neck-deep in cold water after some special sort of fish to vary our diet. I sank to pleading with the peasants not to make a noise, plied them with vodka, bribed them, made them all sorts of promises. And did a host of other silly things.

In the end the rain stopped and the ground dried out. Sometimes I rose at about four in the morning and went into the garden where the flowers sparkled with dew. Birds sang, insects hummed, and there was not a cloud in the sky. The garden, meadows and river were lovely, but I could not get the peasants and the carts and the engineer out of my mind. Masha and I sometimes drove off to the fields in a racing trap to look at the oats, she at the reins and I sitting behind. She held her shoulders rather high and the wind played with her hair.

'Keep to the right!' she shouted to anyone coming the other way.

'You're a real driver,' I told her once.

'Very likely. After all, my grandfather—the engineer's father—was one. Didn't you know?' she asked, turning to me and starting to mimic the way coachmen shout and sing.

'Splendid!' I thought as I listened to her. 'Absolutely splendid!' Then I remembered the peasants and their carts and the engineer. . . .

XIII

Dr. Blagovo arrived on his bicycle and my sister took to coming out. There was more talk about manual labour, progress and the mysterious Unknown awaiting mankind in the distant future.

The doctor did not like us farming because it left less time for arguing, and said that ploughing, mowing and grazing calves were no work for a free man. In due course, he said, mankind would assign these cruder aspects of the life-struggle to animals and machines and would spend all its time on scientific research. My sister kept asking us to let her go home early and when she stayed late or spent the night there was no end of a fuss.

'Heavens, what a child you are,' Masha reproached her. 'This is really too silly.'

'I know,' my sister agreed. 'I can see how silly it is, but what if I just can't help myself? I feel I'm doing wrong.'

Haymaking made my whole body ache because the work was new to me. Sitting and talking on the terrace with the others in the evening, I was always falling asleep. They would roar with laughter, wake me up and sit me down at the supper table, but drowsiness still came over me. I felt like one in a trance—seeing lights, faces, plates and hearing voices that made no sense. I rose early in the mornings and picked up my scythe at once or went over to the building site and worked there all day.

When I stayed at home on Sundays or other holidays, I noticed that my wife and sister were hiding something from me and actually seemed to be avoiding me. Masha was as loving as ever, but she had something on her mind that she kept from me. The peasants were getting more and more on her nerves, there was no doubt about that, and she was finding the life more depressing, but she had stopped complaining to me. She would rather talk to the doctor than me these days—why, I had no idea.

At haymaking and harvesting-time it was the custom in our province for farm-workers to go to the big house in the evenings for a round of vodka—even the young girls had a glass. We did not keep up this practice, so mowers and peasant women hung about our yard till late at night waiting for their vodka and then went off swearing. Meanwhile Masha, frowning grimly, kept quiet or muttered irritably to the doctor, 'Savages! Brutes!'

Newcomers to the country always meet a cool, almost hostile reception, like new boys at school, and this is what happened to us. At first we were taken for stupid, silly people who had only bought an estate because we did not know what to do with our money.

We were a laughing-stock. The peasants grazed their cattle in our woods and even in our garden. They drove our cows and horses off to the village, then came and demanded money for the damage that they had done. The inhabitants of an entire village would come into the yard and make a row about our trespassing on 'old Bull Neck Meadow' or some such place when we cut hay. Not knowing the exact boundaries of our own property yet, we took their word for it and paid for the damage. Then it would turn out that we had been mowing our own land after all. They stripped the bark from the lime-trees in our wood. One Dubechnya man, a thoroughpaced shark who sold vodka without a licence, bribed our labourers to help him work all sorts of dirty swindles on us by changing the new wheels on our carts for old, running off with our ploughing harness, then selling it back to us, and so on.

But the incidents at the Kurilovka building site upset us most, with women stealing planks, bricks, tiles and iron at night. The village elder would take witnesses and search their huts and they would be fined two roubles apiece at a village meeting. Then the money would be spent on drinks all round for the village.

Masha was furious when she heard. 'What swine!' she used to say to the doctor or my sister. 'It's awful! Ghastly!'

I often heard her saying how sorry she was that she ever started building that school.

'Do get one thing straight, Masha,' the doctor would urge. 'If you build that school and go round doing good, it's not the peasants you do it for. You do it for civilization, for the future. And the worse those peasants are, the more reason there is for building them a school, don't you see?'

But he didn't sound at all sure of himself and I felt that he hated the peasants as much as Masha did.

Masha often went to the mill and took my sister with her, both of them laughing and saying that they went to look at Stephen because he was so handsome. It was only in masculine company that he was so taciturn and slow off the mark, as it turned out, for with women he was very free and easy and rattled away like anything.

One day I went to the river to bathe and chanced to overhear them. Masha and Cleopatra, both in white, were sitting on the bank in the broad shade of a willow, while Stephen stood near by talking, with his hands behind his back.

'Call them peasants human?' he said. 'They ain't, begging your pardon. Brutes and cheats, that's what they are. What kind of life does the peasant live? Eating and drinking is all he thinks of—cheap grub and a chance to shout his silly head off at the tavern. He ain't got no conversation, no manners, no dignity. A clodhopper, that's what he is! He lives in filth, his wife lives in filth and his children live in filth. Goes to bed with his clothes on, he does, fishes the spuds out of the stew with his fingers and drinks kvass with beetles in it—can't even bother to blow them away!'

'But he's so poor, you see,' my sister put in.

'What's that got to do with it? True, he's hard up, but there's different ways of being hard up, miss. If someone's in prison, say, or blind or crippled—well, that's something you wouldn't wish on anyone. But if he's free and has his head screwed on, if he has eyes in his head and his two hands and his strength and his God—then what else does he need?

'It's not poverty, miss, it's all self-indulgence and ignorance. If decent, educated folk like you take pity on him and decide to help him out, the low creature will only spend your money on drink. Worse still, he'll open a dram-shop of his own and use your money to rob his mates. You talk about poverty. But what about your rich peasant? Does he live any better. He's just as big a swine, begging your pardon, the brawling, bawling, bullying lout, broader than he's long, him and his fat, red snout! I'd like to take a swing at the blackguard and knock his teeth out, that I would. Take Larion from Dubechnya. He's well off, but I bet he strips your trees along with the poorest of them. He's a foul-mouthed fellow, his children are the same, and when he's drunk he falls flat on his face in a puddle and sleeps it off.

'They're worthless, miss, the whole lot of them, it's sheer hell living in a village with them. I'm sick and tired of that village. I've food to eat and clothes on my back, thanks be to God above. I've served my time in the dragoons, done a three years' stint as village elder and now I'm free as a bird. I live where I like. I won't live in the village and no one can make me. People go on about my wife. They say I ought to live in a hut with my wife. Why should I? I ain't her hired man.'

'Tell us, Stephen, did you marry for love?' asked Masha.

'Love! What—in a village?' Stephen answered with a laugh. 'If you really want to know, miss, this is my second marriage. I don't come from Kurilovka. I'm from Zalegoshch, but I became a Kurilovka man when I got married. The thing was, my father wouldn't divide up his land and there were five of us brothers. So I said goodbye and made myself scarce. Went to another village to live with my wife's family. My first wife died young.'

'How was that?'

'Sheer stupidity. Kept crying, she did, crying all the time for no reason at all. And took ill, always drinking herbal stuff to make herself pretty. Must have harmed her innards. And my second wife, the one at Kurilovka—why, there's nothing to her. She's just a peasant woman from the village—that's all. I thought she was all right when we were courting. She's young, I thought, and clean-looking, and they live decently. Her mother seemed to belong to some funny religious sect and drank coffee, but the main thing was, you see, they did live decently. So I got married. Next day we're sitting down to dinner and I ask my mother-in-law for a spoon. She hands me one and I see her wipe it with her finger. So much for you, I think. And so much for my "living decently"! I stayed on there for a year and then left.

'Perhaps I should have married a town girl,' he went on after a bit. 'They say a wife should help her husband. But what do I need with help? I help myself. I want someone to talk to. And I don't mean just a lot of blah, blah, blah, either. I mean something with a bit of sense and feeling to it. What's the use of living if you can't have a good talk?'

Stephen suddenly stopped and started his weary, monotonous humming. This meant that he had spotted me.

Masha often went to the mill and obviously enjoyed talking to Stephen. What she liked about him was that when he cursed those peasants he meant every word he said. Whenever she came back from the mill the village idiot who guarded our orchard shouted, 'Ah, there goes our lass. Hullo there, wench!' And he barked at her like a dog.

She used to stop and look at him carefully as if she found an answer to her thoughts in this idiot barking. Very likely it had the same appeal for her as Stephen's curses. There was always news for her at home—the village geese had trampled on the cabbage in our kitchen-garden, say, or Larion had stolen the reins. She would shrug her shoulders. 'What do you expect from these people?' she asked sardonically.

She was furious and things were really beginning to get her down, but I was growing used to the peasants and found myself more and more drawn to them. They were mainly highly strung, irritable people who had had a raw deal and whose imaginations had been crushed. Ignorant men with limited, dull horizons, they all had the same obsession with grey earth, grey days, black bread. They tried to cheat, but showed as much sense over it as an ostrich sticking its head in the sand and thinking that it can't be seen. They couldn't even count. They wouldn't take twenty roubles to help with our haymaking, but would do it for half a keg of vodka, when for twenty roubles they could buy four whole kegs.

Oh yes, there was dirt, drunkenness, stupidity and cheating, but all the same you felt that by and large the peasant's life had a firm, healthy base. He might look like some great lumbering beast as he followed his wooden plough. He might dull his wits with vodka. Still, when you looked closer, you saw something vital and significant there which was lacking in Masha and the doctor for instance. I mean his belief that what really matters on this earth is truth, and that truth and nothing but the truth can save him and our whole people. This is why he loves justice more than anything in the world. I used to tell my wife that she could not see the glass for the dirty marks on the pane. She either gave no answer or just hummed like Stephen.

Pale with indignation, this clever, good-natured girl would talk to the doctor in quavering tones about drunkenness and dishonesty. She had such a short memory, that's what I found so staggering. How could she forget that her father the engineer also drank—heavily too —or that Dubechnya had been bought on the proceeds of a whole chain of monstrous, barefaced swindles? How could she?

XIV

My sister too lived a life of her own which she carefully hid from me. She and Masha often whispered to each other. When I went near her she seemed to cringe, and a pleading, guilty look came into her eyes. Obviously she had something on her mind to make her afraid or ashamed. By sticking close to Masha she managed to avoid meeting me in the garden and being left alone with me. I hardly had a chance to talk to her except at dinner.

One evening I was coming quietly through the garden on my way back from the building site in the dusk. My sister was walking near a spreading old apple-tree, making no sound—she might have been a ghost. Nor did she notice me or hear my steps. She wore black and was walking up and down quickly, in a straight line, looking at the ground. An apple fell from a tree. The sound made her jump and she paused, holding her hands to her temples. It was then that I went up to her.

Tears came to my eyes and somehow my thoughts turned to our mother and our childhood. A feeling of great tenderness suddenly swept over me and I put my arm round her shoulders and kissed her.

'What's the matter?' I asked. 'You're unhappy, I've seen that for some time. Tell me, what's wrong.'

'I'm frightened . . .' she said, shuddering.

'But what's the matter?' I insisted. 'For God's sake come out with it.'

'All right, I'll tell you, I'll tell you all about it. I can't bear keeping things from you, it distresses me. Misail, I'm in love . . .' she went on in a whisper. 'I love him, I love him. . . . I'm happy, but why am I so scared?'

Steps were heard and Dr. Blagovo appeared between the trees in a silk shirt and top-boots—they had clearly arranged to meet here by the apple-tree. Seeing him, she rushed towards him impulsively with an agonized cry as if someone was trying to take him from her.

'Vladimir! Vladimir!'

She clung to him and gazed hungrily into his eyes, and only then did I notice how pale and thin she had grown of late. What really brought it home to me was the lace collar that I remembered from some time back—it hung more loosely than ever round her long, thin neck. The doctor was embarrassed, but recovered at once and stroked her hair.

'There, there . . .' he said. 'Why so upset? I'm here now, you see.'

We did not speak, but just looked at each other in some embarrassment. Then we all three walked off together.

'Civilized life hasn't even started in Russia,' the doctor was telling me. 'Old people try to console themselves—if there's nothing doing now, they say, something was at least going on in the forties and sixties. That's all very well for the old, but you and I are young and we aren't yet in our second childhood, so we can't comfort ourselves with such illusions. Russia began in 862 A.D. but *civilized* Russia still hasn't got off the mark at all, as I see it.'

I did not follow his arguments. It was all a bit odd somehow. I did not want to believe that my sister was in love and that here she was walking along, holding a stranger's arm and gazing fondly at him. My sister, that highly strung, terrified, downtrodden, enslaved creature, loved a married man with children. I felt vaguely sorry—what about, I don't quite know. I felt a distaste for the doctor's company somehow and could not see what future this love might have.

XV

Masha and I drove over to Kurilovka for the dedication of the school.

'Autumn, autumn, autumn . . . ' said Masha quietly, looking round her. 'Summer's over. The birds have gone and only the willows are green.'

Summer was indeed over. The days were fine and warm, but there was a nip in the morning air, shepherds wore their sheepskin coats and dew lay all day long on the asters in our garden. There were plaintive sounds all the time, but whether they were from shutters grumbling on their rusty hinges or cranes flying past, you could not tell. It was a wonderful sensation, it made you feel so full of life.

'Summer's over . . .' said Masha. 'Now you and I can see where we stand. We've done a lot of work, a lot of thinking. We're better for it—all credit to us—and we've managed to lead better lives. But has our progress had any noticeable effect on life around us? Has it done anyone else any good? No. Ignorance, physical uncleanliness, drunkenness, the appallingly high infant mortality-rate—none of that's changed. You've ploughed and sowed, while I've spent money and read books, but what good has that been to anyone? All our work, all our fine ideas have clearly been only for ourselves.'

This kind of argument disturbed me and I did not know what to think.

'We've been sincere from start to finish,' I said. 'You can't go wrong if you're sincere.'

'No one's denying that. We had the right ideas, but were wrong in the way we applied them. The main thing is, we've gone about things in the wrong way, haven't we? You want to help people, but by buying an estate you lose all chance of helping them from the outset. Then if you work, dress and eat like a peasant, you somehow lend your support to those heavy, clumsy clothes, ghastly huts and stupid beards.

'On the other hand, suppose you work for a long time, give your life to it and achieve some practical results in the end. What do those results mean? What *can* they mean in the face of such elemental forces as wholesale ignorance, famine, cold and degeneracy? They're a drop in the ocean! What's needed here is quite a different line of attack, something powerful, bold, swift. If you really want to be some use, leave your usual narrow daily round and try to influence the masses directly. What's really needed is noisy, vigorous propaganda. Why is art—music for instance—so alive? Why is it so popular and genuinely powerful? Because your musician or singer makes his impact on thousands at a time.

'Wonderful, wonderful art!' she went on, looking thoughtfully at the sky. 'Art gives you wings—sweeps you off far, far away. If you're sick and tired of filth and petty, niggling concerns—if you're baffled, aggrieved, indignant—you can only find peace and satisfaction in beauty.'

The weather was bright and cheerful as we reached Kurilovka. They were threshing in some of the farm-yards and there was a smell of rye straw. There was a bright red mountain-ash beyond some wattle fences and wherever you looked the trees were gold and red. The church bells were ringing and icons were being carried in procession to the school. You could hear them singing, 'Holy Mother, Intercessor.' The air was clear and the pigeons flew high.

The service was held in a classroom. Then the Kurilovka peasants brought Masha an icon, and those of Dubechnya gave her a large loaf of bread and a gilt salt-cellar. Masha burst into tears.

'If we've said anything we shouldn't or been any trouble, pray forgive us,' said one old man, bowing to her and me.

As we drove home Masha kept looking back at the school. The green roof, painted by me, remained in sight for a long time, glittering in the sunlight. Glancing at it now, Masha was saying goodbye, I felt.

XVI

She packed and went to town that evening.

She had taken to going to town often lately and spending the night there. I could not work while she was away, my arms felt limp and weak, our huge yard seemed like some dismal, disgusting waste plot and the garden was full of angry noises. The house, the trees, the horses—none of these were 'ours' to me while she was away.

I did not leave the house, but just sat at her table near the cupboard with her books on farming—old favourites no longer needed, they seemed to look at me with such embarrassment. For hours on end, while it struck seven, eight, nine, and the pitch-black autumn night darkened the windows, I looked at her old glove or the pen that she had always used, or her little scissors. I did nothing and saw quite clearly that anything I'd done before—ploughing, mowing or felling—had only been done because she wanted it. If she had sent me to clean out a deep well, standing waist-deep in water, I would have plunged straight in without bothering whether the job needed doing or not. Now that she was no longer near me, Dubechnya seemed sheer chaos, with its ruins, untidiness, banging shutters and round-the-clock pilfering. Why work in a place like that? Why should I? Why bother my head about the future when I felt the ground slipping from under my feet, felt that my role in Dubechnya was played out—felt in fact that I was heading for the same fate as those books on farming. And what agony the lonely night hours were! I listened and worried, expecting any moment to hear a voice shouting that it was time I left. Dubechnya was no loss, but I mourned my lost love, for the autumn of our love had clearly come. What happiness to love and be loved! And how dreadful to feel yourself falling off that lofty pinnacle.

Masha came back from town next afternoon. Annoyed about something, but trying to hide it, she only asked why all the double window-frames had been put in for winter—said it was enough to choke anyone. So I took two frames out. Though not hungry, we sat down to supper.

'Go and wash your hands. You smell of putty,' my wife said.

She had brought some new illustrated magazines from town and we looked at them together after supper. There were supplements with fashion-plates and patterns which Masha glanced through and put on one side to look at properly later. But one dress with a wide, smooth, bell-shaped skirt and full sleeves caught her fancy and she gazed at it for a minute with grave attention.

'That's not bad,' she said.

'Yes, it would really suit you,' I said. 'It really would.'

I looked fondly at the dress, admiring this grey blob just because she liked it.

'It's a wonderful, splendid dress!' I went on fondly. 'Lovely, marvellous Masha! Darling Masha!'

My tears splashed on the picture.

'My splendid Masha . . .' I muttered. 'My lovely, darling Masha . . . .'

She went to bed and I sat up for an hour looking at the illustrations.

'You shouldn't have taken those frames out,' she said from the bedroom. 'It might be cold. There, just feel that draught!'

I read something from the 'miscellaneous' column—a recipe for cheap ink and something about the largest diamond in the world. My eye was caught once more by the picture of the dress that she had liked and I imagined her at a ball with a fan, bare-shouldered, brilliant, superb, knowing all about music, painting and literature. How small and brief my own role seemed!

Our meeting and married life had only been one episode, and there would be plenty more of them in the life of this vigorous, gifted woman. As I have said already, all the best things in life were at her service, hers for the asking. Even ideas and intellectual fashions only served her as a source of pleasure, lending variety to her life, while I was just the cab-driver who had conveyed her from one amusement to another. Now I was no longer needed and she would sail away, leaving me high and dry.

As if in answer to my thoughts a frantic yell came from outside.

'He-e-elp!'

It was a shrill voice, like a woman's. As if mimicking it, the wind, moaning in the chimney, gave out the same shrill note. Half a minute passed and through the howling wind I heard the cry again.

'He-e-elp!'

This time it seemed to come from the far end of the yard.

'Do you hear that, Misail?' my wife asked quietly. 'Do you hear?'

She came out of the bedroom in her nightdress with her hair down and listened, looking at the dark window.

'Someone's being murdered,' she said. 'This really is the last straw.'

I took my gun and went out. It was very dark outside and the wind was so strong that I could hardly stand. I went over to the gate and listened. The trees roared, the wind whistled, and a low, lazy howl came from the garden—the village idiot's dog, no doubt. Outside the gate it was pitch dark with not one light on the railway-line. From near the lodge where the railway office had been last year suddenly came a strangled cry.

'He-e-elp!'

'Who's there?' I shouted.

Two men were struggling. One was shoving, the other resisting and both were breathing hard.

'Let go!' said one of them and I recognized Ivan Cheprakov. It was he who had been shouting in that shrill voice like a woman's. 'Let go, blast you, or I'll bite your hands!'

I recognized the other one as Moses. Separating them, I could not resist hitting him twice in the face and he fell down. Then he stood up and I hit him again.

'Gentleman was trying to kill me,' he muttered. 'Trying to get into his Mum's chest of drawers, he was. . . . I'm aiming to lock him up in the lodge, sir, to be on the safe side, like.'

Cheprakov was drunk and did not recognize me. He drew deep breaths, as if filling his lungs to shout 'help' again.

I left them and went back to the house where my wife was lying on the bed, now fully dressed. I told her what had happened outside, not even hiding the fact that I had hit Moses.

'It's so frightening living in the country,' she said. 'What a confoundedly long night this is.'

A little later we heard the cry again.

'He-e-elp!'

'I'll go and separate them,' I said.

'No, they can tear each other's throats out for all I care,' she said with a look of disdain.

She gazed at the ceiling, listening, and I sat near her, not daring to open my mouth, feeling that this cry for help outside and the long night were all my fault.

We said nothing and I waited impatiently for a glimmer of dawn in the windows. Meanwhile Masha looked as if she had just come out of a trance and was wondering how a clever, well-educated, decent person like her ever became involved with a set of contemptible mediocrities in this miserable provincial dump. How could she sink to letting one of these people attract her and be his wife for more than six months? Myself, Moses, Cheprakov—we were all the same to her, I felt. That drunken, savage cry for help summed it all up—me, our marriage, our farming and the filthy autumn weather. When she sighed or moved into a more comfortable position I read in her face, 'Oh, hurry up, morning!'

In the morning she left.

I stayed on at Dubechnya for another three days waiting for her. Then I piled all our things in one room, locked it, and walked to town. When I rang the engineer's bell it was already evening and on Great Dvoryansky Street the lamps were lit. There was no one in, Paul told me. Mr. Dolzhikov had gone to St. Petersburg and Miss Masha must be at rehearsal at the Azhogins'.

I remember how nervous I was as I went on to the Azhogins'. I remember my heart throbbing and fluttering as I mounted the stairs and stood for a while on the top landing, not venturing inside that temple of the muses. In the ballroom—on a small table, on the grand piano and on stage—candles were burning, everywhere in threes. The first performance was billed for the thirteenth and this first rehearsal was on Monday, an unlucky day. All part of the struggle against superstition.

The drama-fanciers were there already. The eldest, middle and youngest sisters were walking about the stage and reading out their parts from notebooks. Radish stood a little apart, quite still, with the side of his head against a wall, reverently watching the stage as he waited for them to start rehearsing. Nothing had changed.

I set off to pay my respects to the lady of the house, but everyone suddenly began hushing and gesticulating to me to step quietly. There was silence. The piano lid was put up and a lady sat down, screwing up her short-sighted eyes at the music. Then my dear Masha went up to the piano. She was superbly dressed and looked beautiful, but in some new and special way, for she was nothing like the Masha who had come out to see me at the mill that spring. She began singing, 'O radiant night, why do I love thee?'

This was the very first time since we had met that I had heard her sing. She had a fine, mellow, strong voice and as she sang I felt as if I was eating a sweet, ripe, fragrant melon. When she finished, everyone clapped and she smiled delightedly, fluttering her eyes, turning the pages of the music and smoothing her dress. She was like a bird that has broken out of its cage at last and preens its wings in freedom. Her hair was combed back behind her ears and she had a truculent, challenging look, as if she wanted to defy us all or shout at us as she shouted at her horses, 'Come on, my beauties!'

At that moment she must have looked just like her grandfather the coachman.

'You here too?' she said, offering her hand. 'Did you hear me sing? Well, what do you think? It's a good thing you're here,' she went on without waiting for an answer. 'I'm leaving tonight for St. Petersburg. I shan't be away long—you don't mind my going, do you?'

At midnight I took her to the station. She embraced me affectionately—to thank me for not asking unnecessary questions, most likely—and promised to write. I held her hands for a while and kissed them, hardly able to keep back my tears and not saying a word.

When she had gone I stood watching the lights disappear and caressed her in my imagination.

'Darling Masha,' I said in a low voice. 'Wonderful Masha. . . .'

I spent the night at Karpovna's house in Makarikha. Next morning Radish and I upholstered some furniture for a rich businessman who was marrying his daughter to a doctor.

XVII

My sister came to tea on Sunday afternoon.

'I read a lot these days,' she said, showing me some books that she had borrowed from the public library on the way. 'I'm so grateful to your wife and Vladimir for making me aware of myself. They've been my salvation, made me feel like a real person at last. There was a time when I lay awake at nights worrying. "Oh dear", I'd think, "we've used too much sugar this week. Oh, what if I put too much salt on the cucumbers?" Now I can't sleep either, but I've other things on my mind. It's agony to think that half my life has gone by in this stupid, feeble way. I despise my past life. I'm ashamed of it, and I think of Father as an enemy these days. Oh, I'm so grateful to your wife. And what about Vladimir? He's such a wonderful man. They've opened my eyes.'

'It's bad that you can't sleep at night,' I said.

'You mean I'm ill? Not at all. Vladimir listened to my chest and gave me a clean bill of health, but health isn't what counts, it isn't all that important. . . . Am I doing the right thing? That's what I want to know.'

She needed moral support, that was clear enough. With Masha gone and Dr. Blagovo in St. Petersburg there was no one left in town except me to tell her that she was on the right track. She would stare into my eyes and try to read my secret thoughts. And if I was pensive in her presence or said nothing she always thought that it was her fault and felt depressed. I always had to be on my guard and when she asked me if she was doing right, I hastened to assure her that she was and that I greatly respected her.

'Do you know, they've given me a part at the Azhogins'?' she went on. 'I want to act. I want to live—in fact I want to experience everything. I'm no good at all and my part's only ten lines, but still this is a far, far better and nobler thing than pouring out tea five times a day and seeing if the cook's been eating too much. Above all, Father must be shown that I'm capable of protest.'

After tea she lay down on my bed for some time with her eyes shut, very pale.

'How weak of me,' she said, getting up. 'Vladimir says all the women and girls in this town are anaemic from sheer idleness. Isn't Vladimir clever? He's right, he's so so right. We must work!'

Two days later she turned up for rehearsal at the Azhogins' with a notebook, wearing a black dress, a coral necklace and a brooch that looked like a piece of puff-pastry from a distance. She had large ear-rings, each with a jewel shining in it. It embarrassed me to look at her and what struck me was the lack of taste. I was not the only one to notice those unfortunate ear-rings and jewels and her strange get-up, for I saw smiles and heard someone laugh and say, 'Cleopatra of Egypt'.

She was trying to be urbane, nonchalant, at ease, but that only made her look grotesque and affected. Her natural and becoming air had deserted her.

'I just told Father I was going to rehearsal,' she began, coming up to me. 'He shouted at me—said he wouldn't give me his blessing and actually came near to striking me. Just fancy, I don't know my part,' she said, looking at the notebook. 'I'm bound to make a mess of it. And so I've burnt my boats,' she went on, much agitated. 'I've burnt my boats. . . .'

She thought that everyone was looking at her, staggered by the momentous step she had taken and expecting something extraordinary from her. No one ever does notice people as drab and trivial as she and I, but you could never get her to see that.

She was not on until the third act and her part—that of a guest, a provincial busybody—just involved standing by a door for a short time, as if eavesdropping, and then making a short speech. For at least an hour and a half before she was due on—while people came and went on the stage, recited, drank tea and argued—she did not leave my side, constantly mumbling her part and nervously crumpling the notebook.

Thinking that everyone was watching her and waiting for her to go on, she patted her hair with shaking hand.

'I'm sure to make a mess of it . . .' she told me. 'I feel awful, you've no idea. I'm so terrified, it's as if I was going to be led out to execution.'

Her cue came at last.

'Cleopatra Poloznev! You're on,' said the stage-manager.

She walked into the centre of the stage looking horrorstruck, ugly and clumsy, and stood for half a minute as if paralysed, not moving at all except for the large ear-rings swinging from her ears.

'You may use your notebook as it's the first time,' someone said.

Seeing that she was shaking too much to speak or open her notebook and was not concerned with her part at all, I was about to go and have a word with her when suddenly she fell on her knees in the middle of the stage and burst out sobbing.

All was agitation and uproar. Only I stood there leaning against the scenery at one side, overwhelmed by these proceedings. I hadn't the faintest idea what to do. I saw them pick her up and take her off. I saw Anyuta Blagovo come up to me—I had not noticed her in the hall before and she seemed to have sprung from nowhere. She wore her hat and veil and had her usual look of having just dropped in for a moment.

'I told her not to take a part,' she said angrily, jerking out each word abruptly and blushing. 'It's sheer lunacy! Why didn't you stop her?'

Mrs. Azhogin rushed up, looking thin and flat-chested in a short blouse with short sleeves and tobacco ash down the front.

'My dear, this is too ghastly,' she said, wringing her hands and staring into my face as usual. 'Ghastly! Your sister's in a certain condition . . . she's, er, pregnant! Please take her away, do you mind . . .?'

She was actually panting with emotion. Her three daughters, just as thin and flat-chested as their mother, stood near by, huddled timidly together. They were paralysed with fright. You might have thought an escaped convict had been caught in their house. ('Oh, what a disgrace!' 'Oh, what a dreadful business!') Yet this worthy family had spent its life fighting superstition. Three candles, the number thirteen and unlucky Monday—these in their view clearly exhausted the catalogue of human superstition and error.

'Please . . . do you mind . . . ?' said Mrs. Azhogin, pursing her lips as she said 'do you'. 'Do you mind taking her home?'

XVIII

Soon after that my sister and I went downstairs. I tried to shield her with my coat and we hurried along, choosing side streets where there were no lamps and avoiding passers-by. We might have been running away. She had stopped crying and looked at me dry-eyed. It was only about twenty minutes' walk to Makarikha where I was taking her and, curiously enough, we managed to call to mind our entire lives in that short time. We went into everything, considered where we stood and made plans. . . .

We decided that we could not go on living in this town and would move somewhere else as soon as I had some money. People had already gone to bed in some houses, and in others they were playing cards. We hated and feared those houses. We spoke of the fanaticism, hard hearts and worthlessness of these respectable families, these lovers of dramatic art whom we had so alarmed.

'Are these stupid, cruel, lazy, dishonest people any better than the drunken, superstitious Kurilovka peasants?' I asked. 'Are they any better than animals, which also panic when some accident disturbs their monotonous lives bounded by instincts?'

What would have become of my sister now if she had gone on living at home? Talking to Father and meeting people she knew every day—what torments she would have endured! I could just picture it. Then I remembered people, all of whom I knew, whose lives had been made more and more of a misery by their nearest and dearest. I remembered the tortured dogs going mad, the live sparrows thrown into water after street urchins had plucked out all their feathers. I remembered the long, long procession of obscure, slow agonies that I had observed continuously in this town ever since I was a boy.

I just could not see what kept these sixty thousand citizens going. Why did they read the Gospels? Why did they say their prayers? Or read books and magazines? Not one word of what has been said and written since the beginning of time can have done them any good if we still find the same darkness of the soul and hatred of freedom as a hundred or three hundred years ago. A master carpenter spends his whole life building houses in the town, but he will go on mispronouncing the terms of his trade till his dying day. Likewise these sixty thousand townspeople have been reading and hearing about truth, mercy and freedom for generations, yet their entire progress from cradle to grave is one long lie. And they torment each other, fearing and hating freedom as if it was their worst enemy.

'Well, my fate is decided,' my sister said when we reached home. 'I can't go back *there* after what's happened. God, isn't that marvellous! I feel so much easier in my mind.'

She went straight to bed. Tears shone on her eyelashes, but she looked happy. She slept sweetly and soundly and obviously really was relaxed and easier in her mind. It was a long, long time since she had slept like that.

Thus began our life together. She was always singing and saying how well she felt. We borrowed books from the library, but I took them back unread because she could not read these days. She only felt like dreaming and talking of the future. She darned my underwear or helped Karpovna at the stove. She was always humming or talking about her Vladimir—how clever, well mannered and kind he was, and how amazingly learned. I would agree, though I no longer liked her doctor. She wanted to do a job and earn her own living. She said that she was going to be a schoolmistress or nurse as soon as she was well enough, and she meant to scrub floors and do the washing. She was quite devoted to her baby. He wasn't even born yet, but she already knew what his eyes and hands were like and how he laughed. She liked talking about education. As Vladimir was the best man in the world, everything she said about education boiled down to making her boy as fascinating as his father. We had no end of discussions and whatever she said was exciting and exhilarating to her. I sometimes cheered up too without knowing why.

I suppose her dreaminess infected me. I did not read anything either, but just mooned about. Tired as I was, I used to walk up and down the room in the evenings with my hands in my pockets, talking about Masha.

'When do you think she'll be back?' I would ask my sister. 'I think she'll be here by Christmas at the latest. What is there for her to do there?'

'She must be coming very soon, or else she'd write.'

'Very true,' I always agreed, knowing full well that there was nothing to bring Masha back to our town.

I missed her dreadfully. Unable to deceive myself any longer, I tried to get other people to deceive me. My sister waited for her doctor and I waited for Masha, and we both talked and laughed all the time without noticing that we were keeping Karpovna awake. She lay on her stove.

'The samovar was humming this morning, oh dearie me it was,' she kept muttering. 'That means bad luck, my dears. Bad luck, that means.'

No one came near us except the postman who brought my sister letters from the doctor, and Prokofy who sometimes looked in during the evening, stared at my sister without speaking, then went off.

'Every class should stick to its own rules,' he would say from his kitchen. 'And them as is too proud to understand that will find this life a vale of tears.'

He loved this phrase, 'Vale of tears'. I was going through the market one day—Christmas week had arrived—when he called me over to his butcher's stall. Without offering to shake hands, he announced that he had something important to discuss. Vodka and frost had made his face red, and by him at the counter stood Nikolka—he of the villainous face—holding a bloody knife.

'I want a word or two with you,' Prokofy began. 'This business can't go on because you can see for yourself that this here vale of tears is going to get you and us a bad name. Ma's too sorry for you of course to say anything unpleasant about your sister moving to other quarters on account of her being in the family way. But I don't want her around any more because her behaviour is something what I can't approve of.'

I took the point and left his stall. That day my sister and I moved to Radish's place. We could not afford a cab, so we walked and I carried our stuff in a bundle on my back. My sister did not carry anything, but kept panting and coughing and asking if we would get there soon.

XIX

A letter did arrive from Masha in the end.

My dear, kind M. (she wrote), my good, gentle 'angel of mercy', as the old painter calls you, goodbye. Father and I are going to America for the Exhibition. In a few days I shall see the ocean—it's dreadful to think how far from Dubechnya. It's distant and unfathomable like the sky and I so long to go there, to be free. I feel on top of the world, I'm crazy—you can see for yourself what a muddle this letter is.

My dear, please give me my freedom. Please hurry up and break the thread that still binds us together. Meeting you and knowing you was like a ray of sunshine that lit up my existence. But becoming your wife was a mistake, as you see yourself. The thought of my mistake depresses me. I beg you on my knees, my generous darling, please, please send a wire quickly before I sail over the ocean. Say you agree to put right our common mistake and remove this one stone which weighs down my wings. My father will make the arrangements and he promises not to bother you too much with formalities. So may I be free to do as I like? Do say yes.

Be happy and God bless you. Forgive me my sins.

I'm alive and well. I spend money like water and do lots of silly things. I thank God every minute of the day that a bad woman like me has no children. I'm still singing and doing rather well at it, but my singing isn't just a hobby. No, it's my haven, my cell where I retreat to find peace. King David had a ring with the inscription, 'All things pass'. When I'm sad those words cheer me up, and when I'm cheerful they make me sad. I've got myself a ring like that with Hebrew letters on it, a talisman to prevent me being carried away too much. Things pass. Life too will pass, so one doesn't need anything. Perhaps one needs nothing but a sense of freedom, because when someone's free he needs nothing, nothing at all. So do break the thread. My best love to you and your sister. Forgive and forget

your M.

My sister lay in one room and Radish, who had been ill again and was getting better, lay in another. Just as I received this letter my sister went quietly into the painter's room, sat down beside him and started reading aloud. She read him Ostrovsky or Gogol every day, and he solemnly listened, gazing into space, not laughing.

'All things are possible, indeed they are,' he muttered from time to time with a shake of his head.

When a play portrayed something base or ugly, he jabbed his finger at the book. 'That's lies for you,' he would gloat. 'That's what lying does for you.'

He liked plays for their plot, their moral and their complex artistic structure, and was full of admiration for the authors, whom he never named, always referring to them as 'he'. ('How neatly he tied all that up.')

This time my sister only read one page quietly and could not go on because her voice gave out. Radish took her arm and moved his parched lips.

'The soul of the righteous man is white and smooth as chalk,' he said in hoarse, barely audible tones. 'But the soul of the sinful man is like unto pumice-stone. The soul of the righteous man is like clear oil, but the soul of the sinful man is like tar. We must labour, we must mourn, we must fall sick,' he went on.

'He who labours not and mourns not, shall not inherit the Kingdom of Heaven. Woe, woe unto them that are well fed, woe unto the mighty, woe unto the rich, woe unto the money-lenders, for the Kingdom of Heaven is not theirs. Grass doth wither, iron doth rust. . . .'

'And lies do rot the soul,' my sister went on with a laugh.

I read the letter again. Then the soldier came into the kitchen—the one who twice a week brought us tea, French bread and grouse, all smelling of scent, from an unknown source. I was out of work and had to stay at home for days on end, and whoever sent us those rolls must have known that we were hard up.

I heard my sister talking to the soldier and laughing happily. Then she ate a roll, lying down.

'Anyuta Blagovo and I,' said she, 'knew from the start that you were right to turn down your job and become a painter. But we feared to say so out loud. Tell me, what is it that stops people saying what they think—what is this strange compulsion? Take Anyuta Blagovo. She loves you, adores you and knows that you're absolutely right. She loves me like a sister and knows I'm doing the right thing too—and envies me, I dare say, in her heart of hearts. But something stops her visiting us. She shuns us and she's scared.'

My sister folded her arms on her breast.

'If you only knew how she loves you!' she said excitedly. 'I'm the only person she's told about her love—and then secretly, in the dark. She used to take me to a dark avenue in the garden and whisper how precious you are to her. She'll never marry because she loves you, you'll see. Aren't you sorry for her?'

'Yes.'

'It's she who sent the bread. She really is a funny girl. Why make such a secret of it? I was funny and silly myself once, but now I've left that place and I'm afraid of no one. I think and say what I like and I'm happy. Living at home I had no idea what happiness was, but now I wouldn't change places with a queen.'

Blagovo arrived. He had obtained his higher medical degree and was now staying with his father in our town. He was on holiday and said he was soon going to St. Petersburg, as he wanted to work on inoculation for typhus—and cholera too, I think. He meant to finish his training abroad and then become a professor. He had left the army and wore generously cut cheviot jackets, very wide trousers and superb ties. My sister was crazy about his pins and studs and the red silk handkerchief that he kept in his top jacket pocket—as a jaunty touch, presumably. Having nothing else to do one day, we tried to remember how many suits he had, and decided that it was at least ten.

He obviously still loved my sister, but never, even in jest, suggested taking her to St. Petersburg or abroad. I could not see what was going to happen to her if she survived—or to her child. But she was forever mooning about and gave the future no serious thought. She said that he should go where he liked. So long as he was happy he might even desert her. What had already happened was enough for her.

When he came to see us, he usually listened most carefully to her chest and saw that she drank milk with drops in it. He did the same this time, listening to her chest and making her drink her glass of milk with something in it that made our rooms smell of creosote afterwards.

'There's a good girl,' he said, taking the glass from her. 'You shouldn't talk too much. You've been chattering away like nobody's business lately. Try not to talk, will you?'

She laughed. Then he came into Radish's room where I was sitting and gave me a friendly pat on the shoulder.

He bent over the sick man. 'Well, how are things, old fellow?'

'Well, sir . . .' said Radish, moving his lips slowly. 'Permit me to report, sir. . . . We none of us live for ever, it's all God's will. . . . Permit me to tell you the truth . . . you won't go to heaven, sir.'

'Never mind,' joked the doctor. 'Someone has to go to hell.'

Suddenly a strange feeling came over me and I seemed to be dreaming. It was a winter night and I was in the slaughter-house yard, standing by Prokofy. He smelt of pepper vodka. I tried to pull myself together and rubbed my eyes, whereupon I saw myself going for my interview with the Governor. Nothing of this sort has ever happened to me before or since and I can only put down these strange, dreamlike memories to nervous exhaustion. I lived through the scene at the slaughter-house and my interview with the Governor, dimly conscious all the time that none of it was real.

When I came to, I found myself outside, standing by a street-lamp with the doctor.

'Oh, what a miserable business,' he was saying, with tears streaming down his cheeks. 'She's so cheerful, always laughing, full of hope. But her condition's hopeless, old boy. Your friend Radish hates me, thinks I've treated her badly and is always trying to bring it home to me. He's right in his way, but I have my own point of view too and don't regret the past a bit. One must love—we should all love, shouldn't we? There'd be no life without love, and anyone who fears love and runs away from it, well, he's not free.'

He gradually turned to other topics, talking about science and his thesis, which had gone down well in St. Petersburg. He was quite carried away as he talked, forgetting my sister, his own troubles and me. Life fascinated him.

'Masha has America and her ring with the inscription on it,' I thought, 'and he has his higher degree and academic career. Only my sister and I are stuck in the old rut.'

I said goodbye to him and went up to a street-lamp to read the letter again. And I remembered her so vividly coming to see me at the mill one spring morning and lying down with her fur jacket over her, wanting to look like a simple peasant woman. Then there had been another morning when we were pulling a fish-trap out of the water and huge raindrops fell on us from the riverside willows and made us laugh. . . .

The lights were out in our house in Great Dvoryansky Street. I climbed the fence and went through the back door into the kitchen, as in the old days, to fetch a lantern. There was no one in the kitchen. By the stove the samovar was hissing in readiness for Father. 'Who pours out Father's tea these days?' I wondered. I took the lantern, went out to the shack, made up a bed from old newspapers and lay down. The pegs on the walls looked as stern as ever and their shadows flickered. It was cold. I felt as if my sister was just about to come in with my supper, but then I suddenly remembered that she was ill in bed in Radish's house, and it seemed strange that I should have climbed the fence and be lying in this unheated shed. My head was swimming and grotesque visions passed before my eyes.

The bell rang. I remembered how it sounded from childhood—first the wire rustling on the wall, then the short, plaintive note in the kitchen. Father must have come back from his club. I got up and went into the kitchen. When Aksinya the cook saw me she threw up her arms and burst out crying for some reason.

'My boy!' she said softly. 'My dear! Oh goodness me!'

In her agitation she started crumpling her apron. There were gallon jars of berries in vodka standing in the window. I poured out a cupful and gulped it down, for I badly needed a drink. Aksinya had just scrubbed the table and benches, and the kitchen smelt like any other bright, cosy kitchen where the cook keeps things spick and span. This smell and the chirp of crickets always attracted us children to the kitchen and put us in the mood for fairy-tales and card games. . . .

'But where's Cleopatra?' asked Aksinya softly, flustered and holding her breath. 'And where's your cap, my dear? I hear your wife's gone off to St. Petersburg.'

She had worked for us in Mother's time and used to bath Cleopatra and me. She still thought of us as children who had to be told what to do. In about a quarter of an hour she had put to me all the arguments which, wise old servant that she was, she had been piling up in the quiet of the kitchen since our last meeting. She said that the doctor could be made to marry Cleopatra—he only needed to be given a bit of a fright. And then, if the application was drawn up properly, the bishop would dissolve his first marriage. She said that I should sell Dubechnya without telling my wife and put the money into a bank account of my own, and that Father might forgive my sister and me if we threw ourselves at his feet and asked him properly. She said that we should offer a special service to Our Lady. . . .

'Now go and talk to him, dear,' she said, hearing Father cough. 'Go and talk to him—bow down before him. Your head won't fall off.'

I went. Father was sitting at a table sketching out the plan of a villa with Gothic windows and a fat turret like the watch-tower of a fire-station, something thoroughly stick-in-the-mud and second-rate. I went into his study and stood where I could see this sketch. Why I had called on Father I did not know, but when I saw his lean face, red neck and shadow on the wall, I remember, I wanted to throw my arms round his neck and prostrate myself before him as Aksinya had instructed me. But the sight of that villa with its Gothic windows and fat turret held me back.

'Good evening,' I said.

He looked at me and immediately looked down at his sketch.

'What do you want?' he asked after a while.

'I've come to say that my sister's very ill. She can't live long,' I added in a hollow voice.

'What do you expect?' sighed Father, taking off his spectacles and putting them on the table. 'You reap what you have sown.'

'What you have sown,' he repeated, getting up from the table, 'you reap. Remember coming to see me two years ago? In this very room I asked you, implored you to leave the path of error. I reminded you of duty, honour, and what you owe to those ancestors whose traditions we should hold sacred. And did you listen to me? You scorned my advice, stubbornly clinging to your false ideas. Furthermore, you also led your sister into your own evil ways and made her lose her virtue and all sense of shame. Now you're both in trouble. Well, what do you expect? What you have sown you reap!'

He walked up and down the study as he spoke, probably thinking that I had come to apologize—perhaps beg for my sister and myself. Cold and shivering feverishly, I could hardly find my voice.

'I must ask you to remember something too,' I said hoarsely. 'On this very spot I implored you to try and see my point of view and help me decide how to live and what to live for. You replied by bringing in our ancestors and my great-uncle the poet. Now I tell you your only daughter's dying, you're off about ancestors and traditions again. . . . How can you be so frivolous in your old age when you haven't all that long to live—some five or ten years perhaps?'

'What have you come for?' asked my father sternly, obviously offended at being called frivolous.

'I don't know. I love you and I'm sorry we're so far apart, more sorry than I can say—so I came. I still love you, but my sister's finished with you. She can't forgive you and she never will. Your very name fills her with disgust for the past and for life itself.'

'Well, whose fault is that?' Father shouted. 'It's all your doing, you scoundrel.'

'All right,' I said, 'we'll call it my fault. I admit I'm very much to blame. But why is your way of life—which you think binding on us too—so dismal and mediocre? You've been building houses for thirty years now, but why do none of them contain people who could tell me how to live decently? There isn't an honest man in the whole town! Those houses of yours are sinks of iniquity where mothers and daughters have their lives made a misery and children are tortured.

'My poor mother!' I went on frantically. 'My poor sister! A man must dull his wits with vodka, cards and tittle-tattle, must be a vile hypocrite, must have spent dozens of years drawing up plan after plan, not to notice the horrors lurking inside these houses. Our town's been here for hundreds of years and all that time it hasn't given the country one useful citizen! Not one! Anything the least bit bright and lively has pretty short shrift from you! This is a town of shopkeepers, publicans, office-clerks and hypocrites. It's no use to anyone. If the earth suddenly swallowed it up, no one would care.'

'I won't listen to you, you scoundrel!' said Father, taking a ruler from the table. 'You're drunk! How dare you come and see your father in this condition! I tell you for the last time—and you can pass it on to your depraved sister—you'll get nothing out of me. I've hardened my heart to my disobedient children and if they suffer for their disobedience and obstinacy, they'll have no sympathy from me. You can go back where you came from! You were sent to punish me—such was God's will—but I suffer this affliction humbly. Like Job, I take comfort in my sufferings and in unceasing labour. Mend your ways or never darken my doors again. I'm a fair-minded man and I tell you all this for your own good. And if you want it to do you any good, just you remember these words—and what I said before—for as long as you live.'

I gave up and left. What happened that night or the next day I do not remember.

I am told that I wandered the streets bareheaded, staggering and singing noisily, with crowds of boys running after me and shouting, 'Better-than-nothing! Better-than-nothing!'

XX

If I wanted to have a ring I should choose the inscription, 'Nothing passes away'. In my view nothing does pass away entirely and the smallest step we take influences our present and future.

My experiences have not been in vain. The townspeople have been touched by my great misfortunes and the way I have put up with them. No one calls me 'Better-than-nothing' any more and they do not laugh at me or throw water at me when I go past the shops. They are used to my being a worker and no longer find it funny if a gentleman carries paint-buckets and puts in windows. Far from it—they like giving me jobs and I rate as a first-class workman these days and the best contractor after Radish. His health is better and he still paints belfry domes without scaffolding, but cannot manage his men any more. I run round town looking for jobs instead of him these days. I hire men and fire them and borrow money at high interest. Now that I am a contractor myself, I see how a man can run round town for three days chasing up roofers for the sake of some twopenny-halfpenny job. People are civil to me and speak to me politely. When I work on a house I am given tea and they send to ask if I want a meal. Children and girls often come and give me sad, quizzical looks.

One day I was working in the Governor's garden, painting a summer-house to look like marble. The Governor was taking a stroll and came into the summer-house. Having nothing better to do, he started talking to me and I reminded him how he had once summoned me for interview. He stared at my face for a moment, then opened his mouth like the letter O and shrugged his shoulders.

'I don't remember,' he said.

I look older now. I do not talk much, I am austere and stern, and I rarely laugh. They say that I have begun to look like Radish and, like him, bore my mates with my futile exhortations.

Masha Dolzhikov, my ex-wife, now lives abroad and her father the engineer is building a line somewhere in eastern Russia and buying estates there. Dr. Blagovo is abroad too. Dubechnya has reverted to Mrs. Cheprakov, who bought it back after getting the engineer to knock twenty per cent off the price. Moses wears a bowler hat these days. He often comes to town on business in a racing trap and stops by the bank. He is said to have bought up a mortgaged estate and is always enquiring about Dubechnya at the bank because he means to buy that as well.

The wretched Ivan Cheprakov drifted about town for some time doing nothing, always on the booze. I did try to fix him up with us and he joined us for a time painting roofs and putting in windows. He rather took to it actually and stole his linseed-oil, asked for his tips and drank his dram like any other self-respecting decorator. But he soon grew thoroughly fed up with the work and went back to Dubechnya. Later on some of the lads told me that he had been trying to get them to help him kill Moses one night and rob Mrs. Cheprakov.

Father has aged a great deal. He is very bent and goes for walks near his house in the evenings. I never visit him.

During the cholera epidemic Prokofy dosed shopkeepers with pepper vodka and tar and charged them for it. I read in our newspaper that he had been flogged for making nasty remarks about doctors while sitting in his meat stall. His shop-boy Nikolka died of cholera. Karpovna is still alive, and she still loves and fears her Prokofy. When she sees me she shakes her head sadly. 'You'll come to a bad end!' she sighs.

Every working day I am at it from morning to night. On holidays, in fine weather, I pick up my little niece—my sister expected a boy, but had a girl—and walk slowly to the cemetery. There I stand or sit, gazing for a while at the grave so dear to me and tell the little girl that her mother lies there.

I sometimes find Anyuta Blagovo at the graveside. We greet each other and stand in silence or talk about Cleopatra and her little girl and how sad life is. Then we leave the cemetery and walk along in silence and she walks more slowly so as to be with me as long as possible. The little girl, gay and happy, screwing up her eyes in the bright sunlight and laughing, holds out her hands to Anyuta. We stop and both fondle the dear child.

As we enter the town Anyuta Blagovo, flushed and agitated, says goodbye to me. Then she goes her way alone—dignified and prim. No one in the street would think to look at her that she had just been walking at my side and had even fondled the little girl.

IN THE HOLLOW

I

UKLEYEVO village was at the bottom of a hollow. Only its belfry and the chimneys of its calico-printing factories could be seen from the main road and railway station. When travellers asked what village it was, they would be told 'where the sexton ate all the caviare at the funeral'.

Once, after a funeral at factory-owner Kostyukov's place, an elderly sexton had spotted some unpressed caviare among the eatables and begun gulping it down. People jostled him, tugged his sleeve, but he was in a sort of ecstatic trance: felt nothing, just went on eating. He wolfed the lot, and the jar had held about four pounds! This had been some time ago and the sexton had long since died, yet they still remembered that caviare. Was life there really so miserable? Or were people just incapable of noticing anything but this trivial episode, now ten years old? Anyway, it was all one ever heard about Ukleyevo village.

Malaria was endemic in the place. There was gluey mud, even in summer: especially beneath the fences broadly overshadowed by ancient stooping willows. It always smelt of factory waste, and o acetic acid as used in processing cotton. The factories—three calico print-works, one tannery—were not in the actual village, but on the outskirts or some distance away. They were small concerns, employing no more than four hundred workers all told. The tannery often made the stream stink, its waste polluted the meadow, the villagers' cattle suffered from anthrax. There had been an order to close it down, and it did indeed rate as closed. But it functioned clandestinely—the police inspector and the county health officer were in the know, and each was paid his ten roubles a month by the owner. There were only two decent stone-built, iron-roofed houses in the whole village. One contained the local council offices, while the other—two-storeyed, right opposite the church—was the home of Gregory Tsybukin, a shopkeeper from Yepifan.

Gregory kept a grocery store, but only as a cover for dealing in vodka, cattle, skins, grain, pigs and whatever else was going. For instance, when there was a demand to export peasant bonnets as ladies' headgear, he made thirty copecks a pair on the deal. He bought standing timber, lent money at interest. He was, by and large, a resourceful old boy.

He had two sons. The elder, Anisim, was in the police detective branch, and was seldom at home. The younger, Stephen, had gone into the business, and assisted his father, but they didn't expect real help from him as he was deaf and ailing. His wife Aksinya was a beautiful, well-built woman. She sported her hat and sunshade of a Sunday, rose early, went to bed late, and was on the go all day in barn, cellar and shop—skirts hitched up, keys jingling. It made old man Tsybukin happy to look at her, and his eyes would light up—yet he was sorry that she was not married to his elder son, but to the younger: deaf and clearly no connoisseur of feminine beauty!

The old boy had always been domestically inclined, and loved his family more than anything on earth: especially his elder, detective son and his other son's wife. No sooner had Aksinya married her deaf husband than she was already showing an unusual head for business. She knew who could and could not be given credit, she kept her keys on her, not trusting even her husband with them, she clicked away at her counting-frame. She looked horses in the mouth like a peasant, and she was always laughing or shouting. Whatever she did or said, the old man just doted on her.

'Good for you, daughter!' he would mutter. 'Well done, my lovely darling——'

He had been a widower, but one year after his son's marriage had again succumbed to wedlock. They found him a girl of good family, called Barbara, twenty miles from Ukleyevo. Though not in her first youth, she was a fine figure of a woman. And no sooner had she settled into her little first-floor room than everything in the house was sparkling like a new pin. Lamps burned before icons, tables were covered with snow-white table-cloths, red-eyed flowers appeared on window-sills and in the front garden, meals were no longer eaten from a common bowl—everyone had his own little dish. Barbara's warm, friendly smile seemed to make the whole house smile. Also—and this was new—beggars and various pilgrims began to call. The piteous whining of the Ukleyevo women was heard outside the windows, as also was the apologetic coughing of their frail, haggard menfolk dismissed from the works for drunkenness. Barbara gave them money, food, old clothes. When she was a bit more sure of herself she also took to fetching them odd things from the shop. The deaf man once saw her taking two two-ounce packets of tea, which disconcerted him.

'Mum just took two packets of tea,' he informed his father later. 'Who shall I charge it to?'

The old man made no answer—just stood and thought, twitching his eyebrows—then went upstairs to his wife.

'Barbara, dear,' said he affectionately, 'if you want something in the shop you take it. Take as much as you like, don't you hesitate.'

Next day the deaf man ran across the yard shouting 'if you want something, Mum, you take it.'

There was something fresh, cheerful and light-hearted about her alms-giving, just as there was in those icon-lamps and little red flowers. Just before fasts, or on the village saint's-day (it actually lasted three days), they used to palm off putrid salt beef on the villagers: stuff with so vile a stench that you could hardly go near the barrel. And they let drunks pawn their scythes, their caps and their women's kerchiefs, while mill-hands—befuddled by foul vodka—sprawled in the mud, the very air seeming clogged by a dense miasma of sin . . . at which times it rather helped to remember that over there in the house was a neat, quiet woman who had nothing to do with that beef or vodka. On such oppressive, hazy occasions her charity operated as a safety valve.

These were busy days at the Tsybukins'. Aksinya would be spluttering as she washed herself in the passage before sun-up, while the kitchen samovar hissed and droned like a prophet of doom. Gregory—a nice, clean little old fellow in his long black frock-coat, nankeen trousers and sparkling jack-boots—paced the rooms, tapping his heels like 'My Husband's Dear Old Dad' in the popular song. They would open the shop. When it was light the fast droshky would be brought to the porch, and in the old man would jump, jauntily, pulling his large peaked cap down over his ears. No one looking at him would have thought him fifty-six years old. His wife and daughter-in-law would see him off. Now, at such times, when he wore his nice, clean frock-coat and the great black three-hundred-rouble stallion was hitched to the droshky, the old man disliked the yokels coming up to complain and beg favours. He hated peasants, they riled him.

'Why are you hanging round? You clear off,' he would yell wrathfully if he saw one waiting by the gate. Or, if it was a beggar, he would shout that God would 'pervide'.

When he was away on business his wife, in her dark clothes and black apron, would tidy the house or help in the kitchen. Aksinya served in the shop, and you could hear the jingle of bottles and coins out in the yard while she laughed or shouted and her offended customers raged. That the clandestine vodka trade was in full swing in the shop was also evident.

The deaf husband would also sit in the shop, or pace the street bareheaded, hands in pockets, looking absently at huts and sky. They drank tea half a dozen times a day in the house and sat down to about four meals. In the evening they counted the takings and entered them, after which they slept soundly.

All three Ukleyevo print-works were connected by telephone, as were the homes of the owners: Khrymins, Khrymin Sons and Kostyukov. The parish offices had been connected up too, but that instrument soon stopped working, having become infested with bugs and cockroaches. The parish chairman could hardly read, and he began every word in his documents with a capital letter, but when the telephone stopped working he said, yes, it was going to be 'a bit difficult, like, without that there telephone'.

Khrymins were always suing Khrymin Sons, while Khrymin Sons sometimes quarrelled among themselves and went to law, whereupon their works would stand idle for a month or two until they made it up again—which amused the Ukleyevites, seeing that each squabble provoked much discussion and tittle-tattle. On Sundays Kostyukov and Khrymin Sons would go out driving and career through Ukleyevo running down the calves. Rustling her starched skirts and dressed up to the nines, Aksinya would parade in the street near her shop until Khrymin Sons swooped down and whisked her off as if abducting her by force. Then old Tsybukin would drive out too, to show off his new horse, taking Barbara with him.

In the evening, when the driving was over and folk were going to bed, an expensive-sounding accordion would be played in Khrymin Sons' grounds, and if there was a moon these sounds thrilled and gladdened the heart. No longer did Ukleyevo seem quite such a dump.

II

The elder son Anisim came back very seldom, only on the major saints' days, but he often got people from the village to take home presents and letters beautifully written in someone else's hand. They were always on a good-quality paper, they had an official look about them, and they abounded in expressions never used by Anisim in conversation, such as 'dearest Mum and Dad, I send you a pound of herbal tea for the gratification of your physical requirements.'

At the foot of each letter was scratched ANISIM TSYBUKIN, as if with a cross-nibbed pen, and beneath this, in the same ornate hand as before, the word AGENT.

The letters were read aloud several times.

'Ah well, he wouldn't stay at home, he would be a scholar,' said the old man, much moved and crimson with excitement. 'So be it then. Everyone should go his own way.'

Once, just before Shrovetide, there was heavy rain and sleet. The old man and Barbara went to the window for a look—and behold Anisim sleighing in from the station. Completely unexpected, he entered anxiously as if he had something on his mind, and kept this up during the rest of his time there. He seemed a bit off-hand too, and was in no hurry to leave. Could he have lost his job? That's what it looked like. Barbara was glad to see him and kept giving him rather arch looks, sighing and shaking her head.

'Now, goodness me, this won't do at all,' she clucked. 'Here's a lad turned twenty-seven—and he's still the gay bachelor! Goodness gracious me!'

From another room her quiet, level speech sounded like a continuous susurration. She took to whispering to the old man and Aksinya, and their faces also adopted that arch, mysteriously conspiratorial look.

They decided to marry Anisim off.

'Your younger brother's been wed long since,' clucked Barbara. 'But you're unspliced still, like a cockerel at market—it ain't right, that. You can marry, God willing, and then do as you please: go back to work, and your wife can stay at home and help. You've got into bad ways, my lad, I can see that. Forgotten what's what, you have. Proper shockers you town folks are, goodness gracious me!'

When Tsybukins married they had the pick of the best-looking girls, seeing that they were rich. For Anisim too a beautiful bride was found. His own looks were drab and unprepossessing. His build was frail and sickly, he was short of stature, he had plump, bulging cheeks which looked as if he was puffing them out. He had a sharp, unwinking stare and a sparse, gingery beard which, in pensive mood, he was always chewing at. He liked his dram, too—that showed in his face and walk. But when informed that a very beautiful bride had been found for him, he said that he was, 'well, not exactly misshapen' himself.

'We Tsybukins are a good-looking breed, and that's a fact.'

Adjoining the local town was the village of Torguyevo, half of which had recently been amalgamated with the town, the other half remaining a village. In the town part lived a certain widow in a cottage which she owned. She had a sister who was very poor and went out to work by the day. This sister had a daughter, Lipa, who was a hired drudge like her mother. Lipa's beauty was the talk of Torguyevo. The trouble was, though, she was so terribly poor. The view was that some elderly man or widower would marry her, overlooking her poverty—or else, 'you know, just live with her'—and then the mother would be provided for as well. Hearing of Lipa from local marriage-brokers, Barbara went over to Torguyevo.

Then a bride-showing was laid on at the aunt's house—it was all done properly with the usual snacks and drinks. Lipa wore a new pink dress specially made for the occasion, and a crimson ribbon flamed in her hair. She was a frail, slim, pale little thing with fine, delicate, features, sunburnt from work in the open air. A sad, nervous smile played on her face. And there was a childlike look, trustful and inquisitive, about her eyes.

She was young—no more than a little girl, her bosom barely developed—but already of marriageable age. She really was beautiful, having only one feature which might seem unattractive: large arms, like a man's, now dangling idly like two great claws.

'There's no dowry, but that don't bother us,' the old man told the aunt. 'We took a girl from a poor family for our son Stephen too, and we're as pleased as could be. About the house, in the shop . . . oh, she's a real treasure.'

Lipa stood by the door, and seemed to be trying to tell them to 'do what you like with me, I trust you.'

Her mother Praskovya, the hired hand, skulked in the kitchen almost too shy to breathe. In her youth a merchant whose floors she was scrubbing once flew into a rage and stamped his feet at her. She had been terribly frightened, it had given her rather a turn, and that terror had remained with her all her life: a terror which kept her arms and legs for ever trembling—her cheeks too. From her seat in the kitchen she tried to hear what the guests were saying, and she kept crossing herself, pressing her fingers to her forehead and glancing at the icon. Slightly drunk, Anisim kept opening the kitchen door.

'Why sit out here, dearest Mum?' he would ask jauntily. 'We've been missing you.'

Praskovya timidly pressed her hands to her gaunt, emaciated bosom.

'Oh, you shouldn't, sir, really,' she answered. 'It's far too good of you, sir.'

They inspected the bride, they named the wedding day—after which Anisim kept pacing the rooms at home and whistling. Or he would suddenly remember something, start brooding and fix a piercing stare on the floor as if his eyes sought to penetrate deep into the earth. He evinced neither pleasure at the prospect of marrying soon (the week after Easter) nor any wish to see his bride either, he only whistled. He was only marrying because his father and stepmother wanted him to, that was obvious—and because it's a village custom: the son takes a wife to help in the house. When he left for town again he did so without haste. This time his whole conduct had differed from that of his previous visits: he had been particularly off-hand and said all the wrong things.

III

In Shikalovo village lived two dressmakers—sisters, belonging to the Flagellant sect. They were given the order for the wedding clothes, they often came over for fittings, and they drank tea for hours. For Barbara they made a brown dress trimmed with black lace and bugles, and for Aksinya a light green one with a train and a yellow bodice. When the dressmakers had finished, Tsybukin paid them: not in cash, but in goods from his shop. They went away sadly, holding bundles of tallow candles and sardines for which they had no use at all, and when they came out of the village into open country they sat on a tussock and wept.

Three days before the wedding Anisim turned up in a completely new outfit: shiny rubber galoshes, a red cord with bobbles instead of a tie. A greatcoat, also new, was slung loosely over his shoulders.

He prayed solemnly before the icon, greeted his father—and gave him ten silver roubles and ten fifty-copeck pieces. He gave the same to Barbara, and he gave Aksinya twenty quarter-roubles. The main charm of these gifts was this: the coins were all brand new, in mint condition, and glinted in the sunlight. Trying to look solemn and earnest, Anisim pulled a long face, puffed out his cheeks and gave off a whiff of spirits. He'd popped into the bar at every station, very likely. Once again there was something off-hand, something rather otiose, about the fellow. Then Anisim and the old man had tea while Barbara fingered the bright new roubles and asked about folk from their village who had gone to live in town.

'They're all right, praise the Lord—doing well, they are,' said Anisim. 'Oh, there has been an incident, though, in Ivan Yegorov's domestic life. His old woman Sophia passed on. The consumption, it was. The caterers handled the wake at two-and-a-half roubles a head. There was wine too. There was peasants there—some of our lot—and they charged two-and-a-half roubles for them too, though they never ate nothing. What do them bumpkins know about sauce?'

'Two-and-a-half roubles each!' The old man shook his head.

'What else do you expect? It ain't like a village. You go into a restaurant for a bite, you order a few things, a few of your pals look in, you have a drink—and then, lo and behold, it's already dawn, and it's fork out your three or four roubles a head if you please. And when Samorodov's there, he wants his coffee and brandy after everything—and with brandy at "sixty copecks the glass, sir"!'

The old man was ecstatic. 'What nonsense he does talk!'

'I spend all my time with Samorodov these days. He's the one who writes my letters to you—oh, he's a great writer, is Samorodov.'

Anisim turned to Barbara. 'You'd never believe me, Mum,' he went on cheerfully, 'if I told you what Samorodov's like. We call him Mukhtar because he looks like an Armenian: black all over. Read him like a book, I do—I know all his business like the palm of my hand, Mum. And don't he feel it! He's always making up to me, won't leave me alone, we're thick as thieves now, we are. He's a bit scared of me, but he can't do without me. Where I go he goes. I've got a real good eye, Mum, that I have. Like when I see a peasant selling a shirt in the flea-market. "Hey there," says I, "that's stolen property!" And I'm always right, the shirt *is* stolen, it turns out——'

'But how can you tell?' asked Barbara.

'I *can't* tell, I've just got the eye for it. I don't know nothing about that shirt, I somehow just feel it's stolen, and that's that. That's what they say in the office. "Anisim's gone sniping," say they: looking for stolen goods, that is. True enough, anyone can steal things—it's keeping them that counts. Big as the world is, there ain't nowhere to hide the swag.'

'Last week a ram and two ewes were stolen from the Guntorevs here in the village,' sighed Barbara. 'Goodness gracious me! There was no one to look for them.'

'Very well, I might take it on—I wouldn't mind.'

The wedding day arrived. It was a cool April day, but bright and brisk. Troikas and two-horse carriages—harness-bells jingling, with gaudy ribbons on yokes and manes—had been driving round Ukleyevo since early morning. Disturbed by all the coming and going, rooks chattered in the willows and starlings nearly burst their lungs, seeming to celebrate the Tsybukin wedding with their non-stop singing.

Indoors the tables were already groaning with long fishes, hams, stuffed birds, boxes of sprats, various salted and pickled items, and an array of vodka and wine bottles. There was a smell of salami and stale lobster. Near those tables, clattering his heels and sharpening knife on knife, paraded the old man. They kept calling Barbara and asking for something, and she—panting, looking distracted—would run into the kitchen where Kostyukov's chef and Khrymin Sons' cook had been hard at work since dawn. Hair curled, in corsets but no dress, new boots squeaking, Aksinya whirled round the yard with flashes of bare knee and breast. It was noisy, there was cursing and swearing. Passers-by paused at the wide open gate, and could sense that something most unusual was afoot.

'They've gone for the bride.'

Harness-bells jingled, then died away far beyond the village.

At about half-past two a crowd ran up, and the bells were heard again. They were bringing the bride!

The church was full, the candelabra blazed, the choristers sang from sheet music—old Tsybukin's wish, this. The glittering lights, the bright dresses blinded Lipa, the choir's loud voices rang like hammers in her head. Her corset—the first she had ever worn—and her shoes were pinching her: she looked as if she had just come out of a faint, gazing about her but not understanding. Anisim, in his black frock-coat with his bit of red cord for a tie, was plunged in thought, staring fixedly and hastily crossing himself whenever a great shout came from the choir. He was deeply moved, to the point of tears. He had known this church since he was a little boy. His mother of blessed memory had brought him here for the sacraments, he had once sung in the boys' choir. Each little nook, each icon . . . he remembered them all so well. Now he was being married here because that was the done thing, but his mind was elsewhere, he no longer thought of his wedding, somehow—had forgotten it entirely. He could not see the icons for tears, there was a lump in his throat. He was praying, he was begging God that those fell disasters about to burst on him any day now . . . that they might somehow pass him by as clouds pass over a village in time of drought without shedding one drop of rain. And what of the weight of accumulated sin in his past—the many sins which had ensnared him beyond redemption, sins past praying forgiveness for, even? Pray forgiveness, though, he did—he even sobbed aloud, but no one heeded.

They just thought he'd had a drop too much.

A child's tearful cry rang out. 'Mummy, darling! Take me away from here!'

'Silence there!' the priest shouted.

On their way back from church the peasants thronged after them, and there were more crowds near shop and gate, and beneath the windows facing the yard. Village women had come to sing the bridal songs. No sooner had the young couple crossed the threshold than the choristers, waiting ready in the hall with that sheet music, shrieked for all they were worth. The band, specially hired from town, struck up. Tall goblets of Cossack 'bubbly' were offered round, and the jobbing carpenter Yelizarov—a tall, lean old man with brows so bushy that they nearly masked his eyes—addressed the newly-weds.

'Anisim and you, child, love each other and lead godly lives, my children, and the Holy Mother will not forsake you.' He leant on the old man's shoulder and sobbed.

'Gregory Tsybukin, let us weep aloud, let us weep tears of joy!' he said in a reedy little voice followed by a sudden loud guffaw.

'And this new daughter-in-law of yours is a real good-looker too,' he went on in a loud, deep voice. 'She has everything in the right place, like: all smooth stuff, it won't rattle, the whole mechanics is in tip-top order—plenty of screws.'

He came from out Yegoryevsk way, but had worked in the Ukleyevo mills and near-by parts since youth—he'd settled down. He had looked just as old, lean and lanky as he was now for as long as folk remembered. For years he had had the nickname 'Lofty'. For over forty years he had done nothing but maintenance work at the mills, which is perhaps why he judged everyone and everything solely in terms of their durability: did they need repair? Before sitting down at table he had tested a few chairs for soundness, also prodding the cold salmon.

After the 'bubbly' they all took their places at table. The guests spoke and moved their chairs, the choir sang in the hall, the band played, while the women in the yard simultaneously sang their folk songs in unison: a ghastly, grotesque medley of noise which made your head spin.

Now crying, now laughing aloud, Lofty fidgeted in his chair, elbowed his neighbours, wouldn't let them get a word in edgeways.

'Children, children, children,' he muttered rapidly. 'Aksinya, my dear, and Barbara, let us all live in peace and harmony, my darling little hatchets——'

No great drinker, he was quite merry, now, on one glass of 'English bitters'. This revolting brew, made of God knows what, stunned all who drank it as if they had been slugged. Tongues became entwined.

There were clergy here, there were clerks from the mills with their wives, there were traders and pub-keepers from other villages. The parish chairman and his clerk—they'd been working together for fourteen years now, and never during all that time had they signed a single document, nor let a soul leave their office, without cheating and insulting somebody—sat side by side: fat and smug, both of them . . . and seemingly so steeped in skulduggery that the very skin of their faces had a curiously depraved texture. The clerk's scrawny, cross-eyed wife had brought all her children along. She was squinting vulture-like at the bowls, grabbing whatever came her way and putting it in her own and the children's pockets.

Lipa sat there like a statue with the same look on her face as in church. Not having exchanged a single word with her since their first meeting, Anisim still didn't know what her voice sounded like. Now, as they sat side by side, he still wasn't speaking, but drank those 'English bitters'. Then, when he was tipsy, he addressed Lipa's aunt—sitting opposite.

'I have a friend, name of Samorodov. He's rather special, like. He's a cut above the rank and file, and he has something to say for himself. But I read him like a book, Aunty—and don't he feel it! May we now drink Samorodov's health together, Aunty dear?'

Barbara hovered round the table pressing the guests to eat—puffed, flustered, obviously glad that there were so many dishes. It was all on so lavish a scale that no one could sneer at them now. The sun went down, but the meal went on. No longer did they know what they were eating or drinking, nor could they hear what was said, but now and then when the band was quiet some village woman's shout carried clearly from the yard.

'Rotten swine, grinding the faces of the poor! May you rot in hell!'

In the evening they danced to the band. Khrymin Sons had

brought their own drink, and during the quadrille one of them held a bottle in each hand and a glass in his mouth, which was all great fun. In mid-quadrille they suddenly launched into a squatting dance. Green Aksinya kept flashing past with a breath of wind from her train. Someone had trodden on one of her flounces.

'Hey, her skirting board's come loose, children!' shouted Lofty.

Aksinya had naïve grey eyes which rarely blinked and a naïve smile for ever playing on her face. In those unblinking eyes, in the small head on the long neck, in her litheness, there was something of the snake. Dressed in green, yellow-bodiced, smiling, she looked like a viper: coiled, head uplifted in the young rye, as it watches someone go past in spring time. The Khrymins took liberties with her, and it was only too obvious that she had long been on the closest terms with the eldest. The deaf husband sensed nothing, though—he wasn't looking at her, but sat with his legs crossed, eating nuts and cracking them loudly with his teeth. It sounded like pistol shots.

Out came old Tsybukin himself into the middle and flipped a handkerchief to show that he too wanted to do the squat-dance. A roar of approval ran through the crowded house and yard.

''Tis the old gaffer himself going to dance!'

Barbara danced, while the old man only waved his handkerchief and shuffled his heels, but the folk out in the yard—clinging to each other as they peered through the windows—were in ecstasy and straightway forgave him everything: his money, his insults. Voices were heard in the crowd.

'Good old Gregory!' they laughed. 'That's it, you have a go! So you ain't past it, eh? Ha, Ha.'

It all ended late, after one in the morning. Anisim staggered round choir and band, giving everyone a new half-rouble as a parting gift, while the old man—steady on his feet, but vaguely limping—saw his guests off, telling everyone that the wedding had 'cost me a cool two thousand'.

As they were dispersing it turned out that someone had taken the Shikalovo pub-keeper's new jacket, leaving an old one behind in its place. Anisim flared up.

'Stop, everyone! I'm going to make a search,' he shouted. 'I know who took that. Hold it!'

He ran out into the street, started chasing someone.

They caught Anisim, they dragged him back by the arms. They thrust him—drunk, crimson with rage, wet with sweat—into the room where Aunty had been undressing Lipa. And locked him in.

IV

Five days passed. Anisim was ready to leave, and went upstairs to say good-bye to Barbara. Her icon-lamps were all lit, there was a smell of incense and she sat by the window knitting a red woollen stocking.

'You didn't stay long,' said she. 'Got bored, eh? Goodness gracious me. We do ourselves well, we don't want for anything. And your wedding was done right and proper—two thousand it cost, the old man said. We live off the fat of the land in fact, but it's a dull life, this is. Too hard on them peasants, we are. It grieves me so, dear, to think how we wrong them. Bartering horses, buying things, hiring workmen . . . it's all fraud, fraud, fraud, Lord help us. The olive oil in the shop's sour and rancid—no better than tar, it isn't. How come we can't sell proper oil, eh? You tell me that.'

'None of my business, Mum.'

'But we all die in the end, don't we? You really should talk to your father, dear me you should.'

'Talk to him yourself.'

'Not me. If I do he only answers same as you: it ain't none of my business. Whose business it is . . . that'll be settled in the next world. God's judgement is righteous.'

'Of course it won't be settled,' sighed Anisim. 'There ain't no such thing as God anyway, is there, Mum? So much for your next world!'

Barbara looked at him in amazement, laughed and threw up her arms. That she so genuinely marvelled at his words, that she really did think him a freak . . . it quite disconcerted him.

'Perhaps there is a God, and it's just me that can't believe,' he said. 'I felt a bit funny at the wedding—like when you take an egg from the hen, and there's a chick squeaking in it. It was that way with my conscience—it suddenly started squeaking, and during the service I kept thinking that God does exist. Then I come out of church and the feeling's gone. Anyway, how can *I* tell if there's a God or not? That's not what they taught us as kids. From when we was babes in arms we was taught only one thing: you keep your place. Now, Dad don't believe in God either, do he? You once mentioned some sheep being stolen from Guntorevs'. It was a Shikalovo peasant stole 'em, I discovered. He stole them, but it's Dad who's got the skins. There's your religion for you!'

Anisim winked and shook his head.

'The parish chairman don't believe in God either,' he went on. 'Nor does the clerk, nor does the sexton. If they go to church, if they keep the fasts, they only do it so folks won't speak badly of them, and to be on the safe side—what if there should really be a Judgment Day? Folk are so feeble nowadays, don't respect their parents and all that—so people think it's the end of the world. Nonsense! The way I see it is this, Mum: all this grief, it comes from folk not having enough conscience. I read 'em like a book, Mum, I know what's what. If a man has a stolen shirt, I can tell. Or take someone sitting in a pub—all you can see is him drinking his tea, no more than that. But *I* see that, tea or no tea, he ain't got no conscience. You can search all day and still not see one man with a conscience. And for why? Because they don't know if there's a God or not. Well, good-bye, Mum. Long life and good health to you, don't think too badly of me.'

Anisim bowed low to Barbara.

'We thanks you for everything, Mum,' he added. 'You've been real good to our family, you have. You're a very proper sort of a woman, and I'm real pleased with you.'

Deeply touched, Anisim went out, but came back again.

'Samorodov's got me involved in some deal,' said he. 'It's riches or ruination for me. If it don't go right, do comfort the old man, won't you, Mum?'

'Oh dear, whatever next! Goodness gracious me! God have mercy on us!' she clucked. 'Now, you be nice to your wife, Anisim. You look as if you'd taken agin each other. You might at least laugh a bit, really!'

'Yes, she's a strange one,' sighed Anisim. 'Doesn't understand nothing, never says nothing. She's very young, though—wait till she grows up.'

Near the porch stood a tall, sleek, white stallion harnessed to a dog-cart. Old Tsybukin took a run up, jumped jauntily aboard, seized the reins. Anisim kissed Barbara, Aksinya and his brother. Lipa too stood in the porch—stock still, eyes averted, looking as if she hadn't come out to see him off but had just somehow happened to be there. Anisim went up, lightly brushed her cheek with his lips, and said good-bye.

Not looking at him, she gave a somewhat strange smile. Her face trembled, and everyone felt rather sorry for her. Anisim too leapt aboard, and sat with arms akimbo, thinking himself handsome.

As they drove up out of the hollow Anisim kept looking back at the village. It was a warm, bright day. The cattle had been driven out for the first time, girls and women were walking about near the herd wearing holiday dresses. A brown bull bellowed, enjoying his freedom and pawing the ground with his front hooves. Larks sang everywhere, both above and below. Anisim looked round at the church so neat and white—it had just been whitewashed—and remembered worshipping there five days ago. He looked round at the school with its green roof, at the stream where he had once bathed and fished—and joy stirred within his breast. If only the earth would suddenly throw up a wall to bar his way and leave him alone with his memories.

They went into the station buffet for a glass of sherry. Wanting to pay, the old man felt in his pocket for his purse.

'This one's on me,' said Anisim.

Delighted, the old man clapped him on the shoulder, and winked at the barman to show what a fine son he had.

'Why don't you stay at home and join the business, Anisim,' he asked. 'You'd be a real asset. I'd make you a mint of money, son.'

'It's quite out of the question, Dad.'

The sherry was rather bitter and smelt of sealing-wax, but they had another glass.

When the old man arrived home from the station he at first failed to recognize his younger daughter-in-law. No sooner had her husband left the premises than Lipa became transformed, suddenly cheering up. Barefoot, in a worn old skirt, sleeves rolled up to her shoulders, she was washing the staircase in the hall and singing in a thin, silvery little voice. And when she carried out the great pail of dirty water, looking into the sun with her childlike smile, she might have been another lark herself.

Walking past the porch, an old labourer shook his head and cleared his throat. 'Fine women, Mr. Gregory, your son's wives. God has blessed you with real treasures, sir.'

V

On Friday the eighth of July 'Lofty' Yelizarov and Lipa were on their way back from making a pilgrimage to Kazanskoye village in honour of Our Lady of Kazan, whose festival this was. Far behind walked Lipa's mother Praskovya—being ailing and short of breath, she always did lag behind. It was late afternoon. Listening admiringly to Lipa, Lofty kept sighing and mumbling.

'I'm very fond of jam, I am, Mr. Yelizarov,' said Lipa. 'I sit in my own little corner drinking my tea and jam. Or Barbara and I have it together, and she tells some sad story, like. They have lots of jam—four jars at a time. "You have some, Lipa," they tell me. "You help yourself." '

'Aha! Four jars, eh?'

'They do themselves proud. They have white rolls with their tea, and there's as much beef as you like. They live well, but it's so frightening there, Mr. Yelizarov—it don't half scare me.'

'What have you to fear, child?' asked Lofty, looking round to see if Praskovya was very far behind.

'At first, after the wedding, I was scared of Mr. Anisim. He never done nothing, he weren't nasty to me—it's just that when he comes near me a shudder goes through every bone in me body. And I don't sleep a wink at nights, just keep shivering and praying. Now I'm afeared of Aksinya, Mr. Yelizarov. She seems all right, she's always laughing—it's just that you see her look out of the window sometimes with them angry green eyes afire, like a sheep's in the shed. Them Khrymin Sons are always on at her. Your old man has a bit of land at Butyokino—over a hundred acres, they tell her. There's sand, they tell her, and water too. So you build a brickyard on it in your own name, say they, and we'll go shares with you. Bricks fetch twenty roubles a thousand now—it's good business, that is. Well, at dinner yesterday Aksinya tells the old man she wants to start this brickyard at Butyokino—wants to go into business for herself. She's laughing as she says it, but Mr. Gregory gives her a black look—he don't like it, that's clear enough. "So long as I'm alive," says he, "we ain't going to split up, we must stick together." Well, she flashes them eyes and kind of grinds her teeth. We had pancakes, but she wouldn't eat none.'

'Oh, so she wouldn't eat none?' Lofty was surprised.

'And another thing—when does she sleep if you please?' Lipa went on. 'She'll sleep half an hour, then up she'll jump, rummage round everywhere to see if the peasants have set anything on fire or stolen anything. She scares me, Mr. Yelizarov. And after the wedding them Khrymin Sons never went to bed. They went to town to have the law on each other, and it was all Aksinya's doing—or so folks say. Two of them brothers promised to build her the works, but that annoyed the third one and their mill was shut for a month—my uncle Prokhor was out of work and had to go round begging for scraps. "Why don't you go a-ploughing for a bit, Uncle," I ask him. "Or saw some wood. Why bring shame on yourself?" "I've lost the habit of farm work," says he. "There ain't nothing I can do, Lipa dear."'

They paused near a grove of young aspens to rest and wait for Praskovya. Yelizarov had been doing contract work for years, but he didn't keep a horse. He travelled the whole county on foot with a little bag of bread and onions—walked with long strides, swinging his arms, so that he was hard to keep up with.

At the entrance to the copse was a boundary post, and Yelizarov touched it to see if it was sound. Up came Praskovya, panting. Her wrinkled face, with its perpetual look of fear, beamed happiness. She had been to church today like a real person, then she had visited the fair and drunk pear kvass. It was such a rare treat, she even felt as if she had enjoyed herself today for the first time in her life. After a rest the three of them went on together. The sun was setting, its rays piercing the copse and shining on tree trunks. There was a murmur of voices ahead of them. The Ukleyevo girls had gone a long way in front, but had tarried in this copse—to pick mushrooms, probably.

'Hey there, lasses!' shouted Yelizarov. 'Hallo my beauties.'

'That's old Lofty, that is,' they laughed in reply. 'Silly old geezer!' The laughter echoed after them.

The copse was behind them, now, the tops of the mill chimneys had come into view, the belfry cross glittered. Here was the village 'where the sexton ate all the caviare at the funeral'. They were nearly home, they only had to go down into that great ravine. Lipa and Praskovya, who had been walking barefoot, sat on the grass to put their shoes on, and the carpenter sat down beside them. From up here Ukleyevo—with its willows, white church and stream—seemed pretty and peaceful. The only eyesores were the mill roofs, painted a gloomy greyish colour for economy reasons. On the far slope they could see rye: stooks and sheaves of it here and there, as if scattered by a storm, and newly reaped swathes. The oats were ripe and gleamed like mother-of-pearl in the sun. It was harvest time, but today was a day off. Tomorrow, Saturday, they would get in the rye and cart hay. Then it would be Sunday, another holiday. There was a rumbling of distant thunder every day, it was steamy and looked like rain. Gazing at the fields, now, they all hoped to harvest their crops in time, God willing. It was a cheerful, joyous—yet uneasy—feeling.

'Reapers come dear nowadays,' said Praskovya. 'One rouble forty a day.'

More and more folk were rolling in from Kazanskoye fair: peasant women, mill-hands in new caps, beggars, children.

A cart would drive past, raising the dust, with an unsold horse trotting behind it and seeming glad not to have been bought. Someone would drag a reluctant cow by the horns. Or another cart would come along with drunken peasants dangling their legs. An old woman led a little boy in a large hat and large boots. Exhausted by the heat and his heavy boots, which stopped him bending his knees, he was yet blowing non-stop for all he was worth at a toy trumpet. Even when they had reached the bottom and turned into the village street that trumpet could still be heard.

'There's something wrong with our mill-owners,' said Yelizarov. 'Real vexing, it is. Kostyukov's annoyed with me. "You used too many laths on them cornices," says he. "What do you mean, too many?" says I. "I used what I needed, Mr. Kostyukov," I tells him. "I don't eat 'em with me porridge, them laths." "How dare you talk to me like that?" he asks. "You oaf, you so-and-so! You forget your place. It was me as first set you up in business," he shouts. "You think you're very clever," says I. "But I still drank tea every day even when I didn't have me own business." "You're all swindlers," says he. I says nothing. "Oho!" I thinks. "We may be swindlers in this world, but you'll be swindlers in the next!" On the day after that he caves in. "Don't you be vexed, my good man," says he. "Don't you mind what I said. If," says he, "I said a bit too much—well, I'm a member of the chamber of commerce, so I'm a better man than you are, and you'd better not answer me back." "You," says I, "may well be a member of the chamber of commerce, while I'm just a carpenter. True enough. But Saint Joseph was a carpenter too," says I. "It's righteous, our work is, and pleasing to God. And if," says I, "you think you're a better man than me, Mr. Kostyukov, then the best of good luck to you, sir." After this—after this here talk, I mean—I get to thinking: what *is* better: big businessman or carpenter? I reckon it's the carpenter, children.

'That's the way of it,' Lofty added after a moment's thought. 'It's the one as labours and puts up with things as is better.'

The sun had gone down, and a dense, milk-white mist was rising over the river, in the churchyard and in the clearings near the mills. Now, with darkness so quickly descending, with the lights flashing down there, with the mist seeming to cloak a bottomless abyss, Lipa and her mother, who had been born beggars and were ready to live as such to the end—sacrificing to others everything but their frightened, gentle souls—briefly fancied perhaps that in the unnumbered, never-ending catalogue of lives in this vast, mysterious universe, they too amounted to something. Perhaps even they were 'better' than someone? It was good to be sitting up here, and they smiled merrily, forgetting that they did, after all, have to go back down to the bottom.

They reached home at last. By the gate, near the shop, reapers sat around on the ground. Tsybukin's fellow-Ukleyevites usually refused to work for him, so he had to hire strangers—now, in the darkness, they all seemed to have long black beards. The shop was open, and through the door the deaf man could be seen playing draughts with a boy. The reapers sang softly, barely audibly, or loudly demanded yesterday's pay, but that had been kept back to stop them leaving before the morning. Old Tsybukin—minus his frock-coat, in waistcoat and shirt sleeves—was having tea with Aksinya beneath the birch-tree by the porch. There was a lighted lamp on the table.

'Hey there, Gaffer!' drawled a teasing voice behind the gate—one of the reapers. 'At least pay us the half, Gaffer!'

There was laughter, after which they again sang, barely audibly. Lofty sat down to tea as well, and began a yarn.

'Well, there we are at the fair. We're having a good time, children—a real good time, praise be—when a rather nasty thing happens. Blacksmith Sashka buys some tobacco, and he gives the shopkeeper a half-rouble piece, like. But it was a bad one.'

Lofty glanced round. He was trying to whisper, but spoke in a hoarse, strangled voice which everyone could hear.

'It was a bad half-rouble, that. "Where did you get it?" they ask. "Anisim Tsybukin give it me when I was a guest at his wedding," says he. They call the sergeant, they take him off. You'd better watch out, old Gregory—there might be talk or summat——'

'Gaffer,' drawled the same teasing voice behind the gate. 'Hey there, Gaffer!'

Silence followed.

'Ah, children, children, children,' muttered Lofty rapidly, and stood up. He was practically dozing off. 'Well, thanks for the tea and sugar, children. Time for bed. I'm a-mouldering away, I am—me joists are all a-rotting, ho, ho, ho!

'Time I was in me grave,' he said as he left. And sobbed.

Old Tsybukin did not finish his tea, but sat brooding and looking as if he was listening to Lofty's footsteps, though he was now far down the street.

'He was lying, was Blacksmith Sashka, I reckon,' said Aksinya, guessing his thoughts.

Gregory went indoors and came back a bit later with a bundle which he untied. The brand-new roubles glinted, and he took one, bit it, threw it down on the tray. Then he threw down another.

'Them roubles really are forged,' said he, looking at Aksinya as if in a quandry. 'It's the same ones—them as Anisim brought from town that time, the ones he gave us. Now, you take them, my girl,' he whispered, thrusting the bundle in her hands. 'Take them and throw them down the well, confound them. And mind there ain't no talk! I hope it's going to be all right. Now clear away the samovar and put that light out.'

Sitting in the shed, Lipa and Praskovya saw the lights going out one after the other. Only from Barbara's upstairs room did the blue and red icon-lamps still shed a glow of peace and blissful ignorance. Praskovya just couldn't accept her daughter's marriage to a rich man. She would cringe timidly in the passage during her visits, and smile pleadingly—and they would send tea and sugar out. Lipa couldn't resign herself to it either. After her husband had left she stopped using her bed, and would just lie down any old where in kitchen or shed. Every day she scrubbed floors or laundered, feeling like a charwoman. Now, after having returned from their pious mission, they had had tea in the kitchen with the cook, and had then gone into the shed and lain down on the straw between sledge and wall. It was dark and smelt of horse-collars. The lights round the house went out. Then they heard the deaf man locking up the shop and the reapers dossing down in the yard. Far away, at Khrymin Sons', someone was playing that expensive-sounding accordion.

Praskovya and Lipa began to doze off.

The moon was already bright when they were woken by footsteps. By the entrance to the shed stood Aksinya carrying her bedding.

'Perhaps it's cooler out here,' she said, coming in and lying down almost on the threshold, all bathed in moonlight.

Unable to sleep, she breathed heavily, tossing and turning about in the heat and throwing almost all the clothes off her. What a fine, proud beast she looked in the magical moonlight! A little later more steps were heard, and the old man showed up in the doorway, entirely white.

'You in here, Aksinya?' he called.

'Yes,' she responded angrily.

'Remember me telling you to throw them coins down the well just now? Did you do it?'

'Throw good money down a well—no fear! I gave it to them reapers.'

'God, oh God!' exclaimed the old man, horror-struck. 'You *are* a wild woman, God you are!'

With a gesture of annoyance he went muttering on his way. Not long afterwards Aksinya sat up with a deep, exasperated sigh, got to her feet and went out with an armful of bedding.

'Oh, Mother dear, why did you make me marry into this house?' Lipa asked.

'Folks must get wed, child. It ain't us decides these things.'

Grief and despair seemed about to overwhelm them. But they could sense someone looking down on them from heaven's height, from that starry dark-blue vault: someone who saw all that went on in Ukleyevo, and kept watch. However great the evil, the night was still calm and splendid. God's truth—no less calm, no less splendid—still stood, and would remain, in his creation. All things on earth were only waiting to mingle with that truth, as the moonlight mingles with the night.

Comforted, they fell asleep in each other's arms.

VI

News of Anisim's arrest for coining and uttering counterfeit money had arrived long ago. Months—more than half a year—went by, the long winter ended, spring came on, and Anisim's imprisonment became an accepted fact in his house and village. Anyone passing the house or shop at night would remember that he was in jail. The tolling of the bells in the parish church was also a reminder, somehow, that he was in prison awaiting trial.

A shadow seemed to lie over the premises. The house looked dirtier, the roof was rusty, the heavy, iron-bound, green-painted shop door had shrivelled until it was 'proper mortified', according to the deaf man. Old Tsybukin seemed a bit dingy himself. He had long stopped trimming his hair and beard, he looked shaggy, he was no longer leaping jauntily aboard that four-wheeler, nor did he shout at beggars that God would 'pervide'. His powers were waning, that was abundantly clear. Folk feared him less, now, and the local police sergeant sent in a report on the shop—even though he was still getting his usual cut. Three times the old man was summoned to town to stand trial for illicit vodka-dealing, but the case was repeatedly adjourned because of the witnesses' non-appearance. He was worn to a shadow.

He was for ever visiting his son, hiring lawyers, making submissions, presenting churches with banners. On the chief warder of Anisim's prison he bestowed a silver glass-holder with an enamelled inscription—MODERATION IN ALL THINGS—and a long spoon.

'There's no one, no one to put in a proper word for us,' clucked Barbara. 'Gracious me, you should get one of the nobs to write to the powers that be. They might at least give him bail—why torment the lad?'

She too was grieved, but she had put on weight, her complexion was whiter, and she still lit the icon-lamps, still kept the house clean, still regaled her guests with jam and apple-cheese.

The deaf man and Aksinya served in the shop. That new business—the Butyokino brickyard—had been started up, and Aksinya went over almost daily in the four-wheeler. She always drove herself, and when she met anyone she knew she would stretch up her neck like a snake in the young rye, smiling her naïve, enigmatic smile.

Lipa was always playing with her baby, born just before Lent. He was a tiny, emaciated, pathetic little thing. How strange that he could cry and see, that he rated as a human being and was even called Nikifor! As he lay in his cradle Lipa would go towards the door, bow and wish 'a very good day to you, Master Nikifor Tsybukin!' Then she would rush headlong to him and kiss him, before going back to the door, bowing and again wishing a very good day to 'Master Nikifor Tsybukin'. He would kick up his little red legs—crying and chuckling at the same time, like Yelizarov the carpenter.

A date had been fixed for the trial at last, and the old man left five days early. Then they heard that some peasants from the village had been called as witnesses. Their old labourer went too, having also had a summons.

The trial was on a Thursday. But Sunday passed and the old man still wasn't back, there was still no news. Late on the Tuesday afternoon Barbara sat by an open window listening for his return. Lipa was playing with her baby in the next room.

'You're going to be a big, big man,' she gleefully exclaimed, throwing him up in her arms. 'You'll be a peasant and we'll go and work in the fields together, that we shall.'

'Well, really!' Barbara was offended. '"Work in the fields!" What do you mean, you silly girl? We'll make a merchant of him.'

Lipa started singing softly, but forgot herself a little later and repeated that he would grow up to be a big, big man and a peasant, and that they would go and work in the fields together.

'Oh, really! You're at it again!'

Carrying Nikifor in her arms, Lipa paused in the doorway.

'Why do I love him so much, Mother?' she asked. 'Why do I feel so sorry for him?' she went on in a quavering voice, her eyes shining with tears. 'Who is he? What's he really like? He's light as a feather or a crumb, but I love him—I love him as a real person. He can't do anything, see, he can't speak, but I always know what he wants by the look in his dear little eyes.'

Barbara pricked up her ears, and a distant sound was heard: the evening train coming into the station. Might the old man be on it? She no longer heard what Lipa was saying, she couldn't take it in, she was not conscious of the passage of time, she just shook all over: not from fear, from overwhelming curiosity. She saw a cartful of peasants clatter swiftly by: the witnesses on their way home from the station. As the cart sped past the shop their old labourer jumped off it and came into the yard. Folk were heard greeting him out there, asking questions.

'Deprived of rights and property,' he said loudly. 'And six years' hard labour in Siberia.'

Aksinya was heard coming out of the shop by the back door. She had been serving paraffin, she had a bottle in one hand and a can in the other, and there were silver coins in her mouth.

'Where's Father?' she mumbled.

'At the station,' answered the labourer. 'Says he'll come on later when it's dark.'

When the news of Anisim's hard-labour sentence spread through the household, the cook suddenly started keening out in the kitchen—supposing this to be what propriety dictated.

'Why, oh why, have you forsaken us, Anisim, son of Gregory, light of our lives——'

The dogs, disturbed, started barking. Barbara ran to the window.

'Stop it, Stepanida, do!' she shouted to the cook in an anguished paroxysm, straining her voice to the limit. 'For Christ's sake stop tormenting us!'

They forgot to put on the samovar, they couldn't keep their minds on anything any more. Lipa alone had no idea what it was all about, but went on nursing her baby.

When the old man arrived from the station they asked him no questions. He greeted them, then paced the house in silence. He ate no supper.

'There ain't no one to put in a word for us,' clucked Barbara when they were alone together. 'I told you to see some of the nobs, but you wouldn't listen. We should make an application——'

'I *have* been putting in a word for us!' said the old man with an impatient gesture. 'When Anisim was sentenced I went to the gent as was defending him. "There's nothing to be done now," says he. "It's too late." Anisim himself says it's too late. Still, I did speak to one lawyer when I came out of court, gave him something in advance. I'll wait another week and then go back again. It's all God's will.'

Again the old man paced about the house in silence, then returned to Barbara.

'I must be unwell,' said he. 'In my head there's an—er, a sort of a fog. I can't think straight.'

He closed the door so that Lipa should not hear.

'It's money that's troubling me,' he went on quietly. 'Remember Anisim bringing me some new rouble and half-rouble coins? Before his wedding it was, the week after Easter. I hid one packet of 'em, but I got the others all mixed up with me own. Now, me Uncle Dmitry, God rest his soul . . . used to fetch merchandise from Moscow and the Crimea in his time. He had a wife, did Uncle. And while he was a-fetching of his goods, this wife of his would be having fun with other men. Six children she bore. How dear old Uncle used to laugh when he'd had a drop to drink! "I can't make out them kids," says he. "Which of 'em is true coin and which is the counterfeit?" A bit of a light-weight was Uncle. Now it's the same with me: I can't make out which of me money's true coin and which is the counterfeit. It all seems counterfeit.'

'Oh, really, get away with you!'

'I buy a ticket at the station in town, I pay me three roubles—and then I feel they must be bad ones. It don't half scare me. Unwell, I must be.'

'None of us will last for ever, goodness me, it stands to reason,' declared Barbara with a shake of her head. 'That's what you should be thinking of, Gregory. Something might happen to you—you never know, you're not young any more. You watch they don't harm your grandson when you're dead and gone—oh, they'll do that child an injury, I fear, that they will. He ain't got no father, properly speaking, and his mother's young and silly. You might put the little lad down for something, Gregory, if only some land: that Butyokino, say. You think about it,' Barbara pressed him. 'He's a pretty little lad, it's such a shame. You go and write the paper tomorrow. No sense in waiting.'

'Now, I'd quite forgotten my little grandson,' said Tsybukin. 'I must say hallo to him. The boy's all right, you tell me? Well well, so may he grow up, God willing!'

He opened the door and beckoned Lipa, who came up with the baby in her arms.

'Lipa dear, you ask for anything you need,' said he. 'And you must eat whatever you like—we don't grudge you nothing so long as you keep well.' He made the sign of the cross over the child. 'And you look after my little grandson. My son's gone, so there's only my grandson left.'

Tears coursed down his cheeks. He sobbed and moved away. Soon afterwards he went to bed and slept soundly after seven sleepless nights.

VII

The old man had made a short visit to town. Someone told Aksinya that he had gone to a lawyer's to make a will—and that he was leaving Butyokino, that same Butyokino where she was firing bricks, to his grandson Nikifor. She learnt this one morning when the old man and Barbara were sitting under the birch-tree drinking tea. She locked the shop doors, front and back, collected all the keys, and flung them at the old man's feet.

'I ain't a-going to work for you no longer!' she shouted, and suddenly burst out sobbing. 'I ain't no daughter of yours, it seems, I'm your servant. Everyone's laughing at me: "See what a good maid them Tsybukins have found!" I never asked you for no job. I ain't no beggar—I ain't common, like, I do have a father and mother.'

Not wiping her tears, she glared at the old man—eyes swimming, vicious, squinting with rage. Her face and neck were red with strain.

'I ain't going to be your servant no longer,' she went on, yelling for all she was worth. 'Worn to a shred, I am! Oh yes, when it comes to work, minding the shop day in day out, and sneaking out to fetch the vodka of a night—then *I* can do it! But when there's land going begging you give it to that jail-bird's woman and her brat! She's the mistress, she's the fine lady round here, and I'm her drudge. Give her the lot, the convict's woman! May it choke her! I'm going home. And you can find yourself some other ninny, you rotten swine!'

Never in his life had the old man used bad language or punished children. That any member of his family could be rude to him, or treat him disrespectfully . . . the very idea was inconceivable. Absolutely terrified, he rushed into the house and hid behind a cupboard, while Barbara was so flabbergasted that she couldn't get up from her chair, but just waved both arms about as if trying to ward off a bee.

'Dear, oh dear, what can this be?' she muttered in horror. 'Why does she shout like this? Goodness gracious me! Folks may hear. Not so loud, oh dear, less noise, please!'

'They've given Butyokino to the jail-bird's moll!' Aksinya shouted. 'Well, you can give her the lot now, I don't want nothing from you! You can go to hell! A lot of gangsters, you are. I've seen enough, I don't care. Rich and poor, old and young . . . they've robbed all who came their way, the crooks! Who sold vodka without a licence? And what of them forgeries? They stuff their coffers with false coin, and now they don't need me no more!'

By now a crowd had gathered at the open gates, and folk were staring into the yard.

'Let 'em stare!' shouted Aksinya. 'I'll disgrace you yet, I'll make you burn with shame, you'll crawl to me, you will!

'Hey, Stephen,' she called the deaf man. 'Come on—we're going home this instant: home to me father and me mother. I ain't living with no jail-birds! You get your things together.'

Washing was hanging on the clothes lines in the yard. Snatching down her skirts and blouses, she threw them, still damp, into the deaf man's arms. Then she charged round the washing in the yard in a towering fury, tearing off everything—other people's clothes too—hurling it to the ground and trampling on it.

'Gracious, can't someone stop her?' groaned Barbara. 'What on earth is she at? Let her have Butyokino—give it her, for Christ's sake!'

'Well, well, well!' said people by the gate. 'What a woman! Gone berserk she has, and no mistake!'

Aksinya ran into the kitchen where the washing was being done. Lipa was working on her own, the cook having gone down to the stream to do some rinsing.

The tub and the copper near the stove gave off steam, misting and darkening the stuffy kitchen. On the floor was a heap of clothes still unwashed, and Nikifor had been put near it on a bench so that he wouldn't hurt himself if he fell. He was kicking up his little red legs. When Aksinya came in Lipa had just taken a shift of hers out of the pile, put it in the tub, and was reaching for the large can of boiling water on the table.

'You give that here!' said Aksinya, glaring her hatred, and snatched the shift from the tub. 'You take your dirty hands off of my under-clothes! You're a jail-bird's woman, that's what you are, and you should know your place.'

Lipa looked at her, utterly taken aback, not understanding. But she suddenly caught the look which Aksinya gave the baby . . . and then she *did* understand and turned pale as death.

'You stole my land, now take that!'

Thus speaking, Aksinya seized the can and splashed the boiling water on Nikifor.

There followed a yell like none ever heard in Ukleyevo—that a small, weak creature like Lipa could make such a noise was incredible. A sudden silence fell on the premises. Aksinya went wordlessly into the house with her usual naïve smile.

The deaf man was still out in the yard holding an armful of washing. Then he started hanging it up again—silently, without haste. Not until the cook came back from the stream did anyone dare go in the kitchen and see what was there.

VIII

Nikifor was taken to the local hospital, but was dead by evening. Not waiting to be fetched, Lipa wrapped the body in a little blanket and started to carry him home.

The hospital—newly built, with large windows—stood high on a hill and shone in the setting sun, seeming to be on fire inside. At the foot of the hill was a small village. Lipa walked down the road and sat by a little pond before reaching the village. A woman led a horse to the pond, but it would not drink.

'What more do you want?' asked the woman softly, quite bewildered. 'Ain't that good enough for you?'

A red-shirted boy sat at the water's edge washing his father's boots. Neither in the village nor on the hill was another soul to be seen.

'Won't drink,' said Lipa, looking at the horse.

Then the woman and the boy with the boots left, and there was no one to be seen at all. The sun went to his rest under a coverlet of purple and gold brocade, while long red and mauve clouds watched over his sleep, straddling the sky. From some unknown far-away spot came the doleful, muffled boom of a bittern—it sounded like a cow shut in a shed. Each spring the cry of this mysterious bird was heard, but no one knew what it was or where it lived. Up the hill near the hospital, in the bushes right here by the pond, beyond the village, in the fields all round, nightingales were trilling. A cuckoo was counting someone's age, but kept losing count and going back to the beginning. In the pond frogs bandied enraged croaks, straining their lungs, and you could even hear what they said: 'Hark at *her*! Hark at *her*!' What a racket! All these creatures seemed to be crying and singing with the express aim of making sleep impossible on this spring evening, and of ensuring that all—even those angry frogs—might relish and savour each passing minute. We do only live once, after all.

A silver crescent moon shone in the sky, and there were many stars. Lipa could not remember how long she had been sitting by the pond, but when she got up to go everyone in the little village was asleep, and there was not a light anywhere. It must be eight miles to her home, but she was worn out and had no idea of the way. The moon shone—now in front, now on the right—while that cuckoo, hoarse by now, still teased her with its mocking laughter and a 'Yoo-hoo—you fool—you'll lose—your route!'

Lipa walked quickly, and the kerchief had fallen from her head.

She looked at the sky and wondered: where might her little boy's soul now be—following her, or floating up there with the stars, unmindful of his mother? How lonely it was in the open country at night amid all the singing when you couldn't sing yourself, amid those non-stop cries of joy when you couldn't rejoice yourself . . . with the moon—also solitary—looking down from the sky and not caring whether it was spring or winter, whether people were alive or dead.

It is hard to have no one near you when your heart is broken. If only her mother Praskovya had been there! Or Lofty, or the cook, or one of the peasants.

The bittern gave a slow, protracted boom.

Then, suddenly, a man's voice was distinctly heard. 'Put them horses in, Vavila.'

Ahead of her a bonfire was burning on the roadside. The flames had died down, and there was only a glow of red embers. She heard horses munching. Two carts loomed up in the darkness—one containing a barrel, and another, lower one, with sacks—and two men. One was taking a horse to put it in the shafts, the other stood stock-still near the fire with his hands behind his back. A dog growled near the cart.

The man leading the horse stopped. 'Seems to be someone on the road.'

'Sharik, quiet!' the other shouted to the dog in what sounded like an old man's voice.

Lipa stood still and said 'God be with you.'

The old man came up to her, paused briefly, and wished her good evening.

'Your dog won't bite, will he, Grandpa?'

It's all right, come on—he won't hurt you.'

'I've been to hospital,' said Lipa after a short silence. 'My little son died there. Now I'm taking him home.'

The old man must have disliked hearing this because he stepped back. 'Never mind, dear, it's God's will,' he said rapidly.

He turned to his companion. 'Don't waste time, lad—get a move on.'

'Your yoke ain't here—can't see it,' said the lad.

'You're a proper so-and-so, Vavila.'

Picking up an ember, the old man blew on it, but lit up only his eyes and nose. Then, when the yoke had been found, he took the light over to Lipa and gazed at her. His look expressed sympathy and tenderness.

'You're a mother,' he sighed, shaking his head. 'Every mother loves her child.'

Vavila threw something on the fire, trod it down—and it suddenly grew very dark. The scene disappeared, and they were left with the same old fields, the starlit sky and the racket of the birds preventing each other from sleeping. A corncrake's cry came: from the very spot, seemingly, where the fire had been.

A minute later, though, carts, old man and tall Vavila were seen again. The carts creaked as they came out on to the road.

'Are you holy men?' Lipa asked the old fellow.

'No. We're from Firsanovo.'

'When you looked at me just now my heart melted. And the lad's so quiet—so I thought these must be holy men.'

'Have you far to go?'

'Ukleyevo.'

'Get in, then, we'll take you to Kuzmyonki. You go straight on there, we turn left.'

Vavila got into the cart with the barrel, the old man and Lipa into the other. They set off at a walk, Vavila in front.

'My little boy was in agony all day,' said Lipa. 'He looks at me with them little eyes and says nothing. He wants to tell me, but he can't. Lord God above us! Holy Mother! I keep falling on the floor, I'm so grieved. I stand near his bed and just can't keep me feet. Tell me, Grandpa, why should a little baby suffer so before he dies? When a grown person is in pain, man or woman, their sins are forgiven, but why, oh why should it happen to a baby which ain't never sinned at all?'

'Who knows?' the old man answered.

They drove for half an hour in silence.

'You can't know the rights and wrongs of everything,' the old man said. 'Birds are made with two wings, not four. And for why? Because two's enough to fly with. Man's the same—he ain't made to know everything—only the half or the quarter. What he needs to live . . . that's what he knows.'

'I'd rather walk, now, Grandpa. Me heart's trembling, like.'

'Never mind, you sit tight.'

The old man yawned and made the sign of the cross over his mouth.

'Never mind,' he repeated. 'Your grief ain't so bad. Life is long. There's good and bad, there's all kind of things to come.

'Great is Mother Russia,' said he, looking about him. 'I've been all over Russia, my dear—I've seen it all, I have, believe you me. There's good to come, and there's bad too. I been on village business to Siberia, I been on the Amur, in the Altay. I settled in Siberia—farmed land there—but then I got homesick for Mother Russia and I came back to me native village. We came back home on foot. We're on a ferry once, as I recall, and I'm thin as a rake. All tattered, barefoot and frozen, I am, and I'm sucking a crust, when a gentleman as was going through on the same ferry—if he's passed on since, may he rest in peace—looks at me in pity and his tears start flowing. "Ah me!" says he. "Your bread is black—and so's your prospects." And when I get back home I've nothing to bless meself with, as they say. I did have a wife once, but I left her behind in Siberia—she was buried there. So I worked as a farm-hand. And then what? I'll tell you. There was bad times and good times both, my dear. And now I don't want to die, see—I'd like to live another twenty year. So there must have been more good than bad.

'Great is Mother Russia!' he said, again looking around and glancing back.

'Grandpa, when someone dies . . . how long does his soul wander the earth? How many days?'

'Who can tell? Let's ask Vavila—he's been to school. They teach them everything nowadays.

'Vavila!' called the old man.

'What?'

'When someone dies, Vavila, how many days does his soul walk the earth?'

Vavila stopped the horse before answering. 'Nine days, I reckon. When me Uncle Cyril died, his soul lived on in our hut for thirteen days.'

'How do you know?'

'There were a banging in the stove for thirteen days.'

'Oh well. Drive on,' said the old man, obviously not believing a word.

Near Kuzmyonki the carts turned on to the metalled road and Lipa walked straight on. It was growing light. As she descended into the canyon the huts and church of Ukleyevo were hidden in mist. It was cold, and she still seemed to hear that same cuckoo calling.

Lipa reached home before they had driven the cattle out. Everyone was asleep. She sat on the steps and waited. First to appear was the old man, who took in what had happened at a glance but could not utter a word for a long time: only smacked his lips.

'Ah, Lipa,' said he. 'You didn't save him then, my little grandson.'

They woke Barbara. She threw up her arms, burst out sobbing, and at once started laying out the baby.

'Such a pretty little boy he was,' said she. 'Goodness me, she couldn't even keep the one baby she had—silly little thing!'

They held a requiem in the morning and again in the evening, and buried him next day. At the wake the guests and clergy stuffed themselves—you'd have thought they were starving, they were so greedy! Lipa helped to serve at table.

'Grieve not for the babe, for of such,' said the priest picking up a fork with a pickled mushroom on it, 'is the Kingdom of Heaven.'

Only when they had all left did it really come home to Lipa that Nikifor was—and would be—no more, and she burst out sobbing. But she didn't know what room to go and sob in, for she felt out of place in this house after the child's death—she counted for nothing here, she felt, she was only in the way. And others felt so too.

'Hey, what's all this hullabaloo?' shouted Aksinya, suddenly appearing in the doorway. She was wearing an entirely new outfit for the funeral, and had powdered her face. 'Shut up, you!'

Lipa tried to stop crying, but could not—only sobbed louder than ever.

'Do you hear me?' shouted Aksinya, stamping her foot in a mighty rage. 'Who do you think *you* are? You clear out of here! Don't you never show your face again, you convict scum! Away with you!'

'There, there,' fussed the old man. 'Calm down, Aksinya dear. It's only natural for her to cry—her baby died.'

'"*Only natural*"!' sneered Aksinya. 'She can spend tonight here, but tomorrow she can clear out lock stock and barrel!

'"Only natural"!' she sneered again, and went off to the shop with a laugh.

Early next morning Lipa went to her mother's at Torguyevo.

IX

Today the shop roof and door have been painted and shine like new. The usual cheerful geraniums bloom in the windows, and what happened at the Tsybukins' three years ago is almost forgotten.

Old Gregory Tsybukin still rates as head of the house, but in fact everything has passed into Aksinya's hands. She does the buying and selling, and nothing goes without her say-so. The brickyard is doing well. Bricks are needed for the railway, so the price has gone up to twenty-four roubles a thousand. The local women and girls cart bricks to the station, and load the wagons—all for a quarter of a rouble a day.

Aksinya has gone into partnership with Khrymins, and their works is now called 'Khrymin Sons & Co.'. They have opened a pub near the station, and it's here—not at the works—that the expensive-sounding accordion is played nowadays. The regulars include the postmaster—who has also started up some business of his own—and the station-master. Khrymin Sons have given deaf Stephen a gold watch, and he keeps taking it out of his pocket and holding it to his ear.

In the village Aksinya is said to have 'come on mighty powerful'. And it's true enough that when she drives to the works of a morning—naïvely smiling, handsome and happy—and when she is running that works, she indeed does convey a great air of power. At home, in the village, at the works . . . they're all scared of her. When she goes to the post-office the postmaster jumps to his feet with an 'I humbly beg you to be seated, Mrs. Tsybukin, ma'am.'

A certain dandified squire in his jerkin of fine cloth and patent-leather jack-boots—a middle-aged man—was once selling her a horse, and was so taken with her as they spoke that he let her have it on her own terms. He held her hand for some time, looking into her merry, artful, naïve eyes.

'For a woman like you, madam, there's no pleasure I wouldn't provide,' said he. 'Only tell me when we can meet without interruption.'

'Why, whenever you like.'

Ever since that the middle-aged dandy has driven to the shop almost daily for his glass of beer. The beer is atrocious—bitter as wormwood—but the squire shakes his head and drinks it.

Old Tsybukin takes no more part in business. He keeps no cash on him, for he simply can't tell true coin from false. But he holds his peace, never mentioning this infirmity. He has become rather absent-minded and if they don't give him his meals he never asks for them. They are used to eating without him by now, and Barbara often remarks that her 'old man went to bed without his supper again last night'. She speaks as if it didn't matter because she takes it for granted.

For some reason he goes about in his fur coat, summer and winter alike—it is only on the very hottest days that he doesn't go out at all, but stays at home. After donning that coat, raising the collar and wrapping up well, he usually potters round the village and the road to the station. Or sits on the bench near the church gate from morn till eve. There he sits, not moving. Folk bow as they pass, but he makes no reply: he still dislikes peasants as much as ever. If anyone asks him a question he answers quite rationally and politely—but briefly.

Village gossip says that his son's wife has driven him out of house and home, that she won't feed him, that he lives on what people give him. Some are glad, others are sorry for him.

Barbara is even plumper and paler, and she still goes about doing good—unhampered by Aksinya. They make so much jam nowadays that there's no time to eat it all before the new season's berries are ripe. It candies, and Barbara almost weeps for not knowing what to do with it.

They are beginning to forget Anisim. A letter did once arrive from him—written in verse on a large sheet of paper resembling an official document, and in the same imposing handwriting as before. Obviously he and his friend Samorodov were doing time in the same place. Beneath the verses a single line had been added in an ugly, barely legible hand: 'I'm always ill here, I'm miserable, for Christ's sake help me.'

Late one fine autumn afternoon old Tsybukin was sitting by the church gate with his coat collar up and only his nose and cap peak showing. At the other end of the long bench sat the carpenter Yelizarov, and beside him the school caretaker Jacob: a toothless old fellow of about seventy. Lofty and the caretaker were talking.

'Children should give old folks their food and drink—honour thy father and thy mother,' said Jacob testily. 'But that young woman has thrown her husband's old dad out of his own house, like. Nothing to eat nor drink, the old fellow has—where's he to go now? Three days he ain't had no food.'

Lofty was surprised. 'Three days!'

'Aye, there he sits, never says a word. Proper weak, he is. Why keep quiet about it? They ought to take her to court—she wouldn't get off lightly!'

'Who got off lightly?' asked Lofty, not hearing.

'Eh?'

'The woman's all right. A hard worker, she is. In their line of business you can't manage without it—not without cutting corners, I mean.'

'Out of his own home!' Jacob went on testily. 'Let her build a house herself before she starts throwing folks out of it. What a woman, though! A proper plague, she is.'

Tsybukin listened, but made no move.

'His own house or someone else's . . . what's the difference so long as it's warm and the womenfolk don't quarrel?' laughed Lofty. 'Very fond of my Nastasya, I was as a young fellow. She was a quiet little woman. "You buy a house, Eli," says she—kept on at me all the time, she did with this "you buy a house, Eli" stuff. And when she was a-dying she was on about "you buy yourself a good fast droshky, Eli, so you don't need to walk". But all I ever buys her is gingerbread, that's all.'

'That deaf husband of hers is a fool,' went on Jacob, not hearing. 'A proper dunce he is, a real old goose. Can the likes of him understand? Hit a goose on the head with a stick—it still won't understand.'

Lofty stood up to go home to the works. Jacob got up too, and they set off together, still talking. When they had gone about fifty yards old Tsybukin also stood up and doddered after them, treading gingerly as if walking on ice.

Now the village was plunged in twilight. The sun sparkled only on the top part of the road snaking up the hillside from below. Old women were on their way back from the woods bringing the children and carrying baskets of pink and yellow-white mushrooms. From the station, where they had been loading wagons with bricks, came a group of women and girls, their noses and their cheeks under the eyes red with brick dust. They were singing. In front of all walked Lipa singing in a reedy voice—carolling away as she looked up at the sky and seeming to exult and rejoice that the day, thank God, was over and that she could rest. In the group was her mother Praskovya, the hired drudge, carrying a bundle in her hand and panting as usual.

'Good day, Eli, my dear,' said Lipa, seeing Lofty.

'Good day, Lipa darling.' Lofty was delighted. 'Hey, you women and girls, be nice to the rich carpenter.

'My children, my dear children,' he sobbed. 'Oho, my darling little hatchets!'

Lofty and Jacob were heard talking to each other as they moved off. Then old Tsybukin came up with the crowd, and silence suddenly fell. Lipa and Praskovya had lagged behind a little.

'Good day, Mr. Tsybukin,' said Lipa with a low bow as the old man drew level.

Her mother bowed too. The old man stopped, looked at them both wordlessly, lips shaking, eyes full of tears. Lipa got a piece of buckwheat pasty from her mother's bundle and gave it to him. He took it and started eating.

Now the sun had completely set—even from the top part of the road the fire had faded. It was growing dark and chilly. Lipa and Praskovya went on their way, crossing themselves for a long time afterwards.

NOTES

THE SEIZURE

1 *Moscow Institute of Painting, Sculpture and Architecture*: in north-west Moscow.
the Tver Boulevard: in north-west Moscow.

2 *Against my will to these sad shores . . .*: the Prince's aria from the opera *The Mermaid* (first performed 1856) by A. S. Dargomyzhsky (1813–69), itself based on the dramatic poem *The Mermaid* (1832) by A. S. Pushkin (1799–1837).

3 *Trubny Square . . . Grachovka Road*: in the north of central Moscow.

6 *The Leaflet*: Reference is to *Moskovsky listok* [*The Moscow Leaflet*], a political and literary weekly (1881–1918).

8 *Marshal Bazaine*: François Achille Bazaine (1811–88), French army commander in the Franco-Prussian War, who was court-martialled for dereliction of duty in 1873.
Smolensk: large town, about 240 miles west of Moscow.

9 *Aida*: heroine of Verdi's opera *Aida*, set in ancient Egypt and first produced in Russia in 1875 at St. Petersburg.

13 *The Meadow*: *Niva*, a weekly illustrated magazine for family reading (St. Petersburg, 1870–1918).
. . . today's a Wednesday: for members of the Russian Orthodox Church the Wednesday and Friday of each week were fast-days.

16 *Saratov*: town on the Volga, about 500 miles south-east of Moscow.

18 *Sadovy Street . . . Sukharev Tower . . . Red Gate . . . Basmanny Street . . . Razgulyay*: Vasilyev's walk began in the north of central Moscow (at a point about two miles north of the Kremlin), taking him about five miles in an easterly direction before he turned southwards towards the River Yauza (a tributary of the Moscow River) and the Red Barracks. The whole distance, there and back, must have been at least fifteen miles.

MY WIFE

22 *Tomsk*: town in western Siberia.

25 *Odessa*: the large Russian port on the Black Sea.

26 *Count Sheremetev's*: the Sheremetevs were a famous Russian landowning family. One Count Sheremetev owned 300,000 serfs before the Emancipation of 1861.

27 *after the serfs were freed*: reference is to the Emancipation of the Serfs under Alexander II in 1861.

35 *refuse her a passport*: a Russian citizen was required to possess a passport for purposes of internal as well as external travel. A husband/father had the right to withhold his wife's/daughter's passport, and could thus compel her to reside with him: a frequent cause of protest by nineteenth-century Russian feminists.

48 *Great Morskoy Street*: running south, and then south-west from Palace Square in central St. Petersburg.

my civil service rank is only equivalent to a colonel's: literally, 'I am only a collegiate councillor.' This was the sixth in the Table of Ranks introduced by Peter the Great in 1722 and providing grades for all officials of the government and the court, with equivalents in the armed forces. Only grades three, four and five entitled the holder to be addressed as Your Excellency (*vashe prevoskhoditelstvo*). The correct mode of address for an offical of the sixth grade was Your Supreme Honour (*vashe vysokoblagorodiye*).

56 *Carnot*: Marie François Sadi Carnot (1837–94) became President of France in 1887.

the *Illustrated*: reference is perhaps to the St. Petersburg weekly *Vsemirnaya illyustratsiya* (*World Illustrated*), founded 1869.

serfs . . . Emancipation: see note to p. 27.

THE TWO VOLODYAS

60 *like the old poet Derzhavin blessing the young Pushkin*: reference is to the famous occasion of 8 January 1815 when the elderly poet Gabriel Derzhavin (1743–1816) heard the young poet Alexander Pushkin (1799–1837) recite his *Recollections of Tsarskoye Selo* at the Lyceum of Tsarskoye Selo near St. Petersburg.

68 *Schopenhauers*: the German philosopher Arthur Schopenhauer (1788–1860).

THE BLACK MONK

72 *'Onegin, I cannot deny ...'*: aria from the opera *Eugene Onegin* (1877–8) by P. I. Tchaikovsky (1840–93), based on Pushkin's verse novel *Eugene Onegin* (1823–31); Chekhov's heroine Tanya (short for Tatyana) has the same name as Pushkin's.

74 *Braga's famous Serenade*: the vocal serenade by Gaetano Braga (1829–1907), Italian cellist and operatic composer.
Gaucher: N. Gaucher, a prominent French-born horticulturalist active in the 1880s.
Pesotsky's king of his own little castle: literally, 'Rich and famous is Kochubey.' A line from Pushkin's narrative poem *Poltava* (1829).

82 *'in my Father's house ...'*: John, 14: 2.

87 *The Assumption*: Assumption Day falls on 15 August.

88 *Polycrates*: tyrant of Samos, crucified *c.*522 BC
'Rejoice evermore': 1 Thess. 5: 16.

89 *St. Elias' Eve*: on the eve of 20 July, which is St. Elias' (or Elijah's) Day.

92 *Sevastopol*: Crimean port and naval base.
Yalta: town and seaside resort on the Crimean coast.

A WOMAN'S KINGDOM

101, 112 *the Old Religion ... Reformed Orthodox rites ... a Nonconformist*: reference is to the schismatic branch of Russian Orthodoxy which adhered to the 'Old Belief'—the ritual of the Russian Church as practised before the reforms of the Patriarch Nikon in the mid-seventeenth century. Adherence to the Old Belief was extremely prevalent in the nineteenth-century Russian merchant class.

113 *over his uniform*: uniforms were worn at this period by pupils and staff at state educational institutions; these included the universities and high schools (*gimnazii*).

115 *a senior civil servant*: literally, 'an Actual State Councillor'—the fourth class, in descending order of seniority, in the Table of Ranks (see note to p. 48).
a St. Anne ribbon: the orders, decorations for distinction in

peace or war, had been instituted by Peter the Great in the early eighteenth century. The Order of St. Anne, second class, was worn on a ribbon round the neck.

116 *Leconte de Lisle*: the French poet Charles-Marie-René Leconte de Lisle (1818–94).

117 *Duse*: the Italian actress Eleonora Duse (1858–1924).

119 *her Nonconformist peasant instincts*: those associated with the Old Belief—see note on pp. 101, 112, above.

Jules Verne: the French novelist (1828–1905).

120 *Maupassant*: the French novelist and short-story writer Guy de Maupassant (1850–93).

121 *Turgenev*: I. S. Turgenev, the Russian novelist (1818–83).

125 *Kings*: card game in which the player to win most tricks becomes 'King'.

AT A COUNTRY HOUSE

132 *your most churlish backwoods squire*: literally, 'a bad Sobakevich', reference being to the notoriously curmudgeonly landowner of that name in Part One of Gogol's novel *Dead Souls* (1842).

Goncharov: I. A. Goncharov (1812–91), the Russian novelist, author of *Oblomov*.

Tolstoy: L. N. Tolstoy (1828–1910), the Russian novelist.

136 *Flammarion*: Camille Flammarion (1842–1925), French astronomer and popularizer of astronomy.

137 *Kharkov*: large city in the Ukraine, frequently invoked in Chekhov's fiction as a dump for unwanted objects or persons.

MURDER

138 *Lady Day*: 25 March.

142 *the Fast of St. Peter*: the fast before St. Peter's Day (29 June).

144 *the Molokans*: members of a religious sect which arose in about 1765, they derive their name from drinking milk during Lent.

Forgiveness Day: the last Sunday before Lent, when it is the custom for members of the Russian Orthodox Church to ask each other's forgiveness.

146 *Alexander I*: Tsar Alexander I (1777–1825), who succeeded to the throne in 1801.

147 *an Old Believer*: see notes to pp. 101, 112.

148 *Flagellant meetings*: Flagellants were members of a religious sect which arose in the middle of the seventeenth century.

149 *first be reconciled to thy brother ...*: Matthew v. 24.

150 *poor orphans at the Home*: literally, 'Mariya's orphans'. The Office of the Institutions of the Empress Mariya was a foundation in memory of the Empress Mariya Feodorovna (1759–1829) which administered girls' schools and orphanages in various parts of the country.

Belyov: town about 150 miles south of Moscow.

152 *St. George's Day*: 23 April.

161 *the Dué Roads ... Sakhalin ... Straits of Tartary ... Voyevoda Gaol*: Sakhalin is the large island in the Russian Far East between the Sea of Okhotsk and the Sea of Japan. It is separated from the Russian mainland by the Straits of Tartary. Dué is a small coal-mining settlement on the Sakhalin side of the Straits of Tartary. Sakhalin was used as a penal settlement and was visited by Chekhov in 1890. His so-called 'travel notes'—in fact a serious sociological treatise—were published as *The Island of Sakhalin* in 1893–4. In Chapter viii of this work Chekhov describes a visit to Voyevoda Gaol, built in the 1870s and 'the grimmest of all the Sakhalin prisons'.

162 *a settler*: it was normal for convicts who had completed their sentence to be compelled to reside in the area where they had been in prison, whilst other 'settlers' were people transported to Siberia or outlying parts as exiles without prison sentence.

MY LIFE

165 *Borodino*: the Battle of Borodino took place in west Russia on 26 August 1812 between the Russians and the French and was the most important battle during Napoleon's invasion of Russia in 1812.

marshal of the nobility: the elected leader of the provincial or district gentry, who had certain statutory functions in local government.

173 *Dubechnya*: name of an actual village near Melikhovo, where Chekhov lived.

174 *Kimry*: town on the Volga about 100 miles north of Moscow, a traditional centre of leather and shoemaking 'cottage industries'.

Tula: provincial capital about 120 miles south of Moscow, an old centre of the metal-working industry.

Odessa: the large Russian port on the Black Sea.

187 *a prize collection of gargoyles*: literally, 'Gogol's pig-faced monsters'. The reference is to the extravagant fantasies which occur in much of Gogol's work.

188 *in the days of the Mongols*: the reference is to the 'Tatar yoke', the period in the thirteenth, fourteenth and fifteenth centuries when Russia was under the rule of the Tatars or Mongols.

194 *Make to yourselves friends of the mammon of unrighteousness*: Luke xvi. 9.

204 *a watchman banging his sheet of iron*: Russian watchmen used to make a banging noise in order to warn thieves that they were alert and show their masters that they were awake.

218 *village elder*: it was the practice for the heads of households in a village to elect an elder who became the head of the *mir* or village commune. He presided over and summoned its meetings and was in charge of village administration.

Zalegoshch: name of a village in Tula Province about 40 miles east of Oryol.

220–1 *in the forties and sixties*: periods of intellectual ferment in Russia. The 1840s are associated with aesthetic and philosophical excitement and a relatively romantic, highminded attitude compared with the more practical, utilitarian 1860s, the age of nihilists and radicals.

221 *862 A.D.*: this was the year in which, according to legend, Russian tribes invited the Varangian prince Ryurik and his two brothers to rule over them, thus founding the Russian State.

222 *loaf of bread and a gilt salt-cellar*: reference is to the traditional Russian ceremony of welcome, involving the gift of bread, usually a large, round loaf on a towel, and salt to the person who is to be honoured.

232 *To America for the Exhibition*: reference could be to the World's Columbian Exposition held at Chicago in 1893 to commemorate the 400th anniversary of the discovery of America.

233 *Ostrovsky*: A. N. Ostrovsky (1823–86), the well-known Russian playwright.

IN THE HOLLOW

242 *Yepifan*: village about 150 miles south of Moscow.

251 *Yegoryevsk*: town about 80 miles south-east of Moscow.

259 *a member of the Chamber of Commerce*: literally, 'a merchant of the First Guild': i.e. the more prosperous of the two (at one time three) associations in which Russian businessmen and merchants were enrolled.

271 *Amur*: river in far eastern Siberia. Its first 800 miles form the frontier with China.

Altay: mountainous region of southern Siberia and Mongolia.

THE WORLD'S CLASSICS

A Select List

SERGEI AKSAKOV: A Russian Gentleman
Translated by J. D. Duff
Edited by Edward Crankshaw

A Russian Schoolboy
Translated by J. D. Duff
With an introduction by John Bayley

Years of Childhood
Translated by J. D. Duff
With an introduction by Lord David Cecil

HANS ANDERSEN: Fairy Tales
Translated by L. W. Kingsland
Introduced by Naomi Lewis
Illustrated by Vilheim Pedersen and Lorenz Frølich

THE KORAN
Translated by Arthur J. Arberry

LUDOVICO ARIOSTO: Orlando Furioso
Translated by Guido Waldman

ARISTOTLE: The Nicomachean Ethics
Translated by David Ross

JANE AUSTEN: Emma
Edited by James Kinsley and David Lodge

Mansfield Park
Edited by James Kinsley and John Lucas

Northanger Abbey, Lady Susan, The Watsons, *and* Sanditon
Edited by John Davie

Persuasion
Edited by John Davie

Pride and Prejudice
Edited by James Kinsley and Frank Bradbrook

Sense and Sensibility
Edited by James Kinsley and Claire Lamont

ROBERT BAGE: Hermsprong
Edited by Peter Faulkner

WILLIAM BECKFORD: Vathek
Edited by Roger Lonsdale

MAX BEERBOHM: Seven Men and Two Others
With an introduction by Lord David Cecil

JAMES BOSWELL: Life of Johnson
The Hill/Powell edition, revised by David Fleeman
With an introduction by Pat Rogers

CHARLOTTE BRONTË: Jane Eyre
Edited by Margaret Smith

Shirley
Edited by Margaret Smith and Herbert Rosengarten

EMILY BRONTË: Wuthering Heights
Edited by Ian Jack

JOHN BUNYAN: The Pilgrim's Progress
Edited by N. H. Keeble

FANNY BURNEY: Evelina
Edited by Edward A. Bloom

LEWIS CARROLL: Alice's Adventures in Wonderland
and Through the Looking Glass
Edited by Roger Lancelyn Green
Illustrated by John Tenniel

ELIZABETH GASKELL: Cousin Phillis and Other Tales
Edited by Angus Easson

Cranford
Edited by Elizabeth Porges Watson

Mary Barton
Edited by Edgar Wright

North and South
Edited by Angus Easson

Ruth
Edited by Alan Shelston

Sylvia's Lovers
Edited by Andrew Sanders

THOMAS HARDY: A Pair of Blue Eyes
Edited by Alan Manford

Jude the Obscure
Edited by Patricia Ingham

Under the Greenwood Tree
Edited by Simon Gatrell

The Well-Beloved
Edited by Tom Hetherington

The Woodlanders
Edited by Dale Kramer

ALEXANDER HERZEN: Childhood, Youth and Exile
With an introduction by Isaiah Berlin

Ends and Beginnings
Translated by Constance Garnett
Revised by Humphrey Higgens
Edited by Aileen Kelly

HENRY JAMES: The Ambassadors
Edited by Christopher Butler

The Aspern Papers and Other Stories
Edited by Adrian Poole

The Awkward Age
Edited by Vivien Jones

The Bostonians
Edited by R. D. Gooder

Daisy Miller and Other Stories
Edited by Jean Gooder

The Europeans
Edited by Ian Campbell Ross

The Golden Bowl
Edited by Virginia Llewellyn Smith

The Portrait of a Lady
Edited by Nicola Bradbury
With an introduction by Graham Greene

Roderick Hudson
With an introduction by Tony Tanner

The Spoils of Poynton
Edited by Bernard Richards

Washington Square
Edited by Mark Le Fanu

What Maisie Knew
Edited by Douglas Jefferson

The Wings of the Dove
Edited by Peter Brooks

RUDYARD KIPLING: The Day's Work
Edited by Thomas Pinney

The Jungle Book (in two volumes)
Edited by W. W. Robson

Kim
Edited by Alan Sandison

Life's Handicap
Edited by A. O. J. Cockshut

The Man Who Would be King and Other Stories
Edited by Louis L. Cornell

Plain Tales From the Hills
Edited by Andrew Rutherford

Stalky & Co.
Edited by Isobel Quigly

ANN RADCLIFFE: The Italian
Edited by Frederick Garber

The Mysteries of Udolpho
Edited by Bonamy Dobrée

The Romance of the Forest
Edited by Chloe Chard

SIR WALTER SCOTT: The Heart of Midlothian
Edited by Claire Lamont

Redgauntlet
Edited by Kathryn Sutherland

Waverley
Edited by Claire Lamont